SJ MARTIN

Rebellion

To Margaret.

Enjoy book 2

Sarah Jane
Martin

First published by Moonstorm Books 2021

First edition

This book was professionally typeset on Reedsy. Find out more at reedsy.com

*I dedicate this second book in the Breton Horse Warrior Series to
my hard-working, ever-patient, but often frustrated editor,
Jan Spencelayh*

Contents

List of Characters

- **Morlaix**
- Luc De Malvais: Breton Lord & Leader of the Breton Horse Warriors
- Merewyn De Malvais: Luc's Saxon wife
- Lusian De Malvais: Luc's young son
- Marie De Malvais: Luc's mother the Chatelaine of Morlaix
- Morvan De Malvais: Younger brother of Luc & Horse Warrior
- Sir Gerard: Mentor, swordmaster and friend of the Malvais family
- Briaca: Wayward ward of Marie De Malvais
- Espirit Noir: Luc's famous huge War Destrier bred by Luc's father

- **Gael**
- Ralph De Gael: Rebel leader, Earl of Norfolk & Suffolk, Gael & Montfort
- Emma De Gael: His wife who defended Norwich castle against the Kings Bishops
- Geoffrey Fitz Eustace: Half brother of Ralph De Gael

- Ronec Fitz Eudo: Mercenary in the pay of his Patron Ralph De Gael
- Flek: Mercenary & servant of Ronec Fitz Eudo
- Dorca: Serving girl & Merewyn's maid
- Cadec: Head Stable boy/Groom

- **Anjou**
- Fulk IV: Count of Anjou, constantly attacking Maine and the borders of Brittany
- Pierre D'Avray: Angevin Commander, ruthless, cruel and pitiless.

- **House of Rennes**
- Eudo: the Count of Penthievre
- Alain Rufus: His son, Earl of Richmond, nephew of King William, Luc's Patron.

- **Battle of Dol**
- William the Conqueror: King of England
- Hoel: Duke of Brittany,
- Beorn: Captain of the Vannes Horse Warriors
- Lord Saint-Loup: Lord of Combourg

- **Dinan**
- Lord & Lady St Vere: Castellan of Dinan and Parents of Briaca
- Queen Matilda: Wife of King William
- Constance: William's youngest daughter
- Omar Saleh: Arab Physician

Map

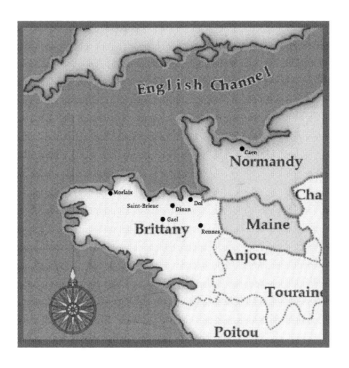

Brittany 1075

Prologue

I n 1075, King William the Conqueror's England is yet again beset by rebellion and strife. This time an alliance of three of his most powerful earls decide to rise against him in Northumberland, led by the formidable and wealthy Ralph De Gael, the Breton Earl of Suffolk and Norfolk. This rebellion is only one of his problems as William is back in Normandy when the rebellion breaks out, dealing with the attacks on his borders in Maine, the province bordered by Normandy, Anjou and Brittany.

His two main enemies, Fulk the Count De Anjou and King Philip of France are just waiting for opportunities to attack him and take back these lands.

Thrown into this maelstrom of rebellion, war and rivalry is Lord Luc De Malvais, the famed Breton Horse Warrior leader and his beautiful Saxon wife, Merewyn. Luc has been recalled to his home in Brittany by his liege Lord Alain Rufus and King William to help maintain peace on the borders and drive Fulk's Angevin raiders from Brittany and Maine.

Brittany is a wild, beautiful but troubled Duchy bordered by the Atlantic on its rugged west coast and by the English Channel to the north. It has had a troubled past and a long-held rivalry with Normandy. However, in 1066, several powerful and independent Breton Lords supported King William in his invasion of England and were richly rewarded.

By 1075, discontent is growing as William interferes once again in Breton affairs by planning to help Duke Hoel of Brittany lay siege to the citadel of Dol, which is held by rebels. There are now powerful alliances ranging against him while Luc De Malvais and his family suddenly find themselves at the centre of a plot to destroy King William.

Chapter One

Merewyn, her knuckles white, tightly gripped the gunwale of the sturdy Cog that was taking them south across the English Channel to Brittany. The fine salt spray from the front of the boat occasionally splashed over her, and she threw her head back and gasped with exhilaration while licking the saltwater from her fingers. To any onlooker, she seemed unconcerned that they had spent several hours at the mercy of a sudden storm.

She was mesmerised by the endless white-topped waves that stretched to the horizon, the smell and noise of the sea, the movement of the creaking boat. This was the first time she had ever seen the ocean or been on a ship. Despite misgivings and anxiety about her quest, she was thrilled to be on deck, even in rough weather, to experience as much as possible. She glanced along to the sturdy but rugged accommodation at the stern; she should have been there with her son Lusian and his nurse, but she needed to be able to breathe; her tension and excitement were too much to contain in those cramped quarters. The sea journey was just

6

as rough as they thought at this time of year; as the small boat climbed and fell with the giant waves, Lusian's nurse Hildegarde was suffering from a bout of seasickness, another reason for Merewyn to risk being out on the deck. Travelling across the sea in November weather was dangerous. Still, it was a risk she had to take, and the irritable captain was paid a considerable amount of silver to undertake this journey with his important passengers.

Sir Gerard, her husband's Steward and veteran Horse Warrior, stood beside her, his feet firmly planted on the heaving deck, one hand on the rail, but silent disapproval emanating from every pore in his body. She knew she was deliberately disobeying her husband's instructions by crossing from England to Brittany, and Gerard did not expect it to end well. He had painstakingly told her several times that no matter how much Luc De Malvais loved both her and his son, he would be furious that Merewyn had left the comparative safety of their home in Ravensworth to try and find him.By insisting on travelling in late autumn, she had put them all in danger. Crossing the channel was a huge risk at this rough time of year, without the further peril of war-torn Brittany.

However, Merewyn felt that she had no choice but to make the journey. It had been eleven long months since Luc was recalled to his homeland on his liege lord's orders. Alain Rufus sent him to serve King William on the unsettled borders of Brittany, Maine and Anjou. She had been devastated to see him go, but he had promised to be back by early summer. It was now late autumn, and no one had heard anything from him for over five months. Her stomach knotted when she thought of Luc, her handsome Breton Horse Warrior, her husband, friend, and lover. They had been through difficult and often life-threatening times together, but she had never been apart from him for this length of time before. It had left a hole in her life, and she knew that she had to go to Brittany to find him, to be by his side, no matter what he was facing. That is, if he was still alive, nobody seemed to know where he was...

They had been married for over four years, and they had a beautiful son Lusian, a miniature Luc with an almost black mop of hair but with his mother's startling green eyes. He was growing up so fast and was already developing his parents' firm and almost wilful characteristics. She was worried that Luc would hardly recognise him; it had been so long now since he had seen him. Merewyn was not afraid; she knew she was capable of facing whatever dangers she would find in Brittany. Raised in a warrior's household, with a father who was a Saxon Thegn, who had fought at Hastings, she was not short of courage. She had also matured early, managing her father's household and home farmlands when her mother died in childbirth nine years ago.

Above all else, Luc was a Breton knight and Horse Warrior; the champion of Alain Rufus, heir to the wealthy House of Rennes, but they both also served William, Duke of Normandy, and King of England. Luc De Malvais was the Marechal of vast lands around Ravensworth in the north of England; he was also the leader of the formidable Breton Horse Warriors, the most fearsome troop of cavalry in Western Europe. She knew that Luc loved her deeply, they had a deep connection between them, but she recognised that he had other obligations as well; he owned extensive estates around the port of Morlaix and down at Malvais in

Vannes.

Suddenly, there was a shout in Breton from the Cog's bows, and Gerard took her arm. 'Land has been sighted; at last, thank the Lord; I thought we would be driven down to Spain by that storm. We will see the shores of Brittany and the bluffs of Morlaix soon,' he said, gazing at the thin strip of coastline in the distance and willing the little boat into safe harbour.

Merewyn's stomach tightened, and she held her breath, raising her hands to her cheeks as she gazed at the dark line on the horizon. This, then, was Brittany, the wild region on the western Atlantic coast of France and the ancestral home of Luc and the De Malvais family. She hugged herself in anticipation. In a few hours, if he was alive and not mortally wounded, she might be with Luc and would feel his strong arms around her. However, Merewyn was not naive; she knew that Luc might not be in Morlaix at his home when they docked. According to Gerard, he could still be fighting elsewhere in Brittany, Maine or Normandy, defending the borders, so inside, she steeled herself for disappointment but prayed he was still alive and unharmed.

From listening to Gerard, she knew that King William had been fighting a campaign on Normandy's borders in the provinces of Maine and Anjou. They were fighting against Count Fulk of Anjou and his allies. William had previously claimed the Province of Maine in 1063 despite opposition from Count Fulk and Conan, Duke of Brittany. Before he invaded England, William was determined to defeat his enemies and secure his borders in Normandy. Therefore, he had seized the neighbouring province of Maine and the fortress and stronghold of Dol before finally agreeing to a peace pact with Count Fulk. However, Duke Conan of Brittany had refused to be pacified by William, whom he saw as an upstart, and he promised to attack Normandy while William was invading England. Conan had signed his death warrant by saying this, and low and behold, he was mysteriously poisoned in late 1066 whilst using a pair of new riding gloves.

This assassination conveniently removed him from Brittany, leaving no heir or Duke of age to take his place, and it left William free to concentrate on invading England. The finger of blame was firmly pointed at William, as he was not only ruthless in getting what he wanted, but he had a long history of poisoning and removing his enemies. Following this, years of war ensued in Brittany and its surrounding provinces, between those who supported William and those who did not.

Merewyn could understand the conflict; she knew that these independent feudal lords in Brittany and other provinces were a law unto themselves. They formed and changed alliances and sides constantly, as it suited their need. However, she could not understand why Luc had not returned home when the recent war had been resolved. Why had he not sent her a letter or message for over five months? This was so unlike him; she was terrified that something had happened to him. He could be badly injured or even dead for all she knew. She could not, and would not, imagine life without him.

Merewyn turned; she smiled at the relief on Gerard's face and returned to the cabin at the stern of the sturdy Cog. She found Lusian full of excitement and energy, galloping his beautifully carved wooden horse along the rough decking while his poor white-faced nurse tried to restrain him. Looking at the horse, she smiled, for it brought back bittersweet memories of life in Ravensworth, the scene of so many happy times for her and her family. She would never have believed that she could fall in love with the enemy of her Saxon people, a hated Norman knight. However, from the moment they had met, there had been an incredible magnetism and attraction between them, which they found difficult to deny or ignore. She was taken aback by how this Norman overlord was slowly accepted and even respected by her people for his firm but fair approach.

She soon discovered that he was a Breton warrior allied to King William; she knew that one day they would have to leave her Saxon family and return to Luc's lands and estates in Brittany. Luc had returned to see his mother and young brother on a few occasions over the last four years, but this time it was different. Alain Rufus, Luc's liege Lord, had arrived with his entourage at Ravensworth and had spent several hours closeted with him. A week later, Luc had packed up and gone. He had ridden out last December on his beautiful Breton stallion, 'Espirit Noir', with his troop of Breton cavalry behind him, leaving a massive hole in her life and an ache in her heart.

At first, some periodic messages and letters had arrived through Alan Rufus at Richmond Castle to let her know Luc was well and hoped to be back by the summer. Sir Gerard acted as Luc's Steward during his absence, and they spent a bitterly cold yuletide together at Ravensworth with Merewyn's father Arlo and her young brother. Still, Luc was sorely missed by them all. Early spring brought a positive message from him that lightened their steps and gave them

11

the hope that he might be back for the summer.

Merewyn knew that Gerard missed Luc almost as much as she did. He had been Luc's mentor and friend since he was a boy in Brittany; he had taught him much of the swordsmanship for which Luc was now famous. Yet, by the end of the summer, there was still no word and no sign of Luc and Merewyn lived with an ache for the man she loved so much. Sleeping alone every night in their large wooden bed, she would often wake with tears on her face and put a hand out to the cold, empty side of the bed where his warm body would usually lie. When she closed her eyes, she could almost feel his touch, remembering how he would curl around her and pull her close as they settled to sleep.

It was at the harvest feast last month that things had come to a head; as the sturdy boat approached the dark Breton shoreline, she thought back to that night...

She had sat at the top table in the Great Hall that was full of her people. There was laughter, good food and flowing drink, and it had brought back memories of other nights in the Great Hall with Luc by her side. In particular, she thought back to the very first night he had arrived, when he had followed her outside to teach her a lesson for her insolence to her Norman overlords. His very touch as he pulled her roughly to him had sent waves of passion through her body, and even now, after five years, his lightest touch still sent fire racing to her loins.

As Merewyn sat in misery, her father, Arlo, had leaned in towards Sir Gerard, and she heard him say, 'Do you have any idea why we have heard nothing? It has been nearly four or five months since his last message; could Malvais indeed be dead.'

Gerard's mouth became a thin line as he snapped at some of the serving boys behind him for more wine, but he did not answer Arlo at first; he just shook his head, shrugged and gazed down into the red wine as he swirled it around in his goblet. She had clutched the edge of the table as she heard his following words.

"Malvais is missing on the borders of Brittany Arlo; there is no doubt of that. Even at his home in Morlaix, they have heard no word of him for several months. I try to keep my hopes alive, but I fear the worst."

Unexpectedly, they heard the sudden sounds of arrival outside the Great Hall and the large Irish dyer hounds set up a torrent of barking and howls. The doors were flung open, Merewyn was immediately on her feet, her hand to her mouth, and her face filled with joy, expecting Luc to walk into the Hall any moment. However, she was to be disappointed as Bodin, the half-brother of Alain Rufus, appeared with his retainers and another man, a stranger, at the back of the Hall. The anguish on Merewyn's face was clear to see, but, as the host, she quickly recovered and smiling, she had moved gracefully down the Hall to greet their friend Bodin Le Ver, who was now Lord of Bedale.

He had settled at the table with them and related the court's gossip; all the news was about the recent rebellions in the north. He had introduced the confident auburn-haired young man as Bardolph, his younger brother. Looking directly at Gerard, he explained that Bardolph was to take over the reins as Marechal and Lord of Ravensworth, and he thanked Gerard for his service to date while Luc was away. Merewyn's hand went to her heart as she wondered if Bodin knew that Luc was injured, or even dead, for Ravensworth to go to another Marechal.

Bodin, having seen her concern, quickly explained. This had been the plan for when Luc returned to Brittany; they were bringing it forward because of the recent rebellions in England and the threat to Normandy and Maine's borders. He knew that they had heard nothing from Luc and admitted it was unusual and troubling. He had taken her hand and reassured them that while Luc may have disappeared if someone had killed him, the news would have spread like wildfire; after all, he was Luc De Malvais, his name known across Western Europe.

Merewyn sat, a fixed smile on her face as the conversations flowed around her, her mind in turmoil while Sir Gerard arranged to show Bardolph around the estates. However, Merewyn had only half listened, for her mind had been in Brittany. Luc was not returning, but she could not understand why he had not let her know; why had he not sent for them?

It was now early October; she knew it would become too dangerous to cross the seas very soon. She had determined to act; she refused to spend another yuletide and the long winter months without him. The arrival of Bardolph had made it easier for her to leave Ravensworth and go to Luc. She was his wife, Lusian was his son, and they needed to look for him, to be by his side. She had decided that they were leaving for Brittany immediately, and nothing and no one would stop her, not Sir Gerard and not Lord Bodin. She was Merewyn De Malvais, no matter the barriers in her way; she knew she would find him wherever he had gone.

Chapter Two

The thunder of hooves reverberated through the ground as the Breton Horse Warriors galloped their huge destriers down the hill towards the river.

They should have been back home in Morlaix over a month ago, but they were still hunting the troop of Angevin soldiers who were wreaking havoc throughout Maine's north-western borders, where they met with Normandy and Brittany. There had been several sightings of this murdering troop in the far distance, but they had just seemed to melt into the forests when pursued. Every one of Luc's men had a burning desire for revenge against the marauders. Village after village on Brittany and Normandy's borders were attacked, the elders and men murdered, and the women raped if they had not managed to hide or escape into the forests in time.

Luc De Malvais was frustrated at their inability to find and kill this group. They constantly seemed to retreat to their hideouts in Maine or back to Anjou, but this was especially so since the savage incident at Gorran on the river Colmont.

The Horse Warriors were tasked with patrolling these borders by King William; he had ordered Luc to protect the people from the plundering contingents of Angevin chasseors. Maine was a troubled province in the Mid-west of France sandwiched as it was between Normandy and Anjou while both sides tried to claim overlordship. It had apparently been given to Rollo of Normandy by King Rudolph of France as early as 924 A.D., but since then, Luc knew it was a cause of disagreement between the rulers of these two powerful principalities, especially between William the Duke of Normandy and Count Fulk IV of Anjou. William had invaded Maine in force in 1063; he intended it for his young son Robert Curthose who he betrothed to the previous heir's daughter Margaret of Maine. Since then, the Angevins had constantly disputed this Norman overlordship and had ravaged the borderlands of Brittany and Normandy.

For months, Luc and his Horse Warriors had challenged and killed several Angevin raiding parties, but one large group constantly evaded them. Luc was desperate to return home; he had been away for far too long; he also had concerns that no messages from his mother at Morlaix had reached them despite the several messengers he had sent. He had decided to split his large troop of Horse Warriors into two; his younger brother Morvan sent north to patrol the Normandy border while he rode up the western border with Brittany. With luck, using this pincer movement, they would find them. They spent several weeks searching until an urgent message arrived from Morvan asking Luc to join him immediately at the large village of Goran. The events of that day would remain etched on his memory forever.

Luc had led his forty-strong troops along the banks of the river Colmont towards the village. As they approached, he could see the plumes of smoke rising above the trees, and he sighed, no doubt, another village was razed to the ground, but this time inside Maine, which puzzled him, they usually raided over the border. They galloped into the main thoroughfare; to find that only a few houses were burning amid the scene of devastation; it looked as if the attackers had been disturbed. The Horse Warriors now regarded the death of these villagers as inevitable in this war of attrition. The bodies of the peasants and landowners who had fought and died protecting their home and families lay scattered outside their homes. They slowed grim-faced to a trot as they headed for the river. If Morvan had not caught the Angevins in the act, Luc knew that they would be long gone, but just in case, he was vigilant as he rode along the banks until he saw Morvan down by the ford on the other side of the river.

There was an expansive grove of trees and a clearing; Morvan raised a hand in greeting as he rode out of the forest to meet his brother as he crossed the ford. Luc hailed him, 'Well Met, Morvan, you disturbed them but did you catch up with them,' he asked while taking the younger man's arm in a warrior clasp. He had shaken his head, his brown eyes staring into Luc's with concern, his face an unusual pallor; Morvan was only two years younger than he was, but Luc knew he was a brave and fearless warrior.

'What is it,' he had asked, still tightly gripping his arm. Morvan had shaken his head, unable to speak at first, and he released his brother's arm; he took a deep breath, 'you had better come and see,' he said, turning his horse to return up the bank to the other side.

Luc and his men rode to join the other troop of Horse Warriors who had dismounted; many men stood or sat dejectedly around the grove of trees. Luc scanned the men for injuries and raised a hand in greeting but received only desultory nods and a few raised fists back. As Morvan led him deeper into the grove, he saw that some of the village men were tied to the tree trunks, but the truth dawned on closer inspection. Ropes tightly secured the two young men's necks and torsos; their heads hung forward on their chests, the slight breeze still ruffled their hair. He recognised the signature laced leather jerkins, the empty sword scabbards; these were his men. These Horse Warriors had been murdered in this grove. He took a breath and turned to Morvan. 'How?' he asked.

Morvan could not meet his eyes, as his own were full of unshed tears; he had looked away into the distance as he answered. 'They were the outriders on our patrol, as you know, they always rode in pairs, the Angevins captured them, and they bound them to the trees and chopped their hands off, leaving them to bleed out.'

Luc contemplated the scene; after many years as a mercenary, he was used to scenes of atrocities; he had seen far worse. Little could surprise him when he witnessed man's inhumanity to man, but this was different; these were his men, he knew them and their families, most were from his lands and estates. He dismounted and slowly walked to stand in front of the two victims. He reached out and lifted the heads of each man, looking long and hard at the drained white faces. He knew each one; the first was Jean Reynard, about twenty-five years old, recently married with a young baby. The second man was much younger, and he heard the cry of anguish behind him as he lifted the young man's head. It was young Doric, the joker in the group, always laughing and full of life, the younger brother of Robert, one of his

Serjeants. The older brother came to stand beside him, and he sank to his knees on the blood-soaked ground, shaken with racking sobs as he stared at his young sibling. Luc rested a hand on the man's shoulder for a while before he turned away and met the shocked and saddened gazes of his men around him. They had ridden and fought together for several years; they were a brotherhood. They rode, drank, joked and played dice together; death in warfare was an acceptable part of their lives, but now two of their own had not been killed in battle but captured and brutally murdered. Luc had noticed the empty wineskins on the ground; the Angevins had sat and watched them die.

'There is more,' said Morvan leading Luc down and along the riverbank, 'we had to kill them quickly to put them out of their misery.' Lying on the banks of the river, half in and half out of the water, were two of the large Morlaix warhorses, two of the big-boned beautiful older horses that his father had bred for battle. Now, they lay glassy-eyed and inert; Luc felt a cold spasm pass through his body as he looked at them. They had been cruelly hamstrung, slashed across their back legs and looking at the marks on the bank, they had floundered in distress for some time before Morvan and his men had calmed them and quickly cut their throats.

Luc felt a cold rage building inside him as he looked down at the beautiful animals. This was personal; this was a message to him from the elusive Angevin leader; the Morlaix warhorses were known and recognised throughout the provinces. Luc did not say a word to Morvan. Instead, he turned and, stone-faced, walked back through his men to his horse. For a few seconds, he rested his forehead on the powerful neck of the huge warhorse before pulling the reins over his head and leading him down to the ford to drink.

'Feed and water your horses, we ride in an hour, we will find those responsible for this, I promise you,' he had shouted to the assembled men.

That had been nearly a month ago, and now, at last, they received a message from a Breton knight living at Laval; he had received news that the Angevins were camped in the forest to the northwest just outside Ernée. Finally, they would find them, and he would exact his revenge; there would be no quarter given.

As they rode towards Ernée, the vedettes returned and confirmed that the enemy camp was about half a mile inside the forest that wrapped itself around the foothills. He again split the Horse Warriors into two groups as they sat waiting for the sun to set behind the western hills; they would attack in a pincer movement at sunset from two directions at once. He sent Morvan off with a wave of his hand, and they moved slowly and quietly into the forest across the swathes of amber coloured leaves that now carpeted the forest floor. The vedettes confirmed that the camp was just ahead in a clearing beside the stream; his men had silenced the Angevin sentries, cutting their throats. As the gloom deepened, Luc waved his troop forward in unison, moving quickly into a wedge shape as the pace escalated to a steady canter through the trees; it was a well-practised manoeuvre, the men ducking to avoid low hanging branches.

They had fought together for years, and it was second nature to them to fall into position; each man knew his role in the formation. The front rows with the heaviest destriers also had the most powerful swordsmen who would slash down mercilessly on the enemy below or beside them. The Horse

Warriors further behind would thrust and stab to finish off the wounded enemy or kill those who had been lucky enough to escape the first onslaught. The horses were just as lethal, trained to attack, bite and strike out on command at the enemy if cornered, or surrounded or, God forbid, if a Horse Warrior became unhorsed by chance. A thick leather buckler with raised iron studs protected the powerful chests of these great destriers; their forelegs also encased in tough leather greaves. They were a formidable sight as they rode towards the enemy.

Luc could now smell the smoke from the Angevin camp-fires, and he tried to curb his impatience and anger to make these men pay for what they had done. They burst into the large clearing, pushed their horses into a gallop and issued a blood-curdling war cry. Almost the entire thirty-strong Angevin group had dismounted and unsaddled their horses; most were sat around campfires in the chilly autumn evening, drinking from wineskins or cooking their food. Panic ensued as the enemy leapt to their feet, grabbing their weapons just as Morvan's force also erupted from the trees on the western slopes. Very few could stand against the might and power of the Breton Horse Warriors, and within minutes, it was a bloodbath as men were killed or mown down and trampled. Luc quickly scanned the group looking for their leader and soon found him, a tall, sharp-faced individual on the very edge of the clearing. He was still dressed in his fine chain mail, topped with a linen surcoat bearing the Angevin crest of lions rampant on an azure background. He stood silently waiting for them to come to him, seemingly unperturbed but his sword raised in readiness, an arrogant aloof sneer on his face.

Luc, the reins now knotted and dropped on his horse's neck, rode straight for him, and he saw the man clench the handle of the sword tightly in both hands, ready to bring the long sword round in a swinging blow. However, Luc swerved Espirit sideways and up into the air, rearing away from danger at the last moment. This meant that the Angevin's sword whistled through the air close to Luc's thigh as he struck out at Luc but fortunately did no damage. The blow's momentum brought the Angevin leader forward, and Luc swung his sword up to meet him, slicing open the right-hand side of his face. The wounded leader staggered back, his hand to the wound in disbelief, the blood running through his fingers; he glared at Luc.

There was still fighting around Luc, and he turned Espirit away from the melee of men and horses pressing against him. He leapt from the saddle to kill the man responsible for torturing his men; turning, sword in hand, he saw the Angevin leader running with two other men through the trees. Luc set off in hot pursuit while shouting 'To me Bretons' at his men. One of the enemy men in front turned to take Luc on; he was an older, scarred warrior with narrow, closely set eyes; he planted his feet firmly and dropped into an experienced crouch. However, he had no chance against the cold anger and skilled swordsmanship of Luc De Malvais, who paused for only a second as he engaged the man's sword but brought the hilt of his second sword up to slam it into the man's face. He calmly thrust his sword into the fallen man's throat, and stepping over the body, he ran on determined to kill the Angevin leader. He could hear some of his men running close behind as he burst into a second clearing where the Angevin horses were hobbled and grazing. He was just in time to see his enemy mounted bareback on a large black horse; the Angevin glanced back at Luc as he reached the far side of the clearing and raised his bloodstained hand in salute as he turned and galloped off through the trees.

Luc gave a cry of pure rage as he watched him disappear; he reluctantly sheathed one sword and stood hands resting on the other as Morvan came riding up beside him. 'We will meet again that Angevin and I, I swear it,' he shouted into the darkening gloom as Morvan nodded and stretched down a hand to pull his brother up behind him.

Chapter Three

Luc De Malvais sat deep in the saddle of his huge Breton stallion, his long legs dangling, his muscular frame relaxed, his hands resting on the pommel, the reins loosely hanging. He smiled as he gazed out at the view ahead of him. They had just navigated the passes of the Arree Mountains, part of the Armorican Massif, and now they were about to head down the valley below to his home in Morlaix on the coast. He had been away for over four months this time, dealing with further skirmishes; King William's enemies, especially Fulk, were nothing if not persistent in their attacks on his forces and surrounding territory. However, although they had searched for weeks, they had not seen the Angevin leader again; presumably, he had gone to ground in Anjou.

Luc knew the impact of these recent years of strife; he could feel the change in Brittany as he travelled through the countryside; the villagers would flee at the sight of an approaching troop of horses when once the children and peasants would have waved from the fields. Too many Breton Lords had formed alliances with opposing sides setting Breton against Breton. Luc was King William's man, mainly because of his allegiance to Alain Rufus, the nephew of William and heir to the House of Rennes. Still, significant forces were ranging themselves against the King. Luc's mind mulled over the problems of this last year; it was this allegiance to Alain Rufus that had kept him in Western France for longer than expected when he wanted to return to Ravensworth in Northern England. He missed his wife, Merewyn, and his son, Lusian, so much, but he knew that duty and loyalty to both his liege lord and the King came first.

As his eyes ranged over the verdant cultivated plains below, he could see the winding river which would lead directly to Morlaix; the sliver of the shining sea in the distance told him they only had three or four hours more to go. His dappled stallion tossed his long black mane and stamped his foot impatiently, telling Luc that they had stood for too long. Luc glanced over at the dark, handsome young man who sat quietly beside him, his brother Morvan, who had followed faithfully at his side on all the recent campaigns, now a seasoned warrior in his own right. Although still in his older brother's shadow, Luc knew that Morvan was building his own fearsome reputation as a swordsman and Horse Warrior.

Luc had been away from his home and family in Brittany for too many years, so it had been good to spend this last year with Morvan, despite being apart from his wife and son in England. He turned and scanned his assembled men spread out behind him. They were relaxing in their saddles, their massive Breton warhorses loosely held so they could graze on the heather shoots and shrubs around them, but they were still a fearsome sight. As his eyes ranged over them, he felt immense pride in what this elite troop of nearly a hundred horse warriors had achieved. They had come off reasonably lightly this year overall, despite the recent clashes with the Angevin troops. Most only had cuts and bruises, the recent exception being the loss of the two men and horses brutally murdered by the Angevin leader.

He knew his Breton Horse Warriors sowed dismay among the enemy soldiers wherever they appeared; their fearless reputation enough to cause chaos and disorder in the enemy. This was precisely what King William had intended when he summoned Luc and his men back to Brittany. However, William had returned to Britain last month when news of another rebellion in England had reached him in Normandy. William, without warning, found himself betrayed by three of his Earls. His warrior Bishops had managed to keep the rebel Earls at bay, but William had to return to England to deal with it. He had left Luc De Malvais to consolidate his alliance with the Breton lords, to ensure that Fulk, the Count De Anjou, and Hoel, the new Duke of Brittany, were kept under control, not an easy task for any man.

Luc ran his hands through his dark mop of hair and stretched his tired shoulders. His heart ached to see his wife and child in Ravensworth, but he saw no way in which he could leave Brittany to see them before next spring or even summer. As he sat there on the cliff, he thought of Merewyn, his beautiful, willowy Saxon beauty; he so longed to gaze into her green eyes, run his fingers over her soft naked skin and through her long silver-blonde hair as he made love to her. They had been apart for far too long; he missed her laughter and the warmth of her unconditional love, both for him and for their son Lusian. His boy would be almost five years old now, Luc suddenly felt afraid that Lusian might forget

26

him, and he frowned in dismay at the thought. Despite his sadness, he knew that it was far too dangerous to bring them to Brittany with so much unrest, so many uneasy alliances. Luc had to concentrate on keeping control of Maine and Brittany's borders and keeping as many of the Breton Lords as possible supporting the King. He sighed at the thought, then sat up, tightened his reins and nodded to Morvan, who raised his hand in acknowledgement.

'On Y Va!' his brother shouted to the assembled men. 'We are heading home to warm, comfortable beds, hot food and ale!' The men gathered their huge, grazing destriers up as they laughed and gave a ragged cheer before following Luc and Morvan down the hillside and along the valley towards Morlaix.

Luc's mood lifted as he thought of his home at Morlaix, with its warm fires and delicious Breton food only two hours ahead of them. His mother would be pleased to have them both home. Since his father's death, she managed and ran the large estates with Morvan, being only occasionally at home to help her when he was not out on patrols or sorties. For the first time, Luc felt weary of war; he longed for a future when he could bring his family to live here, following his dream of breeding the formidable destriers, like his stallion, Espirit Noir. These destriers were huge; Breton warhorses crossed with Arab stallions, brought north through Spain and interbred to give the warhorses intelligence, immense staying power and endurance. He had continued the plan started by his father over ten years before, and he now had over two dozen promising youngsters with more on the way. He needed the time and peace to breed and, more importantly, train them, and he was unlikely to have either for a while. As long as King William and Alain Rufus needed him, his time was not his own. God only knew when the next messenger would arrive, telling him to ride out again, and there may even be one waiting for him when he reached Morlaix.

Several hours later, Luc and his tired men rode in the autumn light of the dusk towards the large stone towers and gates of his home above Morlaix, amid welcoming shouts and cheers from the castle as row after row of Horse Warriors rode under the archway.

The sturdy Breton ship had furled its sail, and the crew were now rowing the Cog up the Dossen Estuary towards the town of Morlaix. Gerard excitedly pointed out to Merewyn the large stone cairn, a prominent landmark on the headland, which had been there since Roman times. Morlaix, she had heard it mentioned many times by Luc; this was his main home, in the imposing castle looking down on the town. It was a small but bustling seaport on the coast of North West Brittany. Gerard pointed out the men cultivating the rich oyster beds, standing thigh-deep in the shallow waters. Along the sides of the river, white-capped Breton women, who worked in the thriving Breton linen industry, were gathering in the cloth put out to dry in the breeze. Merewyn gazed at all of this with tear-filled eyes; she realised that these scenes, so strange to her, were very familiar to Luc; this was his home, and if he was alive, it was about to become hers. She quickly wiped away the tears and stood proudly in the bow with Lusian as they moved closer to the wooden quay.

During the journey, Gerard had explained that Luc's title and lands owed homage to the Lords of Penthievre, the family of Alain Rufus and his father, Eudo. These were independent, powerful and wealthy Dukes in their own right; they had always resisted Conan's ducal authority and that of his successor Hoel, although they did attend the ducal court occasionally when it suited them. She knew, from Luc, the history of his family, the Lords of Malvais; she knew that his father had died at Hastings and that his mother, Marie, had become the Chatelaine of Morlaix in his absence. He had talked with affection of his brother, Morvan, two years younger, who was also becoming a notable warrior. She could not wait to meet his family, and she was sure she would learn to love this wild and beautiful Breton land.

Lusian was bouncing with excitement beside her as he watched the sailors obeying the order to ship the oars, ready to pull up alongside the wooden quay in the dusk. One of their own men was the first off the boat, and he set off at a trot up the hill to the castle to arrange transport for the family and their baggage. Merewyn watched the bustling quayside scene around her and then gazed out at the wide estuary behind her. She breathed in the sharp salt air as she tried to keep her feelings under control, excitement but also apprehension and fear of what she would find. She signalled to her maid Helga to restrain Lusian, who was trying to climb over the gunwale onto the quay, and she turned to smile at Gerard, who smiled back, some of the tension in his face gone now that they had reached Brittany safely, the sea voyage behind them.

Before long, there was a clatter of hooves as the soldier returned with three riding horses and a wooden cart rumbling over the cobbled quayside behind. They descended the boards to the quay and mounted the horses, Gerard lifting a wriggling Lusian in front of him. Then, turning to the soldier,

Gerard asked the question that Merewyn had been burning to ask, 'Is my Lord De Malvais here, Petroc?'

The young man nodded, 'Yes, I believe so, Sir, there are dozens of men and horses filling all of the courtyards in the castle; the carter tells me they have just returned from the borders after over four months away.' Gerard turned and grinned at Merewyn, his concerns forgotten as they turned their horses and headed up the hill towards the castle.

Merewyn, filled with excitement, found her heart was thumping; he was alive, Luc was here, and he was alive. "Away for four months" reverberated through her. 'Is this why Luc has not been in touch?' she asked Gerard.

He shrugged. 'Quite possibly, these are dark and dangerous times on the borders. Come, let us get into the warmth,' he said, as he turned the willing horse back up the hill towards the castle. Merewyn followed, listening to the sounds of a very relieved Helga, now that she was off the boat and chattering happily to the driver of the cart behind them.

Chapter Four

L uc ordered hot water, and, having washed the dust and grime from his body and hair, he had dressed in a soft tunic and fresh dark linen braies to go and greet his mother in the solar. He strode along the stone corridor and gently opened the door a fraction. He paused beyond the threshold, remaining out of sight, and took in the scene in the room, a family scene.

He loved his mother dearly; she was a remarkably strong and elegant woman, with family links to some of the oldest royal families in Europe. His father, Robert, met her in the court of Henry I of France; he had swept her off her feet and away into the wilds of western Brittany where she had thrived, devoting herself to her family and their estates. She had been devastated by his father's early death at Hastings, but he had been a warrior to the end; he had insisted on going to war with William and Alain Rufus. Although Robert was in his fifties at the time, he had still been a tall, fit, muscular man and a formidable fighter. Luc remembered seeing his father galloping his black Breton stallion up the hill at Senlac during the battle, in the front line as usual, but he had not seen him fall. He had, however, found his father's body, looking almost peaceful, his neck broken and his hand still holding the reins of his shivering horse. Luc had brought his father's body home but felt somewhat guilty that he had been of little help to his mother at this time, as his young wife, Heloise, and their newborn child, had died during those months. He had fled away from Morlaix and the pall of death that hung over his home. Fortunately, Gerard went with him and saved him from the worst excesses, but it was a dark time. He was angry at the world, and he had done things as a mercenary of which he was now ashamed. He had given no quarter to surrendering rebel troops, and the captured women had been treated as commodities by his men and the armies they fought alongside.

Mercifully, Gerard had taken him to fight for Alain Rufus at Hastings, where he met Bodin, Count Alain's half-brother. In a matter of weeks, they had become close friends and part of a fighting brotherhood under the House of Rennes' flag. Having seen the fury of the Malvais warhorses in the Battle of Hastings and the havoc that ensued, Alain tasked Luc with forming an elite cavalry of horsemen that became the famed 'Breton Horse Warriors'. These horses trained to fight and strike out with hooves and teeth were terrifying, and their warrior riders were just as lethal with their trademark double swords strapped over their backs. After campaigns in southern Italy for a short while, Luc then returned to England, going north with Alain Rufus to put down the rebellions in Northumberland.

He had visited his home rarely in those years; there were too many memories of his beautiful wife Heloise and his father at Morlaix, so he left his mother as Chatelaine to run the estates with the help of his younger brother Morvan. She had done so with an iron fist in a velvet glove, managing the vast estates with a firm hand, never pausing if she needed to repel bands of marauders. Luc had fully intended to return home in 1070, but, instead, Alain Rufus had installed him as the Marechal of a large section of his estates in the North of England, based in the large village of Ravensworth. These were lands that had belonged to wealthy Saxon Thegns, and it was Luc's task to subdue any further Saxon rebellions while managing the estates and building Norman fortifications.

It was at Ravensworth that he had come across Merewyn, the most beautiful but wilful Saxon rebel he had ever encountered. She had hated him on sight, and he, in turn, was determined to punish her for her insolence and disobedience. Still, the chemistry between them was something he had never experienced before. As a tall and striking Breton warrior, he had made love to dozens of women, but his heart and emotions had never been engaged after the pain of Heloise. Merewyn was different; she crept into his heart, and he admired her fiery spirit. They fell deeply in love but then went through the trauma of Luc's capture and torture by the Saxon rebels. Merewyn, accused of being a Saxon informer who had betrayed Luc, was put on trial. Fortunately, together with her wealthy father and Lord Bodin, he had saved her, as she had only betrayed him under threats and coercion from the Saxon leader. They had married, now had a delightful son, Lusian, and had lived a joyful life in Ravensworth until his recall to Brittany last year. Looking at the warm scene in the solar, he longed with all his heart for the time when she could be here with him in Morlaix when Brittany was finally at peace.

He ran his hands through his dark unruly, still-damp hair, pushed the heavy door fully open and walked into the room.

'Luc! At last!' exclaimed his mother, holding out her hands.

It was a large, well-proportioned room with an enormous stone fireplace in which several large logs were blazing. The room had stone-mullioned dual-aspect windows, which, while shuttered at present, made it a light and airy space in the daytime; the stone walls covered in coloured tapestries depicting hunting or religious scenes. Luc took his mother's hands and kissed them, smiling down at her. She sat holding court in an oversized, carved chair close to the fire.

'You are both back much later than expected,' she complained, pinning him with those piercing blue eyes that he had inherited and quickly scanning his tired face and body for any injuries. He laughed; his mother rarely wasted time on pleasantries.

'Good evening, mother,' he said, his dancing eyes sweeping over the group of people assembled and nodding at Morvan already lounging in a chair opposite.

He turned and greeted Briaca, who was the daughter of one of his mother's oldest friends, sent by her parents to live under Marie's wing for a year to prepare her to be the wife of a Breton knight. However, he had heard there was a hint of scandal around her– the whisper of an unsuitable dalliance, which was why her parents had sent her away. Luc believed that his mother intended her for his brother, Morvan, but he had seen no attraction or interest between them yet. Briaca was the epitome of a Breton beauty; she had ebony-black long shining hair, cornflower blue eyes and creamy white skin, untouched by smallpox. She turned her full charm on Luc as she smiled up at him.

We heard nothing from you, Luc; we were worried?' his mother said in a disapproving tone, bringing his attention back to her.

'Did my messengers not arrive' he asked. 'I sent two over the last few months.' She shook her head, and Luc looked questioningly over at Morvan, who shrugged, 'Look into it tomorrow Morvan, it seems we may have two more men missing.' Luc said with a frown.

'Two missing? What was this? Are you and the men still in one piece? She asked in concern.

'Almost. We lost two of our men and horses, but we have, yet again, chased the Angevin troops back over the border,' Luc said with a grin, making light of the months of skirmishes and hardships and horrors they had endured.

'Good. Let's hope this will be an end to these tiresome incursions into William's lands,' she said, but his light tone did not fool her as she looked at the strained face of her eldest son. Luc nodded, but he knew that these raids were just the beginning; there was trouble on the borders and discontent among many Breton lords as well.

Briaca had watched Luc's arrival and the conversation with his mother, with a fixed, charming smile on her face. However, steely determination lay behind the mask. She had fallen in love with Luc De Malvais since she had come into his orbit eleven months ago. She had spent several days and many evenings in his company; she was aware that they meant her for his brother, Morvan De Malvais, but she was not going to settle for a second son with no land or title. She was determined to have Luc. She heard that he had married a Saxon nobody in the heathen wastes of northern England, but he had not returned to, or seen, this so-called wife for almost a year. Therefore, she reasoned that he could not love her, whereas Briaca was here with him, young, beautiful, and available. She beckoned to her maid in the corner to bring another chair for Luc, and she rose to position it by the fire opposite his mother, delivering a breath-taking smile to him while she did so.

Luc smiled back at Briaca and sank gratefully into the seat, thinking what a stunning beauty she was and how lucky some young knight would be to get her. He watched her for a moment; she was so like his first wife, Heloise, with her dark Breton colouring and deep blue eyes, that his stomach flipped for a second, and he forced himself to look away from her. Watching him, Briaca inwardly preened herself and made sure that mulled spiced wine was at hand, personally pouring him a cup. She had seen the glances, the narrowing of his eyes as he appraised her from her shining black hair to her neat small feet; she was satisfied with the effect she was having on him. Everything was going to plan, but she knew that she needed to play this very carefully, so she modestly lowered her long black lashes and picked up her embroidery.

'So, what news have we received here at Morlaix mother? Your lines of communication and contacts from the ducal courts across Europe are often frighteningly better than mine,' he laughed.

Marie smiled and inclined her head in agreement. 'Mostly what you know already, Ralph De Gael, the Earl of Suffolk and Norfolk, has rebelled against King William in England in alliance with his brother-in-law, the Earl of Hereford and Earl Waltheof of Northumberland,' she said.

'But why would these Earls do this? The King had rewarded them all so well after the conquest,' asked Briaca, in a puzzled tone.

Marie answered the girl, 'Ralph De Gael has never really

forgiven William for poisoning his older brother, Walter, and his wife, Biota, with bride-ale while they were guests at William's castle in Falaise.'

'Yes, but that was nearly ten years ago, and it did allow William to take control of the province of Maine when he needed to secure his southern borders,' said Luc.

'Spoken just like a soldier and a true supporter of your ruthless King,' said Marie, as she raised an eyebrow at her son. 'Some people have long memories, Luc, especially when their families are murdered,' she added. She turned back to Briaca and continued, 'Then, William refused to sanction Ralph De Gaels' marriage to Emma, the Earl of Hereford's daughter. However, Ralph defied William, married Emma anyway and launched the rebellion from his wedding feast in Northumberland, while William was still occupied in Normandy.'

Luc gave a low whistle; this was indeed worrying news; Ralph De Gael, the Earl of both Suffolk and Norfolk and the Lord of Gael and Montfort in Brittany, was a powerful and wealthy adversary with many allies. Now in alliance with other Earls, he had rebelled against King William. 'Always trouble brewing in the North,' he muttered.

'However, the warrior Bishops have apparently held the rebels at bay for King William. Emma De Gael is now under siege in Norwich Castle, and rumour has it that Ralph De Gael has abandoned her and fled England for Denmark to raise an army and a fleet to bring back against William. Or, he might possibly be heading for his home here in Brittany,' she added.

Luc frowned; this all meant further trouble in Brittany. If Ralph Da Gael returned here when Luc had hoped to be released from his service to return to Ravensworth, it could mean all-out warfare and no chance of returning home. He knew that William would not forgive a Breton Earl's betrayal, especially one that he had rewarded so well in the past with lands and gold. It meant that the King would probably pursue Ralph De Gael here.

His mother continued, 'As you have just returned from our eastern borders, I am sure that you are aware of what is happening in Dol.' She asked Luc.

'I know there have been months of disagreements about the new archbishop and that Duke Hoel is threatening to go and remove him reinstate the previous archbishop.' he said in a puzzled voice.

'It is more serious than that; my sources tell me that Hoel is preparing an army to lay siege to Dol in the spring and more worryingly that William may come and support him.' There was a stunned silence at this news as they weighed up the implications of this. Luc shook his head, 'If William is coming to Brittany and Ralph De Gael arrives here as well, then Brittany will become a battleground.' He exclaimed in disbelief.

His mother stood, 'Let us go down to dinner. Briaca, go and tell Mathew we are ready.'

Luc watched as Briaca put away her embroidery and gave him a shy smile. He found himself smiling back, and his eyes swept over her rounded breasts and hips as she swayed gracefully to the top of the stairs. He glanced at his brother, Morvan, who was grinning at him and shaking his head.

'She is a tempting witch,' he mouthed at Luc behind his mother's back.

Luc grinned and shook his head. He needed to get back to

his wife. He so missed curling up around the soft, warm body of a woman, Merewyn's body, the woman he loved dearly. He sighed, and his face sank into a resigned expression that was not lost on his mother as she glanced back at him. She took his arm; she knew how difficult things were for her eldest son, but duty came first; it was the code they had chosen to live by as Breton nobility.

The Great Hall at Morlaix castle was impressive; the largest room in the solid stone-built fortress on the cliff could easily seat up to two hundred and often had. The roof was wooden with carved, arched beams, but the walls were stone and adorned with colourful tapestries in blues, reds and greens, alongside shields and banners on poles. The Malvais coat of arms was prominent, and dozens of large flaming torches lit the scene below. Most of Luc's men were already seated at the long wooden tables that ran lengthways down the Great Hall, the loud sound of their laughter, shouts and chatter greeting them as they descended the stone staircase from the solar. They made their way to the long top-table on the dais, where Briaca stood waiting for them, a vision of Breton beauty that entranced many men on the tables. No sooner were they settled when the men were reaching for the delicious Breton food, rich fish stews, roasted ducks and venison with chunks of fresh bread and rich yellow Breton butter. Suddenly, Luc's attention was attracted by his steward Mathew hurrying up the Hall in some urgency.

'What is it, Mathew?' he said, tearing a chunk of roast venison from the huge joint and lifting it onto his platter.

'We have received a message from the quayside, my Lord, requesting horses and transport. We have visitors arriving,' he said in a breathless voice.

'Did they say who it was, Mathew?' said Luc; it was unusual to get visitors by ship at this time of the year when the seas could be very rough.

'Yes, my Lord, it is Sir Gerard.'

Startled, Luc put down his knife. 'Gerard? Here?'

He turned and looked at his mother, who raised her hands and shrugged. 'There must be a reason, my son. Gerard would never come here at this time of year without orders from you. Now finish your meal. It will all become clear when he arrives.'

Luc grunted his agreement, but his mind was racing; why would Gerard leave Ravensworth? Had something happened to Merewyn or Lusian? He went cold at the thought, and the rich red meat he had looked forward to became tasteless in his mouth.

His mother watched the play of emotions across her son's face. Luc was never one to bare his soul, but he had talked at length when he first arrived back in Brittany about his all-enveloping love for the Saxon beauty he had married and their son Lusian, her first grandson. She had been pleased for him. She could see that Merewyn had managed to heal the dreadful pain he went through, losing his first wife and child, and she hoped to God that whatever news Gerard brought did not include bad tidings about his family.

Luc gave up all pretence at eating, pushed his platter away and drained his wine goblet instead, tapping his fingers impatiently, sending several glances to the door of the antechamber at the back of the Hall.

Briaca had watched all of this with interest; she hoped that whatever news this Sir Gerard brought would aid her in her quest to win Luc De Malvais for herself. She had dressed with care this evening in a deep russet velvet overdress, cut much lower at the front than was seemly in an unmarried maiden, but she knew it emphasised her rounded breasts and creamy white skin to advantage. She had seen Luc's eyes sweep over her again as he settled at the table, and she had taken the chair on his right. Now, sitting beside him, she leaned forward, placing her hand lightly on his arm and, looking up, she gave him the full benefit of that view before leaning over to speak softly in his ear. 'Would you like some more wine, my Lord?' she purred and, smiling, she raised her huge cornflower-blue eyes to his face. Luc gazed down at the beauty close beside him, his eyes drawn to her perfect breasts, and he distractedly smiled down at her and nodded as she filled his goblet.

Looking up again, he became aware that the group of travellers had entered the Hall, and there was Gerard, his friend and mentor, smiling at him; beside him was a tall, hooded and cloaked figure that raised her hands and lifted the hood back from her head. He would have recognised that long silver-blond hair anywhere, and he leapt to his feet, knocking his wine over and his chair backwards in his haste.

Briaca, her arm knocked to one side, watched all this in dismay, narrowing her eyes as she took in all the details of the arrivals. There could be no doubt that this tall, willowy, blonde beauty was Luc's wife; within seconds, he was striding down the Hall towards her leaving Briaca's plans in tatters.

Chapter Five

Merewyn felt the first misgivings as they rode into the grassed outer Bailey of this enormous fortress that was Luc's home. There were dozens of men and huge horses everywhere, tack being cleaned and horses rubbed down by what seemed to be an army of young stable boys and squires. A few Breton horse warriors from Ravensworth hailed Gerard and Merewyn with shouts and a raised clenched fist.

As they rode through the arch and the wooden gates into the large inner cobbled courtyard around a vast stone Donjon, she saw that this was just as crowded and full of bustling servants carrying buckets of water for the large, stone troughs. The scale of the campaign Luc had led almost overwhelmed her; there must be over a hundred people and horses here. She felt further misgivings for several seconds; surely, Luc would understand why they had to come to Brittany, she thought, dismounting as a groom came to take her horse. Gerard lifted Lusian down and carried him up the broad steps to the impressive stone entrance with the De Malvais coat of arms carved above the doorway. Lusian's eyes bubbled with excitement as he took in the bustling scene in the courtyard, and she wondered what he would do when he saw the father he had not seen for almost a year. They had been very close. Luc would take Lusian up before him on the back of Espirit practically every day in Ravensworth, and then suddenly, he was gone.

Luc's castle Steward, Matthew, greeted them with a smile; Sir Gerard was an old friend. He pushed open the heavy door, and they went into a large, stone antechamber. It had carved wood panelling covering the lower stone, something she had never seen before, and wooden benches for supplicants and visitors lined the walls of the room. There was a large, stone fireplace with very welcome blazing logs, and they stood in front of it as Matthew explained that the family were at dinner in the Great Hall with many of the returning horsemen joining them. The noise and shouts from the Great Hall could clearly be heard, and Merewyn realised that her reunion with Luc would be very public, not the private one that she had imagined. She ran the tip of her tongue nervously over her lips and clasped her hands tightly in front of her. Gerard turned and, taking Lusian by the hand, he smiled encouragement at her. She followed him through the door and into the vast, brightly lit Great Hall, and she took in the scene at a glance. Her eyes scanned over the dozens and dozens of men sitting at the trestle tables and then moved up to the top table. Her breath caught in her throat as she saw Luc; there was a very regal, older woman to his left with silver hair held back in a veiled band; she assumed that this was his mother. However, seated to his right, with a hand resting on his upper arm, was a stunningly beautiful young woman with shining black hair and translucent, white skin. She was gazing adoringly up at Luc while he was smiling down into her eyes. As she watched the scene, she saw his dark,

43

handsome head move closer to hers, and the dark beauty whispered something in his ear. Merewyn heard herself give a loud gasp, and conversation stopped at the end of the tables closest to her. Was this girl the reason he had not returned or contacted her? She felt the anger build within her. Gerard enthusiastically greeted the men on the tables close by, and she realised that Luc had seen them; his eyes had narrowed as he stared down the Hall at the group, so she slowly lifted and then lowered her hood to reveal her shining silver-blonde hair.

She watched as Luc leapt to his feet and, within seconds, he was striding down the Great Hall towards them, his face suffused with joy. She laughed with relief and ran into his arms as he picked her up, swinging her around and then enveloping her in an all-consuming kiss that left no doubt about his love for her. The Breton Horse Warriors cheered and banged their tankards and fists on the tables. Half of them had been with Luc at Ravensworth; they adored Merewyn; she was *their* Saxon beauty as well.

Merewyn nestled within Luc's arms, her head against his chest, just breathing in the smell of him. She didn't want to let him go but could feel an insistent pulling at her cloak. Lusian had fought his way out of Gerard's hold and now wanted as much attention. She stepped reluctantly out of Luc's hold and smiled, 'My Lord, I think your son would like to greet you. Say hello to your father, Lusian,' she said.

Luc looked down at the dark little boy, regarding him solemnly from large green eyes. There was no fear or apprehension there, more of a challenging stare. Luc laughed and swept him up into a hug; he could not believe how much his son had grown. At nearly five years old, he was a very tall boy and the image of his father. He felt suddenly saddened that he had missed so much of his life over the last year as he threw the laughing boy in the air and caught him.

'Come and meet my mother; she is so impatient to meet you and her grandson,' he said as he shouldered Lusian to more cheers from his men and took Merewyn by the hand, leading her up to his mother, who had come round the table and was now smiling down at them as she stepped down from the dais. While Marie was greeting her daughter-in-law and grandson, Luc enveloped Gerard in a bear hug, clapping him on the back.

'I am pleased to see you, my old friend, but…' he raised his eyebrows and indicated his wife and son.

Gerard shrugged and gave a rueful smile. 'There was little I could do, my Lord, to stop her, short of locking her up, especially after Bardolph arrived as the new Marechal of Ravensworth and you were missing.'

Luc gave a rueful smile at the thought of his headstrong wife riding roughshod over Gerard and his instructions. 'We will talk later, my friend, but they could not have come to Brittany at a worse time; the situation is increasingly dangerous,' he said, shaking his head.

He brought Morvan over to meet his family. 'This is my sensible younger brother,' he said, slapping Morvan on the back.

Merewyn gazed up at Morvan, he was very like Luc, but he had his father's wide brown eyes flecked with gold. 'You didn't mention that he was just as handsome as you,' she laughed.

Morvan coloured up slightly, which she found enchanting, but he deflected her attention by introducing Briaca, his mother's ward staying with them for a while. The girl was even more beautiful at close quarters, and Merewyn could see why any man would find her attractive. However, as she smiled and bowed to Merewyn, she noticed that the smile did not reach those big cornflower-blue eyes. Instead, Merewyn felt that this haughty beauty was assessing her as Luc's wife.

Briaca had watched the joyful family reunion with gritted teeth while she fixed a sweet painted smile on her face. This unwelcome arrival may be a setback, but she was still determined to have him one way or another; she just needed to come up with a plan to remove this Saxon interloper. More chairs were brought as they all gathered around the top table, eating, laughing and catching up on the news from Ravensworth. Briaca was unceremoniously pushed out to the end of the table to make way for Merewyn and Gerard. Lusian, bouncing on his father's knee, enjoyed all of his new family's attention, especially from his uncle, who was also a brave warrior, like his father.

Morvan was delighted to meet his stunningly beautiful sister-in-law; Luc had talked so much about her as they sat around the campfires on a night. She was a tall, elegant woman like his mother, but with a sparkle in her eye and a ready smile. He could see the happiness shining in her eyes as she gazed at Luc, and he was pleased for his brother. He hoped he would find a woman who would love him as much as that one day. On that thought, his eyes moved to the end of the table where a much darker beauty sat facing him. He looked at the fixed smile and the narrowed blue eyes and thought, Yes… That one will not like being eclipsed by another, brighter beauty at Morlaix. He knew his mother hoped that he and Briaca would make a match of it; after all, he was a second son, and she was the heir to her father's extensive estates in Dinan. However, Morvan was not taken in by Briaca; it was not only her beauty that was dark. He could see past the façade, and he did not like what he had witnessed; he had watched her try her wiles on his brother, aiming for a bigger catch. At that moment, her eyes met his, and he lifted his goblet in salute with a mocking smile. He saw her lips narrow and the fury in her eyes. Yes, he thought, she would make any man's life hell, and he turned back, instead, to enjoy watching the lively scene around Luc.

Before long, Merewyn signalled for Helga to come and take Lusian to bed; his head was nodding against his father's shoulder. However, after greeting Helga, a familiar Saxon family retainer, Luc refused to hand him over. He announced to the table that he would be retiring to his chambers with his family, and, taking Merewyn by the hand and carrying his son, they mounted the stone staircase to the upper floor. Beds were now set up in the room adjacent to Luc's chamber for Lusian and Helga, and Merewyn stood beside Luc gazing down at their son, now curled up asleep on his bed, his hand curled around the leg of his carved horse. She looked up at Luc, and the tenderness on his face as he gazed at his son filled her heart with joy. They quietly left the room, and, for the first time since they had arrived, Merewyn felt nervous as Luc took her hand and led her into his chamber. It had been nearly a year since she had lain with him, and she, unaccountably, felt suddenly shy. As they entered the room, she gazed in awe at this commodious bedroom and solar. It had large, stone, mullioned-glass windows and logs burning brightly in a substantial, stone fireplace. Several large, wooden chests lay against the walls, which, again, had been lined with wood on the lower section. Colourful tapestries and flags adorned the stone walls, and, in particular, her attention was drawn to an eye-catching and unusual tapestry above the bed. It was of a white unicorn drinking at a pool in the forest. Luc stood back looking at his wife as she gazed at the tapestry, her hair shining in the firelight. He could hardly believe she was here. He came up behind her pulling her close against him, sliding his hands around her waist and dropping his head to smell and feel the touch of her hair on his face.

'Unicorns are a symbol of purity and grace,' he murmured, breathing in the smell of her. 'There are many legends surrounding unicorns in Brittany, I thought you should take it as your emblem, so I commissioned this tapestry for you,' he whispered, as he revelled in the feel of her soft, warm body against his. He moved his hands up to cup her breasts. He had wanted her for so long that he groaned as he pulled her harder against him.

Merewyn was deliriously happy; she had been somewhat overawed at first by the size and extent of his family home. She had known, of course, that he was a wealthy Breton Lord and that he had inherited even more land and wealth from his first wife, Heloise, but to see that wealth reflected in every aspect of their new life was a revelation to her. With the furniture, the silver tableware, the rich linen and huge tapestries everywhere, his family lived like minor royalty; she must have seen at least fifty servants and retainers since she had arrived.

Now, however, she just wanted to be with Luc, her husband, her lover. She needed him, wanting to enjoy every inch of the long, hard body that she had missed so much. A quiver of excitement raced down through her body to her groin as he pulled her against him. He swept her hair to one side and began gently kissing and biting the back of her neck. She could feel herself melting against him, and she gasped as his hands caressed her breasts and found her hardening nipples. Oh, how she had missed Luc making love to her. He groaned, and she could feel his hard erection pressing against her. She put her head back and met his searching lips until he spun her around and pulled her to him, kissing her deeply, his strong hands holding her head. He moved back and slowly unlaced her over-gown. He drew it down over her shoulders to drop at her feet, and she stood expectantly in her linen chemise, her eyes never leaving his face and those steel-blue eyes that reflected her passion.

The warmth of the fire was on her back; her long silver-blonde hair was unbound and hung over one shoulder, and the light from the flames outlined her perfect body. Luc pulled off his tunic and stood bare-chested in front of her, gazing at her with an expression of utmost love on his face. However, she could see and feel his need for her, the prominent bulge in his braies evidence of that. Her eyes hungrily devoured his hard-muscled torso as he slowly undid the ties around his waist and allowed the linen garment to drop to the ground. She followed the lines down his toned torso and the dark, almost black line of hair that spread down to his groin and his hard prominent manhood.

He put his hands on her shoulders and stepped purposefully towards her drawing her linen chemise over her head. As he wrapped her naked body in his arms, she could feel the heat of his large erection pulsing and demanding against her stomach. He lifted her effortlessly up into his arms and carried her to the bed, placing her gently in the middle of the soft fur coverlet. He lay down beside her and took her face in his hands

'Let's enjoy these next few days together, Merewyn. I have missed you so much; I want you, and I intend to have you now and hopefully several more times before the dawn. I want your bare skin touching mine; I need to bury myself within you.'

Merewyn laughed and smiled up at him, her eyes full of joy as he gently spread her legs and knelt between them, running his hands up the soft flesh of her thighs so that she gasped with pleasure, need for him coursing through her body. He leaned forward, supported on his elbows. She could feel the heat from his long body against her. Then he kissed her deeply again. Merewyn felt her body rising, involuntarily, to meet his, as she squirmed with desire beneath him, her mound pushing hard against his manhood inviting him to enter her. However, Luc knelt up, running his hands down over her shoulders and arms, caressing her breasts, enjoying having her there ready for him after so long apart. He just brushed between her legs, and then he stroked the inside flesh at the top of her thighs.

His eyes scanned her body in an unmistakable caress, and she whispered, 'Luc, I need you inside me.' However, as he moved to position himself, she realised what he had said. 'Do we only have a few days, Luc? When do you leave?' she asked.

He reluctantly stopped caressing her and sat back on his heels, smiling down but with a semi-frown on his brow. 'I will not be leaving, Merewyn, but you will be. I will arrange for a boat to return you to England before the seas become totally impassable.'

Merewyn raised herself onto her elbows and looked at him in horror. 'No,' she managed to say and then louder. 'No! I am not leaving you again!' she shouted.

Luc looked at her perplexed; he was not used to people disobeying him. 'I am not giving you a choice, Merewyn; you have put yourself and my son in danger by coming here at this time. William is dealing with several rebellions, and Brittany is torn apart by opposing alliances for and against him. I will not have my wife and son here at risk in the middle of this turmoil and war, causing distractions. Did you not understand the letters and orders that I sent to you?'

Merewyn had listened to this in disbelief at first, but now she could feel the anger building inside her. 'I have had no letters or communication from you for over five months. I thought you were wounded or even dead,' she said, her voice breaking on the last word.

Luc was confused, 'I sent the last courier to Alain only a month ago and included a missive to you,' he said.

Merewyn hardly heard what he said, taking a deep breath, her green eyes flashing with anger, 'I did not receive it, as for us being distractions,' she spat at him. 'What did I see when I entered tonight, but you distracted by a black-haired beauty with her hands all over your body, and you gazing down at her breasts. Is that why you want us gone from here, Luc?'

At that point, Merewyn's eyes filled with angry tears, but Luc did not see that as he turned and slowly climbed off the bed. Crossing to the small table, he poured himself a goblet of wine. He was trying to make sense of her words; he vaguely remembered talking to Briaca, and he guiltily admitted to himself that he found the dark Breton girl beautiful. But betray Merewyn? He would never do that; he

51

felt righteous anger building inside him as he downed the wine and poured another immediately. Merewyn sat on the bed, arms wrapped around her knees, looking at the back of Luc's long, muscled naked torso, the scars from his ordeal with Braxton, the rebel Saxon leader still prominent across his back. Whenever she saw them, she felt a stab of guilt that she had been responsible for Luc's capture, but he had forgiven her, and now a wave of misery engulfed her at the rift between them. They had never had a cross word in over five years, but this Luc seemed different in Morlaix. She knelt up on the bed; her loosened blonde tresses fell over her breasts.

'You will have to bind me and carry me kicking and screaming onto that boat,' she said, eyes blazing. 'I will not leave you again,' she shouted at him.

Luc downed the second goblet of wine and turned towards her. 'You defied my orders, Merewyn, putting all of you in danger. Are you so selfish that you only thought of yourself?' he asked as he glared back at her. 'You are my wife, Merewyn, and you will do as I say if I have to thrash that into you.' Merewyn said nothing but glared back at him.

Luc hesitated for only a second, thinking how beautiful she looked in the firelight, kneeling up and naked but spitting defiance at him. His glance softened as he realised that this reminded him of Merewyn when he first met her, a furious, Saxon rebel who hated everything Norman and defied him at every turn. Nevertheless, Luc knew he could not have this. He slammed the goblet down onto the table and then strode towards the bed. For the first time, Merewyn felt real apprehension. The sight of this tall, naked, muscular warrior striding towards her with intent written all over his face also triggered a frisson of almost fearful excitement. She had never seen this expression on Luc's face before, mainly because she had never really defied him before.

'You will obey me, Merewyn,' he said in a firm, no-nonsense tone; he stood between her legs gazing down at her, his hands on his hips. She could see that he was still fully aroused.

'You will do as I say, Merewyn. Can't you see I am trying to keep you and Lusian safe?' he asked in an exasperated voice.

'I am not leaving,' she said through gritted teeth, starting to sit up. Luc pushed her back down and, spreading her legs, entered her quickly, kissing her deeply at the same time to silence her. She gasped; this was not quite, what she had imagined for their first night together, but she so wanted and needed him. She loved him, and she tightened her arms around him, running her hands over his muscled shoulders and down his back as she kissed his neck. Suddenly, he slowed and looked down into her eyes. He stopped and held her at a distance. Then, pulling her into his arms, he kissed her eyes and lips.

'I am sorry, Merewyn, I love you so much, but I will not allow you to defy me in this way; we will discuss this calmly tomorrow. Do you understand?'

She nodded as he held her close and began to kiss her deeply again so that waves of desire coursed through her body. He pulled back so that he was just poised at the entrance to her body, tormenting and teasing her with just a hint of penetration. He kissed her nipples, taking them gently between his teeth and biting them. Within moments, she had lost all control and, placing her hands firmly on his hips; she pulled him inside her. She revelled in the hardness and fullness of him as he filled her, his lips and hands still caressing her body. She made repeated soft sounds and then moaned as he quickly brought her to the edge. Before long, she had completely lost control, and her hands gripped the sides of the bed as her body moved with his, giving in to the sensation until she reached a peak and climaxed with a cry of pure ecstasy.

However, Luc was only beginning, and she soon felt the pleasure mounting again as he repeatedly drove into her, putting his hands under her buttocks and pulling her up and onto him. Merewyn opened her eyes and gazed at this man that she loved so much; his dark hair flopped over his forehead, his steel-blue eyes glazed with passion, and she could see the sweat beginning to glisten on his skin in the firelight. Merewyn laid back in a sea of ecstasy, revelling in the feel of his body on top of hers, the delicious weight of him, the musky, masculine smell of him. She ran her hands up through his hair as he moved intensely within her. He was now starting to lose control, and she felt his body tense until he groaned aloud and poured himself into her as she shuddered with the aftershocks of another climax.

They lay entwined on top of the fur coverlet; his body spent and supine in her arms as she vowed to herself that she would do everything in her power not to leave Brittany. She knew, however, that she would have to play this differently. Luc would not tolerate open defiance, so she needed to get allies such as Marie, Morvan and Gerard on her side. Luc's head rested on her breast, and she gently kissed his forehead, telling him how much she had missed his lovemaking. He pulled her tight against him, enveloping her in his arms as he drifted off to sleep. She smiled as she pulled the coverlet up to cover them; the huge fire was banked with logs so they would be warm enough. She listened to his deep breathing, and she could feel the beat of his heart against her breast.

'I will never leave him again,' she whispered to herself repeatedly.

Chapter Six

Merewyn awoke to the sunlight streaming through the unshuttered windows. It took a few seconds for her to realise where she was as she gazed up at the wooden vaulted and carved ceiling above her. As realisation dawned, she instinctively put a hand out to find Luc, but the bed was cold and empty beside her. She sat up, wrapping the fur coverlet around her as she swung her legs out of bed. She winced as she sat on the edge of the bed; after a year without lovemaking, she could certainly feel the aftermath of last night's passion. She smiled at the thought but then remembered the argument that had almost ruined their first night together. The picture of Luc and Briaca came unbidden to her mind, and her eyes narrowed. She was not naïve; she knew that both men and women could be tempted when they were apart for so long, and most men she knew would not hesitate at a quick dalliance if it were on offer. However, she knew that Luc was different; the love they had for each other was so deep, she knew that he would never betray her. However, part of her mind wondered how things might have developed between them if she had not turned up; she had caught the anger in Briaca's eyes at her arrival.

She shook herself to remove such thoughts just as the door

opened to reveal Luc followed by a servant carrying a jug and a large tray; he placed them on the table, bowed and left them alone. There was silence in the room for what seemed an age as Merewyn and Luc regarded each other. He thought she had never looked more beautiful, tousled and rosy from last night's lovemaking, wrapped in the soft fur coverlet with her naked shoulders and long bare legs on show. The sun streaming through the window made her silver-blonde hair shine, and her large eyes gazed intently at him. He was unsure at first of what to say; he was also slightly ashamed of his forceful behaviour last night. He had never had to treat Merewyn like that before but, although he regretted it, he could never let her defy him like that here in Brittany; it was too dangerous for them to stay here. With these thoughts foremost in his mind, he assumed a somewhat sterner expression than he had intended.

'I have had some food brought up for you, Merewyn, to break your fast. Lusian has eaten with us down in the Hall, and my mother has taken him down to the home farm to help collect the duck eggs. I told her we needed some time on our own to talk.'

Merewyn gazed back at him, both love and concern clear to see, and he forced himself to look away.

'I will give you time to dress and eat while I go to the stables. I will see you in the Solar at noon, and we can decide what the arrangements are for your departure.'

Merewyn's heart leapt into her mouth; she could not let him go like this. She had watched him as he entered the room, the emotions playing over his face. She knew he loved her deeply, and she surmised that he was as unhappy as she was about how their first night together had begun. However, as one of the fiercest warriors in Europe, she knew about his pride and sense of righteousness. He was the leader of what was almost an army of men, servants and tenants; he expected and received respect and obedience. She knew that he expected it from her as well. It was very rare that Luc De Malvais came across defiance and disobedience, and, as Gerard had pointed out repeatedly on their journey here, it never ended well for those who defied him or displayed those traits.

As he turned to go, she whispered his name and, as he looked back, she dropped the coverlet and opened her arms, her face full of love for him. Luc hesitated for only a few seconds before he strode across the room and enveloped her soft naked body in his arms, pulling her tight against him as if he would never let her go. He sighed into her hair. The smell of her was intoxicating as he put his fingers under her chin and raised her smiling lips to his. 'Food and Espirit can wait; we have a lot of catching up to do,' he said as he effortlessly picked her up and took her back to bed, a grin on his face.

Merewyn dressed with care in a soft powder-blue over-gown before she went to join Luc in the solar at midday. She knew her most challenging task lay ahead, persuading him that they should be allowed to stay, yet she was determined not to leave him again. Luc was standing in the semi-octagonal embrasure staring out of the windows when she opened the door. She took a deep breath and quickly crossed to his side.

'You look beautiful,' he said, raising her hand to his lips and pulling her to his side with his arm around her.

They stood in silence looking out on the estates' extensive and well-tended fields on this side of the castle. She asked him several questions about the features she could see in the distance while revelling in his close masculinity. The smell of his soft leather doublet was so resonant of their former life together, along with the sight of the dark stubble on his chin and the strong, tanned, sword-hand resting on the stone mullioned windowsill. She wanted to stay like this, leaning against him, breathing him in, the man she loved, but Luc, looking down at her, suddenly took her hands and sat her down on the window seat. Merewyn felt apprehension as she gazed up into his eyes; she could see both determination and resignation in his face, and she steeled herself for what was to come.

Luc sighed as he looked down at his beautiful wife. He wanted nothing more than to keep them in Brittany with him, but he knew it would be too dangerous and a distraction for him given the recent events.

'Merewyn, I have loved having you and Lusian here. I have missed you both so much, but you must trust my judgement on this. There are moves afoot in Brittany amongst the Breton Lords that will put you both in danger. I am fighting for King William on Alain Rufus's orders, my liege lord, and there are now many ruthless forces and enemies pitted against us. You and my son could become a target, and I cannot let that happen, so I must send you back to safety until these wars are over.'

Merewyn looked earnestly into his face and saw that he did indeed regret this, and she found it difficult to fight against such arguments.

'But I cannot leave you again, Luc, it has been too long, and Lusian hardly recognised you.'

He quickly pulled her into his arms and, kissing her,

murmured, 'Do you think I want to lose you again? Don't you realise what you and Lusian mean to me? The nights I have lain in the forest with my men, wrapped in a thin blanket against the cold, all I could think of was you waiting for me in our bed in Ravensworth. My heart has longed for both of you, Merewyn, but I have no choice in this. I have found that a coastal vessel arrives next week that will take you up the coast to Calais, where you can get a second vessel to take you across the channel. So let us enjoy the time we have together,' he said, kissing her tear-drenched eyes and pulling her to her feet to kiss her, his hands sweeping down her spine and stroking the curves of her bottom. 'Let us go and find Lusian,' he growled, 'before I take you back to bed.' Merewyn smiled, and, hand in hand, they went to find their son.

Briaca had waited in the Great Hall for Luc and Merewyn to come down that morning, but it had been a subdued Luc who had appeared. It had been difficult to ignore Luc and his wife's raised voices last night in the castle's echoing stone corridors. Briaca had smiled, pleased that the reunion between them was not going well. She had been unpleasantly surprised last night to find that the Saxon nobody was, in fact, a tall, elegant, wealthy Thegns daughter. During her arrival, she had watched Luc's face and saw that he truly loved his wife, despite being unhappy about her disobeying his orders to stay in England. She watched him sit down beside his mother, who Lusian was entertaining, and she heard him mumble an excuse about Merewyn being tired from the long journey. She decided to volunteer to go with Marie to the Home Farm. She wanted to get to know young Lusian; Briaca needed to find a new way to ensnare Luc and remove Merewyn. She would use any and every opportunity.

The three of them returned to the Hall for a nuncheon to find Luc, Gerard, Merewyn and Morvan deep in discussion. Lusian let go of Briaca's hand and raced to his father, giving Merewyn time to sit back and assess this dark, Breton beauty as she walked up the Hall with Marie. Merewyn admitted to herself that she was undoubtedly stunning and beautifully rounded in all the right places. When she smiled, as she was doing now at Lusian and Luc, it was a sweet smile. But Merewyn had glanced up and caught a cold, calculating look during an unguarded moment at dinner last night. Luc had explained that Briaca was intended for Morvan, so if this was to be her future sister-in-law, Merewyn knew she had to make an effort to be pleasant to the girl, although secretly she thought that Morvan would have his hands full there. However, she stood and thanked both Marie and Briaca for taking the time to entertain Lusian, who was now back on his father's knee. Merewyn signalled for Helga to come and take Lusian to get him washed and fed up in his room.

'It was a delight to spend time with my grandson. He reminds me of you, Luc, at that age, so impetuous and curious,' Marie laughed, while Luc smiled.

'I look forward to spending more time with him over the next few months, getting to know him and you much better,' she said, smiling at Merewyn and placing a hand on her knee. This kindness from Luc's mother, who, she was aware, had wanted a much better match for her widowed son, was almost too much for Merewyn, who raised her eyes to Luc in a mute appeal before dropping her head.

'Unfortunately, this is a brief visit, mother. They will leave next week, once more under the care of Gerard, to return to

Ravensworth,' said Luc, his face an expressionless mask, his eyes gazing into the far reaches of the Hall. Marie looked at her son in amazement and then at Gerard, who just raised his eyebrows and shrugged.

'But why Luc? They will be perfectly safe with me and Gerard at Morlaix,' said Marie.

Merewyn raised her head and smiled at Luc's mother. She realised that she had an ally here, and she needed to use this to her advantage, but very carefully so that she was not blatantly acting in defiance of Luc's wishes.

'We certainly don't want to leave, my Lady, but I understand Luc's concern for us. He sees the much bigger picture of the danger we may be in, so we must follow his instructions,' she said sweetly. Gerard raised an eyebrow at this sudden compliance from Merewyn, and Luc glanced at her, waiting for the sting in the tail, but Merewyn was the epitome of a dutiful wife as she folded her hands in her lap and gazed down at them.

'From what we hear, it is just as dangerous in England at the moment, with Ralph De Gael's rebellion against William happening in different areas of the North and East. His new, young wife, Emma, is now besieged in Norwich Castle, and you are thinking of sending your wife and child back to travel hundreds of miles through many of the areas in England they may be fighting in, to say nothing of a dangerous sea journey. What are you thinking of Luc?' his mother asked in an exasperated tone.

Luc did not answer, and his face set in stern lines of displeasure at this criticism as he stood and, pushing his chair back, drained his tankard. 'Gerard, Morvan, with me. We need to continue training the new men,' he said, striding off down the Hall. Gerard grimaced at Merewyn and Marie, and, sighing, he followed Luc and Morvan.

Marie smiled, 'He always was a very stubborn boy. Don't worry, my dear; I am not going to allow you and my grandson to get on that boat next week if I have to sink it myself,' she said as she rose and left them. Merewyn left with Briaca, decided to make an effort with the girl.

'Tell me, Briaca, how long have you been here at Morlaix? I believe your family have large estates in the North East at Dinan,' she said, smiling at her.

Briaca turned and looked at this Saxon beauty sitting in front of her. She blatantly ran her eyes over her, assessing her from her hair to her kid leather boots, and then gave a tight smile that was not pleasant.

'I have been here for a year; however, I have known the De Malvais family since I was a small child; Luc and his mother have gone out of their way to make me feel part of it. Heloise, Luc's first wife, was my cousin, and I am apparently the image of her. I belong here as a Breton; the Breton spirit runs through us, something you will never understand, and this is why you, as a foreigner and probably a heathen as well, will never understand us. We were building castles like this in Brittany while you Saxons were in mud huts,' she smirked. 'Now I am going to confer with the cook. Marie has given me responsibility for part of the household; she trusts me,' she said as a parting shot. She stood and, with only a nod in Merewyn's direction, headed to the kitchens.

Merewyn felt as though she had been slapped. This young girl must be at least eight years younger than her, yet she had treated her as someone of no importance. The arrogance of the verbal assault astounded Merewyn. There was no doubt that she thought of Merewyn as a foreigner, an interloper, someone of much lower status who would never fit in. Merewyn frowned; did other people think that? Did Luc's family? His men? Would his tenants and servants believe that? If so, her life here would become untenable. For the first time, Merewyn felt unsure of herself, and a cloud descended upon her earlier happiness.

Chapter Seven

Merewyn awoke to Luc kissing her as he prepared to leave the room. She smiled lazily at him. They had made love for hours in the firelight last night, and she felt reassured and happy, basking in his love. She also knew she had the backing of his mother to stay in Brittany, a powerful ally to have on side. As for the poisonous Briaca, she would deal with her in her own time.

'Must you go?' she said, reaching out an arm to pull him, fully clothed, back into bed. Laughing, he shook her off but, taking her hand, he raised it to his lips and kissed her fingers.

'You are delightfully insatiable, my love and, yes, I have to go; one of the houseboys has just told me that two messengers have arrived and are waiting for me downstairs.' He strode towards the door, and, turning, he grinned at her before he disappeared. He looks so boyish when he does that, she thought, so carefree when he has so much responsibility and many difficult decisions to make. She thought for a few moments about the messengers. She knew from experience that they often meant troubling news and upheaval; it was highly likely Luc would have to take the horse warriors and ride out again. That thought made her swing her legs out of bed to get dressed; she needed to find out what was happening.

On descending to the Hall, she could see that everyone was gathered, waiting to hear the news. The first messenger was from Dinan, from Briaca's parents, who insisted that she return to them for the few weeks of the yuletide celebrations. Briaca looked crestfallen at the news, but there was no way she could refuse, and Merewyn was delighted.

'Don't worry, girl, you can return after yuletide for the spring and summer,' said Marie, looking pointedly at Morvan, who pretended not to have heard. However, Briaca turned and bestowed a sweet smile on Luc and his mother.

'With your permission, of course, my Lord,' she said, gracefully bowing her head to them both.

'We will discuss arrangements tonight, my dear. I am sure that Morvan will be delighted to escort you to your home and renew his acquaintance with your parents,' said his mother. Merewyn met Morvan's eyes; he looked anything but delighted, and he quickly replied.

'Luc has business that way next week. There is a stunning Arab mare near Dinan that he wants to look at,' he said, looking pleadingly at Luc. However, Luc was only half listening as he read the missive brought by the second messenger from Alain Rufus. He looked up distractedly and nodded, much to Morvan's relief, before thanking the messenger and sending him down to the kitchens. Merewyn's spirits sank at the thought of Briaca travelling anywhere with Luc. Marie noticed the stern expression on her son's face. 'So what news from Alain Rufus? Anything you can share, Luc?' she asked.

'Well, as usual, mother, your network of informants proved reliable. Ralph De Gael did escape from England, and he has raised a Danish fleet in alliance with Cnut. He has sailed to attack William in the east; however, they are also raiding the channel's coasts and attacking all Norman shipping.'

His eyes narrowed as he glowered across at Merewyn at that point and said in an exasperated tone, 'Well, Merewyn, you have your wish. You cannot sail back to England, and you have brought yourself and my son into danger against my express wishes. I hope that we all do not live to regret your rash actions.' He banged the message in its leather bag down onto the table, turned on his heel and strode down the hall, leaving the others staring after him.

Marie took hold of Merewyn's hand. 'Don't worry, my dear. These storms blow over quickly with my son, as I am sure you know.'

She shook her head, undone again by Marie's kindness. 'We have never argued before,' she said, glancing at Gerard, who stood there, arms folded, with his I-told-you-so expression on his face. However, Briaca was standing beside him, her eyes dancing with delight. At that point, Merewyn drew herself up to her full height and smiled. 'It will be for the best. Lusian and I will be staying by his side where we should be,' she said.

Marie nodded and smiled. 'That's the spirit,' she said.

Morvan made a hopeful move to follow Luc but Gerard put a hand on his arm. 'Leave him be, Morvan. As you know, he will calm down in his own way.' Morvan nodded and reluctantly re-joined the women as requested as they headed to the solar to play with Lusian.

Luc had gone immediately to the stables. He declined the stable boy's help, saddled Espirit himself, and cantered out over the cobbles, through the gate and into the crowded Bailey. The sight of the large Destrier and their grim-faced lord bearing down on them scattered people and animals alike. Luc rode across his lands and forest for most of the day, tiring both himself and Espirit. Finally, in the deepening dusk, he reached the coast and the cliffs near the Roman ruins and dismounted, leaving Espirit to graze. A stiff, late-autumn breeze ruffled his hair as he sat on the ancient stones and gazed at the horizon and the eerie light of the winter sun setting in the west while Espirit cropped the grass nearby.

He was angry and exasperated.

Angry at himself for not foreseeing this situation and sending his family away sooner. He had selfishly kept them here longer for yet another week, which made him as equally culpable as Merewyn. He was frustrated because he could think of nothing to do to alleviate this situation. There was no safe place to send them in Brittany, given the pacts building against William's forces.

The recent message from Alain Rufus had contained alarming information about the extent of these alliances and the likelihood of open warfare. It meant his family would have to stay in Morlaix, which, in turn, meant leaving a larger contingent of his men, and probably Gerard as well, here to defend it. He clenched his jaw and then swore loudly, staring out but not really seeing the wind-whipped sea striking the rocks on the Breton coast. He was completely wrapped up in a reverie of thoughts; he needed to check on some of the disturbing intelligence arriving; several Breton Lords seemed to be joining the King's enemies for a concerted attack against him. The cold rain that suddenly lashed down took him by surprise.

Espirit stamped his feet and shook his rain-spattered mane, prompting Luc to retrieve the loosely knotted reins.

Mounting up, he trotted the Destrier down through the woods, heading for home. By the time he rode slowly back through the gatehouse, both horse and rider were thoroughly drenched, but Luc would allow no one else to see to his horse. This responsibility was always the first rule of a Breton Horse Warrior, no matter what his rank. He was shivering as he finished rubbing the Destrier down with large twisted wisps of straw and, in his sodden garments. It was late as he headed up to the Great Hall, where he knew the family would now be at dinner.

At first sight of him walking up the hall, his leather doublet, braies and overtrews soaked, Briaca had immediately leapt out of her seat and raced to get blankets and cloths. Merewyn watched Luc, his dark forelock plastered against his skin, as he stopped to share a few words with his assembled men on the benches. Some of them had been brave enough to throw a question at their severe-faced lord, having heard that messengers had arrived; they all expected the order to ride out.

From the corner of her eye, Merewyn saw Briaca re-enter the Hall with blankets heading towards Luc. In an instant, Merewyn stepped forward and intercepted her.

'Thank you, Briaca, for bringing me these,' she said, in her clear but sweetest voice as she lifted the blankets from her arms. For a few seconds, Briaca's grip tightened, and her eyes narrowed. 'Do you want me to slap you for insolence and disobedience in front of the whole Hall?' Merewyn whispered as she leaned over the girl. Briaca let a hiss out through her teeth and reluctantly let go.

Merewyn turned, just in time to greet Luc. She scanned the face of the man she loved so much, seeing the strain in his blue eyes and the tension in his neck and shoulders. She dropped into a deep curtsey in front of him to hold out the blankets.

'I am sorry, my Lord, for bringing this added concern to your door. I hope you will forgive me,' she whispered.

Luc looked down at his beautiful wife, closed his eyes and let out the breath he had not even realised he had been holding.

'You know Merewyn that you never have to kneel to me,' he said, taking both her hands and raising her to face him. He took the blanket, dried his head, arms and shoulders and dropped it on an empty bench. He then turned and looked into her eyes with a rueful smile, stroking the side of her face with his finger,

'We will manage this, Merewyn. Yes, you have created problems, but we will find a way to deal with it and keep you both safe.' He kissed her on the forehead and moved towards the stairs. 'Now I am going to get changed,' he said, nodding to his family and running lithely up the stairs.

Merewyn caught Marie's eye as she returned to the table, who nodded and smiled at Merewyn in approval as she gave the order for their dinner to be delayed. The family moved to stand around one of the large roaring fires at the side of the Hall as they waited for Luc. The men on the benches, already being fed vast platters of meat and a rich Breton fish stew, were tucking in regardless.

Morvan escorted Briaca towards the large stone fireplace. 'Well, you were outdone and outmanoeuvred there, my Breton beauty,' he whispered behind his hand.

Briaca gave him the full benefit of her sweetest smile. 'I have no idea to what you are referring, my Lord; I was purely trying to be helpful. And I would have done the same for you, Morvan.'

He looked down into those glittering hard sapphire-blue eyes and gave a burst of laughter that turned several heads in their direction.

'You do not fool me, Briaca. I have watched you, for several months, trying to win the interest of my brother; you will never be someone who will settle for a second son!'

They had reached the others by then. Briaca just gave him a haughty glance and clamped her lips shut on the reply she could have spat at him. She sat quietly on the bench and watched the family group around her, his mother recalling embarrassing tales from Luc and Morvan's childhoods, with Gerard joining in with more risqué memories from their youth. Briaca smiled sweetly but, watching a laughing, handsome Morvan with his arm around Merewyn's shoulders, she suddenly felt excluded. They were all trying to outdo themselves to entertain her, this Saxon outsider. Briaca clenched her fists in her lap as she thought of the effort she had made in the last six months to become the biddable Breton beauty they all wanted, but, for her, the prize had always been Luc De Malvais, and it still was. She was determined she would get rid of Merewyn; she just needed to find the right opportunity. At that moment, Merewyn turned and glanced back to where Briaca was sitting and was taken aback by what she saw on the girl's face,

'Mon Dieu,' she whispered, 'the girl really hates me.' She knew then that in future, she would have to be vigilant around her.

The following week passed in a blur of happiness for Merewyn. She enjoyed the evening family time with Luc and Lusian. Luc and Morvan spent hours each day in the paddocks and on the training ground to ensure that both the men and horses were fit. Luc enjoyed training the young three and four-year-old Destriers to get them ready for battle; usually, he did not have the time, but there seemed to be a lull in news and messengers now, so he was taking advantage of it. Often, there was a small figure with a mop of dark hair running between them, Lusian; he was fearless under the legs of the enormous horses while Merewyn watched him, her heart in her mouth.

'They are almost ready to sell on, Luc,' said Morvan, watching the latest batch go through their paces. We do need that breeding mare we were offered if she is as good as they say. Luc nodded while shouting instructions to the men in the saddles; a young, black stallion was proving far too difficult for the young rider to control.

'Is that the stallion out of Espirit and that black witch of a mare, Midnight, that we had?' asked Luc.

Morvan nodded. 'Yes, she was a filly out of fathers black stallion Demon; she destroyed her stable several times over, gave us two beautiful black colts, one of whom was this one, and she finally escaped. Rumour has it she is running with the wild herds south of here near the coast; I would like to catch her again one day.'

Luc laughed. 'Well, good luck with that; he certainly has her spirit!'

'I know,' said Morvan, 'I am thinking of keeping him for my second string.'

Luc nodded. 'He will be phenomenal in battle, but don't break his spirit.'

Morvan was reluctant to let the topic of selling the surplus drop, as he needed to bring up the two-year-olds for training soon. 'We have over twenty spares for our troop here, which leaves us at least another twelve to sell on; we do have a lot of interest.'

Luc laughed. 'Yes, Morvan, I know. I will be seeing the Arab mare when I go to Dinan in a few days, and I will bring her back if she lives up to the description: intelligent, fast but with plenty of stamina and bone. I will just need to haggle the price down.' Morvan grinned.

The time that Merewyn loved most was after dinner when they would retire to their chambers to talk, play music and plan for the future, sharing their dreams even in this uncertain time. Their lovemaking had slowed in its intensity, but Luc was a vigorous man who would pull her into his arms most nights. It was as they lay sated after such a bout that Luc pulled her close.

'I will be leaving in two days for Dinan,' he said while stroking her long blonde hair.

Merewyn knew that the journey was imminent, and her stomach knotted at the thought of losing him again.

'How long will you be gone?' she asked.

'There was other news and orders in Alain Rufus's message that I did not share widely. As you know, alliances are forming up on one side or the other, and I have been tasked to sound out several Lords in the north-west who are undecided. Therefore, I will be calling on a few on the way to and from Dinan to try and persuade them to support William. I would imagine I will be away for just over a week.'

Luc paused and gazed into the firelight. She could see the determination in his face but a hint of resignation at being parted from his wife and son again. She rested her head on his muscled chest and ran her hands down his sides and along his raised thigh. She loved every inch of Luc's body, loved to run her hands over the flexing muscles, revelling in the feel of his warm skin; she had so missed these moments.

'Yes. Things have been unnaturally quiet for the last month, even on the borders, but this is unusual, and I can only feel that it is the quiet before the storm as people prepare for war. I only hope that we are also prepared with a significant number of alliances before it breaks. Otherwise, we will find ourselves outnumbered.'

Merewyn ran her hand along the inside of his thigh up towards his groin, which brought Luc's attention firmly back to her, and he pushed her back onto the bed laughing.

'Let us think of more pleasant things,' he said as his dark head loomed over her.

Chapter Eight

Two days later, on a cold December morning, Merewyn stood at the top of the steps overlooking the courtyard below; Morvan stood beside her and Lusian was firmly gripped in front of her. From behind her, she could hear Marie shooing Briaca outside as Luc and his troop of Horse Warriors had been waiting for some time. Morvan grasped arms with Luc in farewell. 'Unfortunately, one of our new men, Bertrand, has the gripes, he has run to the privy twice, but he is very keen to be with you; I will send him after you to catch up if he recovers.' Luc nodded and glanced impatiently at the doorway.

'Hurry up, Briaca, you know he hates to keep his horses standing in the cold,' Marie scolded as she came to stand beside Merewyn and her grandson.

'Well, that is one person we won't miss,' Morvan whispered to Merewyn, who smiled and shook her head. Merewyn admitted she was looking forward to spending more time with Marie without Briaca's glowering presence.

However, she had to give it to Briaca; she was indeed the perfect Breton beauty. She watched through narrowed eyes as the girl ran lightly down the steps and offered her hand to Luc to help her to mount. She had dressed for riding but with a fine deep blue woollen hooded cloak that matched her eyes. As she picked up her reins, she looked down at Luc and gave him the full benefit of those huge, blue eyes and a winning smile as he tightened her girth. Merewyn noticed that Luc could not help but smile back at her as she thanked him and rested a small, white hand on his shoulder. She then pulled up her skirt to show a snowy white leg, her tiny feet encased in soft leather boots, which she invited Luc to help guide into the large leather stirrups. Merewyn gritted her teeth as she watched Luc's hands on the girl's lower legs. At that moment, Briaca looked up and sent a triumphant smile in Merewyn's direction.

'An accomplished performance,' laughed Morvan, but Merewyn did not join in, feeling the anger bubbling inside her. Breathing deeply, she thought instead of their time this morning when he told her how much he loved her and how much she meant to him. He had made love to her again with an intensity that revealed how much he would miss her...

Meanwhile, Luc vaulted onto the back of Espirit and, with a wave to his family, he led the group out of the courtyard at a trot. He took fifteen of his men with him, many of whom were recent additions or in need of more training, as it provided an ideal opportunity to spend extended times with their mounts. The first part of the journey was uneventful but slow. However, he sent small groups ahead at full gallop on several occasions, racing each other through dangerous woodland not only as scouts but to cement the vital partnership between man and horse that was integral to the Breton Horse Warriors.

The journey also gave Luc time to think and plan; he had decided to spend the first night at Lannion, the capital of

Tregor and the home of one of his father's oldest friends. He had sent a message ahead to say that they would arrive and stay at the nearby convent. However, Sir Gwilliam would not hear of it, insisting they remain with him, and so as they rode in, Luc looked forward to a convivial night in the company of the old warrior and his sons.

After seeing his men and the horses settled, Luc made his way into the Great Hall, where Briaca was happily holding court in this male domain as Sir Gwilliam's wife had died several years before. They sat down to dinner, and the old knight closely interrogated Luc. They were loyal allies of Alain Rufus, but he wanted to know about King William's plans, and, of course, he wanted more news about the recent rebellions in England and how much damage they had inflicted on the King. Luc answered as truthfully, but as diplomatically, as he could while knowing that he could not pull the wool over the eyes of this shrewd old warrior.

'We will be there fighting by your side, as usual, Malvais, when it comes to war, as we both know it will, but I am unsure about some of the others. This news about Ralph De Gael's possible return is very unsettling, especially with the possibility of war at Dol, which is not so very far from here.' said Sir Gwilliam nodding sagely. Luc nodded in agreement.

Briaca, meanwhile, was in her element, the two sons being very attentive, and, to Luc's amusement at first, she flirted outrageously with them. However, when one of them became too daring and, leaning forward, put two fingers under her chin to bring her face towards his, Luc excused himself from the conversation with Sir Gwilliam and intervened.

'I think it is time you retired, Briaca; we have a long ride tomorrow.

For a moment, he saw a rebellious glint in those large blue eyes, but then she lowered them demurely, smiled, and concurred with his wishes. Luc smiled and inclined his head in a nod to her acquiescence while Sir Gwilliam summoned a maid to accompany her up to a large comfortable room.

He turned to Luc and laughed as he watched her leave, 'Keeping her safe, Malvais? He looked at his two disappointed sons and wagged a finger at them. 'Boys will be boys the world over, and she is an absolute beauty, but she knows it. I am not so old that I do not remember what it would be like to bed that little vixen, that long black hair and white skin against the bedsheets, but it would be fun taming her.' The two young men smacked their lips in appreciation and laughed with their father.

Luc gave a rueful smile and nodded at the old knight, but, privately, he found he was surprisingly and unjustifiably angry that they could talk about her like that. Jealousy was a foreign emotion to him, so he put it down to righteous indignation for his mother's ward. However, part of him agreed that she would probably cause mayhem and trouble wherever she went and, for the first time, he wondered if she was suitable for Morvan or if Morvan was even interested in her. He had seen little sign of courtship from his brother; he treated her more like a troublesome younger sister.

With Briaca gone, the talk between the men turned to more serious discussions, including the recent Angevin attacks over Maine's border. The two young men pulled their chairs closer, Briaca forgotten, and for several hours they discussed the support that Sir Gwilliam could provide to King William when, as it seemed, it would come to war.

'What of De Gael now? Does the King know where he is?'

asked the old knight.

'Our information tells us his Danish fleet was defeated, and he was making his way south from the lowlands. In all likelihood, he will head for his home here in Brittany,' replied a serious-faced Luc.

'Well, that will put the cat amongst the pigeons; De Gael is powerful and well respected here in Brittany, and many lords, who would have remained neutral, may be tempted to take up arms for him against a Norman King. Some Bretons are questioning where their allegiance should lie. Also, Ralph's half-brother Geoffrey Fitz-Eustace has been active in persuading the Breton lords to support De Gael. He has been here, impressing my boys with his court manners, fancy clothes and showy horses.' Added Sir Gwilliam with a sneer.

Luc listened in silence, alarmed by what he was hearing; he knew Geoffrey Fitz-Eustace; he had fought alongside him in the past but had not seen him for several years, he knew that he managed Ralph's large castle and estates at Gael. To hear these concerns voiced aloud by a faithful supporter of the King was alarming. It was a preoccupied Luc, who took his leave of the Tregonian men to head up to his chamber; the situation at Dol with the return of De Gael could be the spark that sets Brittany ablaze.

As a boy, Luc had been here for several visits with his father, so he knew the castle well, but as he approached his room along the torch-lit corridor, he noticed that the door to Briaca's room was slightly ajar. He pushed the door open, expecting to find both her and her maid fast asleep, but he saw that their beds were empty at first glance. The room was unusual; it seemed to have an L shape with a deep stone embrasure round the corner. He padded quietly over to look. On reaching it, he saw that it was, in fact, an octagonal tower at the end with stairs, and a faint light was shining down from above. He slowly climbed the staircase and reached the top; he was met by a blaze of candles in the small octagonal room. A wooden Prie-Dieu was on the far wall with a crucifix on top, and Briaca was kneeling saying her prayers. Her jet-black hair was undone and fell in waves down her back, reaching well below her waist. The soles of her tiny bare white feet peeped out towards him from her nightgown. At first, he stood there mesmerised by the scene before him; then, he spoke almost unwilling to disturb the bowed head.

'Briaca, it is very late, and you will catch cold; you should go to bed,' he whispered.

She nodded her head, bowing to the crucifix, and then slowly and languidly she unfolded, took a step forward and stood facing him. Luc could not prevent himself from gasping. She had moved in front of the bank of candles so that the light was behind her but illuminating the shine of her black hair. The linen nightgown she was wearing of the finest and thinnest chambray was semi-transparent. With the light behind her, he could see every curve of her body. She had the perfect hourglass figure, with large but pert breasts and wide hips. He could clearly see the dark triangle between her legs and the dark aureoles around her nipples. As he gazed at her transfixed, she slowly ran her tongue over her full, slightly open lips and then slowly walked towards him. He could see the desire for him in her eyes as she took her bottom lip between her teeth.

She stood in front of him and rested her hands on his chest; Luc knew that he should back away, but he found his hands encircling her waist and, as her mouth reached up for him, he kissed her. She pressed her soft, rounded body against his hard masculinity, and his hands came up to cup those perfect, rounded breasts. For a few moments, he was out of control as he pulled her closer against him, grinding his groin into her and squeezing her nipples hard until she gasped with shock. As he reached down to grab a handful of that heavy black hair to pull her head back, a single thought occurred to him: this hair falling through his fingers felt so different to Merewyn's fine silver locks, and he froze.

What was he doing?

He pushed her firmly away so that she stumbled and began to fall backwards, but he roughly caught her arm.

'This is madness! What was I thinking? I love my wife! You know I love my wife!'

He turned away and shook his head as if to clear it of the copious amounts of wine he had consumed. Briaca reached out and took his arm. 'You don't understand. I love you, Luc; I wanted you to take me.'

Luc shook her arm off and glared at her, totally shocked at his lack of control and at what she had just admitted to him.

'I should never have kissed you; I am sorry, Briaca, it was unforgivable of me, and we will never speak of this again.' He turned and headed for the doorway. As she called his name, he reluctantly turned to look at her. She still stood, illuminated in all her glory, her eyes blazing.

'I will go to bed, Luc, but I will lie there thinking of your lips on mine, your hands on my breasts, your manhood pressed against me. I will not forget so easily, and I will always be here waiting for you when you need or want me,' she whispered.

Luc stood there spellbound for a few seconds before

walking down the and steps out of the room and closing the door behind him, almost with a sense of relief.

They broke their fast early the following day, and a bleary-eyed Sir Gwilliam rose to wish them Godspeed, offering hospitality on the return journey if Luc needed it. Luc thanked him but was eager to be gone; he had completed his task of reaffirming the knight's allegiance to William, and now he needed to be on his way to deliver Briaca to her parents in Dinan. He watched with a wary eye as the eldest of Sir Gwilliam's sons escorted her to her horse and helped her to mount. She delivered a winning smile to the young man and allowed him to kiss her hand before casting a searching glance at a stern-faced Luc.

'Let's go,' he said, and they trotted out of the gate and through the small village at the foot of the castle. Most of the land ahead was farmed and well managed, so they made good progress; both horses and riders enjoyed a good gallop across the meadows, scattering the small, Breton Ushant sheep in all directions. They slowed to a steady trot and kept that up for some time until they reached the head of the valley.

Luc had avoided conversation with Briaca, ashamed and annoyed at his actions and response last night, but now he stopped and waited for her to catch up.

'We will push on through the wooded foothills and then stop to water the horses on the other side. I expect to catch up with the wagon soon, they had a good few hours start on us, but that will slow us down.'

Briaca nodded demurely and then inquired, 'Where are we staying tonight? Another castle? Another important alliance?'

Luc narrowed his eyes and stared into the distance rather

than meet her eyes before answering.

'I sent a man ahead to arrange rooms for us at a well-known, large inn on the outskirts of Saint-Brieuc; we will reach it in the early evening if we make good time.'

He pressed his lower leg gently against Espirit's side, and the great horse leapt forward and up through the wooded slopes ahead. It was a beautiful but cold, late autumn day as they rode northeast through the valleys, heading towards Dinan.

Luc rode, stern-faced and brooding, rarely glancing behind at the front of the cavalcade; even his men exchanged glances and kept their conversation to subdued whispers. They presumed that the meeting with Sir Gwilliam had not gone well when, in reality, Luc was still furious with himself for the events of the previous night. He replayed the incident repeatedly in his mind, blaming her at first, and he decided that, when they reached Dinan, he would suggest to her parents that she remain there rather than return to Morlaix. Then he berated himself for his actions and the loss of that all-important self-control when confronted with a scantily clad, beautiful young woman who was the image of his first wife. What happened was, in reality, as much his fault. He purposefully replayed his last night with Merewyn in his mind; it had been very passionate and intense. He loved her so much he could not wait to get back to her and his son.

They caught up with the wagon and stopped briefly in a clearing to water the horses and partake of the Steward's fresh bread and cheese from Lannion. Luc helped Briaca to dismount without once looking at her face; he spread a saddle blanket on a log to make sure she was comfortable, and then curtly nodding in her direction, he called her maid over from the wagon and went to join the men.

Briaca watched him under lowered lids from a distance; she listened to the laughter and easy conversation between the men while Luc stood quietly with them. She knew what was happening. Luc was no doubt suffering guilt from his actions last night, but she was not disheartened; she had seen the way he had looked at her in the tower room. Her eyes closed, and she smiled as she relived those moments and the feel of him pressed against her body. He had wanted her, of that she was sure. She knew that she could have him if he were free; she just needed to compromise or remove the Saxon outsider he had married.

In the trees to the north, a group of well-hidden horsemen looked across and down into the clearing. The body of their informer, Bertrand, the young Horse Warrior, lay at their feet, his throat slit from ear to ear. He had been useful for a while and well paid for the information he provided about the movements of Luc De Malvais and his brother over the past six months. This information had allowed them to waylay messengers and plan for tonight's accidental rendezvous.

The group leader, a narrow-faced older man by the name of Flek, bent down and reclaimed the bag of coins that had fallen from the young man's hand. 'He does not need them now, boys, but we do, tonight in the pot room,' he laughed as he pocketed the money; he knew that there would be more coming, his master would pay well for the information he now had, and a messenger had gone to summon him to the Inn. He walked back to his horse and leapt onto its back, 'Ride, we need to make haste if we are all to be in the inn before them tonight,' he said, kicking his horse forward to ride in a northern arc around Luc and his entourage.

For Luc and his men, the rest of the journey was uneventful; travelling with the wagon had slowed their pace, and it was a typical autumn evening as they pulled up outside the Inn nestling in a wide forest clearing on the road into the large hamlet of Saint-Brieuc. The mist had settled on the tops of the trees, and the smoke from the Inn and houses around added to the deepening gloom. Luc breathed in the heady scent of the peat fires and log fires and breathed a sigh of relief that, by lunchtime tomorrow, he would be able to deliver his charge to her parents. It was courtesy to stay the night with them at Dinan, and he also wanted to hear what Briaca's father had heard this far north; he knew that he had contacts all the way up the coast, and they would know or inform him of any landings by Ralph De Gael and his men. They dismounted, and he turned to the welcoming lights of the large two-story, half-timbered building in front of them. The sounds of the large troop of men arriving had brought the stable and potboys running out, but Luc would not let them touch Espirit as usual. A tousle-headed, gangly youth stood just out of range of the Destriers hooves with an expression of awe on his face as Luc dismounted, as Espirit, stamping his feet, eyed up the stranger. He humoured the boy by telling him to run ahead to find the best stall with water and hay while he motioned to one of his men to assist Briaca to dismount.

'Go into the Inn, Briaca; the innkeeper will be waiting to show you and your maid to your room,' he said, leading the huge horse to the stables.

However, Briaca followed and stood in the light of the stable doorway, watching him as he removed the tack.

'Does your horse always come first, Luc,' she said with an

85

amused smile.

He glanced over his shoulder, annoyed to see her there.

'A good mounted warrior always puts his horse first,' he snapped. 'He has saved my life several times over. Why are you not in the Inn as I ordered?' he said, turning a glare on her.

'The Inn is full, and the pot room and corridor are full of men and knights who are also travelling, and the Innkeepers are too busy,' she said with a wan smile.

Luc swore quietly under his breath; he had already noticed that the stables were full of good quality mounts. He finished rubbing Espirit down, ordered the stable boy to bring good oats for him and, taking Briaca firmly by the arm, he led her back into the Inn.

As he pushed the door open, a heady mix of warmth, smoke and noise hit him. She was right, there seemed to be men everywhere, and her timid maid was crouching at the base of the stairs.

'Wait here with your maid,' he ordered, and he entered the large pot room at the front of the Inn. The sight of this main room filled him with dismay; it was packed. At least a troop of a dozen men in there drinking and laughing loudly, and this was before his men joined them. However, the innkeeper spotted him in the doorway and hurried over.

'My Lord De Malvais,' he said, bowing, the noise dropping slightly as the name registered with one or two of the closest men inside; many knew the Breton Horse Lord, and few would ever want to face him. A few familiar faces close to the door nodded to him or raised a hand, and he quietly gave a token gesture of a nod while turning back to the Innkeeper.

'I hope you have kept our rooms, Gavillon,' he said, as he

narrowed his eyes at him.

'Of course, my Lord. I am sorry for the delay, but several unexpected guests all arrived at once; however, my wife will show you both to your rooms,' he assured Luc, whilst waving the harassed innkeeper's wife out from behind the wooden counter. Luc turned at this comment and realised that Briaca had not waited in the hall and was now standing behind him in the crowded pot room. She had dropped her hood to show the long cascades of raven black hair.

The men's laughing and banging of tankards had stopped as they appraised the beautiful young girl, but it included much lip-smacking and ribald comments about what they would like to do to Briaca until Luc turned and glared at them. As he turned back to the troublesome girl, a man had come into the pot room behind her, pushed the maid aside and was running his hands down around Briaca's waist while she tried to dislodge him with her elbows. Luc stepped forward, and reaching over Briaca's head; he dropped the man with one well-aimed powerful punch in his face; the crack of his nose breaking was audible. As the man hit the floor, a deathly silence descended upon the room until the cry went up, 'It's Malvais!' Expressions changed to awe as heads turned. Luc was a legend in his own right, and here he was in the midst of them with a stunningly beautiful woman in tow. A cheer went up, and tankards were raised with much stamping of feet and banging on tables; he was one of theirs, a Breton hero. At that moment, a tall figure stood and detached himself from the group near the fire.

'Luc De Malvais, is it really you, knocking out one of my men? I thought you were in the wilds of northern England with Alain Rufus,' he said as he strode, laughing, towards a surprised Luc.

'Ronec Fitz Eudo! What are you doing here?' asked a grinning Luc. 'I heard you were in Devon and the southwest helping to subdue rebellions for William, but Bodin told me you had then gone back to Italy to warmer climes.'

Ronec laughed. 'I have just returned, and I am so glad to be back home in Brittany. How fortunate to meet you here in this backwater,' he said, gripping Luc in a bear hug and slapping him on the back. He stepped back and held Luc at arm's length. 'You look well, Luc. Marriage obviously suits you especially with such a beautiful wife,' he said, his eyes running over and appraising the smiling Briaca.

Luc shook his head, 'No, this is not my wife Ronec; Merewyn is at home with my son in Morlaix. But yes, my wife is very beautiful, the daughter of a Saxon Thegn.'

Ronec raised an eyebrow and gestured towards Briaca, who demurely lowered her eyes, but she smiled up through her lashes at this tall, handsome knight. 'So… Who is this dark Breton beauty? Is she your mistress?' he asked.

Luc was annoyed that Ronec thought this was a dalliance. He had forgotten what an accomplished flirt Ronec could be, so he quickly interjected, 'No, this is my mother's ward, Briaca Saint Vere. I am returning her to her parents in Dinan for yuletide.' Luc turned to Briaca at that point; she had been exposed to the glances of a room full of men for too long. 'Go with the innkeeper's wife, Briaca; she will take you to your room where your maid will be waiting, and your dinner will be served up there. I will check on you later. Do not come down here again, do you understand?' Briaca looked at him defiantly with her lips pressed together in disappointment.

'Do you understand, Briaca?' Luc repeated, in a more

forceful voice, taking her by the shoulders and stepping over the unconscious intruder's body; he turned her to face the innkeeper's wife at the bottom of the wooden staircase, Ronec followed him out to stand in the hall.

'I understand I am to be shut away in a cold room on my own while you stay here and carouse with your friends,' she said petulantly while moving closer to face him and putting her hand on his arm.

Luc lost all patience at that point. 'Oh, for God's sake, Briaca, there will be a fire in your room. The pot room is no place for a lady, now go,' he said, turning and propelling her to the stairs, watched by a laughing Ronec. She gave him the full effect of the large, pleading, blue eyes as she reluctantly mounted the stairs. Then she stopped.

'Come and say goodnight to me, Luc, please, and check we are safe. It will be lonely up there without you.' Luc looked deep into those blue pools of unshed tears and nodded; after all, this was the girl who had lived in his house for the last year and, he had to admit, he had enjoyed her company. He was probably too harsh because of his reaction to what had happened the previous night; after all, she was a young, innocent girl who had a romantic crush on him, and he was an experienced man who should have known better. He turned back to Ronec, who was standing, arms folded, with a grin on his face.

'That was some performance; she seems quite a handful.'

Luc shook his head, laughing. 'You have no idea Ronec, no idea; Briaca seems to think I will just put my wife aside and choose her instead,' he said in exasperation while calling for some mulled ale and moving to join the group around the fire. Ronec looked thoughtful. Then he smiled as his eyes followed the young girl going up the stairs; an opportunity may have presented itself, he thought as he joined Luc and his men while casting a glance over into the far corner where his man Flek sat with several others…

Luc found that he was more relaxed in this company than he had been for some time. He was happy for Ronec to ply him with questions about the recent campaigns in Anjou and Maine, and, before long, they were recounting tales of past escapades when they were mercenaries together, to an admiring group of men. This, in turn, led Ronec to challenge Luc to a drinking game, one that Luc had always beaten him at before, but still, Ronec always hoped to win. Ronec called for the innkeeper to bring a barrel of his best brandy before going out to answer the call of nature. He seemed to be much longer than expected, but Luc, surrounded by a crowd of men who revelled in being in the company of the famous Malvais, was kept thoroughly entertained. Eventually, Ronec returned and, egged on by the crowd, they broached the cask together, two young warriors reliving former nights of carefree fun, Luc's promise to check in on Briaca wholly forgotten.

Briaca had been quietly pleased with Luc's response downstairs; his eyes had connected with hers in what she thought was a meaningful way. However, she needed a plan; she had almost run out of time before being delivered to Dinan and her parents. She ate a satisfying dinner and then curled up in a fur rug by the fire to wait for Luc to keep his promise to check on them. She had blown out the candle, so the room was lit only by firelight. The hours seemed to tick by so slowly, the raucous noise and laughter from below showed that at least some people were having a good night. Suddenly there was a knock on the door, at last, she thought, as her sleepy maid went to answer it. However, the dark knight who stepped into her room was not Luc De Malvais.

'Get rid of your maid,' he instructed in a voice that brooked no argument. She looked at him in surprise and then nodded; she pulled the rug tighter around her and signalled for the maid to stand outside on the landing. The maid, goggle-eyed at the handsome knight in front of her, reluctantly left the room, pulling the door closed behind her.

Briaca watched him as a rabbit would watch a snake, 'I will scream if you touch me,' she said, retreating further into the chair. Ronec threw his head back and laughed. 'Do you think that would stop me if I wanted you,' he said, sitting on the wooden settle opposite her. She looked at this dark-eyed knight with interest.

'I have a proposition for you, but what we speak of must never leave this room,' he said in a voice laden with meaning. Briaca inclined her head in acquiescence, eager to hear what he had to say despite her apprehension.

'You clearly want Luc De Malvais, I believe,' he said. She nodded, wondering what it was that he proposed.

'Well, tonight I intend to deliver him to you; listen carefully, for this is what I want you to do,' he said.

Briaca walked over to the window; the mist had cleared, and, looking at the position of the moon, she knew it must now be in the early hours. The noise from below had died to a murmur as the mulled ale and brandy took their toll on the young men.

She was crestfallen that Luc had not appeared; she had been so sure that his chivalry would ensure that he came to check on them, and she could feel a raw anger building inside,

Ronec's plan was not going to work. 'He did not come,' she repeated to herself, this time out loud.

She glanced angrily around the room. Her maidservant had come back in and was asleep on a truckle bed; she was now snoring, which infuriated Briaca even more. She got out of the chair and roughly shook the girl. 'Get down and sleep in the kitchen; you are snoring to wake the dead,' she snarled at her. As the girl gathered her clothes, Briaca returned to the fireside, suddenly she heard the clump of heavy boots on the stairs and mumbled voices. She raced across the room and opened the door a crack; her room was right at the end of the corridor; she had a full view of the head of the stairs and the other two doors. Four figures appeared; the big one at the back held a lantern high, and she recognised the Innkeeper. The other two had an unsteady, dark figure between them.

She recognised Luc's dark head in the middle as she heard one man drunkenly mutter, 'What room is he in, do we know?'

'The one at the end Fitz-Eudo told us,' the other taller man replied; he had a narrow unpleasant face and a distinctive scar across his chin.

She did not recognise either of the men, which was good, as it meant they were not from Morlaix; they must be Ronec's men. Briaca gestured to her maid to pass her cloak to cover her nightgown, and shrugging it on; she opened the door wide.

'Bring him in here. Is he drunk again,' she laughed.

The man with the scar nodded and manoeuvred Luc through the doorway and into her room. 'He certainly sank more than most of us tonight,' he said.

'He and Ronec were trying to outdo each other. Malvais won, though, because Ronec fell off the bench, out stone-cold,' the other man added and laughed.

Briaca went over to the bed and pulled back the blankets, 'Just lay him down on here. We will see to him now,' she said, indicating the open-mouthed maid.

The men doffed their caps; the one with the scar on his chin nodded meaningfully at her from the doorway and left. Briaca stood for a moment staring down at a drunken, mumbling Luc. 'Here, girl, help me get his boots off,' she said.

The girl did as she was told, undoing the leather laces and then, raising a troubled face, said, 'But where will you sleep, mistress?'

Briaca smiled and guided her gently to the door. 'Why, in your truckle bed, of course, while you go and sleep in the kitchen. I will send for you when I need you in the morning. It could be a late start,' she said, ruefully indicating the restless figure on the bed. The girl left reluctantly with an unsure glance at her mistress, but Briaca wanted her gone and closed the door behind her; she leant her back against the door, not quite believing how easy it had been, she had him; Luc De Malvais was all hers.

Briaca awoke to hear the room door opening early the following day; she could now see daylight through the cracks in the shutters, so she presumed it was the maid coming back. She was on her side facing away from the door, and Luc was curled tightly around her. She turned to lie on her back, and as she moved, she felt Luc stir, his eyes opened, and he regarded her with some confusion. She smiled but looking up; she was shocked to see Luc's handsome friend and her visitor from last night, Ronec Fitz-Eudo staring down at them from the end of the bed, a grin on his face. She quickly pulled the covers up from her waist to hide her nakedness.

'So, your mother's ward is she?' he laughed. 'Well, we had better not tell your mother or your wife what you have been doing with her!'

Luc closed his eyes again, put a hand to his head and groaned. 'Get out of here, Ronec,' he muttered through gritted teeth.

Ronec laughed. 'I will wait for you downstairs, but do not be long; we have things to discuss,' he said.

As the door closed with a thump behind the departing Ronec, Luc pushed himself up on one elbow, turned and gazed down at the vision of naked loveliness enfolded in his arms. He could not quite believe what he was seeing. He had been dreaming not of Merewyn but of his first wife, Heloise, who had died in childbirth at the tender age of 19. She had been a Breton beauty with black hair and blue eyes. He groaned again and covered his eyes; what had he done?

'What happened?' he murmured.

Briaca smiled. 'You mean, you don't remember, my Lord,' she said sweetly. He shook his head to try to clear it. The last thing he remembered was the drinking game with Ronec, which he thought he had won; he had no memory of anything after that. What did not help was the fact that her soft, rounded naked body was still pressed against him, her arms around his waist and his early morning erection was pressing insistently against her stomach. She daringly put her hand down and took hold of it.

'No!' he exclaimed, his hand taking hold of hers in a vice-like grip to remove it. She pouted with disappointment, and he groaned again.

'You don't remember coming to my room in the early hours

to say goodnight?' She asked. He shook his head in disbelief.

'You came to check on me, but then you sent my maid away. I was sat by the fire. You took the rug from around my shoulders, pulled me into your arms and kissed me goodnight. Then, suddenly, you ripped my nightgown in two, picked me up and threw me onto the bed,' she said, indicating the torn nightgown on the floor. Luc groaned again and closed his eyes as she continued. 'I must admit, I was very willing, even though it was my first time, but you were very impatient. You flung your clothes off and took me.' She paused for effect. 'It was gentler the second time,' she said, watching the emotions play over his face. 'I would love you to do it again now,' she said, raising those luminous blue eyes to his face, dropping her hand back to his manhood and biting her bottom lip.

'No!' Luc almost shouted at her, horrified at what he had done. He gently pushed her away and swung his long legs over the edge of the bed, throwing the covers back. As he did so, he saw the blood on the sheets and on the top of his thighs, and he shuddered. 'No. No, what have I done?' he said, dropping his head into his hands. Briaca knelt up and rested her head on his scarred back, wrapping her arms around his waist.

'Don't worry, Luc; I love you; I won't tell anyone. It will be our shared secret,' she whispered.

Luc sat, overwhelmed with misery and guilt. How could he do this to Merewyn? She would never forgive him. He tried hard to remember the events of last night; he had been drunk, gloriously rip-roaring drunk for the first time in years. He had laughed and relaxed as they had broached another cask of brandy, reminiscing and sharing outrageous tales. He had no memory of coming into her room, but he obviously had, and the evidence was there to see that he had ripped off her nightgown and taken her.

He had no idea what he would do now or what, if anything, to say to his wife. He unpeeled her arms and turned; seeing the hopeful but determined expression on her face, he pushed himself up from the bed in dismay and disgust at himself.

'I am sorry, Briaca, but this should never have happened; I need some fresh air and some time to think.' He walked shakily to his clothes and dressed in silence. He knew this was not Briaca's fault, and he now had a responsibility towards her; he had taken her virginity, his mother's ward, who was almost promised to Morvan. Oh, God! His brother! What would he say to him? He had despoiled his future bride.

Outside, Ronec entered the stables to find his man Flek already there saddling his horse. 'Well done, Flek, I do not think that this could have panned out in a better way,' he laughed. Flek nodded. 'I do hope the information proved helpful Sire, as you know, we have intercepted his messengers for some months, but hearing of this journey, it seemed the perfect opportunity.' Ronec nodded in approbation. He turned to go back to the Inn but stopped at the doorway, 'I need you to take a message to Geoffrey Fitz-Eustace at Gael; he will find much of this information from last night valuable. By the way, Flek, the young Horse Warrior you found, I presume he gave you the information about the Inn. He has certainly proved useful, and he may be so again, but are you sure he won't talk to his compatriots?' 'I assure you, Sire; I promise you his lips are sealed.' Said Flek, with a tight smile, giving a bow of his head.

'I set up the rendezvous here for you to accidentally meet

up with Malvais, Sire. He certainly seemed happy to see you.' Ronec looked thoughtful for a moment as he dropped some coins into his manservant's open hand.

'We were very good friends once, Malvais and I, he is the best of men to have on your side or to have your back, but we have to do something to stop this Norman King just taking what he wants in our lands, even if that means sacrificing former friendships.' He said in a resigned tone as he turned back to the inn to meet Malvais.

Chapter Nine

Merewyn had settled happily into life in the castle in Morlaix; Luc's mother deferred more and more to her son's wife for household decisions, and she had happily unhooked the household keys from her belt and handed them over to Merewyn. She knew that Merewyn had run her father's household as a young girl, so she had no qualms, and, more importantly, it freed her up to spend more time with her grandson.

'They grow up so fast, we seem to have so little time with them before they are taken away for training to follow their fathers into battle and war,' she said, sadly.

Merewyn watched Lusian as he ran ahead through the meadow; he was the image of his father, and she could just imagine him as a young man. Tall and handsome with that same shock of nearly black hair, Lusian already had his first wooden sword and, today, he was to get his first pony.

Gerard was waiting for them with a small, bay gelding; Merewyn was alarmed at the size of it. 'Gerard isn't that too big for him?' she asked in a concerned voice.

Marie laughed. 'Both of my boys were put on bigger horses than this little gelding; he must only be about fourteen hands.'

Lusian stood gazing up at the light chestnut bay horse

in awe. 'Is he really mine?' he asked, looking back at his mother and grandmother for confirmation. Merewyn nodded, her heart still in her mouth as he went immediately to stand beneath the horse's head. Reaching, up he stroked the gelding's soft nose, laughing as the horse gently blew air down onto his fingers.

'His name is Duke,' said Gerard, indicating that Lusian should come round to mount into the light saddle.

'Duke,' proclaimed Lusian, 'after Duke William, who is now our King,' he said with satisfaction.

All of the adults smiled. Lusian was a bright boy who listened with interest and absorbed knowledge from the adults' conversations around him. They watched for a while as Gerard led him around the meadow giving instructions until Lusian impatiently demanded to have the reins.

'Don't worry, Merewyn, this is a very good-natured horse.' said Marie. Let's go back and leave them to it; there are tasks to be done as I expect Luc and the men today or tomorrow, and they will be tired and hungry.' Merewyn was filled with excitement at the thought of Luc's return; it had only been six days, but she had only just found him again, and she missed his company and his lovemaking. She loved those firelight hours when they lay together talking about the future; she could not wait for him to return.

However, Luc did not appear that day, and by the following evening, Merewyn was listening for every sound, waiting for the barks of the castle dogs in the Hall below to betoken an arrival. Marie could see her concerns. 'Don't worry, my dear, Luc will be fine; he will have stayed longer at Briaca's parents, or he has spent longer looking at the Arab mares. I have always given my menfolk three days beyond when they are supposed to arrive before I worry,' she said, laughing.

Merewyn nodded and smiled. 'I know, but I just miss him so much.'

Marie smiled. 'The words of the old French song are so true,' she said; 'love to a man is a thing apart, but woman's whole life,' she said softly. Suddenly, there was a flurry of barking, and Marie smiled. 'And here they are! Let's go down and greet them.'

When they reached the hall, Gerard and Morvan were ahead of them, greeting and backslapping Luc, who looked tired and mud-splattered. Merewyn saw him glance up at her as she descended the stairs, but there was no smile or recognition that he had seen her. They crossed the Hall, and Luc came and greeted them, kissing them both on the cheek and asking after their wellbeing. Merewyn was taken aback; this was a different Luc, so formal and distant, and he barely looked at her. Something was wrong. Was he still angry with her for coming to Brittany? Had he brooded further on it while he was on the road? She decided just to put on a brave face and follow his lead when, in reality, she just wanted him to enfold her in his arms and tell her he had missed her. Maybe he would do that later.

Luc was standing by the fire laughing at something Gerard was recounting, so she sat on the bench and devoured him with her eyes, this man she loved so much. Then he turned.

'I am cold, wet and hungry, ladies, so if you will excuse me, I will go wash and change and greet my son. I presume he is in his room?'

Merewyn made to rise, but he waved her back into her seat and, speaking to a spot above her head, said, 'I will join you shortly.' She watched as he ran lithely up the staircase.

She was very perplexed and turned a questioning glance on Marie, but she was deep in conversation with Morvan and seemed unperturbed.

Luc closed the heavy door to the chamber with a relieved thud. He leaned back against it and took a deep breath; this was proving to be almost impossible. How he could meet her eyes or even touch her after what he had done, he didn't know.

He cast his mind back to that morning at the Inn in Saint-Brieuc. He had left Briaca in the chamber to get dressed and had gone into the yard where he had spent a considerable amount of time stripped down to his braies with his head under the pump. He hoped that the cold water would bring him around to try to get to grips with the reality of what he had done. He was rubbing his upper body down with a cloth when Ronec had appeared; Luc had watched with a wary eye as the tall, handsome warrior strolled over and sat on a nearby wooden cask.

'So, was she as good as she looks, Luc?' he grinned.

Luc had held up a hand to stop him while rubbing his other hand wearily over his eyes, 'This was a mistake, Ronec. As a friend, please do not mention it to anyone. I was so drunk; I have no memory even of going to bed.'

Ronec had laughed, 'My lips are sealed, my friend.' Luc nodded his appreciation. 'Now, on to more important matters, Malvais, I want to come and see these young horses you have been training. Everyone is talking about your Breton warhorses and, if Espirit is their sire, I am very interested,' he had said.

Luc had looked thoughtful for a moment, 'You know you

are welcome at Morlaix any time, Ronec. I am going on to Dinan now, and also I have an Arab mare I need to see close by, but I should be back at Morlaix within a week as we begin the yuletide celebrations. Where are you planning on spending the festival, Ronec?'

He had waited for a reply and gazed at Ronec, who was tight-lipped and staring into the distance. They had fought together for many years, so he was aware of Ronec's troubled past. Ronec was one of the several illegitimate sons of Eudo De Penthievre, the father of Alan Rufus. Eudo had recognised some of these children, such as Bodin and Bardolph, who were now in Yorkshire, but others, such as Ronec, he refused to acknowledge for some reason. Fortunately for Ronec, his mother had become one of Ralph De Gael's mistresses, so he was given a place as a squire, which enabled him to then become a knight through his outstanding prowess in his own right. However, he was landless, so he became a mercenary, selling his sword and his band of men to the highest bidder. He made himself wealthy through the spoils of war, buying several small manors, but he was always on the move, seeming unable to settle. His mother had died, and he had not yet felt the need to take a wife. Instead, he enjoyed numerous dalliances with married and unmarried women alike.

'Come to us for yuletide Ronec; you know my mother will be delighted to see you. She loves a full house at this time of year.'

Ronec had smiled. 'I will keep you to that, Malvais. Now we must be gone; we have business at Gael for several days.' Luc had raised an eyebrow at that news. Was Ronec hoping to sell his services to Ralph De Gael now?

Ronec had raised his hand in salute and left, leaving Luc with the unhappy task of conveying Briaca to her parents in Dinan, their only daughter whom he had just despoiled. He had groaned and covered his face with his hands before slowly walking towards the Inn door.

Now he was home in Morlaix and had to deal with the consequences of his actions to build up the courage to face his wife. He may be the undefeated warrior champion of Alan Rufus, but the thought of telling Merewyn what he had done was more daunting than any swordsman he had ever faced. He loved her so much, and all he wanted to do was sweep her into his arms. But she was fiery, independent and proud; once she knew, it was highly likely that she would leave him and take Lusian with her. He needed to keep her at arms-length until he thought this through and worked out how to deal with it.

Merewyn was confused by Luc's attitude and manner towards her; he was courteous, polite and seemed to be caring, especially with Lusian, but he was totally unlike the loving, passionate man who had left her ten days ago. She listened with interest to the conversation at dinner that night to see if she could glean any clues about the change in his temperament.

Gerard was bringing Luc up to date on recent news. 'Still no sign of Ralph De Gael?' asked Luc.

'No, he achieved little with the Danish fleet and Canute, and they returned to Denmark via Flanders. His wife, Emma, left to hold Norwich Castle, was apparently under siege for some time. She refused to surrender to the King's warrior Bishops, and they finally came to terms. She was given forty days to leave England and return on a safe passage to Brittany.'

Luc raised an eyebrow and shook his head, 'That means that De Gael will return here as well, which could further influence and unsettle any alliances we have made.'

Morvan, who had been listening intently, whistled silently through his teeth. 'That means William will follow. He cannot allow someone of Ralph De Gael's stature to escape or remain unpunished after coordinating such a rebellion; it's treason.'

Luc frowned and nodded. 'What of the other two Earls?' he asked.

Gerard sighed. 'Both Roger, the Earl of Hereford, and Waltheof, the Earl of Northumberland, have been imprisoned and their lands seized, as have all of the English estates of Ralph De Gael in East Anglia. William rarely forgives such actions so they will be harshly punished or lose their lives'

'That only leaves De Gael his estates here in Brittany, so he is a fugitive and in need of money. He will be like a cornered rat,' said Morvan.

Gerard nodded, 'Which makes him even more dangerous, especially to the allies of William in Brittany,' he added, looking pointedly at Luc. For a while, silence reigned as they thought over its implications and applied themselves to the roast meats.

'Luc did you see the Arab mare?' said Morvan. Luc laughed at Morvan's persistence, and his expression lightened.

'I did, and I bought her. She is coming to us as we speak. She is beautiful and a good 16 hands high. She is exactly what we are looking for, perfect confirmation of body. You should see her move, the way she holds herself, but she has a lot of spirit and strength.'

Morvan grinned. They may be on the verge of war, but

the breeding schedule at Morlaix had to go ahead for both of the brothers. They were producing the most sought-after warhorses in Europe, formidable, powerful Destriers that were lethal in battle, but, like any breeding programme, they had to plan years ahead with the best bloodlines. Fortunately, they had Espirit, and now several of his sons were coming along as promising young stallions as well. But they needed to maintain and build on the Arab strain that made these horses combine intelligence with tremendous strength and endurance.

Morvan continued, 'How was Bertrand Luc? Did he recover from his malady? He has the makings of a good Horse Warrior.' Luc looked perplexed for a few moments as he thought back to his week away; at no point had Bertrand joined them; he shared that with Morvan and suggested he check with the horse Serjeants; young Bertrand might still be ill.

'Did we hear any more about our missing messengers, Morvan? His brother shook his head, 'they seem to have disappeared Luc, I sent riders out to check the villages on the roads to Morlaix; nothing has been seen of them.'

'We don't usually lose our messengers; several did not seem to make it to Alain Rufus either; these two were young boys from the estates riding our horses, send some men to the horse fairs Morvan let us see if they have been seen and sold.' He saw the concerned expression on his mother's face and changed the subject.

'That reminds me,' he said, bowing his head to his mother and wife in recognition of the fact that Merewyn was now taking her place as Chatelaine of Morlaix, 'we are expecting guests tomorrow or the next day for yuletide. They may be with us for at least a week,' he said.

Marie smiled. It was so typical of her son to give such short notice. 'May we ask who it is that we are expecting? Someone entertaining, I hope,' she said, raising an eyebrow.

'Entertaining? Yes indeed. I met Ronec on my way to Dinan; it has been too many years since I last saw him.'

'Well… Ronec Fitz Eudo. It has been a long time. How many will there be in the party?' she asked, smiling.

'Probably just Ronec and ten to twenty of his men. He was ever a loner, as you know,' he said.

Merewyn watched Luc's face darken; he toyed with his food and then stared off into the distance. Was this meeting the reason for the change in mood, she wondered, or was it a combination of things with Ralph De Gael's threat and imminent war hanging over them?

Suddenly, Luc stood up and pushed his chair back. 'I am going up to see Lusian before he goes to sleep,' he said and left them.

Merewyn looked at Gerard and Marie wanting answers. 'Who is Ronec Fitz Eudo? Is that another of Eudo De Penthievre's sons, another brother or half-brother of Alain Rufus?' she asked.

Marie looked thoughtful. 'Ronec is one of Eudo's many illegitimate children; he was always a very troubled young man with a huge chip on his shoulder because Eudo has never recognised him. But he is absolutely charming and very convivial. All the girls fell in love with him. But an out and out lovable rascal, wherever there was trouble, Ronec would be in the middle of it; he led Luc into several scrapes, some extremely dangerous. He was always a neck or nothing rider, always taking risks.'

'Yes, but now also a great warrior and respected knight in Brittany. He has certainly earned the money he made to buy several small estates here. He fought with us for several campaigns in England, but then we went north, and he went to help subdue the rebellions in the southwest, in Devon. He fought for and deserved that knighthood from William,' said Gerard.

Merewyn looked perplexed. 'So he supports William?' she asked.

'Ronec supports whoever pays him. He is a mercenary first and foremost,' said Gerard.

'So the meeting with Luc, they are friends?' she asked.

Gerard looked thoughtful. 'They were comrades in arms so became good friends, but Luc is aware that Ronec is unpredictable, and one day he may even end up fighting against him. To make up for his birth, Ronec is driven by money and ambition. He desires wealth but, even more, he desires recognition for his deeds in the hope that his father may one day be proud of him and recognise him.'

Merewyn nodded and then left them to go and find her husband. She found Luc sat on Lusian's bed telling him a story about a great warhorse, an ancestor of Espirit, who led the herds of wild horses in Brittany. She stood for a few minutes at the door and watched them as Lusian's eyes began to close. Luc leaned forward and kissed him on the forehead, their two dark heads together for a few seconds. It was apparent how much Luc loved his son, and now it was as if they had never been apart.

She stayed still in the doorway, not wanting to disturb them, but she watched, perturbed, as Luc sat forward and put his head in his hands. He sat like that for what felt like an age, lost in whatever thoughts were consuming him. She moved slightly to close the door again, and he looked up startled. He realised at once that it was his wife framed in the doorway, and for a fleeting moment, she saw absolute anguish in his face. She moved swiftly forward and put her arms around his head and shoulders pulling him close.

'What is it, my love, what is worrying you?' she murmured into his hair. In response, he just nestled closer into her body and wrapped his arms tightly around her while she rested her head on his. She could hear his ragged breathing, and she knew there was something deeply troubling him. However, she also knew Luc and knew that he would tell her in his own time. Gradually his breathing became regular, and he pushed her gently away and stood up.

'I am weary, Merewyn, let's go to bed,' he said as he moved towards the door with a last glance at his sleeping son.

Once in the chamber, Merewyn undressed slowly while Luc poured a goblet of wine and, instead of coming to bed, he sat in one of the leather-backed chairs in front of the blazing fire.

'Get into bed, Merewyn, before you get cold, I will be there shortly,' he said, gazing into the flames. However, it was several hours later when he eventually joined her. She feigned sleep as he quietly undressed and then slipped under the heavy fur coverlet, lying beside her but not touching her. She could feel the heat from his long, muscled body only inches away from hers, and she longed for him to turn and make love to her. Yet, before long, she heard his breathing change as he dropped into a troubled sleep, twisting and murmuring beside her. She eventually drifted off to sleep, but she woke early in the dawn to find a cold empty space beside her. Luc was gone. She laid there, a weight on her heart, trying to fathom what was wrong. Her hand stroked the cold sheet where he had lain.

Luc walked amongst his young horses in the mist-drenched meadows, his mind racing. This was a new dilemma for him; he had taken and made love to dozens of women in his time, especially during his years as a mercenary, some of them married, almost all of them willing. He was not proud of his past because he had been emotionally numb and angry after his wife and son's death. He never thought he would truly love again, but then he had found Merewyn. She became not only his wife but also his soulmate and friend. They had made exciting plans together for the future; their life would be here in Brittany on his estates with lots of children and horses. Their time together disrupted when he had been recalled to duty in Brittany, but he had never doubted for a second that they would soon be back together.

Now he had put all of that at risk. He knew that other knights' wives accepted the love affairs and dalliances of their husbands, and even some of their wives affairs were tolerated without question. After all, just look at Eudo; he had over a dozen offspring at least, scattered over Western Europe, some acknowledged, some not.

However, his relationship with Merewyn was different; she would find it impossible to accept that he had lain with another woman. Their love was too deep, too intense. He knew that she would never forgive him. He remembered how he had felt when he thought she had betrayed him with the Saxon rebel Braxton Le Gunn; it was as a knife stabbed into his heart; he had never felt anguish like it. He knew once he told Merewyn about Briaca, their relationship would never be the same again, and now the guilt of what he had done was consuming him.

Chapter Ten

L uc re-entered the castle by the postern gate; he walked up from the wall to the courtyard to find it full of men and horses. His mother and Morvan were on the steps to greet the visitors. He realised that Ronec had arrived; he could see the tall warriors dark head as he went up the stairs to greet Luc's mother. Luc was pleased his old friend was here; it would create a wealth of distraction in the castle.

'Ronec!' he shouted. The tall Breton mercenary turned, grinned and raised a hand as Luc crossed the cobbles towards him, weaving a path through the melee of horses and men.

'Morvan go and find the Steward and see to the settling of the additional men and mounts in the Bailey,' he shouted as he took the hand and arm of Ronec in the timeless warrior clasp and slapped him on the back.

'I am glad you decided to come for yuletide; you and your men are very welcome,' he said.

'Well, the hospitality at Morlaix is legendary,' he said, bowing his head to Marie. 'My men were very pleased when I shared where we were heading for Yule. However, I hope you don't mind, I have brought you another guest.' He turned and gestured to the man dismounting from an impressive but showy chestnut stallion.

Luc gave an indiscernible intake of breath and frowned as he recognised the auburn-haired man who had dismounted. Geoffrey Fitz-Eustace, the bastard younger half-brother of Ralph De Gael. They shared the same mother, the Saxon Lady Goda, Geoffrey's father was Eustace Boulogne, but Geoffrey had been accepted and brought up in the Gael household.

Luc fixed a smile of welcome on his face, but he knew that Geoffrey's arrival at Morlaix did not bode well; he would be supporting his brother Ralph as Sir Gwilliam had indicated when they stopped at Lannion. It was also quite likely that he was involved with the recent rebellions in England. He was on the opposing side to both William and Alan Rufus. Why, then, did he choose to come here to Morlaix? He must know that Luc was tied to Alain and the House of Rennes. However, the laws of hospitality reasserted themselves, and Luc stepped forward to greet Geoffrey. After all, they had fought together on the same side at Hastings.

'Welcome to Morlaix. This is my mother, Marie, whom I believe knows your mother very well.' Geoffrey held Luc's gaze for a few seconds; he had seen the fleeting change of expression; he knew precisely what Malvais would be thinking. He was also wary. He may be ten years older than Luc and Ronec, an experienced warrior in his own right, but he knew the formidable reputation of Luc De Malvais and his brother, and he had seen Malvais in action, a sight he would never forget. However, he had been sent by Ralph to try to persuade Malvais to change sides or to try and find some way of neutralising him to keep him out of the impending war. He intended to use Ronec Fitz-Eudo to help him achieve that, knowing of their previous long friendship.

'It has been far too long, Malvais,' he said, turning his full, laconic charm on for Luc and his family and reaching out an arm to clasp Luc's. 'Of course, I remember your beautiful mother,' he said, bowing over her hand like a French courtier. Marie, always susceptible to flattery from a handsome young man, smiled down at him.

'We have not seen you for several years, Geoffrey. I believe you married and now have a son,' she said.

'Yes, Countess, my son, Faramus, is now five years old,' he said, not at all surprised that she would know and remember everything about him.

At that moment, Merewyn appeared at the top of the steps behind them. She had dressed, with care, in her soft powder-blue over-gown, and the morning winter sun shone on her silver-blonde hair. She had Lusian by the hand, and she slowly descended towards the group, who had all turned to watch her.

'Ah! Here is my five-year-old grandson. Lusian, make your bow to the gentlemen,' she said, holding out a hand for him as he ran down the steps to her. Luc smiled at his son as he coolly appraised the knights before giving them a curt bow. He then turned his attention back to his guests, who were staring at Merewyn, transfixed.

'Mon Dieu! You said your wife was beautiful, Luc, but you did not do her credit. She is stunning, a veritable angel,' said Ronec.

'Merewyn is the daughter of a Saxon Thegn and warrior. He fought against us at Hastings, but I now have the honour of calling him a friend, even though I stole his beautiful daughter away from him,' said Luc, smiling at Merewyn as he took her hand and introduced the two guests. Both men bowed and kissed her hand, but Ronec held it for far too long as he gazed up into her huge green eyes.

'A man could lose himself forever in those eyes,' he murmured.

Merewyn had to retrieve her hand and look away. She was unsettled by the pointed attention of this tall, handsome knight. She purposefully moved closer to Luc, flattered, but she could see that he was slightly annoyed by the attention she was garnering from other men.

'You should be a poet instead of a mercenary, Ronec,' Luc commented, with a cynical smile.

'Maybe I will if I can write poems about the beauty of Merewyn De Malvais of Morlaix, see it has a ring about it already,' he suggested with a bow in her direction. Luc laughed aloud. He had forgotten how incorrigible Ronec was when it came to women.

'Come, let us go in and break our fast and then I will take you to the paddocks to show you our young stock,' he said, leading the way up the stairs and into the Great Hall, Lusian bounding along beside them.

Merewyn watched them go through the stone arch until a voice beside her said, 'may I escort you, mistress Merewyn?' She looked up into the smiling, dark-brown eyes of Ronec Fitz-Eudo and shyly took his proffered arm. Suddenly, she smiled back at him; it felt good to get the attention of a man, albeit a charming stranger.

The castle bustled with the extra guests and two dozen additional men and servants to be accommodated, and Merewyn found that she had no time to speak to Luc at all that day. They spent a convivial evening with lots of laughter and stories from earlier days. Merewyn noticed that

114

all mention of the recent rebellions and William's campaign was carefully avoided, although they did all reminisce about Hastings and its aftermath. It was late when Merewyn and Marie went to bed, leaving the men to drink and muse over past battles. She was approaching their chamber door when it opened. A strange man came out; he was tall and well built but, with a narrow face and eyes that were too close together, she challenged him immediately. 'You there? What are you doing in my room?' she asked. The man dropped into a deep bow, 'A thousand pardons, my Lady, I have never been here before, and I am looking for the room of Ronec Fitz-Eudo; I am his manservant.' She was only partly mollified; the man was too obsequious for her liking, though she admitted the huge castle could be confusing. 'What is your name?' she asked.

'Flek, my Lady', he said, bowing his head again. Merewyn looked him up and down; he was clearly a fighting man as well, with a distinctive scar on his chin. She quickly gave him directions and then entered their chamber, immediately scanning the room, but could see nothing amiss. She would mention it to Mathew, their Steward, tomorrow; something was unsettling about the man. She climbed into bed and dropped into a troubled sleep, stirring only briefly as Luc climbed into bed in the early hours, but when she woke, yet again, he was gone.

There was little opportunity for any time with Luc the following day either. Ronec and Geoffrey went with Luc and Morvan to see the promising three-year-old Destriers put through their paces, Morvan had well-schooled them, and by the afternoon, a deal was done, and three of them had been sold. It had started to snow lightly, and Lusian was beside himself with excitement as it began to lay, for he knew that the next day they would be going to bring in the traditional yuletide log to be blessed and dressed for the festive celebrations.

This was always a joyful occasion. The men had been out hunting in the dawn and returned in high spirits with a large male 'tusker', a wild boar, which would be hung and smoked for at least the following week. A hearty meal was served to the returning huntsmen with several cups of spiced wine and mulled ale before they wrapped up again to go and bring in the Yule log. It was a large group that left the castle that afternoon. Marie and Merewyn, wrapped in fur-lined cloaks, and Lusian, bouncing with excitement beside them. Servants carried flaming torches to light the way, and the castle priest strode ahead with the men, carrying a large cross, a boy beside him swinging the incense burner.

There was an air of joy and laughter, banter and playfulness as Lusian threw snowballs at his father and Gerard. Merewyn, watching them, was pleased to see the return of the 'old Luc', and she hoped that whatever had been troubling him was now resolved; he seemed almost carefree today. Merewyn joined in the games with Lusian, and she turned to find Luc stood watching them. She laughed at him, and he smiled back, a smile that lit up his blue eyes. She turned to see that Ronec had also stopped to watch the playful family scene, and she caught an almost wistful expression on his face. As he moved away to follow Luc, it made her wonder about this dark, handsome knight. Was he married? Did he also have a family that he loved? If so, why was he not with them at yuletide? He disturbed her. She loved Luc totally, but she did feel an attraction to the dark-eyed Ronec Fitz

Eudo that was unfathomable.

Before long, the group reached the clearing where a large oak tree awaited them, and the foresters had already cut out a large section of the trunk. The group gathered in a torch-lit circle as the priest blessed the log with incantations in Latin and much swinging of incense. He turned and blessed the group, raising the cross high. Merewyn was entranced; it was very atmospheric in the gathering winter dusk, the almost singsong voice of the priest echoing through the trees. The young serving boys had gathered branches of holly and the big bunches of mistletoe from the oak branches; she could see the combination of the pagan and Christian festivals to bring in a fertile and peaceful season ahead. Just for a minute, it made her homesick for her Saxon home in Ravensworth, where her family and friends would enact similar rituals, and no work would be done in the village for several days.

The servants poured more goblets of spiced wine to the assembled group as Luc directed the placing of ropes on the large log; tradition had it that only the men of the castle, not the servants, would haul it back to the castle. The women laughed at the men who were full of bravado as they took the strain on the ropes; Merewyn was spellbound as she watched Luc laughing at his son, now sitting on the log, determined to ride it back to the castle. As they set off, the snow helped, and the group began to sing the yuletide carol. With half a mile to go uphill to the gates, the strain began to tell, but Luc and Ronec at the front had, of course, turned it into a competition, the strain showing on their faces and their muscles bulging. She noticed that Geffrey Fitz-Eustace remained aloof, pulling on a side rope half-heartedly, a faint smile on his face.

When they reached the Bailey, Luc released the harness

ropes from around his chest and stretched. He turned to thank Ronec and clasp hands but noticed that his friend was already beside Merewyn. Luc frowned as he watched her laugh aloud at something Ronec said. For the first time, Luc felt an angry knot in the pit of his stomach, which he ashamedly recognised as jealousy. He turned that anger on himself. What right did he have to feel jealousy when he was the one who had lain with another woman? He turned away to direct the servants bringing in the huge log to be dressed with holly and mistletoe before it was lit on the start of the twelve-day Yuletide festival.

Merewyn stopped in her tracks. It had been a delightful winter afternoon with a laughing Luc, full of fun, but now she watched his back as he strode up to the Hall, the tension evident in his shoulders. She could not understand what had triggered the change.

Merewyn did not see Luc again until he came to change for dinner; she was determined to find out what was wrong. She sat on the bed as he came in; he nodded at her before he began to strip off his clothes to wash after the day's exertions. She watched as he stood in only his linen braies, tied loosely at his hips. He washed his torso. She loved watching him naked, the muscles moving in his back as he raised the jug of water over his head to pour over his hair and shoulders. It was too much for her, and she crossed the room, swiftly placing her warm hand on his cool skin. She ran her hands down his back. For a moment or two, he stood still, and she heard his breathing change as she moved her hands around his waist and began to go lower. He grasped her wrists to stop her and turned to stare bleakly into her eyes.

'What is it, Luc? What is wrong?' she cried.

He flung his head back and gazed at the wooden ceiling before taking a deep breath, 'We have no time for this Merewyn; they will be waiting for us downstairs.'

She stood forlornly, hands by her sides until her pride took over, and she raised her head. Without a backward glance, she left the room.

Luc dropped to his knees in the chamber, placing his head in his arms on top of the carved wooden chest. He had never felt such despair, and he knew he was no nearer to a solution. If he told her, she would reject him. If he kept quiet, the guilt would eat away at him. Then there was Briaca; what sort of reparation did he owe to that young woman? He dressed quickly, drowning several goblets of rich red wine until he made his way to the Hall.

It was Midwinter's Eve, the night before the Winter Solstice, and the beginning of the twelve-day celebration of Yuletide. This was the time when the villages and estates would mate their animals for the spring. They would choose and slaughter the male animals that they could not feed over the winter, salting and smoking the meat to get them through the barren winter months to come. It also coincided with the fermentation of all the wine and beer from the summer fruits and crops, so it was a time of celebration with plentiful food and drink before what some called 'the famine period'. They had waited for Luc and Merewyn to descend, and she explained all of this to Lusian as his father set fire to the yule log in the massive hearth of the Great Hall. Luc turned and raised his goblet in a midwinter toast, and a rousing chorus of cheers went up from the men on the benches, their numbers swelled to well over a hundred by the arrival of Ronec and his guest. Again, the family and guests had a convivial evening, but Luc did not come to bed at all that night...

Chapter Eleven

The next few days were a haze of misery for Merewyn. She barely saw Luc, who was either out hunting with his friends or helping Morvan and the Steward oversee the cattle's slaughter. He stayed up late at night and rose early every morning, never touching her. Then she could take no more, and she waited up for him in their chamber until the early hours.

She was nodding off curled up in the chair by the fire when he came in, and she watched as he quietly closed the door so as not to wake her. He moved to the bench in the window embrasure to remove his boots, and she heard him sigh. She quickly crossed to his side and dropped to her knees in front of him. 'Let me do that for you, Luc', she said. He was taken aback, but she noticed that his eyes darted immediately away from hers as he began to stand. She gently pushed him back down onto the bench and, undoing the lacing, she pulled off his long leather boots. She took both of his hands in hers.

'What is it, my love? What is wrong? What have I done to upset you? Is this because Lusian and I came here to Morlaix?' she asked.

For a second, Luc gazed down at her, and she saw pure anguish in his eyes. Then, she watched as his beautiful steel-grey eyes hardened and changed. He stood up, pulling his hands from hers so that she fell backwards.

'Does it ever occur to you, my Lady, that not everything turns on you and our relationship? Yes, you are my wife, and yes, you disobeyed me by coming here. But, now you are here, and you need to accept that my life here in Brittany is different from the idyll we had established in Ravensworth.' She could see and feel the anger building in him; he was almost unrecognisable from the controlled and calm Luc that she knew. He peeled off his tunic and stood glaring down at her.

'I have been given the task of bringing together a mix of volatile, independent Breton Lords in an alliance with William, many of whom have their own agenda and would change sides without warning. Into this mix, we have the fleeing treacherous Earl, Ralph De Gael, who many of them see as a hero for rebelling against William. He is probably now making his way to Brittany. No doubt his arrival will stir up a hornets' nest.' He paused for breath.

'Do you know who that is downstairs?' he asked, pulling her roughly to her feet. 'Do you know who I am now entertaining over yuletide thanks to Ronec, a person that I could not turn away due to the law of hospitality?' he spat at her.

Merewyn stared at Luc wide-eyed in alarm while shaking her head. He still gripped both of her upper arms. She stayed silent; she had never seen him like this.

'It is Ralph De Gael's half-brother who is openly recruiting for his brother's return, recruiting against the King and here he is in my home. God knows why Ronec agreed to bring him here or how this visit will look to Alain Rufus when it gets out or, God forbid, to King William.'

He let go of Merewyn, and she quickly stepped back, shaken by his anger, although she knew that she was not the only cause. Luc had crossed to the table and was downing another goblet of wine. Suddenly, he slammed the empty vessel down onto the heavy table and turned to face her, leaning against it.

'What do you want, Merewyn?' he said, in a hoarse, almost unrecognisable voice.

'I am sorry, Luc, for not understanding, but I have missed you. I hardly see you and I just want to know that you still love me,' she whispered. For what seemed a long time, the silence hung in the fire-lit room. She could see Luc's hands gripping the table behind him. She could almost feel the dark, angry intensity of his gaze.

'You want me to show you?' he laughed harshly, and stepping forward, he grabbed her hand and pulled her to the bed. He lifted her and flung her backwards onto the fur coverlet. He quickly placed his muscled thighs on either side of her, pinning her down, and began raining rough searching kisses on her mouth and neck. Merewyn felt a fleeting moment of panic. Luc was obviously already very drunk, and she had never seen him like this. He seemed to be almost out of control, which was unknown for her Horse Warrior. She was not frightened, but she could feel the detachment in him and the unusual harsh frantic nature of his touch; these were not his usual loving caresses.

He urgently ripped out the lacings at the front of her dress and freed her breasts, squeezing and then biting her nipples until she gasped. He stopped for a moment and looked down at her, his face a mask of desire. However, there was

123

something else in his eyes, as if he was in pain. Without a word, he pulled her gown up around her hips and, kneeling up, he untied his braies, his eyes never leaving her face.

He drove into her, pinning her shoulders to the bed, his solid muscular thighs pinning her legs. She tried to caress his shoulders and back, but he quickly reached his climax, and suddenly the tension went out of him as he lay supine on top of her. She heard him sigh into her hair, and she gently stroked his head and shoulders as he quietened. He lay like that, still inside her, for some time while she hardly dared to breathe; just holding him was enough.

However, Luc roused himself, pushing himself up onto his elbows and slowly untangling himself from her body. He stood for a few moments looking down at her. The firelight shone on his beautifully proportioned muscular body, and her eyes travelled slowly up to his face. He looked sad and almost boyish, the long dark lock of hair falling over his brow. She raised a hand to him, but his eyes clouded, and he turned away.

'I am going to get some sleep,' he said, pulling on his discarded braies and his tunic and, turning on his heel, he quietly left the chamber. Merewyn lay very still as she tried to make sense of what had just happened.

She dressed with care the following day, putting on a brave face as she descended the stairs into the Great Hall, where the family and guests were assembling. She nodded a greeting to the crowded table and sat quietly with Lusian to break her fast with bread and the soft flavoursome goat's cheese, but the food was tasteless in her mouth. She raised her eyes to glance down the table and found Marie scrutinising her closely, so she smiled,

'Has Luc gone hunting again?' she asked Morvan.

'No, we have one of our broodmares in foal, and Luc has gone to check on her progress. The foal should arrive later today or tomorrow, and I am sure Lusian would love to see it,' he said. She nodded and smiled as she saw the anticipation on her son's face.

Soon the men departed, and Merewyn and Marie were left alone. 'So what has my thoughtless son done to upset you so much, Merewyn' she said with a penetrating glance and a soft smile. This kindness was almost too much for Merewyn, and, close to tears, she described the almost total change in Luc's behaviour since his return from Dinan.

Marie looked thoughtful. 'Yes, I have noticed a difference; he is drinking far more, and the Steward tells me that Luc has been sleeping on the hard settle in the records room on some nights. He is somewhat abrupt with the servants and grooms as well, which is not like my son. It almost reminds me of how he was in the year after Heloise died when he just went into himself and would listen to no one,' she said, staring into the fire. Merewyn explained what Luc had said about Geoffrey Fitz-Eustace, but Marie just shrugged.

'Usually, my son would take something like that in his stride and put plans in place to mitigate it; he is a consummate tactician as well as a warrior,' she said, shaking her head. 'Leave it with me; we will find the underlying cause of this,' she said, taking Merewyn's hands and squeezing them. She was as good as her word and summoned Gerard to her chamber after nuncheon. However, when questioned, he admitted that he was just as perplexed by Luc's sudden change.

'It is as if all of the joy in life has gone out of him,' he said, shaking his head.

'So what happened at Dinan? Is that where he met with Ronec? Is Fitz Eudo the cause of all this? We know he can be trouble,' she asked.

'No. I think they met amicably on the road and went their separate ways, and Luc did invite him here. He would not have done that if there had been an incident or disagreement,' mused Gerard. Marie nodded and sent him down to the stable yard to talk to Luc and see if he could find out what was troubling him.

Chapter Twelve

Luc did not return to the Hall all day. The family had gathered early in the Great Hall that evening before he arrived. A stage was set up for the strolling players, and Lusian could hardly contain himself; Luc greeted everyone, ruffled Lusian's hair and went to wash and change. Merewyn was relieved to see that he looked more relaxed, laughing and joking with Gerard and Ronec. The players performed a mummer's play for the packed Hall with a brave knight killing a fearsome beast. Lusian sat wide-eyed, clapping enthusiastically as the beast was slain at the end and feinting at it himself with an imaginary sword. Then the players led Lusian to a chair and crowned him as the Lord of Misrule for the night.

He gave several commands, including more honey-dipped almonds to be brought, which made his mother smile. He copied some of the games he remembered from previous events in Ravensworth. Chargers was one, with Luc on Gerard's back and Geoffrey on Ronec's back trying to unseat each other with padded wooden staves. The men in the Hall roared their approval, and bets were placed on who would win. Lusian was delighted when his father won, and Geoffrey went toppling backwards. Merewyn was aware that it was getting late and rowdy in the Hall, so she told Lusian that his rule was over, but he could give one more command before bed. Lusian's mouth set in disapproval; he was having far too much fun, so he decided to put his mother in the middle for the circle game.

'Maid a kissing,' he announced to much hilarity from the assembled men and obvious displeasure on his mother's face as this could become a pretty wild adult game.

He watched with glee as his mother was blindfolded, and he then picked ten of the willing volunteers from the Hall to join his father, Geoffrey and Ronec in the circle. The musicians would play, and when they stopped, Merewyn would move left, around the men in the circle, running her hands over the upper body of the man in front of her who had to keep his hands behind his back. She had to keep count and kiss each man on the cheek. Usually, several of the men would try to steal a better kiss, but the 'Maid in the Ring' would push them playfully away. In the end, the drum would beat into a roll, and she had to count her way back to the man she knew to be her husband or betrothed. It was a fun game as the men jostled each other for position and tried to change places to be kissed twice. It had been known for blows to be exchanged in the past, with one man even picking the maid up and running off with her.

Merewyn, now resigned to the game, took it all in good stead; she knew she had to entertain their guests and men. She also knew that she could easily pick Luc out of the men due to his height and broad shoulders. She knew she could not touch his face or hair, but she could encircle his waist and run her hands over his chest and shoulders. The betting on this was desultory as most men, especially those from

Ravensworth, thought it was a foregone conclusion.

A laughing blindfolded Merewyn made her way around the circle. Each time the music stopped, she played to the audience, laughing and flirting, pretending to be unsure with one of the older grey and whiskered men. She playfully slapped away any man who became too enthusiastic. Finally, the drum began to roll, and there had been two or three of a similar build to Luc, but she was positive that he was number seven, who was taller with a warrior's toned and muscled torso and arms. The Lord of Misrule shouted that she had to find her husband, and she slowly went back round the circle, touching each man on the chest and counting. The assembled men in the Hall counted with her, many now standing on benches to see what was happening. The drum stopped, and she stood before Luc. She put her hands on his shoulders and raised her lips to his.

Luc had enjoyed the evening; he thought things through and convinced himself that he could find a way through this. Briaca must not come back to Morlaix. He had laughed at his young son, commanding grown men and women to do ridiculous and daring things.

He took part in several games, and he was happy as he watched his beautiful wife make her way around the circle in maid-a-kissing. He laughed aloud as some of his Horse Warriors, who had taken a lot of drink, tried to steal a kiss from her and had then thrown a guilty glance at him. Now, though, at last, the drum was beating, and he smiled with confidence as his blindfolded wife counted her way towards him, laughing as she avoided the hands that reached out for her. At last, she was in front of him, but she fleetingly touched his chest and moved on. He gaped in total disbelief as she stopped three men later and stood in front of a tall, dark warrior. She placed her hands on his chest, saying in a loud voice, 'I choose to award the kiss to this man,' as she went on tiptoe to meet his mouth. As her choice became clear, there was uproar at the unexpected result. Many laughed, including Lusian, who did not understand the implications. However, many of the men who had won their bets were banging the tables with their tankards at this turn of events.

Merewyn felt Luc's strong arms come around her as he pulled her close against his body. His mouth descended on hers, possessing her, and she felt his body reacting to her closeness, feeling the male hardness of him pressed against her. A current of passion raced to her groin but, as she reached up to his hair and face, she realised that this man was not Luc. She tried to break away, but he had her waist in a vice-like grip, while one hand held her head as he continued to kiss her, his tongue exploring her mouth. She was horrified by her mistake and frightened by her body's response to this man because she knew instinctively who it would be. He released her and removed her blindfold. Blinking, she looked up into a pair of dark brown eyes that were full of passion. She stepped back, breathless, as a slow, lazy smile spread across his face.

'Well, that was certainly worth waiting for my Lady,' he said, bowing.

The Hall had now erupted into laughter and cheers, and Merewyn knew that, although she had to look shocked initially, she had to laugh as well at her own mistake; this was all part of the game. She stole a sideways glance at Luc and caught the thunderous expression on his face before he shrugged it off to the men slapping him on the back and commiserating with him.

Luc felt a cold fury race through his body as he watched his wife choose another man, and it had to be Ronec. The anger built as he watched the long, passionate kiss between them. His rational mind told him that this was just a game, a yuletide prank, but this was Merewyn, his wife. Another man's hands swept over his wife's body; another man was kissing her deeply, and she seemed to be responding. At that moment, he wanted to pull her away and smash his fist into his friend's face. However, he knew he had to take it in good part, or he would just look ridiculous, a jealous husband. So, he unclenched his fists, took a deep breath and continued joking with the men around him.

He glanced at Ronec and caught his eye; Ronec just smiled and shrugged, his palms held out over to indicate that it was not his fault. Luc nodded and smiled back at his friend, but both of them knew that the smile was not genuine, and it certainly did not reach his eyes. Ronec had seen the thunderous look on Luc's face, and he was delighted. His plan was panning out, the added bonus being the response of Merewyn to his lovemaking, and he was now determined to take that further and seduce her. He wanted her in his bed, and he wanted Malvais and his Horse Warriors out of contention, both in the coming war and with the beautiful and wealthy Merewyn. He smiled. He was now confident he could achieve those goals both for Ralph De Gael and for himself.

Before long, the men were settling down to their drinking games and dice, so she bade goodnight to Luc and their guests and followed Marie up to their chambers, as she knew they would be down there for several hours yet. Marie smiled broadly at her when they reached the landing.

'Well, that put the cat amongst the pigeons,' she laughed.

Merewyn hung her head, but Marie put a finger under her chin and smiled at her.

'It will do Luc good to know that he has competition; he gets far too much of his own way. He is just like his father,' she said, kissing Merewyn on the cheek; she went along to her chamber, still laughing softly.

Luc slept in the solar; he woke stiff and cramped from sleeping on the wooden settle. He had stayed up far too late and drank far too much Rhenish wine, so, throwing a warm cloak over his shoulders, he made his way down to the stables for an early morning ride in the mist to clear his head.

Taking his cloak and tunic off, he washed at the well, pouring nearly a whole bucket of freezing water over his head to wake himself up. As he shook off the droplets and pulled his clothes back on, from the corner of his eye, he caught a slight movement and heard a heated conversation that seemed to be taking place deep within the stables. He walked quietly over and stood in the doorway to listen.

'I am telling you, he won't countenance or consider it.'

As he turned towards the end stalls, he could see that it was Ronec and Geoffrey Fitz-Eustace; they stopped abruptly as they saw him silhouetted in the doorway. Ronec immediately stepped forward, a smile on his face.

'We thought we would join you for your early morning ride this morning Luc to clear our heads after last night's revelry,' he said.

Luc stood in silence and regarded the pair for a few minutes, enough for Fitz-Eustace to feel uncomfortable and move from foot to foot before Luc nodded and headed for the particular box stall where his stallion, Espirit, was impatiently stamping his feet. He affectionately rubbed his neck and began tacking him up. He was not naïve, and the tension between the two men in the stables was palpable; he did not trust either of them, which saddened him as Ronec had been a friend and companion in arms for many years. When he led Espirit out into the courtyard, they were mounted and waiting for him. Fitz-Eustace let out a long whistle of appreciation as he watched the stallion dance sideways across the cobbles. Luc leapt into the saddle and controlled the great horse with ease using only his knees before picking up the reins.

'So this is the famous Breton stallion,' he said to Luc.

'Yes, the sire of the three-year-old youngsters you saw two days ago,' he said; Espirit was now caracoling left and right on the spot in his impatience to be off.

'I don't suppose he is for sale?' asked Fitz-Eustace. Ronec burst into laughter that Fitz-Eustace would even have the temerity to ask.

'Never,' shouted Luc over his shoulder as he cantered out of the courtyard, down across the bailey and out of the gates, heading towards the wooded foothills.

Luc set a punishing pace for a good hour until they came out at the head of the valley, looking out along the coast. The view was breath taking, and you could taste the salt in the stiff breeze from the west. Luc cantered ahead onto the bluff but then gave Espirit his head to crop the salt-soaked grass as he waited for the others to catch up. Both horses were blowing slightly as they galloped up to join him. Ronec gazed at Luc's stallion with admiration.

'He goes like the wind Luc,' he laughed.

'And so will his offspring Ronec, especially from the Arab mare I have just bought.'

Fitz-Eustace cut in. 'I will definitely take all four that we saw put through their paces; we are in great need of such quality warhorses,' he said. Luc narrowed his eyes as he looked at Geoffrey. He did not know him well; he had always been more of a courtier than a warrior, although he had seen him do well in tournaments when they were younger. However, tournaments were different from warfare, and he pondered about the man's need for so many horses so quickly.

'What exactly do you mean when you say 'we' Fitz-Eustace?' he asked, in an emotionless voice but with a raised eyebrow. Luc needed information, so he was determined to play along with them to get it. He knew that the two of them had cornered him this morning for a reason. He glanced at Ronec, who had been watching him intently but who now looked away, avoiding his eyes.

Fitz-Eustace drew himself to his full height in the saddle. 'My brother's wife Emma has arrived at Gael, after months of siege at Norwich castle, they finally allowed her safe passage to leave. My brother, Ralph De Gael, is in Flanders, but he is making his way south and will join us here very soon.' Luc tried to keep a neutral expression on his face. It was just as he had feared, and Brittany once again would become a battleground.

Fitz-Eustace continued, 'I suppose you have heard that Northumberland and Hereford have been imprisoned. No doubt, he has executed them by now, two of the most powerful Earls in England! How can you support such an underhand and murdering king such as William, Malvais?

You know he poisoned our older brother Walter and his wife while they were staying as guests at his castle in Falaise?'

He paused for breath, the emotion becoming too much for him, as Luc did not reply. Then he continued, 'Come and join us, Malvais. We will destroy him and defeat Duke Hoel; we will drive him out and bring peace back to Brittany; you could become a powerful leader here. Surely that is what you want?'

Luc took a deep breath and pinned Fitz-Eustace with a steely gaze. 'My Patron is Alain Rufus, and I am loyal and accountable to him. He is my liege lord, and he supports the king. I cannot betray him, and I am surprised that either of you thought that I would, Ronec,' he said, looking searchingly at his friend.

Ronec needed to keep Luc on his side, and he wanted to be able to stay at Morlaix for several months to take his plan forward, so he just shrugged with a rueful smile and gave a non-committal answer.

'I told them it would be futile, but who can blame them for trying. It would even up the odds to have the most famous warrior in Western Europe and his cavalry fighting on their side,' he said. However, Luc noticed that Ronec could still not look him in the eye.

'So I presume that you have sold your sword, and you are joining them, Ronec?' he queried.

'No, I prefer to stay here for a month or two if you will have me for a little longer Malvais,' he laughed and smiled. It was difficult not to like Ronec, and Luc did feel a small amount of relief knowing that he was not riding off with Fitz-Eustace to join Ralph De Gael. However, he was sure that Ronec had some plan, although he was not quite sure yet what that was.

He thought it probable that Ronec was weighing up which side would win and biding his time before he jumped.

However, more importantly, an approach had been made to him by the rebel De Gael camp. He had to get that information and the news about the imminent arrival of Ralph De Gael to Alan Rufus and the King immediately.

Meanwhile, at Morlaix, Morvan turned a corner on the lower floor to find Ronec's manservant coming out of the records room, a small parchment in his hand. He jumped when he saw Morvan standing in the shadows. Then he quickly bowed his head in acknowledgement and went to walk past. Within seconds, Morvan had a vice-like grip on the wrist holding the parchment. 'You are Ronec's man, are you not,' he asked, moving even closer to confront him. Flek lowered his eyes and backed against the wall, 'Yes, Sire, I am Flek.'

'So why are you coming out of my brother's records room with a letter' he asked.

'Forgive me, Sire, but my master asked me to get a small piece of plain parchment as he needs me to send a message to one of his manors,' he explained. Morvan still gripped the man tightly as he took the scroll from the man's hand. He unrolled it expectantly, but as the man had said, it was empty. Morvan reluctantly let go of the man's wrist. Although the manservant had been telling the truth, Morvan felt there was something suspicious about Flek, who never raised his eyes from the ground.

'Next time, ask the Steward who will find anything that Fitz-Eudo has requested; I do not expect to see you near this room again, he added, dismissing the servant with a wave of his hand. When Morvan reached the door, he looked behind and encountered a pure vitriolic look from the manservant who still stood rooted to the spot before he quickly turned on his way. It was a thoughtful Morvan who entered the room and scanned the tables and scrolls stacked there. His brother was very organised; everything seemed to be in place; however, Morvan crossed to the table and lifted the quill on a whim. Morvan knew his brother used only the more expensive oak gall ink and mainly vellum for Alain Rufus and the King's messages. He raised his finger to the end of the quill, which acted as a reservoir for the ink, and it came away wet with black ink. There was no doubt that this quill had been used very recently. Yet Luc had been out riding since early morning, and Gerard had been on the training ground. Flek had written something in here, using that quill. Morvan turned on his heel and sprinted along the corridor and up into the Hall, but there was no sign of the manservant. From that moment, Morvan resolved to watch him like a hawk.

The three men arrived back at the stables to see two of Geoffrey Fitz-Eustace's men about to leave; they led the horses to the mounting block. Luc barely glanced at them while taking Espirit towards his stall as he was preoccupied, but Morvan was coming down the steps from the Donjon. He suddenly gave a shout, and Luc seeing his brother running down the steps, handed Espirit to a waiting boy and headed back into the cobbled inner bailey. Morvan had dragged one of the Gael men out of the saddle, and as Luc strode over, he had the man tightly by the throat.

'Where did you get the horse?' He yelled at the man, who was gasping for breath. Ronec and Fitz-Eustace, attracted by the shouting, had also arrived at the scene, and the latter drew his sword and turned it on Morvan, who unwillingly let the man go.

At a glare from Luc, Fitz-Eustace reluctantly sheathed his sword.

'Can you tell me why your brother is attacking my Captain,' he asked in an outraged voice. Before Luc could find an answer, Morvan leapt in.

'He is riding one of our missing horses, and I would like to know exactly where he got it from,' he yelled, stepping towards the Captain who had pulled himself to his feet, his hand still rubbing his bruised throat, he backed away against the mounting block. Luc turned and raised an eyebrow at Fitz-Eustace, who was glaring at his Captain and shaking his head.

'Well, can anyone shed any light on why this man is riding one of our Morlaix strawberry roans?' he asked. Fitz-Eustace just shrugged. Quite a crowd had gathered to watch the altercation by now, servants and Horse Warriors alike. The Captain now straightened up and addressed Fitz-Eustace,

'I bought it, my Lord, over a month ago, it was at the horse fair at Loudeac; it had no brand or marks on it,' he said defensively.

Morvan watched the Captain like a hawk, shaking his head in disbelief, but Luc happened to catch an unexpected searching stare from Ronec into the crowd. He saw that Ronec's manservant was standing at the back looking very uncomfortable, and as he saw Luc staring at him, the man lowered his eyes. Fitz-Eustace now shrugged and turned to Luc, 'it seems as if my Captain bought it in good faith. Are you sure it is one of yours? He asked Luc. Before Luc could answer, Morvan replied, 'do you not think we know every horse we breed here? He may not be one of our big Destriers, but that is a quality riding horse, the type we use for our messengers and scouts. I could take you to the paddocks and show you his dam and his brother.' He spat at Fitz- Eustace, whose hand returned to his sword as Morvan stepped forward towards him. Luc put an arm out to hold Morvan back.

'Please remember the laws of hospitality, brother, these are our guests, and there may well be another explanation.' He said meaningfully. Morvan took a deep breath and turned back to the Captain, 'Who did you buy our horse from?' He asked in a deadly cold voice.The Captain gave a quick glance over to the back of the crowd before he answered, and Luc saw Ronec's manservant turn and hurry away.

'It was from one of the usual horse traders, Sire; he had a string of them, there were several traders there, but I do not know his name.' The Captain said plaintively, looking again at Fitz-Eustace. Morvan was clearly not satisfied with this answer, and Luc became even more irritated when Fitz-Eustace took a bag of silver from his belt and threw it at Morvan's feet.

'Here is payment for the horse, now can I send them on their way? They have urgent messages to deliver.' He sneered.

Within seconds, Morvan's sword was in his hand, but again Luc stepped in front of his brother. He bent and picked up the bag of coins, and walking over to Fitz-Eustace, he took the man's hand and placed the bag of coins in his palm. He curled Fitz-Eustace's fingers around it in a crushing grip that made the bones crack.

'We do not want your coin, but we will take our stolen horse back as the messenger that was riding him is missing and possibly dead, but we now have a trail to follow. I believe you now have urgent business, which means you and your men will be leaving at dawn. Do we understand each other?' Fitz Eustace blanched and managed to pull his bruised and crushed hand free; backing away, he nodded and, turning, he swiftly entered the stables followed by Ronec.

Geoffrey Fitz-Eustace left very early the next day, and the ladies made an effort to rise early and join the men to see him off, wishing him Godspeed with a stirrup cup of warm, spiced wine; Luc had not shared with them the reason for his sudden departure.

Before he mounted, Geoffrey had purposefully clasped arms with Luc despite their dispute the previous day,

'Remember you can join us any time Malvais, if you change your mind. You have a reputation as a fair and just man, so you must see the injustice in this murdering King's actions. Think on it; that is all we ask.'

He drank the proffered cup and then raised a hand to his men and led them out through the huge stone arch into the bailey and down to the main gatehouse. As Luc watched him go, he knew that the next time they met, it would highly likely be on a battlefield on opposing sides, Breton against Breton. Luc sighed, shook his head, and then looked at Morvan beside him, staring after the departing men.

'I will arrange for the young horses to be ridden in stages over to Gael, and we will pick up payment from them,' he said.

'Don't bother. Those youngsters will not be going anywhere. Bring Gerard, and I will explain,' he said, turning and heading into the castle.

The three men were closeted together for most of the day in the castle's stone-vaulted records room while Merewyn and Marie entertained Lusian. They watched servants and messengers coming and going all morning with interest. They were joined for lunch by Ronec, who had spent the morning in sword practice with some of Luc's new young recruits.

'Welcome, Ronec. We are pleased to see you as our menfolk have abandoned us,' said Marie. Ronec looked at the closed door leading to the tower and the records room, and he raised an eyebrow. Marie, who had been a consummate courtier in the French court, fended this quickly. 'Neglected estate business, my son has bought an estate which adjoins ours, and he is arranging for more woodland and brush to be cleared for pasture. But he needs permission from Hoel, the Duke of Brittany, to do so, mainly due to some ancient tenure, hence all the messengers,' she smiled.

Merewyn admired her mother-in-law's easy deflection. She had learnt a lot from this great lady in the past few months. However, she also used the moment to study Ronec from under lowered lids. Luc had not been back to their bed for several nights, and he had barely spoken a word to her today, so she had decided to enjoy the attention from this handsome warrior, hoping that Luc would notice how beautiful other men found his wife.

Ronec was charming; he was light-hearted and amusing. She knew he would have a dark and dangerous side, but he did not have the intensity that seemed to emanate from Luc. This made him carefree and good company. He kept the ladies and Lusian entertained for hours in front of the enormous fire that winter's afternoon with tales of conquests and narrow escapes, some not quite suitable for Lusian's ears, but, fortunately, most went over his head. They teased him unmercifully about his love life and lack of a wife or family, which he took in good stead. 'Ladies, although I have loved and left dozens of women, I have never found one that I wanted to marry until now,' he said, gazing at Merewyn but then comically dropping to one knee before Marie and offering her his heart.

Both women burst out laughing and, just at that moment, Luc and the other two men emerged from the tower doorway to find Marie and Merewyn laughing uncontrollably while both were pulling Ronec back to his feet. Suddenly he seized Merewyn's hands, and, humming a well-known ditty loudly, he danced her around the tables and then tried to do the same with Marie, who slapped him away.

'Stop it, you terrible man, you have never grown up Ronec,' she laughed. Merewyn sank back onto the wooden settle, still flushed and laughing; she felt like a young girl again. Then she looked up and saw Luc staring at her. For a few moments, she saw the sadness in his face before it shut down again.

'Oh Luc, what is wrong with you?' she whispered to herself, as he nodded at them all and then headed silently out of the Hall.

Merewyn saw Luc briefly in their chamber before dinner. He had, as usual, spent some time with Lusian at his bedtime before coming to wash and change. She tried to be light-hearted and kept up a stream of conversation, but she found him taciturn, often given monosyllabic answers. As he pulled his tunic over his head, she went to stand close to him, and she placed her hands on his hard muscled chest. 'You do know that we love you, Luc, don't you?' she said, gazing up into his troubled face. He clasped her hands close to his chest, and she could see that his eyes were full of love. She could also feel the hunger in him as he looked at her, pulling her into his arms.

'It will get better, Merewyn, I promise,' he said. 'There are things many afoot, but no matter how preoccupied I am, just know that yes, I love you both,' and he lowered his head to kiss her lips gently. 'Now let us go down to dinner; your admirer will be waiting impatiently', he laughed.

Further, along the corridor, Ronec was quietly pleased with how things were going despite the incident with the horse; he had lambasted Flek for being stupid enough to allow the horse to be brought back to Morlaix. However, he was pleased that Flek had successfully found and copied the most recent message from Alain Rufus, which included a list of those Breton Lords who may be wavering in their allegiance to William, even though he had almost been caught in the act by Morvan. He decided to send Flek to Gael with this valuable information, as it removed the manservant from that young man's orbit.

Chapter Thirteen

Within days, messages of support arrived from notable Breton Lords to answer the request that Luc De Malvais had sent out to them. Luc was mollified but not sanguine about the response; he knew that significant forces could range themselves against the King, including Fulk of Anjou if he entered the fray, which would challenge William's army. Morvan and Gerard were kept fully occupied in drilling and training the new recruits who arrived from Luc's estates almost daily since the message sent out to rally the fyrd, the able foot soldiers in every village that owed their lord service. Luc intended to use them to protect the estates and castles of the Malvais lands once the Breton Horse Warriors had ridden out.

As for Luc, he concentrated on training the horse warriors and building up over a hundred warhorses' fitness and strength. He was preparing for war, and he requested and gathered additional foodstuffs, livestock and supplies. This was hard on his people as they would have a harsh winter ahead, but he had to feed his men and horses. In the meantime, he prayed that no move would be made until late spring or early summer when the weather and the ground would be better. He sent riders and messengers out constantly to bring back any news of troop movement, either near Gael or near Anjou and Maine's borders. However, all seemed quiet at present. He spent several hours each day in the records room planning on the maps, the best route and ground on which to fight to get the most advantage from the Breton cavalry. He was sending such information to the King when there was quite a commotion in the Hall. Within minutes, Morvan appeared in the doorway, a cynical smirk on his face.

'Another messenger? Is it one of ours or from the King?' asked Luc, lowering his eyes once again to the map spread out on the table in front of him.

'Come and greet our visitor, Luc; she is back at least two weeks before she was expected,' he replied with a raised eyebrow. Luc looked startled and followed Morvan into the Hall to be met with the sight of Marie greeting her ward, Briaca. His stomach lurched. He had told her not to return to Morlaix at all, yet here she was. His face froze and then set in harsh lines and his fists clenched at his sides. They had not parted well when he delivered her to her parents; he had been furious with himself and consumed with guilt. He had told her, and her parents that she was to stay in Dinan and under no circumstances was she to travel across Brittany with war imminent. Given the uncertain nature of the alliances, her parents had agreed. She had been furious but had tried to hide it, yet here she was in Morlaix, as beautiful and wilful as ever.

'Luc, Morvan, see who has arrived,' said his mother gesturing to them to come and greet her; at that moment, Briaca raised her eyes to Luc's face and, holding her head high, she gave him a triumphant smile. Luc groaned inside, but the law of hospitality bade him greet her. He took her hands and leaned in to kiss her cheek, but she purposefully gave him her mouth.

'I am delighted to be back here with you all,' she said, gazing meaningfully at Luc in a way he could not mistake while still holding his hands. His mother had turned away, but Morvan saw this interplay and raised his eyebrows at his brother, who just shrugged. This was a different Briaca, much more confident and possessive of Luc, which made him wonder what had happened between them.

Merewyn, who was descending the staircase from the solar, was equally struck by how the girl was looking at Luc. She was irritated to see the girl back so soon and annoyed to see that Luc was still holding her hands. At that moment, Briaca caught sight of Merewyn and sent her a knowing, triumphant smile. Merewyn continued tight-lipped to cross the floor and greet Briaca. She noticed that Luc could not meet her eyes as he stepped back from the girl.

'This is a surprise, Briaca. If you had sent a message ahead, I would have ordered a fire lit in the guest room,' she smiled.

Briaca was almost disconcerted for a fleeting moment as she noticed the heavily embroidered chatelaine slung around Merewyn's hips, suspended from which were the household keys. So, Marie had stepped down, and Merewyn had rightly taken her position as mistress of Morlaix; this was inconvenient but not impossible. She knew that Luc would be hers. It was only a matter of time.

She smiled sweetly at Merewyn. 'I certainly did not mean to put you to any trouble. After all, I feel as if I am already a member of the family,' she said, gazing directly into Luc's eyes.

Ronec had watched this scene with interest. Inwardly, he was grinning, delighted that she had returned to Morlaix as this could play directly into his hands. He lithely uncurled his muscular frame from the chair and, approaching Briaca from behind, he lifted her into the air and swung her around. A look of petulant annoyance crossed her face until she realised it was the handsome knight from the inn.

'So the Breton beauty has come amongst us to brighten our days,' he said, his eyes laughing back at her. 'However, we are all still eclipsed by this maiden of the sun,' he said, taking Merewyn's hand and kissing it. This fulsome praise somewhat mollified Merewyn as she had taken particular care with her appearance this morning, dressing in a sky-blue overdress and Breton lace chemise. Her long, silver-blond tresses were hanging loosely down her back, held only by an embroidered headband.

'Yes, like night and day,' smirked Morvan.

'Or sunrise and sunset, surely,' suggested Ronec gazing at Merewyn and enjoying this mild flirtation.

Luc was not amused. Briaca's return was a complication in his life that he did not need, a clear and present reminder of his guilt. 'Enough of this,' he declared. Bowing to the ladies, he retreated to his maps and lists, followed sheepishly by Morvan.

Left to his own devices, Ronec continued to pay court to Merewyn, but she excused herself as she discussed household matters with Marie. Ronec turned his ready smile on Briaca.

'Well, my lady, come and join me for mulled ale by the fire to warm yourself after such an arduous journey,' he said, offering her his arm. He guided her to the comfortable, leather-backed chairs set close to the massive, stone fireplace while summoning a houseboy for refreshments. While they waited, Ronec leaned against the large stone fireplace's side slab and watched her settle her gown.

'I seem to remember that the last time I saw you, it was under slightly different circumstances,' he said, smiling knowingly down at her. Briaca lowered her eyes as she nodded, recalling his proposition and the fact that she had been lying naked in bed with Luc when Ronec burst into the room.

'I hope, sir, that you will forget that and not mention it here as I am sure that it would be detrimental to both of us at the moment.' She raised her huge, blue eyes in a pleading glance wanting to assess and gauge his intention.

Ronec laughed at her ploy; he was enjoying himself hugely at her expense. He glanced around the empty Hall and boldly leaned forward, running his fingers around the curve of her breast.

'Luc is a fortunate man to have both of you,' he said while thinking about how he would enjoy bedding this little madam. 'However, I can't help thinking that it is a little unfair, almost selfish in fact,' he whispered as he leaned further forward and brushed his lips across hers. Briaca was spellbound for a few seconds. Ronec was an exceptionally attractive man, and she could see how easily women would be drawn in by his charm and audacity. He excited her, and he could be useful to her. He continued to kiss her, his hands holding her head, his tongue pushing its way through her lips when she heard the houseboy returning and suddenly pulled sharply back.

'No!' she said, holding up both hands to ward him off. Ronec leaned back, laughing aloud. 'Well done, my little beauty, I admire your self-control. However, I do think we can continue to be very useful to each other; it is obvious that you still want and intend to have Luc De Malvais. However, he already has a very beautiful wife, so I think I can help you out. You see, I want Merewyn.'

Briaca's mouth dropped open as she issued an 'oh', her eyes widening in surprise. Then, her eyes narrowed, and she stared at him. Ronec laughed again.

'You are so young and transparent, Briaca; you need to work on that, so you are now wondering what is in it for him? Well, I have my own plan, which I am not going to share but let me give you something you will understand. I am a mercenary with some but not a lot of lands; she is lovely and, more importantly, very wealthy in her own right.' Briaca was not naïve, and she knew that there was more to this than that. Underneath that charming, happy-go-lucky exterior, she had seen a brittle, hard determination in the Inn, and he had arranged for Luc to be brought to her room. 'An alliance to achieve our aims?' she questioned.

'Yes, Briaca, but none of this is to be shared; we need to be circumspect; Morvan already has a very suspicious mind. We will work together to widen the rift between Merewyn and Luc. He has already changed since that night at the inn with you, and relations between them are not good; he spends a lot of time sleeping elsewhere. She is patently unhappy, and I intend to bring some happiness back into her life,' he grinned.

Briaca was pleased by the news, and it gave Ronec food for thought as he took a long draught of his mulled ale. Luc had been very drunk that night; his manservant Flek said they had almost carried him to the room that night. Had he even been capable of making love to Briaca? Ronec decided to raise the

149

subject with Luc to gauge his reaction. He was pensive for a moment as he gazed into the flames of the enormous fire.

'So how is your plan progressing,' he asked, raising an eyebrow.

Briaca steeled herself to look him directly in the face. 'We love each other,' she declared.

'Well, that could be a little difficult as he obviously adores his wife and son as well.' He watched with amusement as Briaca's pretty, arched, wing-like brows came down, and she glared back at him.

'Speaking of this passionate love, is there any sign of issue from that night or morning with Luc, or is it too soon?' he questioned.

Briaca's breath caught in her throat. Of course! Why hadn't she thought of that? She could have been carrying Luc's child if her plan had succeeded and Ronec hadn't walked in on them. The problem lay in the fact that Luc had not actually made love to her. She darted a calculating glance at Ronec.

'I should have been, but you put paid to that by bursting in on us at the crack of dawn,' she said.

Ronec laughed. So she had planned the whole thing. She was an unscrupulous, conniving madam, but his desire to bed her increased by the second.

'So what really happened? He asked with a grin. Briaca cast her mind back and replayed in her mind what had happened that night... while giving Ronec a shortened version of it.

...They had placed Luc on the bed, and he had immediately slipped into a more profound, drunken stupor, so Briaca had curled up in the chair beside the fire and waited until his breathing became deep and regular. She then moved over to the bed and undid the lacing at the front and sides of his leather doublet before pulling it gently out from under him. She had lifted his arms and edged the cambric shirt slowly up and over his head, and then she sat down and stared at the bare-chested warrior stretched out on her bed. She had revelled in running her hands over his muscled chest and shoulders, her fingers tracing the outline of several small battle scars and then the hard white lines where she knew he had been captured and flogged by a Saxon rebel.

Luc had remained utterly oblivious to her caress. Suddenly, a plan leapt into her mind. She had rocked back and forwards in delight as she realised what she could do to tie Luc to her forever, but she needed a knife; unfortunately, there was not one to be had in his belt.

Briaca had stood and scanned the room around her until her eyes alighted on the small fruit knife she had been using after dinner. She returned to the bed and placed it carefully on the bolster. She then turned her attention to removing the rest of his clothes, undoing the straps of his chausses and peeling them off one by one. Luc now lay in just his linen braies tied at the waist. He was still breathing deeply as her hands untied them, and she had felt some shyness, but she had been excited at the thought of removing them. She had slowly loosened them and pulled them down over his thighs, lifting each long foot, in turn, to remove them altogether. She stood somewhat overawed at what she had done; she now had Luc, the Lord of Morlaix and leader of the Breton Horse Warriors, naked in her bed.

She had stood and just stared at the masculine perfection that was Luc De Malvais. His noble, chiselled face, strong neck, broad shoulders and the muscled upper arms of a swordsman. The narrow waist and hips led down to the large, muscled thighs and calves of a horseman warrior. However, there had been something almost vulnerable about Luc like this; he had looked practically boyish without the intense gaze and concentrated frown of a Breton Lord. She had climbed onto the bed and knelt beside him, running her hands down the outside of his hard, muscled thighs. Luc did not stir, so she moved to his inner thighs until her hands caressed his manhood, curled in a dark triangle of hair. Luc groaned slightly and murmured something, but she had been disappointed to see no other reaction; he was too drunk.

Luc lay firmly in the middle of the bed, so, picking up the knife, she had sat straddled across his thighs and held her leg over him. She had selected a small vein at the back of her knee, made a cut, and the blood had welled and dripped onto the bed on and between Luc's thighs, staining the sheets. She had smeared more blood onto the top of her thighs. She was pleased with the result as she surveyed the scene. She removed her nightgown, purposefully ripping it and throwing it on the floor, before curling her naked body around Luc and pulling the rough blankets over them both.

Suddenly, Luc had moved, his hand had reached out for her, and he turned his head restlessly. 'Merewyn,' he had said before drifting back off into sleep. She had watched him for a while in the firelight until he had settled; she had nestled against the heat of his body and felt his strong arms go round her and pull her to him as he fell again into a deeper sleep.

'You will be mine, Luc,' she had whispered to him as she finally drifted off...

Having finished her tale, Briaca waited in anticipation of Ronec's response; would he be shocked at what she had done? Ronec gave a soundless whistle as he looked at her. 'So, unfortunately, you are still a virgin, and there will be no sign of a child,' he said, a small smile playing on his lips. 'Well, I think I can give you some help with that; after all, the birth dates of a baby are always so uncertain, and I am certainly willing to oblige. I promise you, my lady, that you certainly won't be disappointed,' he grinned while placing his hand provocatively on his groin.

Briaca felt the heat race to her cheeks. She may be an accomplished flirt, but apart from the fumbles with a willing squire that had resulted in her being sent to Morlaix, she had never had a man, especially not a virile man like Ronec, a warrior. She felt excitement at the thought, and she unconsciously ran her tongue over her bottom lip and took it between her teeth. Ronec laughed as he watched her; he could almost feel her anticipation.

'I will find my way to your room tonight. Keep it unlocked and dismiss your maid. He paused for effect and then leaned in, his breath hot on her neck, and whispered, 'and every night after that.'

He drained his cup, bowed over her hand and strode off down the Hall. She watched him go, her teeth gritted. This was a price to be paid, and it would finally help her get Luc De Malvais. Ronec was tall and dark, which meant that the child would be too. However, as she watched Ronec arrogantly striding away, she also felt a wave of apprehension at the thought of this muscled warrior naked in her bed; he would not be easy to control.

Dinner that evening was a lively affair as Ronec drew a taciturn Luc out of himself with tales of adventures and skirmishes when they had been mercenaries together. Gerard joined in with other humorous stories of their exploits and scrapes. He described how he had despaired of ever keeping these reckless ' necks or nothing' warriors under control.

Only Morvan remained slightly removed from it all. He felt as if he was a spectator at a play, but he could see that the performances were not spontaneous. He could feel the undercurrents and tension around the table. He glanced at his mother, who was usually very percipient, but she was deeply engrossed in and enjoying Gerard's tale of the two brothers trying to break in their first wild Breton stallions.

It was late when the party broke up. Luc, for a change, took his wife's arm and bidding goodnight, he led her upstairs. Briaca and his mother followed, leaving the three men to play a desultory game of dice. Before long, Gerard went down the Hall to talk to the few men left at the long tables. Morvan sat back and eyed Ronec speculatively.

'So Ronec, how long are you planning on staying with us?' he asked.

Ronec smiled. 'A few weeks longer, Morvan, until the weather improves. I am enjoying helping you train the men,' he said, taking another mouthful of wine.

'And if we are summoned to war shortly, as seems possible, will you ride with us, with these men you have helped to train? Or will you, like a true mercenary, go to the highest bidder?' he asked.

Ronec sighed. 'Let us see how things develop, Morvan. It may all come to nothing. With luck, Ralph De Gael will be captured. I know that William's assassins are on his tail as we speak.'

Morvan gazed in silence at Ronec for a good few minutes,

and the tension hung between them. Morvan did not think for a second that Ronec believed that; they both knew that the whole of Brittany was arming and preparing for conflict. As Morvan studied him, he had the uneasy feeling that he was missing something, and he decided to set one of the young squires to watch Ronec's movements. He would also have a word with the Steward to intercept any messages the mercenary might receive. Unfortunately, he did not trust his brother's friend one iota, especially with his links to Gael.

'I see your man Flek has returned,' he said. Ronec did not respond at first but then gave a tight smile, 'Yes, he is very useful in many ways, he has been with me for nearly ten years, an ex-mercenary like Luc and I, very good with a dagger in a fight,' he said pointedly holding Morvan's stare.

Ronec was not deceived ether. Although he smiled at the young man, he knew he would have to watch his back with Morvan; that puzzled glance and those questions had shown that his suspicions were raised. However, he judged that Briaca would now have had time to prepare herself and have got rid of her maid, so he stood and stretched and bade Morvan goodnight. He made his way to his chamber and dismissed his manservant Flek after removing his tunic and chausses. He moved quietly along the dim corridor to the large, carved, wooden door of the other guest room. Lifting the latch, he entered the large chamber, which was only lit by firelight. A quick scan of the room showed him that she was alone, and he closed the door gently behind him, bolting it shut behind him.

Briaca sat in the middle of the fur coverlet, looking apprehensive but with a firm set to her mouth. He smiled encouragingly at her and confidently walked to the end of

155

the large bed. Without saying a word, he lifted his linen under-tunic over his head and stood bare-chested in the firelight, gazing down at her. She had unbound her long, black hair, which fell past her waist, but she still wore a delicately embroidered linen chemise, which showed all of her curves to advantage.

'Come here,' he said. At first, she seemed transfixed, and he wondered if she might have changed her mind as she stared at him. However, she slowly moved to the edge of the bed, putting her small, bare feet on the floor between his legs. He pulled her to her feet, pulling her tight against his body. She gasped as she felt the strength and power in him, but she was more conscious of his large erection pressed against her stomach as she raised her wide, blue eyes to his deep, dark, brown ones.

Ronec gazed down at her. He revelled in the shyness and uncertainty he could see on her face. He was sure she had never actually been with a man, and he smiled at the thought of what he would teach her over the next few nights.

'Untie my braies,' he demanded. For a minute, she did not move; then, he heard her swallow nervously as she shyly undid the ties that held them on his waist. They dropped, unceremoniously, to the floor, and he stepped out of them and kicked them away, standing naked in front of her.

Briaca could hardly breathe. This naked warrior was inches away from her, and she could not take her eyes off his body as she stood there. Although unsure what to do or say next, she surprised herself by how much she wanted to feel his naked body against hers.

'You will be gentle with me, won't you,' she said, the desire for him clear in her awed expression.

156

He gave a confident smile, and his eyes gleamed. 'Maybe I will be at first, but I want to make you squeal in ecstasy, Briaca,' he said, running his hands firmly down the outside of her arms. Then his hands were wrapped up in her hair, grabbing it tightly and pulling her mouth towards his. He kissed her thoroughly, his tongue deep inside her mouth, and she was breathless as he lifted her chemise and pulled it over her head, staring with desire at her rounded body and magnificent breasts, her skin an alabaster white.

'You are stunningly beautiful,' he whispered, running his hands over her body. 'Now, let us give Malvais some evidence to ensure he thinks he deflowered you on that night,' he laughed.

Picking her up, he unceremoniously dumped her back onto the fur coverlet. Kneeling on the bed at her feet, he pulled her legs apart and ran his hands to the top of her thighs.

She could feel his large muscular thighs forcing her legs wider apart. For the first time in her life, Briaca felt entirely out of control, and she revelled in it as he slowly lowered his body onto hers. His hand guided his manhood so that the head rested just slightly inside her. He was poised to take her, and she sank her teeth into his broad, muscular shoulder in excitement and desire as he firmly forced his way into her, and she stifled a scream.

Chapter Fourteen

I t was several weeks later, and the family were breaking their fast when the Steward announced that a boat from England had entered the harbour. They all knew that this was highly unusual at this rough time of year, so it must be an important messenger from England. They waited impatiently for further news until a young Breton soldier appeared at the back of the Hall bearing the House of Rennes' badge. Luc beckoned him forward.

'My Lord, I give you greeting. I bear tidings from Count Alan Rufus,' he announced, bowing and handing over a sizeable salt-stained leather pouch.

'A rough journey was it?' said Luc raising an eyebrow at the water-stained cloak.

The young man grinned and nodded while Merewyn directed the Steward to take him to the kitchens for some warm pottage, and Luc opened the leather pouch up and scanned the contents. There were two missives; the earlier one detailed Ralph De Gael's escape and the defeat of the Danish fleet he had assembled. It also described the imprisonment and execution of the Earls who had rebelled against William. Luc shared the contents of this with the others around the table, explaining William's actions and indicating that it had left Ralph De Gael no choice but to retreat to Brittany and prepare his forces to meet William in battle.

Morvan carefully studied Ronec's face to see if there was any reaction to the news, but he gave little away, adopting an interested expression on his face but not overly so.

The second message was for Luc's eyes only, and he retreated to the records room to digest its contents.

Alain firstly enquired after Merewyn's journey; he hoped that they had all arrived safely in Morlaix. Luc read the following lines with a rising sense of dismay. William would be arriving with his army at St Malo in the next few weeks, and Luc was to gather the Horse Warriors to rendezvous with him at Dinan; further messages would arrive when the King disembarked his army.

However, he raised concern in his own family; Luc gave a sharp intake of breath at what he read. Alain's father, Eudo, the Count of Penthievre, had decided to change sides and support Ralph De Gael. This was not only a shock that would reverberate throughout Brittany but also highly embarrassing for Alain, who was William's nephew and loyal supporter. William had rewarded Alain many times over with wealth and lands in gratitude for his loyalty and service. Still, his father, the Head of the House of Rennes, was now going over to fight on the side of William's enemies.

Alain ordered Luc to go to Rennes, to talk some sense into his father Eudo and point out the implications of such actions for him and the House of Rennes before it became common knowledge. Luc thought this through for over an hour and then called a servant to bring Gerard and Morvan in so he could share the news with them; both men were equally shocked at Eudo's change of heart.

'The House of Rennes has always supported William of Normandy. Eudo supplied William with hundreds of troops and cavalry for England's invasion, including the boats to ship them across,' exclaimed Gerard.

'This means he will be effectively fighting against his son and the Breton Horse Warriors,' said Morvan in disbelief.

'Yes,' said Luc, standing up and restlessly striding around the chamber. 'We are talking about a civil war in Brittany, our own men fighting against troops who have fought with and beside us in the past at the Battle of Hastings.'

All three stood in silence for a few moments as they considered the implications of Eudo's betrayal.

'We must keep this quiet', said Morvan, glancing meaning-fully at Luc.

Luc nodded. 'You mean Ronec, I presume. I do wonder at times where his loyalties lie,' said Luc pensively. 'Gerard. Prepare for an immediate journey to Rennes. We will take twenty of the men,' said Luc, as he left the office to go and break the news of his imminent departure to his mother and Merewyn. As they descended the stairs from the tower into the Hall, they could hear the tinkling sound of Merewyn's laughter combined with Ronec's deep laugh.

'What are they doing out there?' said an exasperated Luc to Morvan.

'They were playing some kind of hide and seek game with Lusian as I came through. The rain is heavy outside, and Ronec seems committed to entertaining both Lusian and the three ladies; you know what a flirt he is,' said Morvan.

Gerard intervened. 'Why don't you go and spend some time with Lusian and Merewyn, Luc? I can see to all the men and provisions.'

Luc paused before he opened the door into the Hall. 'We are leaving tomorrow, so I should spend some time with them.'

'I know how shocked you are about Count Eudo, as are we all, but we are always prepared to ride, and it should only take us two days to get there,' said Gerard. Luc agreed and went through the door into the Hall.

Merewyn and Briaca had blindfolded Ronec, who was stumbling into benches and tables while trying to catch Lusian. All three teased the large warrior by running close to him and laughing as he tried to grab them. As Luc watched, Ronec suddenly lunged to the left and caught Merewyn. Pulling her to him, he whipped off the blindfold and declared her caught, except he did not let her go. Instead, he whirled her in his arms as she laughed like a young girl again.

Luc's mouth tightened, and he frowned. There was no doubt that Ronec was flirting with his wife, and she seemed to be enjoying it. He could feel the anger and frustration building inside him. Instead of going and joining in with the laughter, he found himself striding down the Hall shouting, 'Enough games for now! I wish to speak with my wife privately.' He saw Merewyn's face fall and Lusian's disappointment, but that only made him brusquer.

'I am sure that Gerard would appreciate your help in the barn with the men, Ronec,' said Luc, his tone of voice not allowing a choice.

Merewyn eyed Luc with trepidation; all the fun was suddenly gone from the afternoon as she viewed her taciturn husband. She loved Luc, and she knew that he would always be the leader of the Breton Horse warriors first, but she remembered and longed for the carefree laughing days at Ravensworth where they had walked hand in hand as lovers. Alienated by his stern, uncompromising visage as he stood by the fire, she found herself stiffening, so she presented a very formal response to him.

'My Lord. You wished to speak to me,' she said, raising her chin and meeting his stormy steel blue eyes. Luc did not answer immediately, but then he turned to Briaca. 'Please take Lusian up to my mother in the solar, Briaca, and find him a quieter pastime.'

Briaca bowed her head and gave him a sweet smile but then turned and said, 'I would also like a moment of your time, my Lord. Sometime this evening?' Luc met her eyes, and the silence deepened between them. He had treated her with cold politeness since her arrival. He was still angry with her for not obeying his orders to stay away. However, he now saw that her eyes were filling with tears, and the last thing he needed was an emotional scene with Briaca in front of his wife. His eyes softened, and he answered her softly.

'As you wish, Briaca, I will find you later.'

Merewyn had watched the interplay between them. There was no doubt in her mind that the girl was in love with Luc and who would blame her, she thought, looking at the profile of her tall, strikingly handsome warrior. However, he sighed as he turned back to her. She stepped forward and put her hand on the side of his face, stroking down the square jawline. Suddenly, he pulled her close to him and held her for several minutes before he kissed her forehead, then slowly held her at arm's length. In those few moments of warmth, with his arms around her, he had come to an unusual decision.

'Merewyn, I am riding out tomorrow to Rennes on the

orders of Alain Rufus. I intend to be gone for over a week depending on what happens when I see Count Eudo; he is threatening to change sides.' He could see how shocked she was by this news as she realised the implications, but she squeezed his hands.

'We will miss you, I swore I would never leave you again, but I understand how important this is,' she said.

'Then come with me,' he said, taking her by surprise. 'It may even temper the meeting with Eudo and allay his suspicions slightly,' Merewyn was thrilled that he wanted her by his side; she knew that Lusian would be safe here and happy with his grandmother.

'Of course, I will come with you, and it will give me a chance to see more of Brittany as it will now be my home. I will go and start preparing immediately,' she said before racing towards the stairs.

Luc watched her go, a smile on his face. She looked so happy and so girlish that he could almost see that tear-stained rebel waif he had first fallen in love with in that high meadow near Richmond. He was also pleased that she would be by his side and removed from the vicinity of Ronec, who could practice his charms on Briaca instead. His face settled into sterner lines as he thought of Briaca. He now needed to go and speak to her and leave her in no doubt that she would be returning home as soon as he could arrange Morvan and an escort.

Luc encountered Briaca just as she left Lusian's room, her beautiful face lighting up at the sight of him, and his heart sank.

'You wanted to speak to me. Is it important?' he said, keeping a suitable distance between them. She, however, quickly stepped forward to reach up and place her hands on his broad chest, those huge blue eyes, so like Heloise gazing up at him.

'Luc, you know how I feel about you, and you told me that you have feelings for me,' she whispered.

'Did I?' he said, damning himself for that night at the Inn when he was so drunk he could not remember what he had said or done.

Briaca smiled. 'You know you did. I am just surprised that you have not been to visit me in my room. I have waited for you every night,' she lied.

Luc groaned and took hold of her hands. 'Briaca, that night at the Inn was a terrible mistake. I do not know what came over me. I love my wife deeply and would never want to hurt her,' he said, brushing away one of the tears that were beginning to fall from her now brimming eyes.

'You told me that you loved me, that you would find a way for us to be together,' she said in a wistful voice.

'Briaca, that will never come to pass; I told you not to come back here; you should have stayed with your parents,' he said in a louder, exasperated tone.

Merewyn, who had just reached the top of the stairs, clearly heard Luc's words. She rounded the corner and could see Luc holding a tear-stained Briaca. She took in the scene at a glance and hesitated for a second, considering whether she should stay in the shadows to see what happened next. However, common sense took over, and she trusted Luc, who did look very uncomfortable. She knew that the little Breton beauty believed she was in love with Luc, but it seemed she was finding out that it wasn't reciprocated.

'Is everything alright Luc,' she asked as she gracefully

swayed along the corridor towards them, her head held high. She saw Luc's face cloud over, and his eyes darted away from her as he immediately pushed Briaca away. From Briaca, she received a glare of anger and hatred that almost took her aback before the girl looked away.

Luc muttered something about the girl being frightened for her parents in the coming war. 'Go and see to Lusian, Merewyn, I will take Briaca to my mother.'

Merewyn stood looking at him for what seemed an eternity to Luc before she nodded and went in, shutting the door quietly behind her. He breathed a sigh of relief and bundled Briaca along the corridor towards the solar. Passing one of the larger stone window embrasures, he pulled her firmly into it.

'Briaca, you must stop this. I love Merewyn. I will arrange for you to travel with us tomorrow, and Morvan will escort you home,' he said in a harsh voice.

Briaca glanced up at this stern-faced Luc who was leaning into the window, his arms firmly folded and his eyes a dark steel unforgiving blue. She knew that look; he was not one for compromises. However, she was about to change his mind because the nightly visits from Ronec over the last few weeks had paid off, and she was now pregnant.

'No, you won't Luc, I am going nowhere. I can't possibly go home because I am carrying your child, and I just know it will be a Breton blue-eyed son, a half-brother for Lusian,' she said smiling.

Luc felt his stomach knot and plunge. With a sharp intake of breath, he managed to gasp out, 'No! It cannot be true! Dear God, it can't be,' as he turned away and repeatedly slammed his fists into the stone wall. He stopped, suddenly dropping his hands to his sides and, leaning forward, he placed his forehead against the cold stonework of the wall. He closed his eyes and was filled with such a deep feeling of despair. It had only been once. Was he just unlucky, or was this fate dealing him a testing hand? Did he not have enough to worry about with the looming war?

He finally took a deep breath and turned to face Briaca standing there looking forlorn, twisting a wet kerchief in her hands and quietly sobbing. She was so young, barely nineteen years old; it was his fault she was in this predicament. He stepped towards her and took her into his arms, holding her until her tears subsided.

'Go to my mother, Briaca. I must go and think about what is best to be done,' he said, running his hand through his hair. He watched as she raised her tear-drenched eyes to his, and then, bowing her head, she nodded and, without a further sound, made her way along the corridor.

Left alone, Luc was filled with a sense of hopelessness as he made his way quickly back through the Hall and then outside. He went straight to the stables, put a bridle on Espirit, leapt onto his bare back and cantered down and out of the castle, pushing him into a flat-out gallop across the meadow. Luc bent forward over his neck, horse and rider as one.

When he reached the woods, he slowed to a walk and reaching a small clearing, he dropped the reins and let out a cry of rage and anguish that echoed through the surrounding trees for a few seconds. He sat there for some time while Espirit grazed, mulling the situation over in his mind. He had brought this situation entirely on himself because of one night of drunkenness, the first night that he had lost control since the death of Heloise and his child, and that was nearly ten years ago.

He knew that Merewyn would never forgive his trans-gression, and the child would always be there to remind them, no matter in which manor or house he placed the mother because Briaca and the unborn child were now his responsibility. He groaned aloud again. This was not the child's fault; no matter what it was, boy or girl, it must be recognised, protected and loved, and this was why he knew that Merewyn would leave him. He finally picked up the reins and headed for home. He would have to tell his mother, Briaca would start to show soon. He blanched at the thought of his mother's reaction; this girl was under her protection, about to be betrothed to his brother Morvan. He groaned again at the thought of telling his brother. Then there was Gerard, who was like a father to him, who would greet this news with disbelief and disappointment in Luc; he adored Merewyn and Lusian.

He brought his mind back to the present as he rode towards his home. They were leaving early for Rennes, and they had hundreds of Horse Warriors to prepare for war. He would make his decision about Briaca when he returned, he had orders from his liege lord, and they had to take priority. Dusk was falling as he entered the inner bailey, but there was still a hive of activity around him; horses were being washed and groomed and tack polished until it shone. Luc insisted on very high standards whenever the Horse Warriors rode out, and Gerard and Morvan maintained that discipline. Luc could hear Gerard bellowing at some poor individual in the barracks who had let rust develop on his chain mail, which should have been oiled and cleaned. Morvan's responsibility was always with the warhorses, and he knew his brother would be somewhere in the enormous stable block or tack rooms. He dismounted and led Espirit back to his stall. Sure enough, he caught a glimpse of Morvan with the blacksmith, inspecting the hooves of several horses.

Luc rubbed Espirit down and turned to find Morvan at the end of the stall, leaning on the wooden partition, watching him intently. Luc straightened up and took a long appraising look at his younger brother. He had changed beyond all recognition from the tall, gangly young man he had left at home when he went with his father to fight for William at Hastings in 1066. He was now a broad, muscled warrior and superb rider, having spent years in the sword yard and in the saddle while Luc was in England. He also had a very level head on his shoulders and was passionate about the breed of horses they were developing at Morlaix.

'You seem to be very preoccupied, Luc. Is it just the foolish actions of Eudo, or is it something else? You know you can always talk to me,' he said while watching his brother's eyes and expression. Luc could see that he was obviously worried about him.

Luc sighed. 'I have a lot to think about, Morvan, but unfortunately, nothing you can help me with.' He smiled and slapped his brother on the back as he walked back towards the castle. Morvan watched him go; he could almost feel the tension emanating from his brother. He thought back to when he had first seen a change in Luc's behaviour, and it was after the trip to Dinan, so he was sure all of this had something to do with Ronec. Luc had not been the same since he met up with him.

Morvan left the stables and headed for the Béhourd, the training ground for the men. He knew that Ronec was there training the men in ground fighting techniques for the times when they found themselves unhorsed. Luc and Gerard took the sword training very seriously, and every horse warrior had to undergo several hours of training a day in the saddle and on foot. Morvan watched Ronec. As the dusk fell, he was still instructing two of the new young recruits in Pell training. The Pell was a thick wooden trunk six foot high, and the men practised the more vicious strokes, thrusting, cutting and slicing, which they could do without inflicting an injury on their opponent. The young men used wooden swords double the standard weight to build up their upper body and arm strength.

Gerard stood leaning on the fence, watching their progress. 'Good timing, Morvan, you can help in the final tournament. These men need a challenge. Morvan nodded in acquiescence and waited as Ronec strolled over to join them, leaving the men to practise the final strokes.

'I have just left Luc. I am somewhat concerned about him,' said Morvan, moving to confront Ronec. Gerard raised an eyebrow and glanced from one knight to the other.

'Am I missing something here, Morvan?' he said, moving to stand close to the two men.

'That is exactly what I wanted to ask Ronec. Luc has changed since he met up with you on the road to Dinan,' he said, staring into Ronec's dark brown eyes.

Ronec took a step back. It was not in his interests to become entangled with Luc's belligerent brother, so he laughed and shrugged it off.

'We were together for only a short time, drinking and reminiscing. Luc enjoyed himself that night, Morvan, relaxed and happy. I have not seen him so drunk since we were together in the lowlands,' he said, smiling at Gerard and bringing up shared memories. He began to walk back towards the Pell but turned around to face them and added, 'I think you need to look a bit closer to home for what happened later that night,' he said and grinned.

Morvan looked at Gerard, who was looking puzzled; however, Morvan had understood the implication of Ronec's barbed comment.

'Briaca', he spat out the name as Gerard's eyes widened.

'No!' thundered Gerard. 'Luc would never do that to Merewyn.'

Ronec smiled, but it wasn't a pleasant smile. 'I walked in on them the next morning, and he looked very happy with that naked black-haired beauty in his arms,' he said before turning on his heel and heading for the Pell.

Gerard and Morvan stood in silence in the deepening dusk, both of them shocked by what they had just heard.

'So she finally got what she wanted,' said Morvan in a low voice.

'You knew this would happen?' said Gerard.

'I had my suspicions. She never wanted me, Luc was always the prize, and she was determined to have him by any means, it seems,' said Morvan.

'It can't be true, and if it is, what happens now? How can he deal with two of them under the same roof? Is he hoping to set her up on the estate in her own house?' asked Gerard, in an incredulous voice.

Morvan just shook his head. 'I have no idea Gerard, but in the short time I have known her, I cannot see Merewyn accepting that.'

Gerard stood for a few moments, his face contorted in

anger at the situation that Luc had created.

'Merewyn will never stand for that; she will leave and take Lusian with her. We must talk to Luc, find out if all Ronec has said is true and try to prevent this happening.'

Ronec, meanwhile, had quietly smiled as he walked away. He was aware of the effect his words would have on the two men. He hoped they would confront Luc. He needed Malvais to be distracted, he wanted Merewyn to find out about Briaca, and he would be there to pick up the pieces when she did, as a friend, of course, to support her.

However, no one had the opportunity to talk to Luc as he disappeared into the tower room to work on strategy and had his food delivered to him there. Therefore, it was left up to Merewyn to announce cheerfully to the table that she was to accompany Luc to Rennes. Unaware of several undercurrents, the announcement did not have the effect she expected. There was a strained silence. Gerard and Morvan glanced at each other in surprise, given the afternoon's revelations, but then recovered quickly to say they would be pleased to have her with them. Marie already knew of the move and was happy to have her grandson to herself. Briaca was furious. She had just imparted startling news to Luc, and yet now he decides to take his wife with him on a two-week journey to meet Count Eudo; Ronec was taken aback. He knew a journey was afoot because of the preparations, but he had purposefully not shown much interest. Now, however, Merewyn had shared the destination. He was not taken in by the story that Luc was taking his wife to be presented to Count Eudo. This was to do with the alliances, and Ralph or Geoffrey may well pay for such information; he needed Flek to find out.

He glanced at Briaca, and he could see the fury in her face; she must learn to hide that. She was so transparent, but she was still so young and had much to learn. He shook his head at her, and she obediently lowered her eyes... The news that Luc and Merewyn were leaving immediately altered Ronec's plans. There was no way he was staying at Morlaix, despite the nightly charms of Briaca. He needed to be as close to Merewyn and Luc as possible to remove Luc De Malvais as a threat to Ralph De Gael. Morvan, who had been vigilantly watching Ronec, saw the exchange between them and realised that Ronec had some sort of influence over Briaca. He determined to speak to her alone before they left on the morrow.

Merewyn was happy. She was oblivious to the tensions around the table; her whole focus was on Luc and their time together. However, glancing at the scowling, subdued Briaca, she experienced a moment of satisfaction, knowing that he would be away from her. She retired early to her chamber, waiting for Luc to appear, but she eventually fell asleep in the large bed on her own.

In the tower room, Luc stretched himself out on the hard settle wrapped in a blanket. He could not trust himself to go to bed with Merewyn; he was dangerously close to telling her everything and asking for her forgiveness. His mind churned over the various plans on how to deal with it but, when the first fingers of light hit the wall, he was no nearer to a solution, and sleep had eluded him once again.

Morvan caught Briaca on her own in the Solar, putting her embroidery away. He stood and studied her from the doorway; she was so beautiful on the outside, but he knew she was selfish, cunning and manipulative on the inside, and he had no regrets in keeping her at arm's length over the last year. She spotted him and gave a half-smile; she found him pleasant enough but inconsequential.

'Well, Briaca, how are you going to get by without Luc for the next few weeks?' he asked with a grin. She turned and eyed him speculatively. She realised it was no accident that he was here in the Solar. He knew something, but she was not sure what that was.

'I am sure we will all miss him, Morvan, he is the Lord of Morlaix, and every castle is better for having its master in residence,' she said sweetly. Morvan gave a low whistle of appreciation. 'You are good, Briaca; I will give you that,' he said. She narrowed her eyes at him. 'Go away, Morvan, if you are just here to annoy and insult me,' she said, closing the embroidery box lid with a thump.

Morvan tried a more direct approach. 'I know about you and Luc at Saint-Brieuc,' he said, leaning on the back of the carved settle. She stopped and looked him up and down.

'So what do you intend to do if that is indeed the case, run to your mother and tell tales?' she hissed. 'Luc loves me, and we will be together.'

'Is that why he is taking Merewyn to Rennes and not you?' he laughed.

'I have a hold over Luc that neither his wife nor you can break. Luc will do as I bid him,' she said.

He found it took the greatest willpower not to shake her; she really was a nasty piece of work. He turned and headed out of the door, thinking what a lucky escape he had had; marriage to that black-haired witch would be a living hell. He left her with a parting shot.

'Take care, Briaca; everyone here loves Merewyn. You may

be alluring, but your beauty is just on the outside. It will never bring you happiness; you are too dark on the inside.'

Although she shrugged off the exchange with Morvan, Briaca felt somewhat troubled if not a little rattled as she entered her chamber. If Morvan knew about the Inn, did that mean that Marie De Malvais knew as well? If that was the case, she expected the conversation with Marie to be a difficult one, but she was a consummate actress, and she felt sure that she would win her over. After all, she would be happy to have another grandchild. No sooner had she undressed down to her shift than her door quietly opened, and Ronec entered the room. She raised her eyebrows in a questioning look.

'Why are you here? We have achieved our aim, and he now knows that I am carrying his child.'

Ronec laughed as he slowly unfastened his soft leather doublet and carelessly dropped it to the floor. Briaca watched with a sense of fascination as he sat on her bed and beckoned her over.

'Come here. You can unfasten my boots,'

Briaca snorted in derision, 'I am not your servant, do it yourself.'

Ronec's eyes sparkled, and he pulled his linen tunic over his head to reveal his broad, muscled chest with its light covering of dark, crisp hair. Briaca found that she was involuntarily running her tongue over her lips at the sight of him; after all, their lovemaking had been passionate and exciting since that very first night. Ronec narrowed his eyes and looked at her.

'I will give you precisely three seconds to get over here and do as I say, or I will come and get you, and I will not be gentle; you might see another side of me,' he threatened.

174

The silence hung between them as she weighed up her options. He made as if to rise off the bed, and she immediately shrugged and moved forward.

'I will do as you say, but only this once; this liaison must end.' She pulled up her linen shift and knelt at his feet; untying the laces at the back of his soft leather boots, she slowly pulled off each one in turn. Ronec looked down at the top of her head and allowed himself a triumphant smile. He intended to enjoy every inch of her tonight on what would probably be their last night together. He reached out, and, taking her by the shoulders, he pulled her firmly forward between his legs, hooking his feet over hers and holding her in place. He put his hand under her chin and brought her mouth up to meet his, kissing her deeply.

'This will be our last night together Briaca, let us just enjoy each other. I have enjoyed teaching you about lovemaking. I will always fondly remember our nights together, but now I have to leave with Luc and Merewyn tomorrow morning to take my plan forward and, of course, leave the field free for you to have Malvais.' As he spoke, he untied the top of his braies and released his manhood.

Briaca watched him fascinated. She did not like to admit it, especially to him, but she enjoyed being with Ronec, and now she wanted him inside her. He excited her.

He reached out, took hold of her long hair on either side of her head, and pulled her face down towards his groin.

'Now for your next lesson in how to please your man,' he said, grinning down at her.

Chapter Fifteen

The Great Hall was full of bustling servants and men early the following day when Merewyn descended to break her fast before they set off.

'I am ready to leave as soon as you bid, my Lord,' she said. Merewyn had chosen serviceable, warm riding clothes, including a fur-lined green woollen cloak with a large hood. However, her beauty still seemed to light up the dark Hall, and Luc noticed that conversation stopped at several tables as the Horse Warriors stared in appreciation at his blonde wife. He smiled back at her and indicated the empty chair beside him.

'We leave shortly, Merewyn. Have a good meal as it will be three or four hours before we stop.'

At that moment, Ronec surprised them all by striding up the Hall, obviously having come from outside. Morvan narrowed his eyes, suspicious that Ronec had been out so early. He did not trust Ronec at all, especially after what he had seen and heard last night. However, Ronec was his usual, convivial, charming self and after chiding Luc for working so hard the previous evening, he turned his attention to Merewyn.

'Good morning, my Lady. You light up this dim Hall like

a bright morning star with your presence,' he said, kissing her hand and raising his mischievous dark brown eyes to hers. Luc frowned as he watched Merewyn glow under the compliments. Morvan watched this interplay with derision.

'Ever the gallant, Ronec. I hope your protection will come to something more solid than pretty words when you are left to look after my mother and Briaca while we are gone,' he said meaningfully. Ronec paused for a few seconds as it dawned on him that Morvan might become a problem. Briaca had related some of her conversation with Morvan from the previous evening, but he obviously had further suspicions. Did he know anything? Alternatively, was he just fishing?

Luc watched the verbal fencing between his brother and friend with amusement, but Ronec's following sentence took him entirely by surprise.

'Unfortunately, I will not be able to accede to your wishes, Morvan, as I received a message late last night to leave for Gael immediately. So I will be travelling with you today, enjoying your company for half of your journey until I turn south.'

Ronec smiled meaningfully at Merewyn as he spoke, and under his direct and daring gaze, she found she had to lower her eyes to her bread and soft cheese. She had very conflicting emotions about Ronec. There was no doubt that any red-blooded woman would be physically attracted to him; he was a handsome warrior in his prime with a sparkle in his eye and a very tactile approach. She had to admit that she was also enjoying the attention, which was something that had been lacking in Luc almost since she arrived. However, she was in no doubt that if given the slightest encouragement, he would try to take things further and that she could not allow; she recognised that he had a reckless streak despite his friendship with Luc. He might see this as a game, but Luc certainly would not.

Morvan watched this interplay with mounting anger. His suspicions immediately aroused, he found that he heartily disliked this smiling mercenary. Pushing his trencher away, he stood and announced that he was going to give the horses a final check. In reality, he was heading to find the Steward; he knew that Mathew was outside supervising the loading of the provisions and horse fodder for the journey.

'Mathew, did Ronec Fitz Eudo receive a message in the early hours of the morning or late last night?' he asked. Mathew put his lists down and looked puzzled.

'None that came through me, my Lord, but that knight has his own messengers who tend to come and go very frequently and at all hours, including his man Flek,' he said, in a pointed but disapproving way.

'He does?' questioned Morvan. Did Luc know of this, he wondered.

'Yes, sir, but they still have to gain entry through the gatehouse. Rollo is still on duty down there, and he would know of any messengers that arrived in the last twelve hours or so. There is something else you should know, my Lord, about his night-time activities.'

Morvan listened with interest to the information Mathew shared, thanked him and headed swiftly down to the gatehouse, every part of him on full alert. Now convinced that Ronec Fitz-Eudo was up to no good, he intended to watch him and Flek like a hawk and prove it. There was also the troubling disappearance of Bertrand and his horse; he liked

mother's ward,' he spat at Ronec. Both men were now on their feet and glaring at each other, and Morvan saw Ronec's hand go to the hilt of his sword.

'Oh, please do, Ronec; I would relish the chance to teach you a lesson,' he said, while forcibly pushing Ronec backwards with both hands to give himself some space. However, both Gerard and Luc's attention, drawn to the raised voices, stepped forward to intervene.

'What is going on here?' shouted Gerard, stepping between them.

'Don't we have enough to do facing a real enemy rather than fighting between ourselves?' said Luc, grasping his brother's arm and pulling him to one side.

'That is just the problem Luc, I think he is the enemy in more ways than one,' Morvan said through gritted teeth at an angry, stern-faced Ronec.

'That is nonsense, Morvan, and you know it. You are just jealous because I was flirting with Briaca,' said Ronec.

'That's enough, both of you! Morvan, go and get the men moving,' ordered Luc. Morvan moved off but with a poisonous glance at Ronec.

Luc turned to his friend. 'What happened, Ronec?' he said softly while looking carefully at his friend's face.

'He is a young hothead Luc, who is imagining things that are not true,' he said.

Luc stared at the rigid, departing back of Morvan. 'Yes, he is slightly younger than both of us, but it is rare to see him lose his temper unless he has a reason.'

Ronec gave a rueful smile. 'I admit I may have wound him up somewhat, and then I overreacted to his aggressive response. Do not worry, Luc; I will go and apologise to him,' he said, looking slightly sheepish.

'Leave it a while; let him calm down. Let's saddle up. Where are we staying tonight, Gerard? He asked.

'The inn at Saint Brieuc, Luc. It's the one we usually use when travelling northeast.'

Luc stopped in his tracks and glanced at Ronec, who could not help giving a bark of laughter. Luc put his hand to cover his eyes and groaned inwardly, the same Inn where Ronec had found him naked in bed with Briaca. His spirits sank. It was likely he could even be in the same room, the same bed, but this time with Merewyn. He glared pointedly at Ronec, daring him to say a word, but the mercenary just shrugged and walked away, his shoulders shaking with laughter. It was a frowning, preoccupied Luc who returned to Merewyn.

'What was all that about?' she asked.

'An argument over nothing. The men are apprehensive about the coming conflict, and tempers can flare for no reason. Do not let it worry you. Come! We must get moving if we are to make the Inn before dark,' he said, pulling her to her feet and marching ahead of her to the horses. Merewyn was dismayed; he seemed to blow so hot and cold with her. She no longer knew what to expect day by day.

They mounted up and headed through the thick woodland, the forest floor a carpet of autumn leaves. Morvan, who had calmed down, chose to ride, as usual, beside Luc at the front.

'It is unusual for you to let your emotions get the better of you in a situation like that, Morvan. Have we taught you nothing? What really happened?' said Luc, watching his brother's face.

'I am sorry, Luc, I know he is your friend and a compatriot in arms going back many years, but I do not trust him. I found that he has sent five messages to Gael since Fitz-Eustace left and received several replies. However, there was no messenger as he claimed yesterday or last night. He is here with us for a reason.' Luc frowned. He found it difficult to believe any ill of his old friend.

'It may be that he did not want to be left at Morlaix with the women, Morvan, and he was due to leave to travel to Gael shortly as we know.'

Morvan shook his head. 'Be careful, Luc and watch him and that man of his. That is all I am asking.'

Luc nodded. 'I will, but you must keep your temper under check and be courteous in his presence. You are a knight, Morvan, and you hold the De Malvais name. Make us proud of you.'

Just then, one of the outriders came galloping up at speed; he pulled to a halt in front of Luc. 'My Lord, we have found something you will want to see, he exclaimed.

Luc signalled behind for Gerard to come forward. 'Morvan stays with Merewyn, Gerard with me', he said, pushing his horse on to follow the young scout. As they cantered through the trees onto the ridge, Luc realised that Ronec was with them as well. They moved along the ridge to a small clearing and slight dip; the young warrior stopped and pointed at a dark shape on the ground; they all realised that it was a body. Gerard was off his horse first and strode over to turn it over with his foot. Animals had scavenged the corpse, but it was still recognisable as young Bertrand's remains from his leather doublet and sword scabbards.

Gerard swore loudly; he had been a pleasant and promising young warrior, now lost, 'his throat has been cut,' he announced on closer inspection. Luc nodded and looked

183

around the clearing for any clues; there were no apparent signs of a scuffle, no sliding hoof marks if he had been unhorsed. He turned and looked at Ronec and was surprised to see his friends face suffused with anger, which was odd, as he had not known the young Breton. Ronec realised he was being watched and gave a sigh, 'such a waste of life; it must have been a robbery, his swords and horse gone, the horse alone would fetch a high price,' he said. Luc nodded, but he was not convinced; this was the fifth man they had lost in as many months; he knew the Angevins had a long grasp and could easily be picking off lone warriors such as Bertrand and his messengers.

'Gerard, get two of the servants up here, we will bury him here, and you can let his family know on our return, arrange for the usual reparation.' Sir Gerard nodded in agreement; unlike many lords, Luc gave support to a family on his estates who lost a son or husband in his service. They rode grim-faced back to the group, and Luc related to Merewyn and Morvan what they had found. Morvan was puzzled that he had died like that, and he turned in sympathy to the Horse Warriors around him to raise a fist in salute to the young man, which they all returned. As he turned back to Luc, he caught a look of pure fury on Ronec's face as he looked at his man Flek; he saw the manservant flinch at the glare and hasten away to his horse. It was a subdued group that set off on the rest of the journey.

However, after a few hours, as expected, Ronec once more gravitated to Merewyn's side, declaring that he had come to lighten their mood. Before long, she found herself laughing out loud again as he related scandalous tales of some of the top Breton families. Luc had taken Ronec's flirtation in good stead before; he knew that he meant no harm, and he also knew that his wife loved him; she would not have her head turned by this handsome warrior. However, since Morvan had shared his concerns, Luc found himself glancing back and looking at Ronec in a different light. He found the sight of Ronec moving his horse up against hers, his dark head constantly leaning in to whisper to his wife, annoying, especially as he obviously amused her.

A few miles before the Inn, the dusk began to fall, and the party reached a series of water meadows with raised flat grassy banks. It was a beautiful spot in the summer with a sea of wild watercress and abundant waterfowl. In the early spring, it had a different type of bleak beauty. The dark bare trees surrounding the meadows had distinctive round bundles of mistletoe in their branches and, with the sun setting behind them, the light had an eerie quality. They sat for a while and gazed at the scene, Ronec and Merewyn pulling to one side.

'Let us liven up this ride, shall we, and race around the banks? You keep boasting of how fleet your Arab mare is,' Ronec said to Merewyn.

The wild child inside Merewyn bubbled to the surface. She hesitated for only a second before digging her heels in and galloping off with a head start, startling the other riders and horses.

Luc was alarmed at first, not being party to the conversation and thinking that Merewyn's horse had bolted; however, he became occupied in reining in Espirit, who, dancing on the spot, wanted to join in. He soon saw that she was turning and laughing over her shoulder and realised she was in complete control of the mare. With a shout of laughter and then a loud hunting, 'Halloo!' Ronec set off in hot pursuit on his big, rangy, chestnut warhorse.

Morvan's youngster was more skittish than the older warhorse, and it slid down the grassy bank towards the water, with Morvan frantically trying to hold and quieten the young stallion. Unfortunately, it could not get a purchase on the slippery leaf-covered surface, and it ended up hock deep in the flooded meadow. Morvan, fuming, had to dismount in the freezing water and lead it back up the steep sides to join the group further on at a lower point.

Luc cantered ahead to catch up with the two miscreants. He could see that Ronec had caught up, they were neck and neck racing along the grass, but gradually Ronec was edging ahead. Merewyn tried her best on the new mare, but Ronec's large stallion just ate up the ground with his giant stride, and she knew he was gaining on her. Suddenly, he was ahead, and as they reached the end of the meadows, he turned, laughing, and waited for her.

'That was a very underhand tactic, my Lady, and you knocked Morvan down the embankment into the water,' he laughed at the thought. Merewyn looked horrified, but she was giggling. She had totally enjoyed the exhilaration and, if she was honest, the feeling of being pursued.

'I demand a forfeit for your cheating and, of course, a prize for winning. You do know I always win, don't you, Merewyn?' he said, bringing his horse close to hers so that their flanks were touching and his leg pressed firmly against hers. 'You do realise that I always get what I want?' he said, staring pointedly at her mouth.

Merewyn lowered her eyes and felt a blush build in her cheeks. She knew what he wanted, and it made her feel like a young girl again.

'A kiss at the very least,' he said as his eyes travelled down to her breasts. Merewyn knew she had to take control.

'I concede, Sir Knight, and you have earned a kiss, but only on my hand,' she said, demurely holding her hand out to him. Neither of them had realised that Luc had galloped after them.

Luc was now close enough to see, but not hear, the conversation. He saw her hold out her hand to Ronec's face; then she put out her other hand to touch his shoulder, and she moved into his arms on his horse where he was thoroughly kissing her. Stone cold anger welled up in Luc. How could she be so faithless? He glanced over his shoulder in front of his men as well. He slowed Espirit down to a fast walk and pulled up quietly behind them.

'I would be grateful if you would put my wife down, Ronec,' he said in an ice-laden voice.

Both of them pulled back in dismay, and Merewyn, suddenly released, slid down backwards between the two horses. Bruised, she scrambled to her feet and tried to remount. Ronec, looking contrite, wanted to blame himself. However, Luc, ignoring him, was glaring down at Merewyn.

'I am going ahead to the Inn. I will speak to you there, and you can explain yourself,' he said in the same icy, emotionless tone. As Luc whirled his horse and galloped off, raising a cloud of autumn leaves, Merewyn turned on Ronec, glaring at him.

'What were you thinking of?' she hissed at him. 'You took my hand and pulled me off my horse into your lap in front of my husband. I have no idea what to say to him!'

Ronec pulled his horse close beside hers, dismounted and

took her hand. 'I would do it again, Merewyn. You do know that I have fallen in love with you?' he said.

Merewyn's stomach knotted at the expression in his eyes. 'But Ronec, you know that I am married, and no matter how infuriating he can be, I love him, and I will always be faithful to him,' she said. She sighed as she looked at this tall, handsome knight in front of her. Any woman would be lucky to win his love, she thought.

Ronec's gaze changed, and his face became serious as he sighed. 'Even though he is not faithful to you, Merewyn?' he said.

Merewyn's eyes opened wide in shock. 'Luc would never do that to me,' she said in a plaintive voice.

'But he has Merewyn. I have seen it with my own eyes; I walked in on them naked in bed together. Can't you guess who it is? You have watched them together.'

'Briaca,' Merewyn said in a hoarse whisper.

Ronec watched the emotions play across Merewyn's face; his plan could not have worked out any better. He had enraged Luc, caused a rift between them and delivered the coup-de-grace with the news of Luc's faithlessness.

'Just remember, Merewyn, that I will always be here for you, whenever you need me,' he said, caressing her long slim fingers before returning her hand.

'Now you must go before he decides to come back and kill me, or his brother does,' he laughed, remounting his horse and watching Morvan riding towards them, a thunderous expression on his face. Morvan leapt off his horse and helped Merewyn to remount, his face stony with disapproval, but she did not speak to him as she laboured under the crushing weight of Luc's betrayal.

188

Merewyn sat stunned for a while in the saddle until she turned and set off at a swift trot after Morvan and the men. Heading through the trees towards the Inn, her mind was in turmoil. Luc has been unfaithful, kept repeating itself in her head. Of course, it had to be Briaca. All the hateful looks, the poisonous glances at her, then her possessive attitude towards him, her hand always resting on his arm or chest. The way she found them alone together in corridors. Was that where he had been spending his time? All of those nights when he did not come to their bed, was he in her room, she wondered? How the girl must be laughing at her. A wave of hurt and anger swept through her, and by the time she pulled the mare up outside the large Inn, pushing her way through the melee of men and horses outside, she remembered nothing of the ride, just a burning sense of betrayal. She handed the mare to a young stable boy, and, taking a deep breath, she headed inside to confront Luc.

Chapter Sixteen

The innkeeper's wife was hovering just inside the hall, waiting to take her to her room.

'Is my husband already there?' she asked. 'No, my Lady, he is in the pot room with the others,' she replied, indicating a door to the right behind which emanated a lot of noise from men happy to slake their thirst after a full day's ride. She took a deep breath and opened the door onto the packed room. These were her husband's men, so conversation lowered, and many bowed their heads to her. She could see Luc leaning on the fireplace mantle, deep in conversation with Morvan; there was no sign of Ronec. His eyes met hers, but they were stony cold, and she turned away to follow the plump woman up the narrow wooden staircase to the rooms above.

She sat on the bed; she was tired, aching and dirty from the ride, and she needed to wash, change and gather her thoughts before she met with Luc. She was still reeling from the implications of what she had learned from Ronec. As she pondered on his words, she did wonder what his purpose had been in telling her. It occurred to her that Ronec had known about this for some time; Luc knew that Ronec had found them together, yet he had welcomed Ronec to stay at

Morlaix for months as if what he was doing with Briaca was unimportant. In addition, what of Morvan and Gerard did they know? Was she the only one that had not seen this?

She became even angrier. She would have sworn that Luc would be faithful to her, but now she thought back to when she had seen them together at the castle. There had been an intimacy between them, the way Briaca could not keep her hands off him. One thing she was sure of was the pain that knifed through her at the thought of Luc with Briaca in his arms, making love to her, stroking Briaca's body the way he had stroked hers, entering her and making her moan with pleasure. She did not know how she could ever forgive him.

The inn servant brought her dinner, serving it on a side table in front of the burning logs in the fireplace. She dismissed her maidservant and sat staring into the flames. She could not face the food; instead, holding a cup of hot-spiced wine in her hand, the questions she wanted to throw at Luc were going around in her brain.

Luc had downed several drinks with Gerard when Ronec entered the room. Luc glared across at him as he did not acknowledge the brothers but turned and joined a group in the far corner.

'So he has finally shown his true colours and fallen from grace,' snorted Morvan. Luc shook his head. The last thing he wanted was for his brother to continue the dissent between them, and he still thought that Ronec might prove helpful; after all, he was Eudo's son, albeit illegitimate.

'I found his attention to Merewyn to be somewhat annoying, and I responded badly to her and him - ironic after I gave you advice about over-reacting,' he laughed.

'Yes, everyone has noticed that he singles her out, and the

women always seem to enjoy his charm and wit,' he said, shooting a dark glance of dislike in Ronec's direction.

Luc put a hand on his brother's arm. 'I can fight my own battles, thank you, brother, and although I am very angry with him at the moment, we may need Ronec to help us to persuade his father to join us, so leave it.' There was no mistaking Luc's tone, so Morvan reluctantly nodded, privately hoping that he would soon be able to prove to Luc that he was right. Then he would be sure to pay Ronec back for his wrongdoings. A messenger had been waiting for Luc at the Inn, and he now shared with the two men the contents of the missive he had received.

'King William has landed at St. Malo; he is disembarking his army and marching to Dinan; we are to rendezvous there in two days, which means an early start tomorrow for Rennes. Gerard send messages immediately for all of our Horse Warrior contingents to meet us here, including the one from Vannes.'

Luc saluted the two men, drained his cup and headed upstairs for the confrontation with Merewyn. He would be the first to admit that he had neglected her recently, but she had crossed a line today. Light flirtations were normal everywhere and were tolerated and even accepted in the circles they mixed in; he would expect his wife to have admirers. However, what he watched today had produced a wave of anger and jealousy in him that was unusual. It was the fact that she would want and allow another man to kiss her like that, which enraged him. In addition, he would now have to send her back to Morlaix; they were now riding on to war to support William and Duke Hoel at the siege of Dol.

He pushed open the room door and saw Merewyn sat in the

firelight, her long silver-blonde hair unbraided and shining. She looked so beautiful and young that she took his breath away. He closed the door and moved swiftly across the room to reprimand her for her behaviour but also to repair the rift between them. Halfway across the room, he was stopped in his tracks by a pair of blazing, green, angry eyes.

'You did not have to leave your companions to check on me, my Lord; I am very happy enjoying the solitude. It has certainly given me the time to think about our marriage,' she declared in a low but emphatic tone. Luc was taken aback by her attitude; he had expected her to be apologetic and contrite.

'I think, Madame, that you need to give me an explanation of your behaviour today when I found you in the arms of another man, kissing him passionately,' declared Luc, moving to stand closer.

Merewyn found that she could hold her anger in no longer, 'So, Luc De Malvais, do you have one set of rules for your behaviour and another for mine? How does that fit with your knights' code? Where is your sense of honour and trust, or does loyalty not extend to your wife?'

She could feel tears of anger filling her eyes, so she turned away from him back to the fire and rested her hands on the ledge above the hearth while she got herself under control. Luc stood still in the centre of the room, and the silence hung for some time between them. He was in no doubt now that Ronec had told her about Briaca. He was unsure at first what to say; then he made the mistake of trying to bluster his way out of it.

'I presume that Ronec has been spreading tales and rumours about me and our exploits? So, has your loyalty as my wife transferred itself to believing a mercenary knight who likes to seduce the wives of others?' he demanded indignantly.

That he would try to avoid the issue just made Merewyn angrier. 'Just tell me the truth, Luc. I would rather know the truth, and I want to hear it from you; you owe me that,' she declared, eyes blazing.

Luc suddenly found that he could not speak, and he certainly could not meet her eyes. He stood as if transfixed, staring at the floor, his arms by his sides, his dark hair falling over his forehead. At that moment, Merewyn knew that it was true, and her world collapsed.

She clung to the back of the chair for support and quietly said, 'It is Briaca, isn't it?' Luc raised his eyes to hers; she could see the pain there but also the guilt on his face.

'Oh, Luc! No! No! How could you do this to us, to me? You even brought her back to live with us in our home, at Morlaix. Is this why you never come to my bed? Are you swiving her every night instead?' she demanded.

Luc's head came up sharply at that. 'Do you think so little of me that you think I would ever do that to you, Merewyn?' he said, his face a mask of misery. He sat on the edge of the bed, his head in his hands while Merewyn stood in front of the hearth, her body heaving with emotion, her fists clenched.

'Yes, I admit that I slept with Briaca, but only once. It was the biggest mistake of my life, but I was very drunk and honestly, I do not even remember it. I do not know or understand myself why it happened or why I woke up with her that morning. It has tormented me ever since, which is why I found it so difficult to be with you at Morlaix; I was consumed with guilt at what I had done.'

Merewyn could see the anguish on her husband's face, but she felt hollow and empty inside when she thought of him taking Briaca to bed and so angry that he thought so little of her and Lusian that he could do something like this to them. Did their love mean nothing to him?

'Where did you do it, Luc? In Morlaix? In Dinan?' She asked in a voice that resonated with anger.

Luc sighed and raised pleading eyes to her face, 'Please do not do this, Merewyn,' he said.

'Where, Luc? Was it while Lusian and I slept in rooms close by?' she demanded.

Luc could feel his anger building at her probing, but even more, he felt anger at himself for having brought them to this. She had every right to ask; the shame and remorse he felt were consuming him.

'It was here, Merewyn! Here in this inn on the way to Dinan. I had far too much to drink, and I woke to find her naked in bed beside me and... God forgive me.... I had taken her virginity. You cannot make me feel any worse than I do at the moment; the pangs of conscience and the self-condemnation have kept me awake night after night.' he admitted.

Merewyn was only slightly mollified that it had not taken place in their home. The tears were coming because she realised the impact that night he had spent with Briaca would have on their relationship. It would never be the same again. Her Breton warrior, her brave knight, the famous Luc De Malvais, had feet of clay.

To Luc, who was now watching her closely, it was soul-crushing to see the effect that his admission was having on his beautiful wife, but he knew that he had to bare his soul and tell the whole. 'There is more Merewyn,' he said in a low voice, his eyes sliding away as he could not watch her face when he told her.

Merewyn felt her stomach knot; were there other women as well? She gripped the back of the chair, and the silence hung in the firelit room as she waited for him to speak. She could see the reluctance in his face as he obviously struggled to tell her something equally damning. He stood and restlessly strode across the room until he came and paused in front of her and let out an exasperated breath.

'Merewyn, I told her not to come back to Morlaix under any circumstances. I was more surprised and angrier than any of you when she appeared, disobeying my orders to stay with her parents. But there was a reason why she returned, a reason why she could not stay with them.' He paused, and Merewyn suddenly knew what he was going to say. Inside she was screaming No! No, not this!

'She is carrying my child, Merewyn, the result of one drunken night of madness,' he said, as he sank onto the wooden settle on the opposite side of the fire, his head in his hands.

Merewyn felt rage and hopelessness bubble up inside her; this child would be a continual reminder of Luc's infidelity. And what of Briaca? She would have to be provided for with an establishment to bring up his son or daughter; they would never be free of her in their lives.

'Get out,' she said in a quiet voice but one that brooked no argument. Luc raised his head and looked at her; he could see the cold fury in her eyes.

'Merewyn, please. You must forgive me. I love you and Lusian so much; let us try and work a way through this,' he pleaded.

196

'Get out!' she shouted at him.

Luc pushed himself unsteadily to his feet and slowly made his way to the door where he turned and gave her a last, heart-breaking look of longing before he left, closing the door behind him, his marriage in tatters.

Chapter Seventeen

onec was still enjoying the company of the noisy group in the corner, but he had positioned himself so that he could see the open doorway and the staircase beyond. He had watched Luc drain his drink and go up to his wife. Before long, he saw him come down again, his face like thunder. He saw Luc glance into the pot room before turning for the Inn's front door and disappearing out into the night.

Ronec smiled, very satisfied that everything was falling into place and, now that he had his opportunity, he drained his drink and quietly left to mount the stairs to Merewyn's room. He stood outside the door for a few minutes listening to the sobbing from within, and then he knocked gently and entered the room. He found Merewyn stood in her riding clothes, frantically stuffing clothes into a saddlebag on the bed, tears of fury and grief staining her cheeks.

'Merewyn, I had to see you to ensure you were all right. He has not hurt you, has he?' asked Ronec, putting an arm around her shoulders with a look of care and concern on his face. It was too much for Merewyn, and she collapsed into his arms. He held her close while she cried out, and then he raised her tear-stained face to his and kissed her eyes.

'I am here for you, Merewyn; I would never betray you, and you know I am in love with you.' Merewyn nodded and rested her head on his broad chest.

'What do you want to do? I can see that you are packing, but it would be better to stay the night and leave in the morning. It is cold and dark out there,' he suggested.

'You do not understand, Ronec, I cannot stay here in this Inn. It was here that he betrayed me with Briaca," she said, raising her pain-filled eyes to his face.

'Yes, I know Merewyn. I walked in on them here that morning, in this very room, naked in that same bed,' he said.

That was the final straw for Merewyn. Part of her had hoped it would go away but standing here looking at the bed and imagining them both entwined and naked in it made it very real and ten times as painful.

'He said he was drunk and didn't know what he was doing,' she said plaintively.

Ronec snorted with derision. 'Well, he knew what he was doing the next morning when I disturbed them. And then he kept us all waiting for a few hours while he took her again and again,' lied Ronec.

Merewyn was filled with despair and sank into the chair; Luc had not only betrayed her, but he had also lied to her, and she had to leave this Inn now before he came back. 'Ronec, I have to go, I have to go now, back to Morlaix to get my son, and you must help me,' she pleaded.

'Of course, I will, Merewyn; that is why I am here. Gather your things; mine are still packed. I will go and saddle the horses and send my men on ahead.'

Before he left, Ronec pulled her close, stroking her hair, and smiled quietly to himself. She showed no resistance to his hands moving down over her back, pulling her closer. This would be easier than he expected; she would be his now, he would make sure of it. He left her sitting there, shouted Flek from his room and headed to the stables, where he suddenly turned and took Flek by the throat, pinning him against the wall. 'So how much did you get for the horses, Flek,' he said through gritted teeth. Flek, his hands clawing for air, made some gasping sounds until Ronec dropped him to the ground, where he repeatedly kicked his man.

'Next time you follow my instructions, you do not blindly decide to murder what could have been a very useful informer; yes, I recognised your style, the throat cut from ear to ear, almost a trademark now, isn't it Flek?' The manservant stayed on the ground and kept his mouth shut; after years with this knight, he knew when to keep quiet.

Sometime later, led by Ronec, Merewyn descended the stairs at the Inn. Turning back in the hall, they went through the kitchens, passing a few very surprised servants. He led her out to the stables where the horses were saddled and waiting. He helped her mount her Arab mare and smiled up at her. She was very pale as she smiled wanly back at him.

'We must make haste, Ronec; we can't let him catch us,' she said, the thought of a vengeful Luc De Malvais on their trail making her shiver. She did not doubt that if she took this step to go with Ronec, Luc would kill him, probably in fair combat, but Luc would not lose; he was a fearsome swordsman, he never did.

'Don't worry, Merewyn, I am taking you somewhere safe where he will not be able to find you. It will give you time to decide what you want to do.'

She nodded her thanks, and he led them quietly out across the stable yard and on to the highway. He turned off after a short while on the road to the south, the road to Gael. Things had worked out beyond his expectation, thanks to Briaca. He had expected, if necessary, to be forced to kidnap Merewyn, but now he was taking her as a valuable hostage to Ralph De Gael and his allies. They intended to use her as bait to trap Luc De Malvais, to cut the head off the Breton Horse Warriors by neutralising their fearless leader.

Luc had stormed out of the inn; for once in his life, he felt powerless to change the situation; he knew there was no going back from this once the truth was out. He blamed himself totally, and now that she knew about the child, he knew that she would never forgive him; it would be a constant reminder. This filled him with a sense of loss that he had not known since his first wife, Heloise, had died in childbirth. He stood outside the Inn and gulped in mouthfuls of the cold night air. He needed to walk, to think, to try to find a way through this nightmare.

It was a clear moonlit night, and he remembered a hill and shrine behind the Inn. He strode through the trees and set off up the steep incline until, an hour later, he came to the crest and in a deep round depression, there was a jumble of ruins surrounded by dolmans, some upright, some fallen. He saw that people had left small offerings on a flat slab of stone. Above it was a tall carved stone, in the moonlight, he could see the outline of Cernunnos, the horned god, a pagan shrine for a pagan god who could reputedly persuade prey and predator lie down together. He was not surprised to see the offerings; the old religions still thrived in the wild

201

countryside. Luc wrapped his warm, woollen cloak around him and sat on the slab, leaning his back against the carved upright.

His mind retraced all that was said between them. It seemed like an impasse, but he refused to give up; he loved Merewyn, and he was determined to win her back, to show her that this was not who he was. It was sheltered in the dip amongst the ancient ruins, and soon a feeling of utter weariness washed over Luc. Before long, his eyes closed as he gave in to utter exhaustion and fell into a troubled sleep.

Luc woke in the chilly, damp dawn. It took him a few moments to realise where he was, and then he uncurled his long legs from their cold, cramped position and pushed himself to his feet. The ruins looked eerie, rising from the swirling mist around them. He shivered and shook himself, a dead weight settling upon his shoulders as he remembered what had happened last night. However, he set off down the hill with a determination to make Merewyn forgive him.

He pushed open the Inn's heavy door and took the stairs two at a time to reach their room. He quietly opened the door. The shuttered room was in darkness, and the log fire had long since died without being banked up for the night. In the darkness, he made his way over to the bed and sat gently down on the edge, reaching out a hand to find the shape of the woman he loved, hoping that she would not repudiate him.

He immediately realised that the bed was cold and empty. He whirled around, scanning the dim room and marched over to the shutters, opening them to let the grey, early morning light into the room. There was no sign of Merewyn.

All of her clothes and bags had gone; the bed had not been slept in.

He stood, hands-on-hips, looking at his own saddle roll and bags lying on the floor. She had obviously moved to another room, not wanting to spend a night with him. He would find her maid to ascertain where she was sleeping. He flung the room door open, and despite the hour being early, he bellowed for the innkeeper. A sleepy, bare-chested Morvan appeared in the doorway opposite, hastily tying his braies.

'What is it Luc, what is wrong? You are yelling fit to wake the dead,' he muttered, holding a hand to his head, having drunk far too much red wine the night before.

Without answering, Luc brushed him aside and clattered down the stairs to find some servants. Having heard the commotion, the hastily dressed innkeeper's wife was emerging from the kitchen, tucking her hair into her cap as she came.

'What is amiss, my Lord?' she asked, frantically smoothing down her apron.

'Has my wife moved to another room?' he demanded of her.

'No, my Lord, we have no spare rooms with such a large company as yours,' she answered, head on one side trying to assess the problem.

'Then where is she?' he yelled.

She cowered back and then turned and beckoned the young serving girl over from the group who had crowded around the kitchen door to see what all the noise was.

'Sylvie, come here and answer the Lord. Have you seen the Lady De Malvais this morning?' she asked. The girl hesitated for a second, overawed by Luc's presence as she stared at her feet. 'Not this morning, but she came through the kitchens last night, Sir, with another soldier,' she said.

Luc felt a moment of dismay, and turning; he sprinted out of the Inn door towards the stables. Morvan, running down the stairs, now fully dressed, followed him outside. Luc saw at first glance that Merewyn's mare was gone; he looked at the empty stall and turned a shocked face to his brother.

'She has gone Morvan, she has left me, and I must catch her,' he shouted, heading towards the stall where Espirit was stabled.

'Wait a minute, Luc, do not be rash. You boy! Come here,' he said to the young tow-headed stable boy standing open-mouthed at the door. 'Do you know what time the lady left here?' he said, pointing to the empty stall.

The bemused boy looked from one angry warrior to the other. 'They left when it was well dark, Sire; the moon was very high.' Morvan thanked him, and, throwing him a coin, he turned and looked at Luc's stricken face.

'They have six to seven hours start on us, Luc, and we have no idea which road they have taken.' He looked away, disturbed by the naked pain he saw in his brother's eyes.

'They?' said Luc, looking puzzled.

'Ronec's horse has gone as well, Luc,' said Morvan in a quiet voice, indicating the empty stall further up the row where the large chestnut had been stabled.

As the truth dawned on Luc, he let out a roar of anguish and rage and slammed his curled fists against the stable wall. He had lost her; she had gone with Ronec to pay him back for his betrayal of her. The thought of Merewyn in Ronec's arms, in Ronec's bed, filled him with a wave of burning anger. However, as the pain sliced through him, he realised this was how Merewyn must have felt when she found out about him and Briaca. No wonder she had left. At that thought, the anger seemed to leave him, and he sat dejectedly on the side of the water trough while Morvan stared at him in alarm. He had never seen his brother like this, so dispirited. Luc was always so in control of his emotions and life; after all, this was the legendary Luc De Malvais, horse warrior and leader. However, now all Morvan could see was the anguish and loss emanating from Luc, who sat still, with his shoulders slumped and his head in his hands.

Morvan was at a loss as to what to do or say. Fortunately, at that moment, Gerard appeared. Woken by the ruckus and the shouting inside the inn, he had spoken to the innkeeper's wife, and now he stomped across the cobbles to where Luc was sitting. He took in the situation at a glance. Nodding to Morvan, he roughly pulled Luc to his feet, not pulling any punches as he rounded on him.

'Why did she leave Luc? Merewyn loves you. She braved wars and crossed the winter seas to be by your side. So what did you do to drive her away?' he demanded, wanting to know but at the same time dreading to hear that what Ronec had told them was, in fact, true.

Luc found it difficult to meet their eyes, so he fixed on a point in the distance and searched for the words to explain.

'I betrayed her. I swived Briaca, and even though it was only the once, she is now carrying my child,' he said in a flat, emotionless voice.

Gerard glared at Luc as if he did not recognise him. 'You damned fool. I didn't believe it when Ronec hinted at it. How could you do that when I know how much you love Merewyn? How could you let that happen, and where did this happen?' he spat at Luc.

Luc dropped his head in shame; Gerard had always been like a second father, and Luc knew how disappointed he would be in him.

'I know what happened,' said Morvan. Both men turned and looked at him. 'She set her cap at Luc from the moment she arrived; she was never going to settle for me; she wanted bigger fish. She thought that Merewyn would never materialise. I watched her trying to seduce you week after week at Morlaix, and it looks as if she finally succeeded. She is a witch, Luc; no matter how beautiful, she is dark inside, poisonous. I could see the triumph shining out of her eyes when she suddenly arrived back at Morlaix after Yuletide, and that was because she had successfully trapped you. You just played right into her hands,' he said, shaking his head in rueful disbelief.

'It still takes two to get into a bed and swive. What were you thinking, Luc? Obviously not about Merewyn and Lusian,' Gerard raged while striding up and down.

'I was very drunk. I have no memory of the night or her until I woke up with her the next morning, her blood on the sheets. Don't you think I hate myself too, Gerard, for betraying Merewyn and for deflowering a young girl, my Mother's ward, who was with us for protection? However, nobody protected her from me. So much for me being an honourable knight,' said Luc. 'I must get Merewyn back! You must help me!' he cried.

Gerard shook his head. 'We don't even know where they have gone, Luc, and by our reckoning, they have almost a half day's start. Your first priority is to Alain Rufus, your liege lord, and the orders he has given you to go to Rennes and persuade his father to remain loyal. He would not expect you to drop everything to go on a wild goose chase in different directions because you have betrayed your wife. Duty first, family later has always been our mantra, and it cannot change on a whim.'

Luc groaned. 'Every night she spends with him will tear a strip off my heart. I must find her soon,' he turned away, his jaw clenched, despair written on his face, and then he sighed and went on in a resigned voice. 'But, as usual, you are right, Gerard, I have an obligation to continue to Rennes. Finding Merewyn will have to wait.' Morvan stood white-faced, his nostrils flaring, the anger building in him as he thought of Ronec. 'How did she find out about Briaca, Luc?' he asked.

'Apparently, Ronec hinted at it. He knew it was here at the Inn; he walked in on us in bed together that morning. Merewyn asked me outright if it was true. It was pointless trying to lie as Briaca is carrying my child, so I told her everything, and I asked her to forgive me. However, as you would expect, she was blazing with anger, and now I have lost her; she has left me and gone with him.' His voice cracking with pain, Luc turned and began walking slowly towards the Inn.

'You are not in this on your own, Luc; I will find her and bring her back, I promise,' shouted Morvan. 'You go to Rennes and carry on with your mission. I will follow and find them. I will track them down, and I swear I will bring her back. I am sure that Ronec is behind all of this,' he added. Luc stopped and faced his brother and his friend Gerard. 'No Morvan, by my actions. I have brought all of this on myself,' he said in a resigned tone.

'Luc, I have seen him going to Briaca's room on a night. I

don't trust him, so I have been watching him for weeks,' said Morvan. Luc's bowed head jerked up, and his steel-blue eyes stared at Morvan in disbelief. 'What?' he cried, unable to take in what he was hearing?

Gerard nodded in agreement. 'It is common knowledge amongst the servants in Morlaix what he was doing, but at the time, I was unaware of your liaison with her, so I didn't interfere. It was just Ronec and another of his flirtations. I knew that Morvan certainly did not want her, and I thought they might make a match of it; after all, she is an heiress,' he said.

'How long has this liaison been going on, Morvan? This might mean that the child is not even mine,' Luc said, eyes blazing.

'Not long after she returned to Morlaix, I believe, but in the reckoning, it would be a good four weeks after you took her,' he said.

'So it could still be mine. I will get the truth out of her if I have to shake her to do so,' he said, fury building up inside him that the pair of them had betrayed or used him. He would never forgive Ronec, whom he had considered a friend, a comrade in arms.

'Go to Rennes, Luc; your duty comes first. Morvan will track and follow Merewyn and bring her back. I will await your return here at the Inn. You should be back in a few days, and I want to wait for the contingent of our men from Vannes,' said Gerard.

Luc nodded and went to retrieve his saddlebags, shouting at his men to saddle up as he strode into the Inn.

Luc watched Morvan and two of his men ride out of the stable yard with a raised hand as he mounted Espirit and waited for his men to form up behind him. Several grooms and potboys came out to watch, open-mouthed at the sight of the famous Breton Horse Warriors. These hardened swordsmen were a remarkable sight on their huge warhorses; their unusual double swords crossed over their backs like a badge of honour as they trotted out behind Luc De Malvais on the road to Rennes.

Gerard, however, had his own agenda; he wanted to question the people at the Inn to find out exactly what had happened on the night when Luc had bedded Briaca. Watching them leave, he felt proud of what Luc had achieved with these men; several hundred were now fully trained and ready for combat at Morlaix with their incredible horses, and there were more at Vannes. However, as he turned towards the Inn, he sighed. Luc had enough of a task with Eudo, a powerful old warlord, who was unpredictable and cunning, used to getting his own way, without the added worry of losing Merewyn as well.

He shook his head in frustration as he opened the door to the Inn to begin questioning the servants. He was determined to find the truth, for such an act was so out of character for Luc. He had brought him up like a son and trained him to be the best swordsman in Western Europe. He was an honourable knight who valued truth and loyalty. Everything about this situation with Briaca felt wrong.

Chapter Eighteen

Merewyn was cold, tired and dispirited when Ronec finally called a halt on top of a small hill at the head of a wooded valley. He pulled his horse close beside hers and took her cold hands in his, rubbing them to try to get some warmth back into them. She smiled weakly at him; she was overwhelmed by the knowledge that she had left Luc after his betrayal. Every time she thought of them in bed together, the pain was unbearable.

They had ridden fast and relentlessly for hours, heading south through rich and forested lands, stopping only briefly to stretch their legs and give the horses a breather. Merewyn felt as if she was constantly looking over her shoulder, expecting Luc to follow them, and she knew that Ronec was continually looking back and listening. Dawn had broken, and the mist was very low to the ground so that they could see the vista ahead.

'We are nearly there, Merewyn; I can see the castle walls from here. It will only be another hour or so, and then we will have hot food and a warm bed for you,' he said, stroking her frozen cheek with his finger. Boldly, he leaned forward and tilted her cold lips to meet his. Merewyn, enveloped in a sea of hopelessness, allowed him to kiss her and even managed a wan smile as he pulled back and contemplated her face.

'I do love you, Merewyn and I will protect you,' he said in a tender voice. This was almost too much for her; she closed her eyes; Ronec, seeing her exhaustion, decided to move on immediately and get her to shelter.

They rode on in silence into the bottom of the valley. Merewyn barely noticed the richly cultivated fields, but as they approached the demesne lands around the castle, she could not fail to see the hundreds of tents and men surrounding them. She had presumed that Ronec was taking her south to one of his small estates, but this considerable fortress was well beyond the purse of a mercenary knight; this was an army preparing for war. She was taken aback by what she saw as she trotted her mare ahead to pull up alongside Ronec. She noticed many hands raised and shouted greetings as they rode in; he was obviously well known here. Her knowledge of Brittany was limited, so as she scanned the scene, she wondered if this was Eudo's fortress at Rennes. After all, Ronec was one of his many sons born out of wedlock, and he had fought beside his half-brothers such as Bodin with Luc. She felt a sense of panic; if this were Rennes, Luc would be heading here as well.

'Where are we, Ronec?' she said in a worried whisper.

Ronec turned and smiled. 'Don't worry, Merewyn; I have brought you to the safest place possible. This is the fortress of Gael, and the Lady Emma will be delighted to see you. She is one of your countrywomen, a brave, fearless young woman who held Norwich Castle on her own against the king's warrior Bishops.'

Merewyn was alarmed at being in Gael. She knew enough

to understand that Ralph De Gael was fleeing from William, but she felt slightly mollified knowing that Lady Emma was here. She determined to stay for only a few days before she returned to Morlaix to collect Lusian and return to her father in England; she would go back to Ravensworth.

They rode through the considerable stone Gatehouse into the inner courtyard, and Ronec leapt from his horse to help her dismount. As Merewyn's frozen feet touched the ground, she was so stiff and exhausted; her knees gave way immediately. Ronec swept her up into his arms, and, holding her tight against his broad, muscled chest, he kissed the top of her head. With a triumphant smile on his face, he carried her into the castle, the home of Ralph de Gael, the rebel Earl who was at that moment riding south through France with the remains of his army.

She was sound asleep as Ronec carried her up to the chamber prepared for them, and, sweeping the coverlet back, he laid Merewyn carefully on the bed. He removed her soft leather boots and unlaced and gently removed her over-gown, leaving her in just her linen chemise, which outlined her body's long elegant sweeping curves. He loosened her long, silver tresses while Merewyn barely stirred. He sat on the bed and gazed at this beauty, and he could not help himself as he ran his hands over her chemise to caress her body from her neck to her feet. Merewyn moaned and then turned on her side, curling into a ball.

He smiled. 'You are mine, Merewyn and I will possess you later,' he said as he pulled up the thick fur coverlet and put more logs on the already blazing fire before he left to speak with Lady Emma. When he returned that night, Merewyn was still asleep, the lines of exhaustion and dark shadows under her eyes plain to see. Ronec quietly removed his clothes and climbed into the large bed with her, pulling her gently into his arms. He had to use the utmost restraint not to take her there, and then, he was so aroused. However, that was not part of his plan; he was playing a longer game. He would make Merewyn fall in love with him; she was no longer just a means to an end to distract Malvais from his duty and ensure the Horse Warriors did not get to Dol. He wanted this wealthy Thegns daughter, so he was going to win her over and prove that he was not like Luc De Malvais, the man who she thought had betrayed her. He grinned at the thought and pulled her even closer, wrapping his legs around hers. He smiled even more when she wrapped her arms around his naked waist and nestled down into his arms.

Chapter Nineteen

At the head of his men, Luc had ridden along the banks of the River Ille towards Rennes. He knew that shortly it would meet in a confluence with the River Vilaine, which ran through the town. He sat on Espirit on the northern bank of the river and ran his hands through his dark hair; he had never felt so bleak, not for a long time, and he was trying not to convey this to his men. He had an empty, hollow feeling inside and cold anger at himself for causing the rift between them. As for Ronec, he wanted to kill him as he recalled Ronec pulling Merewyn off her horse into his arms to kiss her. His men sat patiently behind him, waiting for his next move. Well-trained warriors, they sat in absolute silence save for the occasional snort of a horse or rattle of a bit chain. He turned and waved them on; he knew there was a ford up ahead to cross the rivers into the meadows that surrounded the town, and he just hoped it would be passable as there had been a lot of rain recently.

Rennes, built on a slight hill, was surrounded by ancient ramparts, which had been there since Roman times. Luc cantered his men in close formation behind him across the bubbling ford and through the lush riverside grassland. Looking ahead, he saw that there seemed to be an unnatural amount of activity outside the city walls, and he signalled his men to move into a wide, four-sweep formation. As they cantered closer, he could make out hundreds of tents and banners ahead. To his consternation, he saw that on the far left, there were several Angevin banners. He had spent most of the last year with his men fighting Fulk of Anjou and his forces on the borders of Maine, and he did not expect to find them camped outside the walls of the capital of Brittany. He glanced to either side and could see the grim expressions on the faces of his men as they recognised them as well. He gave the signal to drop to a collected trot, and he moved onto the broad road leading to the main gate.

Luc realised that Eudo was preparing for war; he had gathered hundreds of men outside the city and had formed alliances with Breton Lords who had a reason for discontent with William or with Hoel, the Duke of Brittany. Eudo had his own gripes with Hoel; he had acted as his regent for many years when the boy was young, but then Hoel had imprisoned Eudo, removing him from power.

However, there were still many hands raised and shouted greetings in recognition as they rode up towards the gate. The Breton Horse Warriors and the legend that was Malvais were recognisable anywhere. He gave a cynical smile as he realised they probably thought they were joining Eudo, not that he was here to try to change his mind.

The guards at the gate greeted them and waved them through. As they trotted through the town's narrow, cobbled streets, he slowed them to a walk. The townsfolk drew tight against the walls of the half-timbered houses as the huge warhorses approached. Luc pulled his men to a halt outside the large imposing cathedral where most of the Dukes of

Brittany had acceded to the title. The town was crowded with a busy market at the other end of the large square. He noticed one of Eudo's Serjeants and called him over.

'Where can I find the Count? I need to see him immediately,' he said.

'He is in the Duchesse Tower, my Lord De Malvais; he is meeting with some of the commanders.'

Luc nodded and dismounted, handing the reins to one of his men. 'Find some food for our men, water and feed the horses but stay alert. I have no idea of how long I will be or if we will have to fight our way out of here,' he said. The men nodded; there was a general uneasiness amongst them as they dismounted. They had not expected to find the Angevin enemy at the gates, and hands remained ready to draw their swords if necessary as they led the horses to the long stone troughs close by, their eyes constantly sweeping the square.

Luc strode to the tower nodding to the guards at the door. There was no one there who did not recognise Malvais; they knew he was the Champion of Alain Rufus and the House of Rennes. Luc took a deep breath as he ascended the narrow staircase to the large stone chamber at the top. Like the cathedral, Luc noticed that the tower had been repaired and rebuilt in places; it had undoubtedly needed it. The City of Rennes had often been successful at rebuffing attacks, but the ancient walls showed their age and were beginning to crumble. The sound of voices from above penetrated down to Luc, and he steeled himself for the confrontation to come. He pushed the door open and found Eudo and several other men standing around, many of them staring down at the maps on a large, sturdy wooden table. As he stepped into the room, heads turned, and conversation died.

216

Eudo, the Count of Penthievre, was an impressive, tall and good-looking man. He was now seventy but looked much younger; he had such vitality and virility about him. His shoulder-length grey hair was swept back from a broad brow, and he turned a pair of intelligent, piercing brown eyes on Luc; Ronec's eyes thought Luc unwillingly.

'Malvais, you are a sight for sore eyes,' he laughed at Luc and, striding forward, he grasped Luc's arm in a strong warrior's clasp.

Luc returned it, stepped back and bowed. 'My Lord Count, I bring you a missive from your son.'

Eudo laughed and turned to the room. 'Which one? I lost count some time ago.' The men around the table laughed. Eudo's womanising was well known. He had well over a dozen legitimate and illegitimate children, some recognised and promoted, others, like Ronec, left to find their own way in the world. Luc gave a tight smile and drew forth the leather pouch from inside his doublet. Eudo nodded but held up a hand for him to wait, and he turned to the group of men around the table.

'I think you all know De Malvais, Lord of the Breton Horse Warriors and probably the best swordsman I have ever seen, but who I must now speak to in private,' he said, sweeping an arm in Luc's direction. All of the men bowed, and many knights were past friends who smiled a greeting. Most of them had fought alongside Luc for years. However, one man stood grim-faced and aloof. Pierre D'Avray, the Commander of the Angevin troops sent to Rennes, sported a large red puckered scar down the left side of his face, from his brow to his lips, a deep scar that Luc had given him some months earlier. Luc froze; every hair on the back of his neck

217

seemed to stand up, and his eyes narrowed with intent as he immediately stepped towards the Angevin, drawing his sword in one swift movement. Eudo, still a strong man for his age, grabbed his arm, pulling him back and shouted, 'No, not here, Luc; D'Avray is under my protection,' he said, while impatiently waving the Angevin out. D'Avray sneered at a grim-faced Luc who still held his sword drawn and nodding to Eudo; he briskly left the room ahead of the others who followed him down. Eudo let out a long breath and let go of the Horse Warrior.

'No love lost there then, Luc,' he said, slapping him on the back and trying to lighten the tension in the room. Luc reluctantly sheathed his sword and turned to face the Count De Penthievre.

'No, Sire. He brutally killed two of my young recruits and purposefully crippled their horses; I gave him that scar as he was running away. May I say, my Lord, that I am surprised to see Angevin troops here when we have been fighting them together for years on your borders, often at your request?'

Eudo raised his head from the wine he was pouring and glared at Luc for a few seconds for daring to voice any criticism of his actions, but then he sighed and went to stand at the narrow, stone-mullioned window. 'We have to find allies where we will, Luc, in these troubling times. We are fighting a common cause against Hoel of Brittany. The Duke needs to know that we are not his vassals but independent Breton Lords who decide our own affairs.' Luc was silent and just handed him the missive from his son, Alain Rufus. Eudo read it in silence, and then he gave a bark of laughter.

'So I am embarrassing my wealthy son by forming these unsuitable alliances?' he questioned, his bright, intelligent eyes gazing at Luc. 'I gather that William has landed on the coast and is now marching his army in stages towards Dinan to support Duke Hoel?' he questioned.

'He is, and we have been summoned to meet him there shortly. My Lord Count, for years, you have supported King William; you gave him 5,000 men and over a hundred ships to invade England. He has promoted and rewarded many of your sons with great tracts of land and wealth in England, so why now would you turn against the King?' Luc asked. Eudo gazed thoughtfully out across the tented meadows below. 'For precisely that reason, Luc; William has become too powerful. He is the King of England, not of Brittany. He is also the Duke of Normandy and Overlord of Maine but not of Brittany. Here he is again, landing at St Malo, incursive as usual and supporting Hoel against us.' He paused and sighed and gestured to Luc, 'Come and sit by the fire, Malvais; you must have had a long ride.'

They talked for another hour, and Eudo ordered refreshments brought, but all of Luc's arguments were to no avail. Luc's loyalty lay with Alain Rufus and the King, but he could also understand Eudo's perspective. He tried one last time. 'But Duke Hoel is family; he is married to your sister, Sire.'

Eudo laughed. 'The importance of family is greatly overestimated, Luc. I know this is difficult for you because we have always been on the same side, and no Breton Lord wants to face our own Breton Horse Warriors, but it may well come to that,' he said sadly.

Luc sat watching the old warrior's face, trying to think of any arguments to convince him to avoid what would be a civil war, Breton against Breton. However, he could see it would be pointless; Eudo had chosen his course, albeit a different one to his son Alain Rufus and Luc.

'Stay with us for a few days, Malvais and spend some time with the Breton Lords assembling here. They will be able to convince you that our cause is a right and just one,' Eudo suggested.

'Unfortunately, my Lord, I cannot do that. Pressing matters await, but we will accept your hospitality for tonight, and I promise to keep my men away from the Angevins, but I may just kill Pierre D'Avray next time we meet,' he said.

Eudo snorted with laughter, 'yes, but not in my Hall Luc. I wish you were with us and not against us, but I respect and understand your loyalty to my son and the King,' he said.

'My Lord Count, there is one more thing,' said Luc, not sure at first how to broach it.

'Your other son, Ronec Fitz-Eudo, is he working with you and for Ralph De Gael?'

'Eudo raised both eyebrows. 'I have not seen Ronec for many years, Luc, although I hear he has made quite a name for himself as a mercenary. Why do you ask?'

Luc paused, not wanting to give too much away. 'He is a brave warrior, one that I have fought beside and considered a friend. However, he is now proving otherwise; he seems to have his own agenda.'

Eudo looked thoughtful. 'There are few friends in this game, Luc, as you will find out, especially for a roaming mercenary. They will all go to the highest bidder, and what price loyalty or friendship then?' he asked. Luc nodded and thanked him.

'However, I have one of De Gael's men here tonight, recently arrived. I will see what I can find out without giving too many of our secrets away,' he laughed.

Luc made his way back to his men. He had carried out his duty, presented the letter and many futile arguments for Eudo, but he had been unable to change the Count's course of action. The old warrior had too much of a grudge against Hoel, Duke of Brittany; there were still scores to settle there. His men now accommodated in the barracks, Eudo's Steward had allocated Luc a comfortable room in the castle, so he sat down and quickly wrote a message to Alain Rufus and another to William. The inclusion of so many Angevin troops was alarming. They needed to know this information immediately; he knew the King had arrived on the shores of Brittany, so he found one of his men and sent him galloping into the night. He attended the large dinner that evening and found enough old comrades to have a convivial evening; he had fought alongside most of them. Fortunately, the Angevin Commander was not present, on the orders of Eudo Luc wondered?

Eudo raised a goblet to him in salute at one point, and he noticed he was talking to a swarthy, young Knight he did not know. Was this the man from Gael? Nothing further transpired, and Luc retired early, as he knew they would have to leave immediately at dawn on the morrow. An hour later, he was woken by a knock on the door, and a manservant stood there to escort him to Count Eudo's room.

Luc quickly dressed and followed the man along the fortress's ancient corridors until shown into a chamber decorated in rich tapestries and flags bearing the House of Rennes' insignia. Eudo was seated at a table with several papers in front of him. He was sanding a parchment, which he folded and gave to Luc.

'This is for my son, Alain, to explain my actions. I am sure

221

he will understand. I have told him you were very persuasive, but in the words of Julius Caesar, "Alea iacta est", the die has been cast. Now, as for Ronec, yes, you were right, he has been in the employ of the De Gaels for some time, almost six months; he is expected there any day. He will be commanding a contingent of De Gael's forces. So at least one of my sons is fighting on the same side as me,' he laughed. Luc was taken aback by this news, so his friend was now his enemy, and he had stayed so long to gather information at Morlaix to send to Fitz-Eustace; this was all part of their plot to draw in and then destroy King William.

'If I may suggest one possible strategy to keep both sides placated, Sire.' Luc said. Eudo looked at him with interest and nodded. 'I suggest that you take your men to Dol and join De Gael but keep them in reserve. Keep a low profile with your banners at the back of the army, and I will persuade William that yours is but a token gesture. You do know that all of this is a plan to destroy King William,' he said. Eudo could not meet Luc's eyes as he nodded, but he looked thoughtful as he thanked Luc for the suggestion about his place in the forthcoming battle. The room was silent for a few seconds, both men wrapped in their own thoughts about the paths they had chosen, this time in different directions. Then Eudo broke the silence, 'You may want to pass on one warning to William,' he said, contemplating Luc with concern. Luc waited apprehensively, wondering what Eudo was about to impart.

'De Gael has been sending secret envoys to Philip of France for some months, King Philip has wanted a foothold in Maine for some time, but even more, he wants the Vexin, the province on the northern border of Normandy. He may take advantage of the situation while William and his army are here in Brittany to invade the Vexin.' Luc nodded while he considered this disturbing information; he must get this news to William urgently.

Luc thanked the Count for his hospitality and bowed to take his leave when Eudo called after him. 'By the way, Luc, how is your very beautiful wife? You have brought her to Brittany, I believe. I hear men talking of nothing but the beauty of this Saxon maiden.'

Luc paused and gazed at the floor for a few seconds. 'Ronec has taken her, Sir, and this is why I must make haste as I intend to go and get her back.'

Eudo snorted with disbelief at the foolhardiness of his son. 'The fruit does not fall far from the tree,' he said, beginning to laugh, but he paused. 'Good luck in finding her; she may be at one of his manors Malvais, possibly the large one he was recently given at Loudeac, but try not to kill my son over a woman,' he said, serious for a second.

'I may not kill him, my Lord, but I intend to make him suffer,' said Luc in an ice-cold voice. Eudo nodded and then shrugged as Luc went out, closing the door behind him, the name Loudeac resonating, as that was where the horse fair was held, where the horses of his missing messengers had been sold.

They left Rennes in the early morning mist as soon as the gates opened. Luc noticed a few scarred knuckles amongst his men, and he hoped that they had not caused too much trouble in the taverns, but they seemed to be in good spirits. Luc was now impatient to be at Saint-Brieuc, so he set a punishing pace; he had already sent an envoy to find William on the road to Dinan. He was now hoping that his brother had found Merewyn and persuaded her to return. If not, he would be riding for Gael, fully armed with all of his men.

Chapter Twenty

Morvan had difficulty tracking Ronec and Merewyn, as he had no indication of which direction they rode in. They searched the villages and roads on the way to Morlaix, thinking that Merewyn might want to go straight back to Lusian, but he found no sign that they had passed that way. Retracing his steps, he took a lesser-known track south through the forests and finally, he found a woodsman and his family who had seen a group of riders passing that way late at night.

It suddenly occurred to Morvan that Ronec could be taking her to Gael, into the enemy camp. At first, he could not believe that he would do that, but then it made chilling sense. He urged his huge Destrier forward, his men galloping behind. He received further confirmation at an inn on a small crossroads where Ronec had stopped for mulled ale and a brief rest; he had obviously been forcing the pace. Morvan bought food and fodder for his men and their horses, and then he followed the runaways south. It would take them at least another four hours to Gael, but he was content that he had found their trail, even though they were now nearly a day behind. As he rode, he worked on a plan of how to get into the fortress at Gael and find her. It would be difficult, as he was easily recognisable, but his two men without their horses might get inside unnoticed.

Merewyn felt warm and safe as she floated towards consciousness. She became conscious of the long, warm, naked body wrapped around her; a strong-muscled thigh draped possessively over her bare legs and an arm wrapped around her waist.

Her head nestled under his chin, and for a few moments, she thought she was back in Ravensworth with Luc. A wave of joy nearly overwhelmed her. She rested her hands on his chest but then, with a sickening jolt, reality dawned. She had left Luc; he had betrayed her. She was also aware that the crisp curly, dark hair on the chest under her hands belonged to another man, a naked man. It all came rushing back. This must be Ronec. She was in bed naked with Ronec, and she panicked. What had she done? She ran her hand gently down her side and realised that she was, in fact, still in her linen chemise. He had undressed her, and she was in his bed. Had he made love to her?

She gently moved her head and shoulders back so that she could look at him. He was still asleep, and his long, dark lashes lay on his cheeks. He looked much younger and more vulnerable than the large, laughing, charming warrior that she was used to seeing. Her hand was still on his broad, muscled chest against the abundant curly chest hair, so different to Luc, whose chest hair was smoother. Luc. Even his name caused a pang of pain to shoot through her. How could he have betrayed her?

She suddenly realised that she could not hear the deep, restful breaths coming from Ronec and looked up to find him regarding her with those deep, brown eyes and that lazy smile.

'Good morning, my Lady,' he said in a deep but amused voice. Aware of his naked proximity, she found it difficult to meet his eyes, and she shyly looked down. He made her feel like a young girl again. 'I hope you slept well,' he asked.

She nodded. Now he was awake and moving; she was even more aware of his muscled body pressed against hers. However, she had to ask the question....

'Did we...' she started but could not finish the sentence.

Ronec laughed. 'Of course not, what do you take me for? Do you think I would take advantage of you when you were that exhausted? Make no mistake, when we make love, and I hope it will be soon, it will be because you want it as much as I do,' he said.

'You were dangerously cold and tired, so I banked up the fire, put you into bed and, knowing this was the best way to warm you through, I got in with you.' He gave her a mischievous smile.

He was hard to resist, and she found herself smiling back. He laughed and pulled her closer. His lips descended on hers, and she felt his body react to the closeness, his manhood pressing against her.

'I think I need to get out of this bed and leave you alone, Merewyn, before I do make love to you,' he said, swinging his legs out of bed. He leant over and pulled the fur coverlet up to her chin.

'Stay warm in there. I will organise some breakfast and a maid to help you wash and dress.' He smiled and walked, naked, over to the chest against the wall to put on his clothes.

Merewyn watched him under lowered lids as he stretched.

Like Luc, he was a perfect male specimen, broad shoulders, slim hips and muscular legs from long hours in the saddle. She noticed that he had more battle scars than Luc across his upper torso. She closed her eyes quickly as he turned to look at her, and she heard him go quietly out of the room, closing the large wooden door behind him.

She rolled onto her back and stretched out in the warm bed. It felt so strange to be here in another man's bed, even though she had not betrayed Luc. She forced herself to think about her husband; what would he think if he knew she had spent the night lying in another man's arms, a naked red-blooded warrior like Ronec? She could feel the anger and hurt inside. Luc deserved all that he got now; he had brought this down on them by his thoughtless actions. Did their love mean nothing to him if he could betray her like that with Briaca?

She wondered for a few seconds if she could let Ronec make love to her. She liked him, she was physically attracted to him, but she was not in love with him, not in the all-consuming way she loved Luc. Despite what he had done with Briaca, she had to admit that she still loved Luc; she just could not forgive him. She hated him for destroying their family. Suddenly, she thought about Lusian; what would she tell him about his father when she took him back across the sea to England? She felt the tears coming, and she sobbed into the pillow for what they had lost.

Morvan and his two companions sat quietly in the trees, looking down at the scene in front of them. There were men, tents and horses everywhere. They knew they would stand out immediately on the war Destriers if they rode through the camps to the gatehouse. Morvan watched the activity below for a few moments, then, turning to the others, he said, 'I want you two to go back and set up camp in the clearing we passed, the one below the cliff. I will go and enter Gael on my own, and I will see if I can find out where she is staying in the fortress.'

His two companions reluctantly turned away and left him to ride alone down through the pavilions and tents. He had no problem accessing the town that lay snugly around the fortress walls, although his black warhorse attracted several comments and envious glances. He decided to use the story that he was a mercenary who recently returned from Italy looking for work as he pulled into the yard of one of the inns. The stable boys rushed to take hold of the bridle of such a beautiful black horse. Morvan unhitched his saddlebags and went to ask for a room.

The proprietor was a friendly individual, and Morvan's story went down well. He was given a small but reasonably clean room to wash and then plan his next move. There was no way he could just walk through the gates into the fortress. Over twenty of Ronec's men had stayed with him at Morlaix, he would be recognised, and it was likely they would refuse him entry. He had not parted on good terms with Ronec, but he needed to confirm that they were both here and somehow get a message to Merewyn. Morvan hoped that she was regretting her sudden flight from Luc.

His opportunity came that evening. Several of the castle servants drank in the pot room later in the evening, and many around the large fire were happy to accept drinks from a Breton mercenary looking for news and company. Morvan listened with interest as they boasted about the comings and goings at the fortress, how they all waited for the imminent arrival of their Lord, Ralph De Gael, whom they were confident would lead the assembled army and beat the Norman King. Morvan nodded enthusiastically and raised a toast to his victory. 'I look forward to joining them. I am sure they will need an experienced warrior. Tell me, has my friend Ronec Fitz-Eudo arrived yet? He promised me a place at his side,' he asked.

A garrulous, red-haired house servant nodded emphatically. 'Oh yes, he is here all right, in a privileged room in the castle with the most beautiful woman we have ever seen, in his bed every night.'

Morvan's stomach lurched. He was too late, and his worst fears realised that she had left Luc for Ronec and took her revenge. The man was still talking.

'Hair like silver moonlight she has,' he said, waxing lyrical and making them all laugh. However, one person sat in the shade, well back from the rest, an older man with his hood pulled forward. He laughed along with them, but he listened and watched the Breton warrior who was so free with his silver. He knew that his master would be pleased to hear that Morvan De Malvais was in the local inn asking about him. Flek quickly drained his tankard, pulled his hood closer so Morvan did not see and recognise him, and he left the Inn.

Morvan stayed a while longer, but he left content with the knowledge he had obtained, no matter how unpalatable. Now he knew where she was; he had to get a message to her. Surely, she would not refuse to meet him. He had to persuade her to return to Luc and their son. He refused to think about how Luc would react to the news that Ronec was now her lover. Luc was a proud man, and if, as they suspected, Ronec was manipulating the situation, they needed to find out why. He hoped that Merewyn and Luc would be strong enough to forgive each other for their transgressions.

As he went up the stairs to the room, the very plump innkeeper's wife was coming down, and he squeezed to one side to wave her past when a thought occurred to him.

'I wonder if you can help me,' he said, giving her the full benefit of the Malvais smile. She nodded, rendered temporarily speechless being addressed directly by this tall, handsome warrior.

'I have a lady-love in the castle, and I need to get a message to her without her husband knowing. Can you help me?' he said, giving a shameful lop-sided grin.

The innkeeper's wife's face softened. 'I have a niece who works up there most mornings; I am sure she could get a message to her for you.' She smiled and knowingly winked at him. 'I will send her to you first thing,' she said.

He leaned in and kissed her cheek, which sent her scurrying down the stairs giggling. He sat down and wrote a plaintive note to Merewyn, telling her that Luc was heartbroken and wanted her to come back. He asked her to meet him on the riverbank outside the mill at dusk that night.

The girl knocked on his door early the following morning and shyly took the note once he had explained for whom it was intended. Morvan used the rest of the day to walk around the large encampment. He wanted to assess the forces gathered. He recognised several banners that did not surprise him but others that did, several Breton lords who he thought would have fought for the King. He did not notice that he was being followed for most of the day by Flek, the dark-haired manservant.

In the late afternoon, he returned to the Inn to find the girl waiting for him with a positive reply. As she handed him the note, he noticed that her hand was shaking and she would not meet his eyes, but he put it down to nervousness. He read that Merewyn would meet him, but not until after dusk when the moon rose. Morvan was pleased, and he decided to ride up to the camp to acquaint his men with his change of plan and make sure that they were packed up and ready to leave later that night or very early the following day. As he was remounting, his older companion hailed him; he had obviously been mulling over what Morvan had shared.

'Morvan, are you not suspicious that this is arranged so quickly?' he asked, head cocked quizzically to one side.

Morvan smiled. 'Don't worry, boys, I had inside help in the fortress, and I will be careful. I hope to be back here with Merewyn in a few hours,' he said as mounted and cantered back down to the Inn to have dinner before leaving for his rendezvous.

Merewyn was confused. Her emotions veered from anger to despair as she thought about Luc, but she was here with Ronec. In the short time they had been here, he had treated her with the utmost respect, and indeed, he had not tried to force himself on her. Instead, he saw to her comfort, meeting her every need and request, the warmest cloaks for their afternoon walk, the choicest morsels of food. He had taken her to meet the Lady Emma, who was also young and beautiful. She had been delighted to have an English companion at Gael and had made a fuss of Merewyn, finding her dresses to fit her for the evening dinners in the Hall. Obviously, Ronec had related her story as Emma made no mention of Luc but commented that Merewyn would turn the heads of every man at Gael as she had already done with Ronec Fitz-Eudo. Merewyn blushed, but Emma continued in a conspiratorial whisper behind her hand. 'I have never seen him so obsessed or in love with a woman as he is with you. He cannot take his eyes off you.'

As Merewyn returned to his room that afternoon, she noticed that Ronec was questioning a cowering dishevelled servant girl in the corridor. She noticed his taciturn rough-looking manservant was there as well, an individual she could not like.

'Is there a problem, Ronec?' she asked. At first, Ronec did not look pleased to see her, but he soon smiled and shrugged it off.

'No, Merewyn, my man found a lower-hall serving girl rummaging in our room, where she has no right to be. She is obviously looking for something to steal.' Ronec indicated that Flek should take the girl away and deal with her.

'You look tired, Merewyn, have a rest before this evening. Lady Emma has invited you to dine 'tête-à-tête' tonight in her solar; she so enjoys your company. I am sure you will like that.' He put a possessive arm gently around her shoulders and guided her over to the bed. Standing close in front of her, he gently pushed her down to sit on the end. Taking her face in his hands, he gently kissed her forehead before gazing deeply into her eyes.

'You know how much I love you, Merewyn, and I do want you when you are ready, But, for the moment, just let me take care of you; that is all I ask,' he whispered.

She smiled and nodded. He was so difficult to resist, and she had to admit she was enjoying love and attention from a man after months of tension and estrangement with Luc. Ronec's mouth came softly down on hers, and this time she didn't resist. Instead, she responded, letting his tongue gently explore her mouth, and she ran a hand up into his long hair to pull his head closer. She heard the gasp of breath as he let her go, and she knew that she had gone too far. He was obviously aroused, so she let go of him and turned away. As she walked away, it occurred to her that this was like holding a wolf by the tail.

Ronec closed the room door behind him and took a deep breath. That was so close; he had almost thrown caution to the winds and taken her there and then. Then his face set in grim lines as he thought about his other problem. His manservant had relayed what had happened in the Inn; Morvan was here in Gael. They had then intercepted the servant girl's message who had received a beating and was given instructions to take the reply. This had been delivered, and Morvan would be lured into a trap on the riverbank. He knew that Morvan was now almost as good a swordsman as his brother was, so it would take a few men and a clever plan to catch him completely off guard. He strode off down the corridor to inform Lady Emma that she needed to prepare dinner in her solar tonight; he wanted Merewyn fully occupied while he dealt with the problem of Morvan De Malvais. He smiled at the thought of dealing with that arrogant, interfering, young man and it was not a pleasant smile.

It was a cold night, but well-lit, with a full moon and few clouds as Morvan, wrapped in a thick dark cloak, made his way along the riverbank path that led to the mill. He had skirted the tented encampment with its campfires and sentries, but he had seen no one as he walked under the lee of the castle walls looming above him. He had scouted the area yesterday, and he knew there was a small postern gate in the walls that looked as if it was well used; it was highly likely that Merewyn would come through that. However, when he reached the mill, there was no sign of her. He stamped his feet to keep warm. Another twenty minutes or so passed, and he began to think that she would not show, that she had been unable to get away. He walked back along the riverbank for five minutes to keep warm and then turned to go back for a final look. As he approached the mill, he saw a light flicker inside the building and then disappear. His spirits rose; she had come after all. He opened the heavy wooden door and saw a tall figure in a blue woollen cloak sat by the window in the moonlight; it had the large hood pulled forward that was fashionable with women. He started forward and whispered her name.

'Merewyn.'

He did not see the heavy blow coming across his shoulders. It dropped him to his knees. He was seized and dragged further into the room.

'Take his weapons,' a harsh voice ordered; his swords were pulled from their scabbards, thrown across the room and down through the opening into the fast-running millrace.

He tried to sit up and shake off the arms that held him, but there were too many of them. He felt his arms viciously pulled back and tightly tied at the elbows and wrists behind him. Another blow to his head sent him reeling backwards onto the floor. He heard the scrape of flint hitting stone above him, and a lamp was lit. He stayed down on his side, but he could now see the shapes of three men around him armed with clubs while a fourth held the lamp and raised it high. He cursed his own stupidity of walking so easily into this trap.

The tall man with the lamp stepped forward, and Luc went cold as he recognised Ronec, who he knew would have a strong desire to kill him.

'Pull him up,' he ordered. The men wrenched Morvan into a kneeling position. 'Well, Morvan, this is a surprise. Couldn't Luc be bothered to come and get his wife, so he sends his lapdog instead?' he said, smiling down at the kneeling, bound warrior.

'Luc will kill you for taking Merewyn,' said Morvan through gritted teeth.

'Ah well, that is the point, Morvan, she wanted to come away with me, just as she wants to share my bed every night,' grinned Ronec.

To Ronec's surprise, Morvan laughed and pushed himself up onto his feet.

'Why would Merewyn, a Thegns daughter and the wife of the legendary Luc De Malvais, go off with a landless, penniless bastard like you, Ronec? You are just holding her prisoner,' he spat.

Ronec filled with a cold fury; he had always been sensitive about his birth and his lack of recognition. However, he could not kill Morvan as he wanted to do; he needed him. Yet another pawn in the game to bring Luc De Malvais to heel. He turned away for a second to control his anger and then turned a smiling face on his captive.

'I promise you that you will regret those words, Morvan, but I don't intend to dirty my hands on you. Do not worry; they will not kill you; that is not what I do to a friend's brother,

236

no matter how arrogant he is. But you need teaching a lesson,' he said; he nodded to Flek, then he put up his hood, turned and left the mill.

The first blows rained down in seconds from the club in Flek's hand and, as he fell to the floor, the other men followed, kicking and punching him unmercifully. He tried to curl up to protect his body, but to no avail; it was almost impossible with his arms strapped behind him. As the blows from the clubs rained down amid the waves of pain, he began to lose consciousness.

Chapter Twenty-One

Luc rode towards the inn at Saint-Brieuc in a dispirited frame of mind, which was unusual. He knew that he had done his best with Count Eudo, but, despite the extra days he spent with him, as Eudo implied, the die was already cast, and no other arguments he tried could change the Count's mind. He had sent a messenger to both Alain Rufus and William about the forces arrayed against them at Rennes. The King would probably not be surprised that the Angevin forces were there because Count Fulk had long been a thorn in his side; he was an opportunist, and he would relish this chance to wage war as part of a more considerable force against William. However, the news about Philip of France was far more disturbing as it meant that William might have to split his forces.

It was dark when they trotted into the yard of the Inn. As usual, the stable boys were keen, and Luc knew many of the horses would be taken up to a neighbouring barn for the night to be bedded down. Each warrior would check on their own horse before settling into the pot room for some hot food and a well-deserved drink. Luc had drilled into every man that the care of his horse was a priority. It had taken years to collect, breed and train these horses, and they were worth their weight in gold.

As usual, Luc looked after Espirit, rubbing the great stallion down, ensuring his hay net was filled and his water bucket was full. It was here that Gerard found him. He stood in the doorway and quietly watched for a while, noting the drop of Luc's shoulders and the resigned expression on his face.

'I presume the meeting with Eudo did not go well,' he said. Luc turned and grimaced at Gerard.

'He was courteous enough; he listened to his son's pleas and mine, but there was no turning him from his course; he is determined to fight with the forces gathering against the king. Of more concern were the Angevin troops and their commanders camped around the castle and a possible alliance with France,' he added.

Gerard gave a low whistle. 'That is a day I never thought I would live to see, Breton Lords in alliance with Fulk and in contact with Philip of France. This might take some unravelling. Will Fulk and his forces want to leave eastern Brittany and western Maine when this war is over?' he asked.

Luc groaned and covered his face with his hands. 'Civil wars always leave scars, Gerard, and it looks as if we will be fighting against Breton Lords and troops that fought with us at Hastings, men who were our comrades and friends.'

'Like Ronec, you mean,' Gerard said with a sardonic twist of his mouth.

Luc looked up in hope. 'Is there any news? Is Merewyn here? Has Morvan found her?' he asked, grasping his friend's arm.

Gerard shook his head and patted Luc on the shoulder, 'I have heard nothing yet, but they did have a good start on Morvan. Come inside, get some food, and drink inside you.

239

I will bring you up to date; I have other information,' he said, turning and walking across the cobbles and towards the warm light shining out of the doorway of the Inn.

The large pot room was full, and conversation stilled as Gerard steered Luc to a secluded corner table, ejecting the two occupants with just a raised eyebrow; they all knew who this was in their Inn and happily gave up their seats. Gerard signalled to the innkeeper to bring some mulled ale infused with the region's fiery apple brandy.

Luc sank back gratefully into the corner of the wooden settle and closed his eyes. He felt weary from emotional, mental and physical strain. He had purposefully put Merewyn to the back of his mind so that he could concentrate on the task at hand, but she kept creeping back in. She had left him, and it was his fault, the guilt settling on him like a huge weight that he felt unable to shift. The questions went round and round in his mind. Where was she? Had she gone back to Morlaix? Was she still with Ronec? Did she love the mercenary? She had spent months in his company at Morlaix while Luc had kept his distance from her. Would she take their son back to England before he had a chance to find them? At the thought of losing Lusian as well, another pain went through him.

Gerard watched the play of emotions on Luc's face. He had managed to get Luc through the tough years after his first wife's death, and now he was going to make sure he did not lose this one; Merewyn was perfect for him. The drinks arrived, and he handed the steaming tankard to Luc.

'Here, take a long draft of that and then listen to what I have to say,' he said quietly.

Luc opened his eyes and reluctantly sat forward, almost draining the tankard in front of him. Gerard nodded his approval as Luc wiped his mouth.

'I have been carrying out some investigations of my own about our friend Ronec and the lovely Briaca,' he said, glancing round to make sure that no one could overhear.

He explained that he had talked to the innkeeper and innkeeper's wife, and he had questioned all of the servants who were working here that night.

'One thing was very clear; you almost passed out in the pot room before you went upstairs, and that may have been because Ronec's manservant was seen putting juice of the poppy into your brandy before the drinking competition with Ronec,' he said. Luc had a vague recollection of the competition and the copious amounts of brandy they had consumed.

'Two of the manservants followed by the innkeeper with a lantern carried you up the stairs to your room; you had come round by then but were almost too drunk to stand. They were stopped on the landing by Briaca, who was waiting for you. She told them to bring you into her room and put you into her bed so that she could look after you. The maidservant helped her to remove your clothes while you were comatose on the bed, and Briaca then sent her away. One thing is certain; they said there was no way that you were capable of swiving her, Luc,' he announced with a satisfied smirk.

Luc drained the rest of his drink and signalled for another; he looked puzzled.

'But Gerard, I took her maidenhead. There was blood on the sheets, on me and on her thighs,' he said.

'The maidservant said that before she left the room, Briaca had asked for a small sharp fruit knife. It is an old trick, Luc, a nick in the crook of the arm or on the leg to provide proof of virginity and, of course, at the time you were hungover, befuddled, confused, you would not have noticed any wound. You were not in any state to check any details. She set a trap for you, Luc, and because of Ronec and his underhand tactics, you walked right into it like a lamb to the slaughter,' he said triumphantly.

Luc may have appreciated Gerard's care in working this out, but all he could feel was the anger building inside him. He had known in his heart that he could never betray Merewyn, and now, because of Briaca, she was gone, not only gone but in the arms of Ronec.

'Was Ronec working with her? Did they plan this?' he asked through gritted teeth.

'I am not sure; I genuinely think that was the first time he met her. However, once at Morlaix together after yuletide, I am sure, looking back, there was some collaboration and, if Morvan is right, Ronec saw an opportunity and was in her room nearly every night. There is little doubt that the child she is carrying is his,' he said.

Gerard watched the fury build in Luc as he clenched and unclenched his fists, his mouth a thin white line of anger as he downed a second drink.

'By then, of course, they knew that I had refused to join the alliance or supply the horses they wanted; I had ejected Fitz-Eustace from Morlaix, so is this some act of revenge on me. I had thought him a friend. How deceived we can be at times,' he growled.

Gerard looked thoughtful but shook his head. 'Possibly, but I am still not sure about Ronec's motive. Briaca wanted you; there was no way that she would settle for Morvan, a landless second son. She was sure that you would do the honourable thing, set her up in an establishment and recognise your son. She would also have convinced herself that Merewyn would leave you, she saw how proud she was, and that would leave the field clear for her. The more I think about Ronec's constant flirting with Merewyn; I think he may have truly wanted her. She is very beautiful, Luc and also very wealthy. That is quite a prize for a mercenary like Ronec.'

He sighed and looked intently at Luc. 'Again, the pair of you played straight into his hands, the wronged, heartbroken wife and the handsome mercenary knight close by to whisk her away from the hurt.' Gerard threw up his hands in frustration. 'Let us hope that Morvan caught up with them on the road to Morlaix. All we can do now is wait and hope.'

Luc nodded; the fury and rage had subsided to an evident cold black anger. 'I will find him, and I will kill him if he has laid a finger on her,' he said in an ice-cold voice.

Gerard nodded and signalled for more drinks: it could be a long night.

'You have other things to think about as well, Luc. As you have heard, William landed at St Malo two days ago and has made his way to Dinan; he has gathered his forces there to march on Dol. He may well have received your message and will be sending for you and the men; the rest of our men from Morlaix arrive tomorrow. Put your duty first, leave Merewyn to Morvan and me. We will get her back,' he promised.

It was the early hours of the morning; Luc had just lain down on his bed when he heard the sound of running feet and shouting. This was normal in such a busy Inn, so he lay for a few minutes until he heard Gerard's voice and then, his bedroom door flew open.

'Luc, come quickly. It's Morvan, and he is badly hurt,' shouted Gerard before turning and thundering down the stairs. Luc leapt to his feet, raced along the landing and followed him. As they reached the ground floor, two men were carrying a bloodstained Morvan into the pot room.

'Lay him on the big table and bring some more lights and some cloths and water,' demanded Gerard of the innkeeper, rolling up his sleeves as he spoke. Although clearly unconscious, Morvan moaned with pain as they tried to straighten him out on the table, and Gerard began cutting away clothing to examine him.

'What happened to him?' demanded Luc of Morvan's two companions. The taller and older of the two men turned and faced him; Luc had known him for a long time, a brave and reliable horse warrior.

'Morvan sent a message into the castle and arranged to meet Merewyn on the riverbank at an old mill that night, but it was all too easy, I told him it could be a trap.'

'We told him we would go with him, but he said he had to go alone. We were suspicious from the start because of what we heard from the castle servants about her relationship with Ronec Fitz-Eudo, begging your pardon, Sir,' said the younger warrior sheepishly, unable to meet Luc's eyes. The older man continued while glaring at the younger man. 'So we left the horses and decided to follow Morvan, we stayed back so he couldn't see us, but we would be there if we were needed.'

'Where was this?' demanded Luc.

'At Gael, Sir,' said the young man.

'He took her to Gael's fortress?' Luc said in a puzzled voice as he met Gerard's eyes.

'It looks as if Morvan was right about Ronec all along. He

was a spy for Ralph De Gael and his allies,' said Gerard while cleaning a nasty head wound on Morvan's temple.

'I found that out in Rennes,' said Luc gazing down with concern at his younger brother.

The older warrior continued the tale. 'At first, it was quiet, and nothing happened. He was there walking up and down the riverbank for some time near the mill. Then he disappeared inside for a while. We waited, and we saw him come out again. It was dark, but it looked just like him, the cloak and the long, dark hair. He set off at quite a pace along the path towards us, but then he turned and looked straight at us as he entered the postern gate and went into the castle, and we realised that it was not Morvan but Fitz-Eudo. We went forward as quietly and slowly as possible, as we expected guards outside. However, as we got closer, we could hear laughter and the sounds of a beating. We burst into the mill, and three men were kicking and beating Morvan on the floor. We could see he was in a bad way; they had him trussed up so he could not fight back. We killed two of them for that, sir,' he said proudly. The third man jumped into the millrace and escaped.

Luc slapped both men on their shoulders. 'You probably saved his life, and you managed to get him back here on his horse, a long journey which must have been a difficult task,' he said gratefully.

'We took it in turns to hold him in front of us, sir, and used his horse as a spare; we had to keep going as we thought they would come after us when they found the bodies,' said the older man.

'We are very grateful. Go and see to your horses, then come and have a drink and some food. We have the innkeeper here;

I am sure he can find you something,' said Luc.

Luc turned a concerned face to Gerard. 'How is he,' he asked.

'He will live, but it looks as if he has several broken ribs, a nasty head wound and dozens of cuts and bruises,' Gerrard sighed. I will sit up with him tonight.

Luc looked down at his younger brother's black and blue beaten body and swore to get revenge, 'We will take it in turns, Gerard,' he promised. 'Now let us get some help to get him into a bed. Is there a room on the ground floor?' he asked the worried-looking Innkeeper.

'I will free one up, my lord,' he answered, hurrying off to find his wife to break it to the Serjeant at the back of the Inn that he was about to be thrown out of his room.

Morvan was unconscious for a full day, and Luc had fallen asleep in the chair by the fire for a second night when Morvan finally regained consciousness. Gerard had sat up for the first part of each night as he was worried about the head wound. Luc shouted for Gerard and stood looking down at Morvan. He took his hand and arm in a tight warrior's clasp and said, 'Welcome back.' Morvan managed a weak smile before being subjected to Gerard's thorough examination, which made him grit his teeth in pain.

'Well, apart from a thumping headache, some broken ribs and lots of very deep, sore bruising, nothing else is broken, so I think he will live, although he certainly will not be riding for a while, Luc,' said Gerard. Luc watched his brother's face fall. He was a strong and fierce young warrior who always wanted to be in the thick of the melee, and now he would be bed-bound for several days, if not a week before he could be taken back to Morlaix.

'These things take time to heal, Morvan. I should know,' said Luc, meeting Gerard's eyes. Gerard nodded, remembering when Luc was beaten to within an inch of his life by a group of Saxon rebels five years earlier. No one expected him to survive, but he proved them all wrong.

Morvan started to apologise for failing to bring Merewyn back, but Luc cut him off and, instead, sat on the bed and told him what Gerard had discovered at the Inn. To Luc's dismay, Morvan put his head in his hands. 'That just makes it worse, Luc. You don't understand,' he said, grimacing in pain as he tried to raise himself higher. 'I found Merewyn. She is in the north tower of the fortress at Gael,' he managed to get out.

'I know,' said Luc. 'She is a prisoner there, and I will negotiate, and I will get her back. They probably want the horses they asked for, that we refused to deliver.'

Morvan took a deep breath and found that he could not meet his brother's eyes. He knew how much Luc loved Merewyn and what he was about to tell him would break his heart. 'Merewyn was not abducted, Luc.' She did not set off for Morlaix; she rode willingly to Gael with Ronec. She was running away from you. She is not a prisoner. I questioned the servants, and she is a guest of Lady Emma. She is at dinner with the other guests in the Great Hall every night,' he emphasised. Luc frowned. 'She must really hate me to go willingly to the camp of our enemies,' he said, the hurt and confusion clear to see in his eyes.

'There is more,' said Morvan darting a glance at Gerard, who tried to shake his head in warning.

'Go on,' said Luc in a dangerously quiet tone.

Morvan swallowed and took a deep breath. 'She does not

have her own room; she shares Ronec's bed every night,' he said, finishing in almost a whisper.

The silence and tension hung in the room for several minutes as Luc tried to take it all in and make sense of it. His clear eyes were a hard slate blue, narrowed in disbelief. Without a word, he stood and left the room. Both Gerard and Morvan let out the breath they had been holding, waiting for the storm to break.

'He is at his most dangerous when he is quiet like that. God help them when he finds them,' said Gerard.

Chapter Twenty-Two

Gerard did not see Luc until the next morning in the stables. He was taciturn and pale-faced with dark shadows under his eyes. He snapped orders out to the stable boys and even to his squires, who kept their heads down and rushed to obey his orders. He did not acknowledge Gerard's presence at first, but then he turned his expression stony.

'I have sent a message to Morlaix and Vannes to summon the men to rendezvous here. Most of them should be with us late this evening, and we will ride out to Dinan early tomorrow morning to join with William's forces.' He began to turn away, but Gerard put a hand on his arm.

'But Luc, what are you going to do about Merewyn? Are you just going to leave her there with him? Remember, she still believes that you betrayed her and that Briaca is carrying your child. She feels as if she is the wronged one.'

Luc turned back to face Gerard, His face blazing with fury, and for a second, as Luc clenched his fists, Gerard thought that he might actually hit him. He had never seen Luc like this, so out of control.

'Is that why she leapt into bed with Ronec? Is this her revenge?' he asked. Gerard stayed to give him his due knew when to remain silent.

'No, Gerard, she has chosen her path, and it is not the path that I am on.'

Gerard shook his head. 'But what of your son? What of Lusian? She may go and take him back to England while you are involved in Williams's wars in Brittany.'

'I have sent a missive to Morlaix, to my mother, explaining the situation and instructing her not to let Merewyn through the gates. Lusian is going nowhere. I have also ordered that Briaca be sent with an escort back to Dinan immediately. I will confront her there,' he said in an icy voice before turning on his heel and walking away to join his men.

Gerard stood rooted to the spot for a few moments, taken aback by what he had just heard. He turned and returned to the Inn to check on Morvan. He knew that Luc was hurting and angry, which meant that he was striking out at everyone he cared about as well. He took a deep breath as he walked through to Morvan's room. He could not think of any way to resolve this now, and he did not believe that Luc would ever forgive Merewyn for giving herself to Ronec.

For the second time in a week, Merewyn broached the subject of a return to Morlaix with Ronec. She needed to return to her son and plan her return to Ravensworth. However, each time she mentioned it, Ronec said he would not hear of her travelling on her own in these dangerous times. He intended to take her himself, but he had to wait until the end of the week. Ronec had been as good as his word and not pushed her any further or tried to make love to her, and she respected him for that. He no longer slept naked in the bed beside her as she said it was too much of a temptation, and there was an element of truth in that. Like Luc, he had a warrior's physique, and her eyes did follow him as he paraded naked across the room on a morning to get dressed. He said he respected her wishes, and he now slept on a truckle bed next to her.

There could be no denying that she enjoyed his company; he was an amusing and exciting companion. She was also enjoying spending time with the lovely Lady Emma. However, she was becoming restless; she could not stay here much longer, and she desperately missed Lusian. Watching her that morning, Ronec was aware of Merewyn's increasing discontent and uncertainty. He was also painfully aware that she was still in love with Luc De Malvais, despite the thought that he had betrayed her with Briaca. He knew he needed something to attach her more firmly to him, something to widen the cracks further in her relationship with Luc, so he left her to her embroidery and went to find his manservant.

After nuncheon, he took her for a walk along the inner wall on the battlements. They stood looking down on the hundreds of tents and pavilions below.

'The camp has almost doubled in size since I arrived,' she noted.

'Yes, more troops and Breton Lords are arriving almost daily, more than we expected. I hear Eudo De Penthievre, my esteemed father, is joining us at Dol,' he said, gazing out over the battlements with a tense expression on his face. Merewyn felt for him. A man like Ronec, a victorious warrior in his own right, it must be not easy to have your father ignore your existence. She put her hand on his upper arm and smiled up at him, but he turned away; he did not want the pity he saw in her eyes.

'I know that Luc was travelling to Rennes to try and persuade him to stay loyal to the King,' she said, changing the subject.

'Yes, but apparently he failed, and he was back at the Inn in St Brieuc a few days ago.' This was news to Merewyn. Why was he still there, and how did Ronec know that? Luc should be in Dinan by now with the King. Suddenly a messenger appeared, striding up to Ronec. He held out a message, then turned and with a bow departed. Ronec opened the small piece of folded parchment and started frowning as he read it. Merewyn turned away to let him have some privacy but was brought back with a start.

'Damn the man,' he said. Merewyn raised an eyebrow. 'This is the reply from Malvais; I knew he was back at the Inn, so I sent him a request for Lusian to be brought to Gael or for you and me to be given safe passage to collect him. I know how much you miss him, and I thought Luc might agree for the close friendship we once had,' he said in a wistful tone.

'What does he say?' she said in a whisper.

'That his son will never be leaving Morlaix and that he would be brought up beside Briaca's child, that Briaca would be a mother to them both.' Merewyn gasped in shock, her hands to her cheeks.

'No, he would never be so cruel,' she cried.

Ronec shrugged, and, tearing the parchment in half, he flung it over the battlements. Tears were streaming down Merewyn's cheeks, and he pulled her into his arms and held her tight, kissing the top of her head and allowing a smile of satisfaction to appear for a few fleeting seconds. Merewyn spent the rest of the day in isolation in her room, her emotions ranging from white-hot anger to despair.

252

'How dare he forbid me to see my son? How could he do that to Lusian and me?' she mumbled as she paced the room. Eventually, she curled up under the fur coverlet and dropped into an exhausted and troubled sleep.

She awoke to the sounds of much fanfare and rousing cheers from outside. She climbed out of bed and crossed to the window embrasure but could see little of the front of the citadel. Another grand arrival, she thought as she returned to curl under the covers in the warmth, maybe the great Eudo himself, she sneered. However, soon she could hear the sound of running feet and shouts in the great stone corridors outside and, before long, Ronec appeared, beaming with pleasure. He quickly crossed to her side and held both of her hands,

'Well, Merewyn, you must find your finest gown for this evening. The Earl, Lord Ralph De Gael, has arrived, bringing with him a whole host of knights and hundreds of men, enough to put the fear of God into William.'

Merewyn smiled weakly. Inside, she knew she was in a dangerous and invidious position here in the rebel camp at Gael. She was the wife of a great Breton Lord who was supporting King William and Hoel, Duke of Brittany, against these rebels.

'Was this what you were waiting for, the reason why we could not leave for Morlaix?' she asked.

'Yes, Merewyn, I see my future in serving the House of Gael and Montfort. I also hope that you will be by my side in the future,' he said, taking hold of either side of her face and kissing her deeply. She pulled away. 'I need to go to Morlaix, Ronec. I need to get my son back,' she pleaded.

'Don't worry, Merewyn. I need to spend a few days

discussing strategy with Ralph and his captains, but we will go soon, I promise you. I will send a maid to help you with your hair. You will be the most beautiful woman in the Hall tonight,' he smiled.

She was slightly mollified, and she turned away to prepare her clothes for the celebratory dinner in the Great Hall. Earl Ralph had escaped and managed to make it to Gael; his supporters would be relieved, as would the Lady Emma. However, her mind was still in turmoil since this morning's message; her stomach knotted in anguish at the thought of Luc choosing Briaca as his consort to bring up their son. That left her two alternatives: to flee to Ravensworth on her own or to live a life as Ronec's consort until she could appeal to the Pope for a divorce, which, with her scant knowledge of Pope Gregory, she knew could take years. The problem was that she had no idea what she wanted. Luc had been her world, and she found it hard to believe that, suddenly, he was out of her life. It was so final, and she had to admit to herself, she still loved him.

The maid had still not arrived when Merewyn began to dress for dinner until suddenly; there was a timid knock on the door, and a young dark-haired, waif of a girl appeared.

'The Steward sent me my Lady,' she said in an awed whisper.

Merewyn smiled. 'Come in. You are very late, but you can help me with my hair.' The girl nodded and came to stand behind Merewyn in the light from the candles, while Merewyn described how she wanted it braided across the top of her head but long and loose at the back. The girl ran her fingers through Merewyn's long silver-blonde hair.

'It is so beautiful, my Lady,' she said. Merewyn turned

and smiled at the young girl and suddenly noticed the dark bruises down the side of her face.

'I know you,' she said, standing up. 'I remember you were chastised for stealing by Sir Ronec,' she said accusingly.

'No, my Lady. I swear I was not. I was trying to deliver a note to you,' she pleaded.

Merewyn looked at the girl in disbelief, and then, taking her by the arm, she brought her further into the light.

'You work in the Hall and kitchens as a serving girl. Who would send me a note from there?' she asked.

'I works at the Inn too, my Lady, cleaning for my aunt, the innkeeper's wife. I stays there some nights as well. It was a gentleman knight staying at the Inn. My aunt brung me to him, and he gave me a note to bring to you,' she said wide-eyed.

'So where is the note?' asked Merewyn.

'I was caught trying to find your room by Lord Ronec's servant. Proper hit me he did, and then, outside of this room, they took the note away,'

Merewyn blinked in surprise. 'A gentleman knight at the Inn? Who was he?' she asked, feeling suddenly breathless.

'He was one of those fearsome horse-warriors. He was a fine-looking handsome man,' she smiled.

'Luc?' whispered Merewyn. 'Was it Lord Luc De Malvais? Very tall, dark hair falling over his forehead, blue eyes?' she said quickly.

'No, my Lady. He was tall and dark, but he had longer hair to here,' she said, indicating her thin bony shoulders.

'Morvan. It was Morvan,' said Merewyn more to herself. 'Could you read the note, or did you know what it said?' she asked hopefully. The girl hung her head.

'I can't read my Lady, but I know it was about a meeting because he was badly hurt for being there,' she said. Merewyn looked puzzled for a few moments.

'A meeting? When and who with?' she asked.

'My aunt says he told her he was coming to meet his lady-love, meaning you, but he was ambushed by the castle men and beaten something terrible. He was so badly hurt he was like to die, but his men got him away, they took him back north. My aunt says.'

The girl waited expectantly, but Merewyn just nodded and thanked her, putting her to continue fixing her hair while she mulled over what she had just heard. She had so many questions. Morvan had ridden after them, after all, that night when she fled. Had Luc sent him? Ronec had intercepted the note and set men on Morvan. There was no love lost there, she remembered.

'What is your name?' she asked the girl.

'Dorca, my Lady,' she said, attempting a clumsy bow. Merewyn smiled; she must only be about seventeen years of age.

'Well, Dorca, you can tell the Steward I am pleased with you, and I want you to help me every day, once Sir Ronec and his servant have left the rooms. We will get you some clean clothes and something to bind up your hair. I will also put some arnica on those bruises, and they will soon fade.' Merewyn thought that young Dorca might prove very useful; she was the type that would fade into the background and when cleaned up. Ronec might not recognise her.

Merewyn was somewhat apprehensive and preoccupied as she entered the Great Hall on Ronec's arm that night. She was oblivious to the interest and rapt admiration that her beauty generated in the hundreds of men gathered there, especially the recently arrived knights with Ralph De Gael. Ronec was very aware and allowed himself a small smile of satisfaction as he approached the top table and introduced Merewyn to the rebel Earl.

Merewyn, rising from her bow, found herself gazing into the stern eyes of the infamous Ralph De Gael, frank admiration evident on his face, as he looked her up and down. She could hear Emma, his wife, explaining that she was their guest for a short while. He nodded to them with a smile that did not reach his eyes, and they moved to take their places further along the table beside Geoffrey Fitz-Eustace, who had arrived in the train of his elder half-brother. Merewyn was pleased to see a face she recognised, but she found him dismissive and distant. She realised that she was now of no interest or use to him anymore; his main aim had been to persuade Luc to join the alliance against William.

However, being a few seats away allowed her to study Ralph De Gael surreptitiously. He was powerfully built, and although she knew he was only in his mid-thirties, grey was appearing in his hair and beard. The one thing he certainly had was presence; there was a vitality about him, his eyes darting everywhere, and he threw comments and questions at his followers, often accompanied by a booming laugh. She could see why his supporters rallied to his banners; after all, he had been one of the most powerful and wealthy men in England before his rebellion against William.

As the Earl of Norfolk and Suffolk, he had held vast tracts of land in England, now all lost, although he still owned considerable estates in Brittany. Occasionally, he turned his eyes in her direction with a questioning glance that unsettled her, and a smile, as if he was amused at her predicament. As the evening wore on, the men in the Hall became louder and more boisterous. Several toasts were made to Ralph De Gael and his success in the coming war, which he acknowledged with a raised hand. Merewyn felt very uncomfortable raising her goblet to the man who would be facing Luc on the battlefield. She knew he would be a formidable adversary and more Breton allies seemed to be flocking to his banner daily.

Finally, Ralph De Gael rose to his feet to acknowledge the acclamation from the crowded Hall. He spoke well, thanking them for their support and promising them a resounding victory against William, this Norman interloper who kept interfering in the affairs of Brittany and Anjou. This went down well as the Breton Lords were notoriously proud of their cultural and national heritage. He turned, and, taking Emma by the hand, he pulled her to her feet and asked the Hall to raise a toast to his beautiful wife who had single-handedly held Norwich Castle against the Kings Warrior Bishops.

'With courage like that, we cannot fail,' he shouted to the Hall, who erupted with cheers, most on their feet cheering Emma and banging their fists and tankards on the table. Ralph held up a hand, and they quietened as he continued.

'But we have another beautiful woman here tonight,' he said and turned to raise his goblet to Merewyn, who returned his gaze, wide-eyed at his charisma and presence.

'This is Merewyn De Malvais, a Saxon lady in her own right, wife of the famous Luc De Malvais, the champion of the House of Rennes and the leader of the renowned Breton Horse Warriors.' A hush had fallen on the Hall at these words;

there was hardly a man in the Hall who had not heard of Luc. Many had fought beside him, and most were in awe of him.

'Unfortunately, he is fighting for William, as he is a man of honour to his liege lord Alan Rufus and we accept that decision with regret. But his wife,' he allowed himself a laugh, and he bowed in her direction, 'she is so convinced that we will win and William and his allies will lose that she has left De Malvais to join us as the consort of Ronec Fitz-Eudo. Who is showing her what it is like to be swived by a true, virile, eastern Breton warrior,' he shouted.

The Hall erupted in louder drunken cheers with much lip-smacking, lewd gestures and toasts raised to Ronec.

Merewyn was horrified. Her hands gripped the table, her cheeks red with embarrassment. What would Luc and his family think if this got back to them? She turned helplessly towards Ronec, looking for support and to beg him to take her out of there, but he was on his feet laughing and returning the toasts. She lowered her eyes to the cloth on the table in mortification, hoping that the ground would swallow her up. Ronec sat down and moved close. Placing his arm tightly around her waist, he pulled her to him and kissed her, long and hard, forcing her lips open with his tongue. He grinned down at her and then drained another goblet of wine. His hand moved to her leg, pulled up her gown and beneath the table, he firmly caressed the inside of her thigh, moving slowly to the top of her leg.

He leaned forward to whisper in her ear, 'I am sorry, Merewyn. Unfortunately, I will not be swiving you tonight, as it will be a very late one. However, it will be tomorrow night, I promise you. I have been patient, but I have waited for far too long. It is time you rewarded me for helping you and keeping you safe.' His hand pulled her gown up further and moved to feel and knead between her legs.

She gasped, then grasped his hand and hissed 'No!' He laughed loudly, and she could see he was quite drunk. She stood up suddenly, pushed her chair back and turned to Lady Emma and the Earl.

'With your permission, I will retire as I do not feel well,' she said, casting a glare at Ronec, who just shrugged. Lady Emma nodded and smiled, and Merewyn walked swiftly across the upper dais to the doorway to the private quarters, telling herself not to run.

Ronec was not as drunk as he seemed, and with narrowed eyes, he watched her progress; she would not be running anywhere tomorrow night, he promised himself and smiled. He had achieved his aim of delaying and distracting Malvais, who was apparently still at the Inn and not on his way to join the King. Was he hoping for her return perhaps, he wondered? Ronec had closed as many of Merewyn's escape routes as possible, and now he intended to possess her; first, her body and then her wealth would be his.

Merewyn shut the chamber door behind her and leaned her head against the wood. She welcomed the cold, solid door as her skin felt she was burning up after what had just happened, and she felt a sense of utter hopelessness. She was trapped and had no idea how to extricate herself from this situation. She realised now how difficult it would be to leave Gael. She blamed herself for running blindly from the Inn that night, the anger and hurt getting the better of her. After all, she had the moral high ground at that moment, and Luc was repentant, begging her to forgive him. Then she had allowed Ronec to whisk her away, not caring where they were going, as long as she was far away from Luc. However, he had brought her to Gael instead of Morlaix, and she now found herself in the centre of the rebel camp with nowhere to go.

The tears streamed down her face as she made her way to the bed. Tonight, she realised that Luc would never forgive her; he was a proud warrior, and she had not only run away with another man but shared his room and his bed. Luc would never believe that nothing had happened and, as Morvan had been here, Luc would know, this was why he had forbidden her access to Lusian. Ronec would take her tomorrow night; she saw the look on his face and the lust in his eyes. She was lost and had lost everything she loved. Irretrievably lost, and she could see no way out of it. Sleep eluded her, and when she heard Ronec enter the chamber in the early hours, she feigned sleep as he flung off his clothes and stumbled around the room. Instead of going to his truckle bed, he pulled the fur coverlet back and climbed in with her, draping his long muscular naked frame over hers. Fortunately, the copious amounts of red burgundy he had imbibed soon had him snoring.

Merewyn watched the pale morning light hit the tapestries on the far side of the room as the sun rose. Slowly and gently, she extracted herself from Ronec's limbs and quietly dressed. He stirred just as she was ready to leave the chamber, and she returned to stand by the bed. 'I am going for a walk Ronec, it is a nice bright spring morning out there,' she said.

'You are feeling better then?' he asked in a less than tolerant tone.

'Yes, I am, and some fresh air is just what I need,' she smiled. He was somewhat mollified and grunted acquiescence.

'Take a servant with you if you go further than the castle bailey,' he insisted.

She nodded and left the room with alacrity in case he prevented her from going. She needed to think, and she always thought well when she was walking. Ronec rolled onto his back and thought about what had happened last night. There was no doubt that their relationship had reached a turning point. It was time to make better use of this pawn, especially as Malvais still seemed to be at the Inn in St. Brieuc. He shouted at the top of his voice for his manservant; it was time to send a message.

Gael fortress was a maze of stone corridors, and Merewyn took several wrong turns as she looked for the Steward's room to request the maid Dorca to accompany her on her walk. She finally found the Steward, and he promised to grant her request, telling her to wait upstairs in the Solar where he would send Dorca. The Solar at Gael was a large and impressive room with several fireplaces. Ralph De Gael was a wealthy man, and no expense had been spared with rich tapestries, carved wood settles, stools and chairs. A new and innovative feature was a large deep window embrasure that acted as a balcony with a window seat with small glass windows that opened. Merewyn opened a window and placed herself in the corner in the sun to see the countryside spreading out below, how she longed to be out there, cantering over the fields on her pretty, Arab mare. She decided to go down and visit the stables to see how the stable boys were looking after her.

At that moment, she heard the door open, and she made to rise expecting Dorca, but instead, she heard the voices of two men, realising at once that one of them was Ralph De

Gael with his distinctive, robust and confident voice. She had just decided to make herself known to them when she heard him say, 'What of Malvais and those damned horse warriors? I hear he is mustering over four hundred of them.' The other man replied, and she realised that it was Geoffrey Fitz-Eustace, Ralph's half-brother, who had stayed with them at Morlaix over Yuletide.

'Ronec and I are taking care of Malvais. We began putting the plan into place months ago. We have his wife as a hostage, and next week we will have his son. Malvais will be drawn here to Gael, and we will remove him.'

'Ronec trapped and took Malvais's interfering brother, Morvan, out of the equation too; he won't be riding or fighting for some months,' he added.

Ralph gave a bark of laughter. 'Yes! Ronec Fitz Eudo has done well there; I will reward him,' he said with a smile.

Geoffrey nodded but added, 'I think he has already been rewarded bedding that tasty piece every night. But he is playing the long game; he wants both her and her wealth for his own.'

'We will give him two outlying manors as well. He is a brave warrior with a fearsome reputation, and he brings thirty of his own mercenaries. He was brought up here after his mother came to be my mistress, and we need men like him at Gael,' said Ralph, thoughtfully. 'You have also done well in my absence, Geoffrey. Emma has appreciated your support and advice,' he said, putting an arm around his half-brother's shoulder. 'Now let us go and review the plans we have drawn up for our attack on Hoel at Dol. I intend to leave with our host early tomorrow to break the siege, enter the fortress at Dol and rescue Eudo's nephew, Geoffrey De Grenonat. I also hope that this will draw William firmly into our trap.'

Merewyn sat frozen in the corner of the window seat. She prayed they would not walk this way or that Dorca would not arrive. She dreaded to think what would happen if they found out that she had been party to that conversation. She heard the door opening and closing on the opposite side of the Solar and let out the breath she had been holding, stunned by what she had heard. This then was all part of a larger plot to keep Luc from riding to support William, and she had played right into their hands by fleeing with Ronec, whom she had trusted. She felt the fury build up within her, and she stood up and paced around the room, her fists clenched. Just then, there was a knock on the door, and Dorca came in.

'I believe you have need of me, my lady?' she said, looking pleased.

'Go and get your cloak and then fetch mine from my room. We are going for a walk, and I will tell you how I need your help.'

The girl scurried off, and Merewyn wracked her brain for a way out of this. She needed to escape before they took Lusian or, at the very least, get an urgent message to Luc. He might have now chosen Briaca and her child over her, but she still loved him, and she would not see him lured into a trap. The germ of a plan began to form in her mind as she waited impatiently for Dorca's return.

Chapter Twenty-Three

Luc was angry, furiously angry, at his inability to resolve anything. He still had that deep ache at losing Merewyn. He spent hours on his own, reliving every conversation with her, tortured by the thought of her with Ronec Fitz-Eudo at Gael.

He knew that he should be with the King by now, but because of the extra time he spent at Rennes and the days sitting by the bed while Morvan was unconscious and recovering, he would be at least four days late for the King's muster at Dinan, he doubted that William would wait. He ran his hands through his hair. Most of his men had now arrived from Morlaix over the last few days, and hundreds of them were setting up camp in the woods surrounding the Inn at St Brieuc, the horses filling the meadows around in large herds. However, he was still waiting for the contingent from his estates at Vannes, another hundred Horse Warriors. The innkeeper bowed and scraped with a beaming smile on his face every time he saw Luc. He had never had so much business, and now, he was helping to arrange the victualling of nearly four hundred men. Carts full of provisions were rolling in on an hourly basis.

It was almost noon when Luc decided that he should go

and check on Morvan. He now had his anger under control; he knew it was unjust, the way he had spoken to Gerard and his brother the night before.

He ducked his head to enter the Inn and headed for Morvan's room at the back. He was surprised to find the bed was empty and made his way back to the large pot room at the front where, on opening the door, he found Morvan in a corner propped up by several bolsters and drinking a tankard of mulled ale. Gerard was with him, as was two of the horse Serjeants, whom he sent on their way with a raised eyebrow. The two remaining occupants watched Luc apprehensively.

'Have the men from Vannes arrived yet?' asked Gerard.

'No, and I cannot understand the delay, Beorn is a good man, and I understand that they set off two days ago,' said Luc signalling the potboy for a drink. He sat on the settle beside the fire and regarded his brother, who looked pale, the dark purple bruises on his forehead and cheekbone beginning to turn yellow. Despite Gerard's skilled work with a needle, Luc expected Morvan always to have a two-inch scar above his eyebrow.

'I am somewhat shocked to find you out of bed, though I shouldn't be surprised; however, you must be in pain,' said Luc, smiling at his younger sibling. Both men visibly relaxed at Luc's more agreeable demeanour.

'There was no way I could stay in that room any longer; there must be something I can do, Luc?' he pleaded.

Luc met Gerard's eyes, who looked concerned, but he could understand his brother fretting at his enforced inactivity. He nodded; I will send the quartermaster to you; we will be leaving for Dinan as soon as Beorn arrives from Vannes and has had time to rest the horses. You can check the supplies from here and ensure that the Innkeeper produces the rest of the goods. He will need to be reimbursed for his outgoings. You can then check with the horse Sergeants to assess the fitness of the men and the horses. I want a complete troop tally before we leave in a few hours, but I do not expect you to move from this corner Morvan, bring the Serjeants to you.'

Morvan's face lit with pleasure, and Gerard allowed himself a wry smile at Luc; he knew that Luc would already have completed the latter task, but it would give Morvan something else to think about; Gerard knew the young warrior would be devastated at being left behind. Just then, one of the Serjeants reappeared and approached Luc.

'There is a messenger here, Sire. He is outside, but he insists on speaking with you personally. He says he is from Gael, my Lord.'

Luc looked at Gerard with a raised eyebrow as he indicated to the Serjeant that he should bring him in. The messenger was no other than Ronec's manservant, Flek, and Morvan gave a sharp intake of breath through his teeth, trying to push himself up and grimacing with pain as he spat out, 'You!'

Flek seemed to be surprised to see him sitting there, and he immediately stepped back towards the door, putting his hand to his belt and the dagger there. He quickly interjected, 'I claim the rights of parley, my Lord.'

Luc stood, and reaching up; he placed his hand on the hilt of his sword. 'Judging from my brother's reaction, I see no reason why I should not kill you now,' he said in an icy tone as Gerard also rose to his feet, hand on his sword.

'I am not a soldier, my Lord, kill me, and you will probably never see the Lady Merewyn again,' he said, an alarmed expression on his narrow pockmarked face.

'Your build and speed in reaching for that dagger belies what you say, and no doubt you were one of the group of cowards that lured Morvan into a trap and set on him,' growled Gerard, taking a step forward.

'As all servants do, we follow the orders of our masters,' he said, holding his hands up, palms out, hoping for mitigation. Luc waved Gerard back and dropped his own hands to his side.

'Let us have your message. We will try and respect the rights of parley with honour, unlike Ronec Fitz Eudo,' he said. The man reached into his doublet, brought out a folded parchment, and stepping forward, he placed it on the table before quickly stepping back. Luc read the message, and as he read it, his brows furrowed and his mouth set into a thin, grim line.

'Get out now before I kill you,' he said, in a quiet but deadly voice through gritted teeth. The manservant stood his ground and began to bluster.

'My master and Geoffrey Fitz-Eustace expect an answer, my Lord.' He exclaimed, and then he smirked as if he knew that Luc did not have much choice. Luc reached up again, in a flash, his sword was in his hand, and he had expertly sliced off most of the man's left ear. Flek staggered backwards, his hand clutched to his ear, blood running through his fingers.

'That is a reminder of what you did to my brother. If I see you again, I promise I will kill you.' He stepped forward and gripped the terrified man by the front of his jerkin, wiping the blood from the blade of his sword on the man's sleeve.

'Now get out and tell your masters I do not choose to answer their missive,' he said, pushing the man violently back into the tables and onto the floor. Flek scrambled to his feet, leaving a trail of bloody handprints as he bolted through the door and out of the Inn. A silence descended on the tense room. Gerard and Luc were on their feet, and Morvan bent over was gripping the table in anger.

'He was the one who led them, but he escaped', said Morvan in a voice resonant with pain. Luc nodded, his eyes staring bleakly at the empty doorway, his sword still in his hand.

'What did the message say, Luc?' asked Gerard, in a concerned voice while pushing Morvan gently back onto the bolsters. Luc slowly cleaned the rest of the blade of his sword on a rag and re-sheathed it across his back before he answered.

'As we knew, they have Merewyn, but I do not think she went as willingly as you thought, and she is now a hostage. They also say that Geoffrey Fitz-Eustace will shortly have my son as well. If I do not stand down the Horse Warriors and present myself at Gael within two days, then I will never see them again. Fitz-Eustace will ensure that they are sent south to the Saracens and sold.' The silence hung in the room as Luc's words resonated with each of them.

'No,' whispered Gerard, who loved both Merewyn and Lusian as if they were his own family.

'I always knew that Merewyn would never willingly betray you,' said Morvan. Luc nodded.

'It is a good thing that I sent the message to Morlaix forbidding Lusian to be sent or taken anywhere. He will be well protected. Gerard, go and find two of our swiftest horses and riders. Send them to Morlaix to tell them to go on a full defensive footing, letting no one in or out, friend or foe.' Gerard leapt into action and darted out of the door.

269

'What are you going to do, Luc? Are you going to Gael?' asked Morvan, in a voice hardly above a whisper as if he did not want to hear the answer. Luc's face was set into rigid lines as he ran his fingers through his hair and paced in front of the fire.

'I am afraid I cannot do that, Morvan. I must go to Dinan. This has all been a ploy by Fitz-Eustace, to delay the Horse Warriors from joining the King, conspiring against me using both you and Merewyn. William will think I have failed or even betrayed him; my duty to him and my liege lord must come first. I just hope that the Lady Emma will keep Merewyn safe, for I will go and find her when I am released from my obligations to the King, I will find her, no matter where they send her or imprison her, and then I promise... I will kill Ronec and Fitz-Eustace.' He headed towards the doorway, where he turned and regarded his brother.

'You concentrate on repairing those ribs and doing the tasks that I requested; now I must go and see if Beorn has arrived from Vannes,' he said, leaving the Inn and walking up towards the camp, his heart heavy with the decision he had made.

Two hours later, Luc and Gerard rode out at the head of over four hundred horse warriors. The people poured from their houses in St Brieuc agog at the spectacle in front of them. Morvan pulled himself to his feet, made it slowly, and painfully to the front door of the Inn, where he leaned against the jamb, surrounded by the Innkeeper and his family, come to see the Breton Horse Warriors ride out to war.

As he watched them, in perfect formation, the horses' tails docked for battle, he wondered how many would not return. They would be arrayed against Ralph De Gael's combined forces, the rebel Breton Lords and now the Angevins. He had great faith in the men and in their leaders, but there was many a slip or mistake in the heat of battle. His stomach knotted in exasperation that he was not on his horse riding out with them, especially as many of the riders raised a hand to him with a rueful smile, seeing him left behind. However, he was partly mollified that he had the task of waiting for, or searching for, the missing cohort from Vannes; he had already sent riders out to search the route.

His mind turned to Merewyn, a prisoner at Gael. He just hoped she would understand the decision that Luc had to make and that she could survive in their enemies' hands. He tried not to think about what she might have to endure at the hands of Ronec or Fitz-Eustace when they found that their ploy had not worked. The Breton Horse Warriors would now be there at Dinan and then at Dol, on William's flanks during an attack, if they were not too late.

In the shadows between the houses in St Brieuc, Ronec's maimed manservant, Flek, leaned against the wall holding a cloth to his still-bleeding ear, watching Luc De Malvais ride out with the hundreds of Horse Warriors. He sighed and went to fetch his horse. They were not going to be happy with this information when he reached Gael, but Luc De Malvais was a force to be reckoned with; he shook his head, surely, they had known that a man like him would not submit to blackmail even if it meant sacrificing his wife and child? He mounted his horse while cursing the pain in his ear, the blood still trickling down his neck, and he turned onto the track south to Gael, pushing his horse into a gallop.

Chapter Twenty-Four

Merewyn stood in the stable block in the outer bailey at Gael. She had picked up several small, wrinkled apples, and she fed these to her mare. It took her back to the day at Morlaix when Luc had presented her with this beautiful, sure-footed but fleet Arab horse, and a wave of sadness washed over her. Dorca stood just outside the stable block doorway, chattering away to a tall, freckled young man who ran the stable block. It transpired that he also occasionally helped at the Inn stables, and he clearly liked Dorca a lot.

'Dorca can you ride?' asked Merewyn, bringing the girls attention back inside.

'Yes, my Lady, I used to ride my father's horse. He was a carter and used to bring vittles' and vegetables to all the local inns before he died of the fever.' Merewyn nodded in satisfaction, a plan forming in her mind.

Ronec awoke with a bitter taste in his mouth and a pounding head; they had drunk and then diced until the early hours, toast after toast raised to the campaign's success. However, he needed to dress and check on his men and horses; they were told they were all riding out early the next day. He groaned as he realised he had sent Flek to Saint-Brieuc, just when he needed him to do all the running around this morning.

As he dressed, he thought of Malvais. Would he come galloping down to rescue his wife? Would he be disappointed to find she was not here? Then they would have him. Ralph wanted to cut the head off the wolf so that the horse warriors were leaderless and stuck at Saint-Brieuc. Ronec did not want Malvais killed, just imprisoned, but he planned to send Merewyn out of reach tomorrow morning with four of his men; they would take her to his manor at Loudeac. She would be confined there under lock and key until he returned from the campaign at Dol. Tonight he would finally bed her, the time for games now over. Fitz-Eustace had sent one of his knights to Morlaix to bring her son here. They carried a forged missive with instructions from Merewyn to send Lusian to her. The boy would be held in the tower at Gael to ensure that both Merewyn and Malvais did as they were told. He smiled; his plan was coming to fruition, and he might finally get the recognition he deserved.

Merewyn, meanwhile, had won over Dorca's young man by slipping him a small coin to look after her mare. He mumbled his thanks but assured her he would have taken great care of the mare anyway. She smiled and asked him to find a steady but fleet horse for Dorca to ride that afternoon, as they would be exercising the horses down in the meadow today and probably every afternoon that week. The young man looked puzzled.

'But you are leaving tomorrow, my Lady, immediately after the muster under the banners? I have just finished cleaning your tack, and all the saddlebags have been sent to the Steward.' Merewyn was taken aback but tried not to show it,

'Ah, of course, I had forgotten it was so soon. However, we will go for a good gallop this afternoon, and you may accompany us as our escort,' she added. The young man immediately brightened with a quick glance and smile at Dorca.

Merewyn slowly made her way back into the castle. She left the girl in the Great Hall, telling her to meet her there early afternoon and to dress very warmly for riding. Merewyn intended to ride out and not come back; she had heard that Luc and probably Morvan were still at the Inn, and she knew the track to Saint-Brieuc was north and very straightforward.

Ronec was satisfied with the morning's work; he had met with Ralph De Gael, Geoffrey Fitz-Eustace and their knights to examine the plans for attacking and infiltrating the fortress of Dol. Hoel, the Duke of Brittany, had surrounded the stronghold, they would smash their way through, and Ralph De Gael would ride with over a hundred men into the castle to support Count Eudo's nephew Geoffrey De Grenonat, taking him supplies and men. At the same time, Fitz-Eustace would establish their camp with the rest of the rebel forces east of the town. As he got up to leave the room, Ralph stopped him with a hand on his arm.

'Is there a reply back from Malvais yet?' he asked with a raised eyebrow. Ronec looked up at the impressive figure in front of him,

'No, my Lord Earl, I am just waiting for my man to return from Saint-Brieuc.' Ralph met his gaze for a second and then nodded and turned away, and Ronec headed down to the Great Hall to break his fast.

Geoffrey reassured his half-brother, 'We have managed

to delay the cohort from Vannes arriving at the Inn to join Malvais. We attacked them just outside of Loudeac with the help of the men from Ronec's estate. Several of the horse warriors were killed and injured.'

Ralph raised a cynical eyebrow. 'So, that only leaves us four hundred and eighty plus to deal with,' he said, with a bark of laughter.

Geoffrey looked crestfallen but added, 'One of the scouts around the Inn was taken alive and information extracted from him before we killed him.'

'And what did we discover?' asked Ralph.

'Malvais has been seriously delayed. He is distraught at the loss of his wife and, hopefully, not thinking as strategically as usual. He has not left to join the King yet; he is still at the Inn waiting for the Vannes cohort, and of course, his brother is there, seriously injured.' Ralph nodded and slapped his brother on the back in gratitude.

'Good work, this delay might just give us a chance we need to break through Hoel's siege forces and get into the citadel of Dol, with more supplies and men. Tell the commanders we ride out at dawn.'

Ronec was addressing himself to a large bowl of pottage when his man, Flek, appeared. As Ronec looked up, he was shocked at the state of Flek and said so. Flek just stood there staring at the ground until an exasperated, 'Well?' from Ronec prompted him.

'My Lord, I have been ill-used despite claiming parley. I carried out your orders to the letter, and this is how they treated me.' Ronec regarded Flek with dismay. He had a bloodstained cloth wrapped around his head and ear, his doublet and hands were stained with dried blood, and he looked deathly pale.

'Go and see the Steward. Get yourself cleaned up, Lady Emma's physician will see to any wounds,' he said. Flek made to turn dejectedly away.

'Wait! For God's sake, man, did he send a reply?' snapped Ronec.

'This was his reply, my Lord; he sliced my ear off in a second and then said he would find you and kill you. I watched the inn for a while, despite the bleeding, and I saw them ride out to join the King at Dinan. There were hundreds of them with him at the front.'

Ronec cursed loudly. He slammed his fist down onto the table, upsetting the bowl of pottage, which made him leap to his feet and kick over the bench on which he was sitting. His plan for bringing Malvais to Gael so that they could capture him was in tatters. Flek backed off, bowed and walked dejectedly away, a hand held to his still-bleeding ear.

Merewyn sat patiently in the room with her embroidery; she presented a picture of calm serenity on the surface. Inside, every part of her was tense with both excitement and apprehension. She had prepared layers of clothing to don under her riding cloak when she left, as she knew it would be still quite chill in the forests at night. She had instructed Dorca to do the same. She still had sufficient coin if she needed it, and she had secreted a small dagger in the layers of clothing on top of the chest.

The door opened suddenly, and Ronec strode in, banging it shut behind him. She could see immediately that something was amiss; could he somehow have discovered her plan? Had Dorcas' young man betrayed them? He stood in the centre of the room staring at her but not really seeing her, as if he was deep in thought, his lips clamped tightly together.

Her heart was in her mouth as she asked in a hesitant voice, 'Is all well, my Lord?' He turned to gaze into the fire and stamped a log further into the flames with his foot while the silence hung in the room.

'Your errant husband has refused to parley with Ralph. He does not seem to care that you are here with us,' he sneered. Merewyn's stomach knotted; Ronec's whole attitude had changed, and she did not like the way he was looking at her through narrowed eyes. He was plainly furious that his plans had gone awry.

'Unfortunately, that makes you worthless as a hostage to Ralph De Gael; you are now unnecessary to him. He is a ruthless man who would imprison you or even kill you without a second thought,' he said. Walking over to stand close in front of her, he took the embroidery from her hands and dropped it on the floor. He sighed, and although she was worried by his frustration, she could still see in his face that he cared for her, so she smiled up at him. However, her mouth went dry as he took her hands, pulled her forward and moved them up under his tunic and placed them palm down on his hard, muscled thighs.

'You need to be very grateful to me, Merewyn, for keeping you safe from Ralph De Gael. Malvais has abandoned you and is riding off to Dinan without a backward glance. He badly injured my manservant, who had only taken my message; I was asking for safe passage for us to return to Morlaix so that you could re-join your son. He has denied us that, so that road is closed to us,' he said.

Merewyn's heart sank. Would Luc be that cruel as to deny

her access to Lusian? And with Luc leaving Saint-Brieuc, where could she go? She had thought that their relationship still meant something to Luc, despite what had happened with Briaca.

Ronec's face changed, and she could see the desire in it, which filled her with apprehension. She could feel the heat from his thighs on her palms as he pressed them hard against his muscles. Then he moved her hands further up until they were pressed against his groin on either side of his erect manhood.

'Now you are going to show me just how grateful you can be,' he said, pulling his tunic over his head to reveal his muscled torso, the dark curly hair running from his chest down his flat muscled stomach disappearing under his dark, linen braies.

'Do not move,' he said, moving her hands up as he slowly undid the laces fastening his braies, which dropped to the floor and freed his large, erect manhood. Merewyn was wide-eyed and frozen.

She just managed to gasp, 'No Ronec!' when there was a loud knock on the door. Ronec stood there, thoroughly aroused by the thought of what he was about to do to her; his breath was coming in ragged bursts as he ignored whoever was outside. Then he cursed loudly as the door opened and the Steward entered.

'For God's sake, man, don't you wait to be called in?' shouted Ronec, quickly pulling up his braies. The Steward took in the situation at a glance and suppressed a smile while Merewyn clambered back into the chair.

'Excuse me, my Lord, but it is urgent. The Earl demands your presence immediately in the main pavilion,' he said while waving in a squire holding several saddlebags, which he placed on the bed before hurrying back out of the room. Ronec nodded curtly.

'I will be there,' he said, as the Steward bowed and backed out of the room.

Merewyn sat rigidly, her hands clasping the chair's carved arms as Ronec turned back to her. He looked at her intently, desire for her still written large on his face as he ran his tongue over his lips.

'As you heard, I have to go now, but you can sit there and work out how you will demonstrate your gratitude to me over and over again when I return. I am going to bend you over that bed and make you squeal with pleasure.' He smiled at the thought as he reached down for his tunic and pulled it over his head, and then reluctantly pulled his braies up and tied them at the waist.

As the door closed behind him, Merewyn let out the breath she had been holding. Even now, part of her knew that she could not totally blame Ronec for what had happened; she had used him to run from the Inn and looked to him to protect her here, playing on his feelings and his desire for her. So far, she had managed to keep him at bay, but now, obviously, his patience had run out. She admitted to herself she had been flirting with him for months at Morlaix, enjoying the attention from such an attractive and desirable man, so she had brought this on herself. However, now she knew that there were ulterior motives behind his actions, and she could never forgive him for that or for having Morvan set upon and beaten. She had to leave; it had to be today before he came back. She knew that physically, she would never be able to resist him unless she used the dagger she had secreted, and honestly, she knew he could quickly disarm her as well; he was a trained warrior, a ruthless mercenary, and she would have no chance.

Although her saddlebags were on the bed, she could not risk using them while she was using the pretext of just an hour's ride by the river with a groom. She dressed quickly in several layers and picked up her gloves and heavy winter cloak. As she descended the stone staircase to the Great Hall, her heart was in her mouth. She knew that Ronec had gone out to Ralph's large pavilion, but she did not know how long he would be, and she could envisage him walking in as she was leaving, taking her hand and pulling her back upstairs to finish what he had started. She scanned the Hall. There was no sign of Dorca, but she was earlier than expected. She waved down one of the serving boys and sent him to find her. Merewyn waited next to one of the huge fireplaces, her eyes pinned on the main doors, jumping every time it opened until Dorca finally appeared, out of breath and full of apologies.

'Sorry, my lady, I was sent out to the apothecary by the Steward. Flek has had his ear near sliced off something terrible, and it won't stop bleeding.' Merewyn felt slightly mollified, as she knew that Luc had inflicted that wound on a man she disliked intensely.

'Come, we must make haste. I hope you dressed warmly as I instructed,' she asked. Dorca nodded, and they made their way quickly down to the stables in the bailey where the young man, whose name was Cadec, had been as good as his word; he had saddled Merewyn's mare and provided a neat, sure-footed palfrey for Dorca. He had also saddled one of the job horses for himself.

'It's a good thing you asked me to come, you cannot ride

out through the camp to the river unaccompanied, my Lady, there are hundreds of men milling about down there, and the sight of two beautiful girls might be too much for them,' he said, smiling at Dorca.

Merewyn glanced at the girl objectively and realised she was pretty now she was cleaned up with her hair braided and in some decent clothes, and he was a good-looking dark-eyed young man. She smiled and nodded her approval. This might even work to their advantage; two women escorted might not be challenged going through the gates. However, she was brought down to earth with a thud when she heard Ronec's raised voice. She quickly shrank into the stall behind her mare, out of sight of the doorway. She watched him stride past with Geoffrey Fitz-Eustace; both men looked angry. She waited several minutes until she was sure they had gone up to the Donjon of the castle and were out of sight before she breathed a sigh of relief. Cadec looked at her in a puzzled way, but she brushed it off by leading her mare out to mount, and before long, they were trotting out of the main barbican to put a daring and dangerous escape plan into place.

Ronec's anger and frustration were evident as he ran up the Great Hall's main steps, Geoffrey Fitz-Eustace close behind him.

'So what the hell happened?' he said to him as he entered the Hall and signalled for wine to be brought.

'One of my knights, you may know him, De Fremont, arrived at Morlaix with an escort and was shown up for an audience with the Dowager, Countess Marie De Malvais. However, without warning, he was taken; his men were attacked and overpowered. Several were killed,' spat Fitz-Eustace, barely keeping his temper.

'So they never got a chance to snatch the boy?' asked Ronec.

'Not a sight of him, and they had watched all movement for several days. The entire castle was on a war footing with additional men on the battlements and double-checked at the gates. It was obvious that they had been warned,' he added. Ronec slammed his fist down on the table, and the wine leapt out of the goblets.

'Malvais! Damn that man, always one step ahead,' he stormed. Fitz-Eustace watched his friend becoming angrier and more frustrated.

'We still have his wife as a hostage, but it would have been better with his son as well,' he said. Ronec shook his head in exasperation,

'He knew we had his wife, but he has ridden off to Dinan to join the King without a backward glance. Duty, honour, loyalty comes first to a man like Malvais; it is his code and makes him what he is. I have never seen anyone shed emotions as he can in warfare,' he said thoughtfully.

'But this time when I watched him with Merewyn, I thought we had found something he cared deeply about, something that would affect his judgement and, for a while, he was so tormented about Briaca that I thought it had worked. However, thanks to our friends Morvan and Gerard, that strategy has been laid to bed.'

Fitz-Eustace nodded. 'He may be tormented inside, and I think it is likely that he will come and deal with us later, but you are right, for now, his word to his King is more important, and he will keep it no matter what the personal cost.'

Ronec nodded. 'Well, we have achieved one thing, at least; we have managed to delay him for five days, which means the Breton Horse Warriors will not be invested around the citadel of Dol, and they will still be in Dinan with the King when we arrive in Dol. We will easily be able to break through the meagre siege lines that Duke Hoel has established so that we can support Geoffrey De Grenonat and drive off Duke Hoel's forces before William arrives. We have had word that Eudo of Penthievre has set off with his combined forces of the House of Rennes and Angevin troops; he will arrive tomorrow as well.'

Both men sat in thought for a few minutes and sipped their spiced wine before Ronec broke the silence.

'I will not be riding out with you tomorrow; I will be taking the Lady Merewyn to my Manor at Loudeac where she can be held in seclusion and safety by my men until I return from Dol. I will ride immediately to join you once I know that she is secure.'

Geoffrey was not pleased. He realised that Merewyn had a far greater hold on Ronec than he expected. As his friend rose to his feet and headed for the stairs, he wondered if Merewyn was so desirable to him because she belonged to Luc De Malvais; he had heard the envy and frustration in Ronec's voice when he spoke of him. They may claim to be friends and previous comrades in arms, but it would be hard for a man like Ronec to live or follow in the shadow of the legend that was Malvais.

He knew himself to be a good swordsman, but he knew that Ronec was far better than he was; he had a combination of skill, strength and recklessness that inspired others and made him a desirable addition to any force. However, Malvais was simply the best swordsman he had ever seen. He had never seen him disarmed or beaten, even against two or three men, and he admitted that he was not looking forward to the time when he might have to face him. They had tried to neutralise or remove the threat that was Malvais but had only partly succeeded, so now, he was like a wounded, wild animal and twice as dangerous.

Chapter Twenty-Five

As they rode down the hill away from the barbican gates, Merewyn felt the tension leaving her shoulders. The Serjeant had questioned them at the gate, but she had rebuked him and told him to send for Lady Emma if he was questioning her decision to let them go for a short ride. The man had immediately backed down, looking a trifle shamefaced. They skirted the hundreds of tents and pavilions before breaking into a canter along the southern bank of the River Meu, heading for the ford.

Once out of sight of the castle, Merewyn gave the mare her head. Dorca and the stable boy Cadec tried to keep up with her but were soon left behind. Merewyn felt apprehensive but with a sense of exhilaration as she sat at the end of the meadow, waiting for them to catch up.

'That is a beautiful mare, my Lady; she is as fast as the wind,' said an envious Cadec.

Merewyn sighed. 'Yes, my husband Luc De Malvais gave her to me. She has had several beautiful, strong foals that will become great warhorses, and now she is mine for a year.'

Cadec let out a low whistle. 'Your husband is Malvais, the famous warrior? I thought you were with…?' the question remained unfinished, and Merewyn squirmed inside with embarrassment before answering with a tight smile.

'Lord Ronec was a friend who was helping me for a short time, but now I must return to my husband and my son at Morlaix. Dorca and I are not coming back with you, Cadec; we are riding to the west.'

The older boy looked crestfallen, especially when he looked at Dorca.

'Unfortunately, you may get into trouble because of this, but you must tell them that I ordered you to return to the castle, do you understand?' She asked. The boy nodded, and, opening the purse at her waist, Merewyn extracted three silver coins and placed them into his hand. The boy's eyes opened in amazement; he had never had so much money. He began to stutter his thanks, but Merewyn held up her hand.

'You deserve this for helping us, but I suggest you hide it somewhere very safe as they will probably search you', she added.

She turned to a sad-eyed Dorca and smiled. 'Now we must go, and you must return to the castle, but do so very slowly to give us a head start, as I know they will pursue us.'

She turned her mare, and, with only a backward glance, they entered the dense forests of Poutrecouet, which sur-rounded Gael. She was not taking the road west to Morlaix as she had implied; instead, she cut through the woods across to the track that led north to Saint-Brieuc. She had to reach the Inn. It sounded as if Luc had left, but she hoped that Morvan, or even Gerard, were still there, and she knew that they would help and protect her.

Ronec left Fitz-Eustace and went up to their chamber. If nothing else, he was going to finish what he had started with Merewyn that morning. It was time she began to show her appreciation, especially now that she knew that her husband did not give a damn about her. He pushed open the door to find only his manservant inside, packing the saddlebags for the early start the next day. He glanced quickly around the room. 'Where is she, Flek?' he demanded in a frustrated voice.

'I do not know my Lord, but I would imagine that she is in the solar with the other ladies, or perhaps with Lady Emma?' he suggested.

Ronec glared at the man. Flek was looking slightly better today but still sported a bloodstained bandage over his ear.

'Finish packing and then go and find her. Tell her I want her here, now.'

Flek nodded in assent and continued with his task.

Ronec strode over to the window embrasure and stared out at the forests beyond. He felt at home in Gael; the one thing that Eudo had done for him was to send him as a squire to Ralph De Gael. However, having survived the beatings and the training and finally achieved his knighthood, he had decided to leave to make his own way and fortune in the world, hiring out his sword and the group of men he accumulated to the highest bidder. It had been hard initially, but now his future looked more promising. Ralph had awarded him two small manors on the borders with Maine for his loyalty; although he knew that would entail him provisioning and maintaining an armed presence in those troubled lands, Ralph would expect nothing less. However, that did not distract him from his current plans to compromise Merewyn, keeping her at his manor at Loudeac. Hopefully, she would soon bear his sons; she was still young, and she could use some of her father's money to buy a papal dispensation to divorce Malvais.

For a few seconds, another thought occurred to him; Briaca was carrying his child as well. However, it could never take his name. If it were a boy and survived, it would become Fitz-Malvais, as Luc thought the child was his. That thought irritated him for some reason. He lay down on the bed and remembered those nights with Briaca; she was a passionate wench, and he thought of her fondly, but she was part of the plan to trap Malvais, and Merewyn was still the ultimate and richer prize. He woke over an hour later with Flek shaking his arm.

'My Lord, I have searched the castle and enquired after the mistress Merewyn everywhere, but no one has seen her. So I went down to the gates to see if she had gone for a walk,' he paused as if unsure whether to go on, watching the narrowing of Ronec's eyes as he swung his legs to the ground.

'So where is she Flek?' he asked in an icy voice.

'She has gone riding my Lord, but she has taken two servants with her,' he added, hoping that this would mollify his master. 'I left instructions for us to be told as soon as they return.' He waited for the storm to break, but, surprisingly, Ronec just muttered, 'Good! Make sure they do. And make sure all of the chests are sent on to Loudeac, the Lady Merewyn will be making the manor her future home from tomorrow.'

Flek raised his eyebrows at that news. He had his own thoughts about her afternoon ride, which he kept to himself at present, especially when he heard from the Steward that Dorca, the girl from the Inn, had been acting as Merewyn's maidservant for several days.

Ronec went down to the Hall and partaking of refreshment;

he passed a pleasant enough hour dicing with some of his men and the other knights. However, he looked up every time there was an arrival through the main doors to see if Merewyn returned. Finally, as he noticed the sun was sinking, he sent one of the squires to the stables to see if her horse had returned. The boy was some time, but he returned with a garbled tale of a stable boy returning alone, but who had now suddenly left to visit his mother, as she was ill.

Ronec sat and listened in disbelief and summoned Flek, asking the boy to repeat it for his manservant. He tried to make sense of what he was hearing. So, Merewyn and her maidservant were still riding by the river, but the boy had been called away? Flek raised a questioning eyebrow at his master, and Ronec leapt to his feet and strode out towards the stables, Flek following at a trot. He checked the stall in the stables to find Merewyn's horse was still missing; one of the younger boys was mucking it out.

'You boy! Do you know what time the Lady went riding?' he shouted. The boy was struck dumb at first, but after a hearty clout from Flek, he pulled his forelock.

'They went with Cadec at about midday, your Lordship,' he said, backing away at the expression on Ronec's face.

'Where is this Cadec now?' Flek hissed at the boy, raising his hand again.

'His mother was taken terrible ill, so Bailiff let him go visit, Sir.'

Ronec punched one hand into the other in frustration while the boy flinched.

'Saddle my horse and bring it,' out, he shouted as he headed to find the Bailiff who was in charge of the outside servants and tenants. Ten minutes later, he was cantering out of the castle with Flek and three of his men to find the village only a mile away where the mother of the unfortunate Cadec lived.

Cadec knew that it would be better to disappear for a few days, so he had invented the tale of his mother's illness. He heard the thunder of hooves from inside the tiny cottage, and he bustled his complaining mother and young brother up the ladder to the straw filed loft platform. He listened to the shouts from outside and decided to go out and feign slowness and ignorance after carefully hiding his coins behind a loose stone in the chimney breast.

'That's him!' shouted Flek recognising the young man and swiftly dismounting with the others while Cadec put a confused but worried expression on his face as he was dragged over to Ronec.

'You went riding today with the Lady Merewyn and her maid, is that right?' asked Ronec. The boy nodded and kept his puzzled expression.

'But you abandoned them to see to a sick mother, is that also right? Is your mother sick?' asked Ronec, gesturing towards the cottage.

'Yes, my Lord, but the Lady bade me to go. They were riding further west, and Dorca, the maidservant, knew my mother was ill, so the Lady looked sad and told me to go and be with my mother.' Cadec tried to put the most innocent expression on his face that he could muster.

The silence hung in the air for several seconds as Ronec looked thoughtfully at the boy and then nodded to Flek. The first blows fell on his head and chest. Cadec braced as he had been expecting them. Before long, he was on the ground, and the kicks were coming thick and fast.

'Enough,' said Ronec as they pulled the bruised young man

to his feet but held him tightly.

'So tell me again, but this time the truth. Where were they heading?' he asked.

However, Cadec stuck rigidly to his story despite several more blows, and Ronec was inclined to think he knew no more.

'So she is heading west to Morlaix as I thought, and I intend to catch up with her.'

'Flek, go back to the castle now, get a piece of her clothing, and summon the houndsman. Meet us at the ford.' He turned to give Cadec another look, and he surprised a sudden look of concern on the young man's face, concern for whom? For Merewyn? He frowned. There is more to this; he thought as the boy quickly looked away and shuffled his feet.

'Wait, keep hold of him, Roget, burn the cottage,' he shouted to his men.

Cadec watched with horror as the men piled straw and kindling in front of the cottage and then set fire to it. He strained against the men holding him, 'Sire, my mother and brother are inside, I promise you I know no more,' he shouted in desperation.

Ronec let the flames flicker higher for a few minutes; they were catching quickly on the dry timber structure and would soon reach the thatch. Watching the boy's face, he finally relented, 'Let him go,' he shouted as he turned his horse away and his men mounted up to follow behind him. Cadec, released and thrown to the ground, now leapt to his feet, kicked the burning door open and raced inside. He found his coughing, terrified mother and young brother coming down the loft ladder and, quickly retrieving his coins from the chimney, he pushed them out of the doorway, just as the flames took hold on the roof. Cadec stood, gasping lungful's of fresh air; he glared after the riders, his arms around his family, as he felt the heat from the fire behind him on his back. In his heart, he prayed that Lord Ronec and his men would miss the Lady Merewyn and Dorca and that this knight would get his just deserts from Luc De Malvais if he harmed them.

Chapter Twenty-Six

Luc's spirits had been buoyant as he rode out of Saint-Brieuc. He was imbued with a determination that his duty to his King must come first. However, by the time they had ridden for several hours, rested at the tiny hamlet of Plancoet and watered the horses in the river Aguenon, the anger and frustration had built again inside him. Many of the villagers came out to wave and cheer as they rode through the area that was loyal to Alain Rufus and the King, but many also fell silent when they saw the stern, forbidding expression on his face.

Finally, they approached Dinan, and Luc was surprised to see so few tents and pavilions around the fortress. He settled his men into one of the large meadows and left Gerard in charge as he rode up through the vast gates to pay his respects to the Castellan, Lord St Vere, and his wife. He was quickly shown into the Great Hall, where several knights were congregating. One separated from the group, walking towards Luc, his arms outstretched.

'You are a sight for sore eyes. You had us all worried, Malvais; we thought you had changed sides,' laughed the young man. Luc returned the bear hug and clasped arms with several of the others.

'You should know better than that, San Loup; we just ran into a few problems with Ralph De Gael and his cronies that delayed us. Unfortunately, De Gael is gathering a prodigious amount of allies to his banner. We are in for a tough fight, Michel.' San Loup gestured to the other knights. 'We were left here by William to wait for you. He could not stay any longer. He had to leave to support Duke Hoel, who has surrounded the fortress at Dol. He raised the banners early this morning and has gone on ahead only a few hours ago.'

Luc ran his hands through his hair in exasperation. William had never been a patient man, and Luc blamed himself; he had delayed the King; he was nearly five days later than expected.

'We will rest the horses and men here tonight, and we will all ride out at dawn tomorrow morning,' he declared, to nods of agreement from the assembled men. Refreshments were brought and enjoyed, and then slowly, the knights dispersed to their camps to ready their men for departure the next day. Luc left to sit by the huge fire reflected on what he had just heard. He drank his wine and waved the Steward over for another.

'Saint-Vere does know I am here?' he asked in an exasperated voice. The man nodded and said he would ascertain if his lordship were ready to receive Luc. Another fifteen minutes went by, and Luc was now striding around the Hall when the Steward returned.

'This way, my Lord Malvais,' he said, showing Luc up to the Solar. This was a large family room, facing east with glass-paned, leaded windows that looked out over the river and reflected the wealth Saint-Vere had accumulated as Castellan for the Counts de Penthievre.

As soon as he entered the room, Luc knew why there had

been a delay; Lord Saint-Vere stood by the fireplace, a stern look of disapproval on his face. His wife was sitting in a chair, her bible on her knee, while opposite him and beside her sat Briaca, looking as beautiful and desirable as ever.

Luc gave a formal bow. 'It is good to see you again, my Lord', he said, nodding in greeting to the ladies present. Briaca sat, hands clasped, and did not raise her eyes to his. The silence hung in the air for what seemed like minutes, but then the laws of hospitality reasserted themselves as the Lady Ida put her book on the side table and, walking forward, she held out her hands to take his.

'Welcome Luc, I hope your mother is well,' she said.

'I have not seen her for some weeks, but I believe so,' he answered, looking at the still rigid countenance of Saint-Vere.

Finally, the Castellan spoke. 'I wish I could welcome you with the generosity of my wife, Malvais, but as you can see, our daughter Briaca has returned to us,' he said. Luc looked full at Briaca, and for the first time, she raised her huge blue eyes to his.

'She tells us she is with child and that it is yours, Malvais. This was not what we planned for her when we sent her to live under your mother's protection,' he said, the anger unmistakable in his voice. Luc said nothing as he continued.

'She tells me that you seduced her,' he growled at Luc, who crossed the room to stand in front of Briaca.

'So, you are continuing with this game, Briaca, the lies to destroy my marriage, in the hope that I may turn to you?' he asked with a raised eyebrow. Briaca went deathly pale as her father shouted, 'Explain yourself, Malvais! What do you mean?'

'Your daughter tried to trick me, Saint-Vere. She waited

until I was carried drunk to my room at the Inn, and then she removed my clothes and came naked into my bed to lie beside me, nicking her arm or leg with a fruit knife to make me think I had taken her virginity.' he said in an emotionless voice. Lord Saint-Vere scoffed, 'So how do you explain the child? Another virgin birth perhaps?' he spluttered. His wife tutted at his sacrilege and laid a hand on his arm to calm him.

'I am sorry, Luc. As you can see, we are very angry and upset about what has happened to Briaca and, if this is true, I must apologise for her actions,' she said, glaring down at her daughter. 'Is this true, child?' she said in a disappointed voice.

This was too much for Briaca, who was horrified that Luc had worked out what she had done, and the tears welled and rolled down her cheeks as she nodded to her mother, who turned and then slapped her hard across the face, leaving a huge red welt.

'That is for lying to us and for making your father look like a fool in front of Lord Malvais,' she said, her face a mask of anger at her daughter. 'Do you know whose child it is Malvais? Is it your brother's?' she said hopefully.

'Unfortunately not, I believe the father to be Ronec Fitz-Eudo, a guest in our house over Yuletide,' said Luc.

Saint-Vere was spitting with rage and frustration. 'One of Eudo's bastards,' he spat. 'I think I remember him, a mercenary who has no land,' he added.

'He has wealth now and a few manors, and until recently, I regarded him as a friend. But not now, he is in the pay of Ralph De Gael; he used Briaca as a willing pawn to destroy my marriage and to try and delay me reaching the King.' Saint-Vere looked horrified and glared at his perfidious and treacherous daughter.

'Will he marry her? If not, she is bound for the convent,' he declared.

Luc went deadly quiet and then sighed. 'He might be persuaded to do that; after all, she is a considerable heiress. But there is just one problem.' He paused for a few seconds as all three waited for him to continue. 'I intend to find him, and I will kill him for what he has done,' he said in an ice-cold tone that chilled Briaca to the bone.

Merewyn galloped up the forest track as if the hounds of hell were on her heels. The problem lay with the poorer horseflesh that Dorca was riding, as she was struggling to keep up with the fleet-footed mare. Every few miles, they walked the horses on a loose rein for a while so that Dorcas' palfrey would not be blown, but Merewyn found herself constantly looking back and listening. She knew just how much distance the big warhorses could cover with their endless stamina; their huge strides just ate up the miles, and a few hours start was no guarantee that they would not catch them before they reached the Inn. She just prayed that the ruse had worked and that they were searching the road to Morlaix for them. She felt a little guilty about Cadec, she knew they would find him, but he could not tell them what he did not know.

Unfortunately, for Merewyn, Ronec and his men had met one of their own patrols on the Morlaix road after only five minutes of riding; they had pulled up immediately to question them.

'You there, Serjeant, have you seen two women on horseback on this road? We think they are heading for Morlaix,' shouted Ronec.

'No, my Lord, we are riding from Morlaix. We have been there for a few days on the orders of Fitz-Eustace, watching the castle, but we have seen no riders today, only carters and wagons,' he said.

Ronec circled his horse, waving the patrol on and frantically thinking. Had they pulled off the road when they heard or saw the patrol, he wondered? He knew there was a large hamlet a few miles ahead, so he decided to canter on. His men watered the horses while he questioned the blacksmith, and Flek talked to a few of the villagers, but they drew a blank; no riders had passed through the village apart from the patrol.

Then it dawned on him; she had lied to the young stable boy to throw them off the scent. She had gone north, back to Malvais, damn her. Ronec cursed and leapt into the saddle, waving his men on as they scrambled to mount their horses and follow him. He gave his big-boned chestnut warhorse its head and galloped back towards Gael. He was determined to catch her before she reached Saint-Brieuc. He would make her pay; her and that insolent handmaid of hers had taken him for a fool.

Merewyn was exhausted and cold. Night had come down, and the temperature had dropped, so, after a short rest and some bread and cheese that Cadec had thoughtfully provided, they wearily mounted up again. She winced painfully as she climbed back into the saddle, they had been travelling for about five hours, and she knew it was not much further. She turned and gave Dorca an encouraging smile as she trotted on up the track. They cantered for only a short while, as the horses were tiring as well; a few miles later, she heard the sound she had been dreading, the distant baying of a hound. It was Ronec pursuing her; he had brought the running hounds, the lymers who had a powerful sense of smell, as she suspected he might. It was now a hue and cry and a matter of whether they could escape to the Inn before the hounds found them. She had seen the hunting dogs at home bring down a horse before and tear it to pieces before the terrified fugitive, and she feared for her beautiful little mare. She also knew that if Ronec caught her, his anger would know no bounds, and she would become his prisoner in reality, with all that it would entail. She shouted at Dorca to run and galloped off through the trees ducking wildly to avoid the overhanging and low branches. She cast her mind back to the times she had been hunting with her father and brother, Garrett, in the forests around Ravensworth, and she searched her memory for what the foxes and wolves had done to throw dogs off the scent.

The horses were beginning to flag, so they slowed to a trot, just as they heard the loud clamouring in the distance of dogs who have found the scent, followed by the echoing shouts of men echoing down the valley. Merewyn quailed at the thought of him catching her before they reached the Inn. She knew she would be hauled over to him and tied over his saddle, entirely at his mercy, and she dreaded to think what his men would do with Dorca when Ronec recognised her. This thought spurred her on; the Inn on Saint-Brieuc's outskirts was at the head of this valley. She glanced down to her left and looked at the fast-flowing stream; it was full and deep after the recent rains, and an idea came to her. She waved Dorca to follow her, taking the two horses into the water. It came up to their knees in places as they slowly picked through the rocks and boulders. It took nerves of steel to pick their way as they listened to the louder sounds of pursuit behind. She brought the horses out on the other side and cantered up the left-hand riverbank into the trees before eventually going back towards the wider stream and into the water. She hoped to confuse the hounds enough to give them time to reach the Inn. The hounds now sounded so close it was terrifying, and Dorca's eyes were huge in her pale, waif-like face as, emerging back to join the track, they both broke into a gallop forcing the tired horses on.

Ronec had felt elated for a while when the hounds had undoubtedly found a fresh scent in the clearing. He realised that they were now very close and would catch her before reaching the Inn or Malvais. He smiled at the thought of how he would drag her to her knees and make her pay for humiliating him. Now, however, they had been standing on the edges of the stream for several minutes, as the hounds seem to have lost the scent. They finally found it further up on the opposite bank, but then they lost it again.

'Clever girl, Merewyn,' he muttered from between clenched teeth, his anger building again. Then a thought occurred to him, and he shouted at the houndsman.

'Bring some of the dogs on this side further up. They may have crossed back.'

He waited impatiently as the dogs splashed across, then suddenly, there was a howl, and they were off and running, the horses following at speed up the clearer wooded slopes at the head of the valley.

Merewyn could smell the wood smoke and peat from the houses, and she was sure she could see the odd light up ahead through the trees. She felt a ray of hope. Suddenly, she heard the baying hounds behind her, and Dorca's horse stumbled and went down on its knees, its sides heaving. Merewyn whirled her mare in a circle and cantered back. Fortunately, Dorca was unhurt, and she scrambled to her feet, brushing off mud and leaves.

'Get up behind me quickly,' shouted Merewyn, reaching down a hand and swinging her up.

Merewyn urged the plucky little mare onwards, now carrying both of them; the sound of the pursuit was directly behind them. She burst out of the trees onto the main track and the crossroads that led east through the village and west to the Inn. Merewyn swept around the corner, the mare sliding badly on the damp leaves and mud, but she was sure-footed and kept her course. Glancing back, Merewyn saw the large pack of dogs leaping out of the trees a hundred yards behind them with Ronec galloping behind them on his foam-flecked chestnut Destrier, spurring the big chestnut on now he had his quarry in sight. She saw him grin as he realised he was going to catch them; her heart was in her mouth as she realised he probably would. Suddenly, the large wood-framed Inn was there just in front of them on the bend, and she yelled at Dorca.

'Get ready to jump off and run into the Inn. Save yourself, Dorca.'

Merewyn was perturbed because she saw that the Inn was deathly quiet. There were no horse warriors outside, only a sleepy stable boy waiting as they skidded into the cobbled yard. They were too late. She sobbed in frustration; there was no one here to help them. She did not doubt that Ronec would drag her, kicking and screaming from the Inn, oblivious to any pleas from the Innkeeper or his wife.

Chapter Twenty-Seven

Dorca was running frantically for the Inn door and, Merewyn hearing the loud panting of the dogs and Ronec's chestnut clattering onto the cobbles behind her, threw the reins of the plucky mare to the boy, screaming at him to get the horses to safety in the stables and away from the hounds. She raced in, pushing the heavy oak door shut behind her. She saw Dorca just inside the hallway gasping for breath, terror on her face. Merewyn grabbed her hand.

'Come on,' she yelled; she pushed open the pot room door, standing there dishevelled and panting on the threshold. She blinked at the scene in front of her in the large room.

Ronec watched them dash into the Inn, but he was not worried; he knew that Malvais and his men were gone, and he probably only had an injured Morvan to deal with inside, he would not stop him taking Merewyn. He vaulted out of the saddle, ordered the houndsman to control the barking, snapping hounds and waved several of his men to follow him into the Inn. There was no sign of life in the dimly lit hall, so he drew his sword and stepped forward with his men to push open the pot room door, and there, he stopped dead. Merewyn and her handmaid were in the corner behind Morvan, who stood sword in hand, but about twenty horse warriors, swords drawn, were in front of them. Ronec lowered his sword, his lips tight with anger, and then the old Ronec emerged as he gave a bark of laughter. He knew when he was beaten. Morvan walked slowly forward, hatred and loathing clear on his face.

'Thank you, Beorn; your men can stand down, for now, Ronec Fitz-Eudo is leaving.'

Ronec looked across the room at Merewyn standing proud and beautiful in the candlelight; her head raised high, every inch a Thegns daughter. He met her eyes.

'I do love you, Merewyn,' he said. 'It was not just for Ralph De Gael's plan,' he added as he turned to go. This was too much for Morvan, who gripped his shoulder and spun him around.

'Luc will kill you, Ronec; he is waiting to see you face to face; that is the only reason you are walking out of here alive. And I promise you that if he doesn't, then I will,' he said, in a calm, cold voice.

Ronec, gazing into those hard, blue eyes, and thought yes, he had tempted fate, thrown the dice and lost, and no one would want both of the Malvais brothers as enemies. He did not doubt that one day he would pay the price; his only regret was that he had never made love to Merewyn, never made her his own. He nodded curtly to Morvan, and, with a last long glance at Merewyn, he turned on his heel and left with his men.

Luc declined the offer of dinner with Lord Saint-Vere and his family, claiming he had to plan with his captains for a very early start. Saint-Vere nodded, knowing the real reason; he understood, and he was ashamed of his daughter.

'I am sending my nephew and fifty men with you, Malvais. He is young and full of high spirits; I would be grateful if you would put him under the wing of one of William's more sensible knights,' he said.

Luc nodded and clasped arms with the older man in farewell as he headed out into the night. He stood for a while on the escarpment beyond the keep, gazing down at the hundreds of campfires below in the descending dusk. He had intended to gallop off with his men tomorrow, but now, on William's orders, he had hundreds of foot soldiers, pikemen, archers and a dozen knights who were looking to him for leadership.

For a few moments, he took several deep breaths, breathing in the wood smoke and clearing his head. He suddenly thought of Merewyn, and he felt the usual stab of pain and anguish at the thought of her as a hostage in Ronec's room and Ronec's bed, according to Morvan's spies. The white-hot anger built inside him again, but he purposefully pushed it away, along with all thoughts of her, as he strode down to the pavilions below to coordinate tomorrow's departure with William's knights and his captains.

The war banners were raised in the early dawn with a cacophony of sound. As horns blared, campfires extinguished, tents and pavilions, dismantled to be packed onto carts and wagons, which set off immediately, pulled by burly oxen. He rode around the campground on Espirit to loosen both of their muscles after a night on the ground. Heads turned as he passed, not only at the sight of the enormous dark grey dappled stallion, but this was Malvais, whose reputation was second to none. The men cheered as he rode by, and he raised a fist in salute. He cast an eye over his own horse warriors, who were being checked and assembled by Gerard. Mud was being brushed from horses' coats and short docked tails, and the usual melee of barging, whinnying and snapping teeth was taking place as some of the stallions moved too close together. He laughed aloud as one hapless rider received a hard cuff from Gerard for letting his horse bite its neighbour. The man was lucky; it was a serious offence; a horse bite could be particularly nasty for man and beast and could quickly become infected.

Before long, they were all mounted. Luc glanced at the castle; the early rising sun was just touching the battlements where he could see dozens of people gathered, eager to see the departure.

He whirled his horse around and waved to the squires, who blew several long blasts on the horns. The Breton Horse Warriors moved into a tight formation, five abreast, row after row, after row, over four hundred of them lined up behind Luc and Gerard, harnesses jingling, saddles creaking, the men upright with their signature, laced, leather doublets and crossed swords on their backs. They looked so impressive that even the other knights had expressions of awe on their faces. Luc raised a hand to Saint-Loup, who was in charge of the following cohorts of foot soldiers, and they moved forward out of the meadows onto the road leading to the ford and on to the citadel town of Dol.

Luc knew the pace would be slow to keep the company together, and he estimated that they would not reach William until dusk at the earliest. He sent outriders and scouts ahead through the forests; he would not put it past De Gael to launch lightning attacks to prevent or slow this force's advance from reaching William.

Gerard rode beside him, his face set in grim lines. They were not fatalists, but they were experienced warriors who knew they were riding off to war, and some of their men would not return, or they could be permanently maimed. War could be exciting and exhilarating at first, but they both knew that war was not a game; it would be dangerous, messy and bloody. As they reached the ford at the River Rance, Luc glanced back at the serried ranks making their way down the hill behind them, and he felt proud of his riders' skills. Warhorses were trained, but they had a fiery temperament, and to ride them flank to flank, nose to tail, was no mean feat with some of these stallions. The column must stretch back over a mile, he thought, and then there were the carts, the camp followers, pedlars and hangers-on following behind. The noise of so many horses and men would be heard for miles around; his eyes automatically scanned the treeline for any watching enemy scouts.

Luc cantered through the ford and up the opposite hill. Gerard followed, and they sat on a slight rise watching the moving column as he waved his captains past.

'Thank God we are not moving siege engines as well; they would be a pig to get through that ford and up this hill,' Gerard commented.

Luc nodded as they both remembered a dark day when a vast wooden trebuchet had toppled sideways in a river and killed two men outright, trapping them under the fast-flowing water.

They watched the last of the horse warriors cross, and then they cantered on to return to the front of the column to join the King in his siege and attack on the town of Dol.

Merewyn had let out a breath of relief as Ronec turned and left the Inn, and now she sank back onto the settle and smiled her gratitude at Morvan. The Inn had been so quiet because Morvan had assembled Beorn and the horse warriors from Vannes inside the pot room to describe what their next move would be. She was surprised and relieved when she had flung open the pot room door to find over forty men in there with Morvan. The men had stared in dismay as she had suddenly yelled, 'Help me!' she had slammed the pot room door shut behind her and Dorca, and then pandemonium had broken loose as they all scrambled for swords.

She quietly admitted to herself that she had enjoyed the expression on the faces of Ronec and his men when they had stormed through the pot room door and stopped dead, facing a sea of drawn swords. However, inexplicably, she did experience a fleeting moment of melancholy for the loss of the amusing and flirtatious knight who had kept her entertained during the winter at Morlaix. She had worked out that Ronec enjoyed falling in love, probably with numerous women, although she knew that he had been using her for his own ends.

Merewyn signalled to the shocked Innkeeper to bring refreshments, and she sent a relieved Dorca with him to get a hot meal in the kitchen.

'I was hoping that Luc would still be here, but he has undoubtedly left to join the King?' she asked. Morvan nodded.

'He had no choice, Merewyn, he is Luc De Malvais and duty, honour, loyalty to his Liege Lord and King will always come first, no matter how much he loves you,' he answered.

He watched as a flash of anger lit her eyes.

'If he loves me, then why did he bed Briaca Saint-Vere Morvan? Why has he set her up as his mistress at Morlaix to raise both of his children? He has even stopped me from going to Lusian,' she cried, breaking into a heart-wrenching angry sob. The adrenalin from the flight through the forest had evaporated, leaving her exhausted and heartbroken. Morvan pulled her into his arms and hugged her as much as his broken ribs would allow.

'No, Merewyn, you have heard the lies that Ronec has fed you,' he said, holding her at arm's length, as she raised her tear-drenched huge green eyes to his in hope. He then proceeded to explain the plan that Ronec, Geoffrey Fitz-Eustace and Briaca had hatched between them. Merewyn's mouth dropped open as she listened.

'So Luc did not betray me, and the child is not his', she whispered.

Morvan nodded. 'Briaca has gone. She was sent away from Morlaix, back to her parents. I only hope that Luc does not strangle her if he sees her at Dinan.'

Merewyn could feel the anger and rage building inside her as she thought about what the girl had done to destroy her marriage. It all fell into place now, Luc's distant behaviour and moods, because he was consumed with guilt for what he thought he had done and then the added trauma of a child to explain, as Briaca's pregnancy advanced. No wonder he was tormented. She shook her head in disbelief.

'I must send a message to him, Morvan, to let him know that I have escaped from Gael and that I know everything,' she said, raising pleading eyes to him. Morvan just looked away and stared out into the crowded room.

'What is it, Morvan? What is wrong?' she cried.

Morvan leaned forward and took her hands. 'Yes, it was all a lie, but I do not know if Luc will ever forgive you. You ran away willingly with Ronec Fitz-Eudo, not to Morlaix but to Gael, to the rebel stronghold. You then shared Ronec's bed night after night; you may even be carrying his child.' Suddenly the room seemed to go quiet around her as the horror of Morvan's words penetrated her tired mind. Her eyes opened wide, and she looked at Morvan in shock.

'Yes, I ran away, she gasped. 'Luc had just told me that Briaca was carrying his child. I set off, but I thought we were heading to Morlaix to get Lusian and return to Ravensworth and my father,' she said.

Morvan nodded. 'I went after you. I know where you turned south and headed to Gael. I was there, Merewyn; I talked to the servants. I know you shared his bed every night. Was that your revenge on Luc?' he asked.

'Is that what Luc thinks?' she gasped.

Morvan nodded. Merewyn took a deep breath. 'He never touched me, Morvan. Yes, I slept beside him for two nights, but he never forced me to make love to him. He wanted me to come to him of my own accord. I could not do that, as I still loved Luc, despite what he had done to me. I could not betray him,' she said.

Morvan looked utterly taken aback. 'You must tell Luc this. You must send a message. He is distraught at the thought of you giving yourself to Ronec, and he blames himself for not seeing through Briaca and her lies.'

'No!' shouted Merewyn loudly, standing up and pushing the table back so that several heads turned towards them. 'I am not sending a message; I need to see him face to face to tell him this. I am going to find him,' she declared. Morvan could see the determination on her face and finally nodded.

'Our commander from Vannes, Beorn and his cohort are leaving first thing tomorrow to join Luc. But you cannot go with them, you need to rest yourself and the horses,' he said. She sat down again as a wave of tiredness engulfed her. 'Go to your room; I will have a hot meal sent up. Get a good night's sleep. We will talk tomorrow morning,' he said. She nodded, and he walked her to the bottom of the stairs, where she turned and kissed his cheek and then ran her fingers over his bruised face.

'Thank you, Morvan, for putting yourself in danger for me,' she said, her hand on his shoulder. He smiled down at her, and she could see Luc in that smile which wrenched at her heartstrings as she turned and made her way up the stairs.

Morvan stood for a few moments, watching her go before turning to go to the stable block to check on her mare and the servant's horse. 'What a mess,' he thought and then swore under his breath. 'Someone will pay for this,' he muttered.

Merewyn was already down and breaking her fast amongst the men when he came into the pot room the following day.

'You could have had this sent to your room,' he said, wrinkling his nose at the smells of stale beer and bodies. Several of the Horse Warriors who had overindulged were wrapped in their blankets on the floor and settles. Merewyn smiled, waving a hand at the scene around her.

'I am used to this, Morvan; I was brought up in a Saxon warrior household and village where all of the men tried to outdo each other in drinking prodigious amounts,' she smiled. Morvan grinned back, liking her even more. 'Now, sit down and tell me why William is helping Duke Hoel to 'invest' Dol; I only managed to pick up a few facts at Gael,' she said.

Morvan pulled up a stool and sat down, tearing a large chunk of warm crusty bread to go with his cheese. 'The dispute goes back several years, Merewyn, and it is linked to the church. King William supports Juhel, the archbishop of Dol. However, the inhabitants, merchants and the Lord of Dol wanted the Pope to depose Juhel because he refused to build them an abbey, and they put forward their own candidate. However, neither side won as Juhel was ousted; the Pope brought in his own man as the Bishopric of Dol is a very powerful position. Both sides were furious, but Pope Gregory was playing a longer game. In the past, he has always supported William, keeping him on his side, but not this time.

Over a month ago, Hoel, the Duke of Brittany, decided to attack Dol to force the reinstatement of Juhel as the Archbishop of Dol. This is William's goal as well, so he is riding to support Duke Hoel. Geoffrey De Grenonant, the nephew of Eudo, is holding the Citadel of Dol against them, with the help of a few other rebel Breton Lords. 'Merewyn nodded, a puzzled look on her face.

'So is this why Eudo, the father of Alain Rufus, is going to be fighting against William for the first time?' she asked.

'Yes, combined with the fact that Count Eudo hates Duke Hoel, as the Duke once imprisoned him for several years. Unfortunately, Count Fulk of Anjou also sees this as an opportunity for a war against William and his allies. He has sent Angevin troops to assist Eudo; they are now marching on Dol from the southwest. Then, into this, also comes the rebel Earl, Ralph De Gael, fresh from England, who also hates

William and has raised his banners and is marching from the south on Dol,' explained Morvan.

Merewyn looked alarmed. 'So there are at least three huge alliances against William and Hoel, do they have a chance of winning?' she asked.

Morvan looked thoughtful. 'William has thousands of seasoned troops and, of course, he has the Horse Warriors, if they get there on time. He is also a seasoned commander in battle, his fearsome reputation counts for a lot. At one siege that held out for too long against him, he had the hands and feet of all the survivors chopped off when he starved them out, and they surrendered. The next castle he laid siege to surrendered very quickly.'

Merewyn paled at the thought, but she still feared for Luc in such a battle. He would always be in the thick of it, leading his men. Morvan stood up. 'I expect we will be able to leave tomorrow if Luc's physician allows me to leave,' he said with a rueful grin. Merewyn shook her head.

'Morvan, you cannot ride that distance with broken ribs,' she declared.

'I will strap them up in a stiff leather band. I will be fine, and you will need my help when you meet Luc,' he said. 'He will find it difficult to believe you at first, and he will be furious that you have put yourself in danger by coming to the battlefield. Luc at war is a different man, Merewyn. He will not have time for you, and I am not sure that he will even agree to see you,' he said.

Chapter Twenty-Eight

J ust as dawn was breaking, Luc stood beside King
William, on Mont Dol's crest, a small hill nearly two
hundred feet high, north-west of the town. On top of
the flattened plateau were the small Chapelle of St Michel
and a windmill behind him. The position gave them a perfect
view of the terrain and the surrounding countryside. Luc had
explained to the King that 'Dol' was a Breton word meaning
a low and fertile place, and it was certainly that. The Citadel
was built on a flood plain, the large estuary of the River
Guyoult spreading into extensive and treacherous marshes to
the walled town's north and east. Luc frowned as he surveyed
the scene.

'Sire, that area will be totally inaccessible to the Horse
Warriors,' he said, indicating the few miles or so of marshland
wreathed in mist. William nodded.

'A frontal assault is the best option. Duke Hoel has besieged
the Citadel for over six weeks now. They were on the verge
of surrender when reinforcements arrived a few days ago in
the guise of our enemy Ralph De Gael,' he spat.

Luc remained silent. He had already felt the King's
wrath and displeasure at some length for his tardiness in
arriving at Dinan. He knew that if they had been here, the

Horse Warriors would have driven off De Gael's attack and incursion in a Coup de Main, a pre-emptive strike on the firmer ground in the south, which would have prevented De Gael from reaching the citadel with hundreds of men and supplies. Now, not only was De Gael ensconced with Geoffrey De Grenonant inside the Citadel of Dol, but also new rebel forces were arriving daily from the southeast.

'I see Eudo De Penthievre's banners are flying,' said William, pointing at the rebel encampment with an accusing glance at Malvais. Luc took a deep breath.

'I used every persuasive argument my Lord King; he insists he is not fighting against you. His nephew is holding the Citadel against their mutual enemy, Duke Hoel. He has promised to keep his troops out of it for as long as possible, and he did give us vital information about Philip of France possibly moving to take the Vexin.'

William did not reply but nodded curtly before adding, 'Every man who is not with me is against me, Malvais, no matter how they try to play it. Do not be taken in by these blurred lines that they draw.' He turned his piercing gaze on Luc.

'At the moment, we are employing the Fabian strategy to avoid pitched battles, but it may well come to it that we have no choice but to launch an attack, Malvais. Deploy your men along that ridge to the southwest, which will protect our right flank and prevent them from encircling us. The marshes to the north will provide us with the same amount of protection on our left flank as it provides for the rebels in Dol.'

Luc nodded; he knew the Fabian strategy, a war of attrition in continuous small attacks that would suit his horse warriors and allow them to inflict maximum damage in minimal time.

'Do not fail me, Malvais,' said William, as he turned and made his way back to the large central pavilion on the plateau.

Luc bowed but remained in place on the crest a while longer, analysing every geological feature and how he could use it to his advantage. His gaze returned to the Citadel and Duke Hoel's considerable forces positioned in front of it. He had been to Dol a few times in the past. The city walls were impressive but old, and he was certain parts of them, just like in Rennes, dated back to Roman times. A significant feature of Dol was the fortified cathedral of Saint-Samson, which had actually been built as a defensive bastion into the walls of the town. It looked almost impregnable. He knew, however, that William had taken Dol before, in 1065, from Hoel's predecessor, Duke Conan, so the King was well aware of the town's strengths and weaknesses. This time though, there was a much more extensive array of rebel Breton Lords, and though Luc felt they were evenly matched, he had an uneasiness at Fulk of Anjou's eagerness to send a large contingent of Angevin troops to Dol. How many more might he send and where? With this in mind, he had already sent out his Vedettes mounted pickets at two-mile intervals around the western, southern and eastern approaches. He had done what he could for the present, so he set off to move the Horse Warriors to the long southwestern ridge, as ordered.

Ronec thought of himself as a person who took a light-hearted view of life. He was successful, he had a well-earned reputation as a formidable warrior, and he was gradually accumulating wealth and land. Yet as he threw off his blankets and extracted himself from his truckle bed, he felt disgruntled. His manservant, Flek, was out of bed, had poured his breakfast ale and was brushing the mud from his clothes. He had arrived at Dol three days ago and was pleased to see that Ralph had taken control and was now inside the Citadel. Ronec had joined Geoffrey Fitz-Eustace in the rebel encampment and was now using his own men to defend the camp against the daily attacks launched by William and the Breton Horse Warriors.

Ronec had studied their position with interest; Although Hoel seemed to have several siege machines and dozens of scaling ladders, he appeared to be following a policy of 'Siege en regle', with no direct attacks or bombardment. Instead, he had 'invested' Dol, allowing no one in or out. This strategy had been damaged by Ralph's successful attack and triumphant entry into Dol with most of his forces. Now there was a lull, as both sides seemed to be waiting for the next move. The scouts had reported the arrival of Malvais, with a force of over a thousand strong, including hundreds of Horse Warriors. That news had created a nervous tension in many of the Breton lords, who were reluctant to face them in battle. Not so, for Fulk and his Angevins, who had constantly attacked Maine's borders, they hated the Horse Warriors and wanted revenge.

Ronec had no qualms about fighting fellow Bretons, people who may have even been comrades before. Given the constant shift in alliances, a mercenary could not afford to choose. He dressed quickly and strolled through the camp to the smaller pavilion of Fitz-Eustace. He found him deep in conversation with two other knights, one he knew and a tall saturnine-faced knight with a livid scar on his face whom he had not met before. He saw from his colours that he was Angevin, one of Fulk's knights.

'Ah Ronec, just the man,' said Fitz-Eustace flinging an arm around his shoulder. 'I need you and Pierre D'Avray to go and see what is happening on the southwestern ridge. Garbled reports are coming in about a large force assembling there.

Ronec looked at the Angevin Commander, who stared arrogantly back at him. Ronec smiled; he had experienced years of contempt from knights like this, who looked down on mercenary forces, but always called on them when necessary.

'Let us assemble our men, and we will meet at the large standing stone. We can loop round the enemy forces into the higher forested slopes. That will give us a vantage point,' said Ronec.

D'Avray nodded curtly and left. Ronec raised his eyebrows at Fitz-Eustace, who just shrugged. 'We make alliances where necessary, even with Angevins,' he muttered.

The Menhir or standing stone at the hamlet of Champ-Dolent was nearly nine metres high, conical in shape and easily the largest in Brittany. As Ronec sat on his big-boned chestnut waiting for D'Avray, he looked up at the vast, red, granite stone, wondering who had shaped it and why it was brought here. Brittany was full of these stones, remnants of a long-forgotten people who followed the old ways and the old gods. How many warriors from the past, now long dead, had touched this stone, he wondered, placing his hand on the cold granite? He shook his head and gathered up the reins. He was becoming fanciful when he needed to focus on the task ahead. D'Avray arrived with about fifteen of his men, all in Anjou's blue and gold livery, the gold lions rampant on their shields. Ronec smiled and looked at his own men in their soft brown leather and green or grey cloaks.

'Well, they will certainly see you coming,' he said as he whirled his horse around. D'Avray did not reply but narrowed his light blue eyes and sneered, 'We are loyal troops to Count Fulk of Anjou, not jobbing mercenaries who go to the highest bidder and hide who they ride for.'

Ronec's eyes hardened as he turned and met his gaze, and D'Avray was the first to shrug and look away. He now knew exactly who Ronec Fitz-Eudo was, and he was not stupid enough to make an enemy of him.

Ronec squeezed his horse into a canter and headed west, thinking he may be paid to work with these allies, but that did not mean he had to like them as well. They moved softly through the trees on the slopes, avoiding a vedette, sitting on his horse below them. They came to the edge of the forest and looked across to the slightly raised ridge that stretched below and to the north of them. He recognised the banners of Malvais immediately, a black running horse on a blue background. Luc had chosen the position well, ideal for cavalry, as the slope down from the ridge was gentle but would give them momentum as they raced over the top and down the valley. For a fleeting second, he almost wished he was riding with them, but he had chosen his side.

He scanned the force below and estimated that there must be at least four to five hundred men, servants and camp followers on the ridge. Campfires had been lit, but he knew the horses were tethered in horse lines in full tack; they could be mounted and away in minutes. He glanced at Pierre D'Avray and was taken aback to see the Angevins face twisted in a grimace of hate and fury, his hands balled into tight fists.

He followed the man's glare to the end of the ridge and gave a rueful smile. Sitting apart and upright on his huge, dappled steel-grey Destrier was Luc De Malvais, scanning the forces below in front of the citadel.

'You know of Malvais?' he asked D'Avray. The man's mouth worked for a few moments before he answered.

'He gave me this,' he said, pointing to the line that ran from his forehead, through his brow and down to the corner of his mouth, pulling it down into a puckered scar. Ronec smiled.

'So he let you live, then. I wonder why? If he had wanted you dead, he would have taken your head; I have seen him do so at full gallop, dozens of times.' D'Avray's mouth hardened into a thin line.

'I will make him pay when we join in the battle. I will hunt him out and kill him slowly,' he spat in rage, spittle running from his mouth. At that moment, Luc turned and looked full at them, raising a hand in salute.

'He knows we are here?' asked D'Avray in astonishment as they were still in the tree line. Ronec laughed. 'His scouts will have picked us up as soon as we left the camp. We are talking about Luc De Malvais, and his reputation as a warrior and a commander is well deserved.' To D'Avray's surprise, Ronec rode out of the trees and into plain sight with his men. They stayed like that for what seemed like a long time to D'Avray, staring across at each other before Ronec raised his hand to return the salute and then turned to take the information back to Fitz-Eustace and Fulk.

Luc was lost in thought as he contemplated the placement of Hoel's army below. William held over fifty per cent of his men in reserve at present, but the rest he had placed on the flanks of Hoel's forces in front of the Citadel. To the northwest was the considerable encampment of William and his allies, which ran almost up to the slopes of Mont Dol and Williams's command post. Several pavilions were erected there; he made a mental note to send a small contingent of Horse Warriors to defend Mont Dol. To the northeast of Dol lay the equally large rebel encampment, with half a dozen rebel Breton Lords and the Angevin camp. Luc knew that Ralph De Gael was now inside Dol, which meant that Fitz-Eustace would be in charge of the Citadel's remaining forces. Luc mentally dismissed him; he was a reasonable soldier, but he had no imagination and certainly had no staying power. Luc knew he could carry on a war of attrition with his Horse Warriors on that flank, with impunity.

As far as Luc could see, there would be no full-frontal assault at present. William had brought half a dozen powerful siege machines, and Hoel had assembled dozens of scaling ladders, but they all remained immobile at present. Hoel seemed determined to continue his 'investment' of the Citadel, intent on starving them out and persuading them to leave.

Luc sighed and glanced back at his own men. He could hear the bellows of Gerard as he picked out individuals who may not have been up to his exacting standards. As he smiled, one of his vedettes rode up to tell him that a force of what appeared to be Angevin troops had crossed into the forested slopes to the southeast. He thanked the man. He had been expecting more extensive patrols to assess the strength of his force on the ridge, and he stared straight at the stand of trees for a few minutes, then raising a hand in salute until a line of riders appeared. He recognised the big chestnut horse immediately.

'So Ronec, you are here as I suspected and fighting with the Angevin forces, which means you are not with Merewyn. If my luck holds, I will meet you in battle and pay you back for the ill you have done me,' he swore, as Ronec returned his salute and rode back into the trees.

He turned and rode back to his own pavilion, set up beside the horse lines; he was pleased to see that Beorn was waiting for him.

'Well met, Beorn, we were beginning to think you were staying in Vannes.'

Luc smiled, but it did not reach those steel-grey eyes, and he raised an eyebrow at his Captain usually, a reliable and good man.

'No, my Lord, we were ambushed by De Gael's men on the orders of Fitz-Eustace. They attacked us in a deep gully in the forest as we headed for Saint-Brieuc, killing our two scouts. The men fought bravely, sire, but they took us by surprise. We lost five men, and four more were injured; they kept us pinned down for several days.'

Luc's mouth was a thin, grim line. 'And what of the horses?' he asked.

'The horses were unharmed, my Lord, and we brought them with us as remounts.'

Luc nodded his approval. Maybe Fitz-Eustace would be more of a problem than he had thought if it was his own plan that he had executed, but Luc thought it more likely he was acting on his older brother's orders.

'Go and settle your men in, Beorn; Gerard will allocate tents and supplies. Then I want you to place your men in that stand of trees on the forest line. Set out Vedettes, further than usual, we have had some activity in that area,' he said.

As Beorn left, a squire arrived to summon Luc to William's pavilion on Mont Dol. When he arrived, William was deep in conversation with several commanders and knights. Most, including the King, were stood around a large table on which maps and diagrams were placed. In a chair at the head of the table sat Hoel, the Duke of Brittany, with a self-satisfied expression on his face. Luc could imagine that he would be delighted to let William take control of the strategy behind the siege. However, Hoel suddenly launched into a loud explanation of why he had not bombarded or destroyed the Citadel, explaining how he wanted to reoccupy it, put Archbishop Juhel back into power and place Geoffrey De Grenonant's head on a spike on the gatehouse. Luc bowed to the assembled company and addressed William.

'You sent for me, Sire.' William looked up and nodded.

'Yes, Malvais, I need you to start continual raids on the enemy patrols and encampment. Keep them on their toes, keep them harassed. Send men in at night to cut and stampede their horse lines. I want as much confusion and disorder as possible. My spies tell me that the Breton Lords are already arguing amongst themselves. They are not confident in taking us on in a full-frontal assault while their leader, De Gael, is holed up in the Citadel.'

Luc nodded. 'My men will be glad of the action, Sire.' William smiled. He understood the young warrior's frustration, and cavalry always expected action.

'Your time will come Malvais, I believe we have troops from Anjou against us as well,' he said, sending a piercing glance at Luc and knowing the enmity shared between the Horse Warriors and the Angevins while they had been patrolling the borders of Maine. Luc nodded.

'We will put them to the rout, Sire, as we always do.'

William nodded and returned his attention to the table. Luc, dismissed, returned to his men and Gerard to plan lightning attacks on the enemy, day and night. As he strode purposefully down the slopes of Mont Dol, however, his mind returned to Merewyn. Where was she? Were they treating her well? How could she have given herself to Ronec, or had he just taken her? He clenched his fists at the thought and then sighed; this looked as though it would be a long siege, and she could remain a prisoner at Gael for up to six months or longer. He knew that some sieges lasted for years, but Luc relied on William's natural impatience; he was a man of action. He would not want to sit here for too long.

Chapter Twenty-Nine

It was five days later before the physician that Luc had appointed agreed that Morvan's ribs were healing, and he could risk a short ride. Merewyn had been very frustrated by the wait and enforced stay in the inn when she was desperate to reach Luc and talk to him. However, she knew that she had to wait for Morvan; she felt responsible for the terrible beating he had received, and she knew that Luc would never forgive her if Morvan suffered a relapse. Broken ribs were tricky and could easily pierce a lung if not given time to knit and heal, leading to infection and often death.

She came down that morning to break her fast and found Morvan sat dressed for riding, with packed saddlebags next to him on the floor.

'Can you be ready to leave in an hour, Merewyn?' he asked with a grin. Merewyn's heart flipped; he looked so boyish and so like the light-hearted Luc she remembered from Ravensworth. She glanced sternly down at him.

'I thought we had a few days of only gentle riding for an hour or so first?' she queried. 'It is a five-hour ride to Dinan and then another three on to Dol, at least,' she said.

'I promise you, we will do it over two days,' he said, pleading with her. She looked at those laughing blue eyes. Who could possibly resist this handsome young man, she thought?

'I will go and pack,' she said.

Watching her mount the stairs, Morvan breathed a sigh of relief; he was determined to be at the battle of Dol with Luc; a few broken ribs would not stop him; he would strap them up tightly, and they would leave before the physician knew he had even left.

Luc sat on Espirit's back in the chill evening air. The sun was setting, the smoke from the enemy campfires was blowing towards them, and he could smell roast meats. The campaign of attrition was going well, there had been dozens of casualties, mainly among the Angevin troops, and he had to admit he was targeting their patrols. Their own casualties had been light, a few injuries from the skirmishes, all of them minor ones, and one lamed horse, which would recover.

Suddenly, there was an eruption of noise and cheering from the enemy camp. He could see men leaving their campfires and running towards the centre pavilions. Someone had arrived, or something had happened. He quickly scanned his own lines and over to Mont Dol, but there was no disturbance there at all, so it was unlikely that a stray arrow or crossbow bolt had found Hoel or William. He summoned the Serjeant nearby and told him to send some scouts over to find out from their spies in the camp what was happening.

He heard another horse draw up on his left side and presumed the noise had drawn Gerard over to view the scene below. 'They think they have something to celebrate. I have sent scouts in to find out what is happening,' he said

'I already know,' said a deep voice beside him. 'It is Count

326

Fulk the IV of Anjou arriving to take over the leadership of the campaign. My men have been shadowing him for days; fortunately, he has brought only a few hundred more men with him, as he has a considerable force here. However, with his leadership, you may just get the action you desire for your men, Malvais.' Luc turned and bowed.

'Sire. I am honoured you chose to join my vigil.' William laughed at the Horse Warrior; he admired the young man.

'I watch you every day on this ridge, Malvais, itching for action, assessing the situation, and I sympathise with you. At present, I am placating Duke Hoel. However, I believe that this will change in the next few days. Hoel has, yet again, called for a parley with Ralph De Gael; he is waiting for a reply. I know Fulk. I have fought and defeated him several times. He will want to attack.'

Luc nodded. He hoped so, the morale of his men, although reasonable, could be better, and there was a whisper of disease, possibly cholera, in the camps.

'We do need to end this siege, Sire,' he bravely added. William nodded.

'It is not often I let my knights suggest strategy, they often lack the ability to have that essential overview, but in this, you are right, Malvais. I also have other pressing matters in England; I do not want to linger here much longer. I am pleased to see that Count Eudo has followed your advice and is keeping his men in reserve; I was surprised by his decision to join the rebels, but I understand his antipathy for Hoel; he is an arrogant upstart.'

They sat in silence for a few moments longer.

'I like the perspective from here; it gives a different feel to the battlefield with the enemy camp and lines so close,' said

William.

'I would have thought that the view from Mont Dol was perfect, Sire, the enemy cannot be happy to see that you have such a useful viewpoint.' William laughed; he liked Malvais and had a great deal of respect for the young man's ability and judgement.

'It is a very suitable command post, Malvais. Do you know the legend? Of course, you will; being a Breton, you do love your history and legends. Apparently, St. Michel fought Satan on the top of Mount Dol and drove him off. Very appropriate for the current situation.'

Luc smiled and bowed, as William, laughing at his own humour and this good omen, turned his horse back towards his pavilion.

It was late before Morvan and Merewyn approached Dol in the dusk and gazed down at the hundreds of campfires below. It had taken them three days to get here as the first days' rides had taken a lot out of Morvan, who had been pale with a sheen of sweat on his brow, so she had insisted on calling regular halts. However, each day he had improved, and finally, they could see the Citadel towers of Dol in the distance. A vedette and two sentries had already halted them, but all of them had recognised Morvan and pointed him in the direction of Luc's pavilion. They rode through the camp to shouted greetings and raised fists as they saw Morvan and the wife of Malvais. As they pulled up outside the large tent, Merewyn suddenly felt very nervous, and her hands began to shake; so much had happened since she had last seen her husband. She had no idea how he would react or what he would say, but she knew that she loved him, and she was here to try to put things right.

Morvan gingerly dismounted just as Gerard stepped out of the doorway of the tent. He enveloped Morvan in a bear hug that made him wince until he remembered his broken ribs and laughed. It was only as he placed an arm around the young man's shoulders to lead him inside that he glanced up at the figure on the other horse.

'Merewyn!' he exclaimed. 'By all that is good, it is wonderful to see you here. How did you get away from Gael?' She smiled and gracefully dismounted, waving her maid Dorca on the horse behind her to do the same. Walking over to the older knight, she embraced him.

'I will tell you the story later. Dorca here helped me. Is Luc inside?' she asked plaintively. Gerard shook his head.

'No, he is up at William's command pavilion where they are planning an attack tomorrow. Ralph De Gael refuses to come out of the citadel and negotiate with Hoel or William; the rebel Earl has been encouraged by the arrival of Count Fulk himself in the rebel camp. I can imagine an attack is imminent, as we know, William is not a patient man to wait on their by-your-leave.'

Merewyn's shoulders slumped, and her stomach knotted. So here she was, and yet again, he was somewhere else. However, she was stoic.

'I will come in and wait for him. We want some food and wine if possible Gerard; we have been travelling for several days.' Gerard waved her inside but turned and raised an eyebrow at Morvan, who mouthed back at him,

'All will be well,' and grinned. Gerard still looked sceptical as he busied himself, sending the squire and Dorca for food and pouring a goblet of wine for his unexpected guests.

Merewyn smiled as she glanced around the interior of the large pavilion; it could be nothing but a warrior's tent. There were few niceties, even for a wealthy knight such as Malvais. A table and benches were at one side covered in maps and sketches; there was a rough canvas covering on the floor, a brazier for the cold evenings and two truckle beds for the servants. A second room with the doorway tied back led to Luc's much larger wooden camp bed and a thicker large rush mat on the floor. Armour, weapons and harness were scattered throughout.

She sank back into one of the better folding camp chairs, and Gerard handed her the wine.

'I will wait here for his return, Gerard. Meanwhile, you can tell Morvan and me what has been happening. Gerard pulled up a stool and described the past weeks and the lack of action, although he became more animated when he told of Luc's campaign of attacks on the Angevin patrols.

'So, are we outnumbered?' asked Morvan, looking at the diagram on the table, which showed each side's deployment.

'No, we are pretty evenly matched in numbers, but William, as ever, has the advantage as he has more professional seasoned troops. Many of the rebel lords rely on the peasants and tenants from their lands, armed with pikes and billhooks,' he said.

'So we are attacking tomorrow?' said Morvan with enthusiasm. Gerard snorted with derision.

'You cannot believe that Luc will let you ride into battle like that?' he said, pointing at the strapped ribs. Morvan's face fell, but there was a rebellious cast to his mouth and a glint in his eye. Dorca and the young squire arrived back with some roast chickens and fresh bread, and conversation ceased as they all fell to with a vengeance on the food. However, soon Gerard could see both of them visibly drooping.

'Go and lie down, the pair of you; I promise I will wake you when he returns; it will be late.' Merewyn reluctantly agreed and went through into the curtained room, lying down on Luc's bed. She curled up, convinced that she could smell him on the bolster and coverlet, and before long, she had drifted off to sleep. Morvan wrapped his long wool cloak around him and took one of the servant's truckle beds while Gerard arranged a pallet bed for Dorca on the room's far side. Within minutes, Morvan was snoring, leaving Gerard to wonder again in envy at his ability to sleep anywhere.

Luc returned to find Gerard asleep in the chair in the early hours, the candles guttering and the brazier almost out. Luc stood and stretched before picking up some logs and poking the embers back into life. Gerard jumped awake at the sound, and Luc laughed.

'You did not have to wait up for me, you know, the discussions, or should I say arguments, went on for hours.' Gerard interrupted him.

'Guests arrived,' he said, nodding his head in the direction of the truckle beds, and Luc gave a low whistle.

'I wondered how long it would be before he arrived; he is not one to sit idly by,' he said, gazing fondly down at his sleeping younger brother.

'His ribs are still strapped,' muttered Gerard. 'Your hardest task will be keeping him away from the battle,' he added.

Luc nodded. 'Actually, I have just the place for him. I need a Captain for the patrol I am putting in place to guard Mont Dol and Williams's command tents; I need a mobile force to prevent anyone from getting close. He can organise that, but it will keep him well away from what is happening down below.'

Gerard nodded and then added, 'You have another guest.' Luc poured a cup of ale to quench his thirst.

'Who is it?' he asked, barely listening as he unbuckled his swords from his back and unlaced the leather doublet.

'They are still here, in your bed and on a pallet,' said Gerard, indicating the sleeping Dorca. Luc glanced at the sleeping girl; his brow furrowed as he did not recognise her. Then he strode over to the curtained alcove, sweeping back the canvas ready to evict a visiting knight. He stopped dead as he saw the silver-blonde hair spread on the bolster. Merewyn was in his bed. He ran his hand over his eyes and looked again, walking slowly over to gaze down at her.

'How? Why?' he asked Gerard in a whisper while sitting down gently on the edge of the large camp bed. He picked up a long strand of her silken hair and let it run through his fingers, and then he gently stroked her head, watching her breast rise and fall with each breath.

'She will tell you the story; she managed to escape with the help of her maid, but only just. When she galloped up to the Inn, Ronec and his men were just yards behind her,' said Gerard.

Luc's face hardened. 'He is a dead man. A dead man,' he repeated through gritted teeth.

'Is she....?' he started but could not finish.

'Is she unharmed? Well, I could see no sign of any injuries, but I do not know what happened at Gael; she will only talk to you,' said Gerard. Luc nodded, and Gerard closed the canvas covering and left them.

Luc gazed down at his beautiful wife. He loved her, and

he blamed himself in many ways for what had happened, especially for her decision to leave him; he handled it poorly and drove her away. He should have seen through what Ronec and Briaca were planning. They had far too easily duped him. He had to admit that he had been in thrall to Briaca's breath-taking beauty at times. Merewyn had run from him when he had told her about the child, but she had run into danger, no doubt taken in as he had been by the charming Ronec Fitz-Eudo.

The thought of her in Ronec's bed, with him possessing her body, was like a knife twisting in his guts. Had she acquiesced to Ronec to take revenge on him with Briaca? Or had Ronec forced her? He asked himself. The thought of Ronec with Merewyn in his bed, night after night, filled him with fury, and he got up and strode around the room, his fists clenched. Then he stopped and berated himself for losing control of his anger. He was renowned for his calm in a battle or fight; he needed to put these thoughts away until he had spoken to her tomorrow. He stood there indecisive, had she come back to him because she still loved him or just because she wanted access to Lusian? Did she know the truth yet about Briaca, Ronec, and their schemes? Could he ever forgive her if she had gone willingly into Ronec's arms? These questions and others would keep him awake for hours.

Then he made a decision, he peeled off his linen shirt and slowly drawing back the fur coverlet; he gently climbed in beside her and put his arms around her, tucking her head under his chin. He revelled in the softness of her, the warmth from her body and the smell of her hair. He had missed her so much; he would listen to what she had to say tomorrow.

Chapter Thirty

Ronec was equally frustrated by the inaction of this siege of Dol. He rode out daily on sorties and patrols to test the enemy's defences, but these rides were short. Of more concern had been the constant squabbling of the rebel Breton Lords. Having seen the combined size of William and Hoel's armies, some were getting cold feet; some were already quietly sending some of their men back home. Geoffrey Fitz-Eustace tried to keep them in line, but he did not have Ralph's power and forceful personality.

However, the situation had improved with the unexpected arrival of Count Fulk of Anjou. He took control and sidelined Geoffrey, treating him as just another of his knights. Ronec watched and listened with interest; he had worked for Fulk before when he was much younger. He knew him to be an arrogant, unpleasant and ruthless man who had fought with and permanently imprisoned his older brother to allow him to steal the province of Anjou. Although only thirty-two, he was already on his third wife, and rumours abounded about what had happened to the first two.

Ronec strolled into Fulk's pavilion early the following day to accept his orders. As a knight who had brought over fifty mounted men, he was a man of consequence and as such had a place at the table. As he joined them, he found Fulk's eyes on him and looked up to meet their hooded but direct gaze.

'Ah, Ronec Fitz-Eudo, I have several tasks for you today which will become clear shortly.' Ronec nodded, Fulk knew his worth, and he hoped it would be more than a patrol. He needed a Coup-de-Main, a pre-emptive strike on the flanks of Hoel's army to keep his men sharp and keen. At that moment, Count Eudo de Penthievre joined them. Fulk welcomed him warmly; it was a triumph to have someone with the stature of Eudo join them against King William. Eudo glanced around the table and nodded to the lesser Breton lords; then, his eyes settled on Ronec, the son he had never acknowledged.

'Well, Ronec, I hear good things about you. It seems that sending you to serve under Ralph De Gael paid off.' He gave a tight smile, but Ronec could see that it did not reach his piercing, dark brown eyes. Ronec bowed his head to his father as Eudo continued.

'Are you still holding the wife of Malvais? I believe that Saxon blonde beauty has spent weeks in your bed,' he laughed. The attention of all the men around the table was now held, their eyes on Ronec and Fulk looked on in annoyance at such a distraction.

'I am afraid that we have parted, and I believe she is returning to her son in Morlaix,' said Ronec, with a rueful smile and a shrug. 'However, I enjoyed her many charms for a while.' Eudo narrowed his eyes at his son.

'I consider myself to be somewhat of an expert in dalliance,' he said, grandstanding to the room. The men present, knowing his reputation, appreciated the joke and loud guffaws were heard. They all knew that no one's wife was safe if Eudo was around, and even now, in his seventies, his prowess in the bedroom was legendary. Even Fulk put down his map and smiled. Eudo continued, but his jocular tone had changed. 'I was never stupid enough, though, to kidnap and swive the wife of the most formidable warrior in Europe. Malvais will hunt you down, and he will kill you,' he said, in an icy-cold voice.

The silence in the room was deafening as Ronec looked at the tall, striking, old warrior in front of him, his father and the man he had spent the last ten years trying to impress. He shrugged and smiled again.

'We will see,' he said.

Fulk rapped sharply on the table and brought them back to the task in hand. The next hour was spent discussing various strategies, from a full-frontal assault on William and Hoel's forces to a combined attack bringing Ralph De Gael's forces out of the castle to swell the numbers. Eventually, it was decided to launch a surprise attack on Hoel in the early dawn.

'The Angevin troops and the cavalry can hold the horse warriors at bay with a shield wall and an echelon diagonal attack through the forest onto the ridge,' Fulk decided.

Ronec waited impatiently to see where he would be deployed; he wanted to be in the heart of the battle; he needed to ride into war, stabbing and slashing at the enemy to help him exorcise the demons and the anger that seemed to fill him.

'And where will we be used, Sire?' he asked impatiently of Fulk.

'You are to cut the head off the snake, Ronec Fitz-Eudo. You will take fifty warriors and ride south and west in a wide loop to come around behind William's forces, going as far as the marshes' northwestern edge. I have arranged for a local eel catcher to guide you through the marshes on safe paths so that you will arrive from the mist on the north side of Mont Dol early tomorrow. William and his allies will not be expecting an attack from that area; you will have the element of surprise as he has no men stationed there, apart from the odd lookout that I am sure you can take care of. You will then slaughter every man you find as you make your way up the mound to the pavilions on the top, where you will find and kill William.'

The men's faces around the table reflected the shock that he was feeling; it was probably the most dangerous and daring mission that he had undertaken. William and his knights would not give in easily; they would be ready to die for their king. Ronec took a deep breath and smiled.

'You honour me, my Lord Count. I will indeed attempt to carry out your orders to the letter or die trying.' Ronec looked across at his father. For the first time, he saw surprise and puzzlement on Eudo's face and something else. Could it be pride? The old warrior spoke.

'That, Count Fulk, is a dangerous but clever plan. Without William's support, I am sure that Duke Hoel will retreat like the coward he is, and if my son succeeds in killing William, I believe that I can persuade Malvais to stand the Horse Warriors down and save his men and horses.'

Ronec stared at his father. It had finally happened; his father had recognised him in front of the assembled Breton Lords even if it took a life-threatening mission to do so. For the first time, his father had seen him as a person rather than a by-blow or a name. He felt imbued with triumph and anticipation. He needed to plan this attack carefully. He needed as much information from their informants about what protection William had around Mont Dol and, more importantly, which knights were likely to be there with him, probably very few if the battle started in earnest.

As he opened the flap to leave the pavilion, a hand came down on his shoulder, and he turned to find Count Fulk behind him.

'I admire your courage Fitz-Eudo, so I am giving you one of my best swordsmen to go with you, Pierre D'Avray, Commander of my finest cohort of Angevin troops. I will send him to you now so that you can plan together,' Ronec nodded and thanked the Count, but he grimaced as he turned away; he would probably find the man useful. However, he found him a vicious and cold fish.

Merewyn woke feeling warm and content. As she came to full consciousness, she realised she could feel a man's arms around her and the heat emanating from the body pressed against her back. For a moment, she felt a wave of panic. Confusion set in as she thought that Ronec had found her. She turned her head and saw. Instead, the dark, almost black hair falling across the brow of the man she loved.

'Luc,' she whispered, and those steel-blue eyes opened and gazed into hers. They stayed like that for a few moments, and then he pulled her around and crushed her to him.

'Merewyn. My love. My life. I have missed you so much,' he said.

She pushed him slightly further away so that she could look at him. 'I am sorry I ran from you, Luc. I was hurting so much that I could not stand being with you, thinking of you with Briaca, and when Ronec told me that you were still in her bed every night at Morlaix, it was just too much to bear,' she sobbed. 'However, I know now that it was a plan to destroy our marriage and to keep you from your duty.' She looked up at him with those huge green eyes, and he was lost. He started to shower her face and neck with kisses and then stopped, his eyes clouded and tormented. His voice broke with emotion as he asked the question.

'I have to know, Merewyn, did you give yourself to him in anger at me, or did he hurt you?'

She dropped her eyes, and his stomach knotted, expecting to hear the worst, that she had lain with Ronec for revenge. He could feel the anger at Ronec and his betrayal building again. Then, she looked up at him, her eyes full of unshed tears.

'I will admit there was a time when I was tempted,' she said and paused. 'I was so angry and hurt, and yes, he is a handsome man. However, I could not betray you. For the first week or so, he never asked or forced me to do anything. For the first two nights, we did share a bed, and he lay naked beside me.'

She stopped as she could see the fury in Luc's eyes; she quickly placed her finger on his lips. 'I swear that he did not touch me. No man has ever taken me except you, Luc. I love you so much, but I thought I had lost you forever. I had to escape because things changed at Gael once Ralph De Gael had arrived; they seemed to have no more use for me. Ronec hardened and became more threatening. I found out by accident that I was not only a hostage, but I was to be taken to one of his manors to be held there as his concubine.'

There was a stunned silence as Luc threw the cover off and

swung his legs to the ground.

'He is here, in the rebel camp, I will find him, and I will eviscerate him,' he yelled in an angry but deadly voice. She knelt up and placed her hands on his bare shoulders.

'No, Luc. Do not let this dominate you. They have not won. I am here with you because I love you. We want to leave Dol at the end of this siege and go back to Morlaix and our son Lusian. I would like him to have several brothers or sisters. I have missed some of my courses, and I believe I may be carrying another child. However, if you ask me if it is yours, I will hit you, Luc,' she smiled nervously, waiting for his reaction.

He turned, amazement on his face, and swept her into his arms.

'Merewyn, my love, this is wonderful news. However, it would be best if you were not here in Dol; I need you somewhere safe. I will arrange for you to go to the Chateau de Combourg, it is only an hour south of here and is the home of my good friend Michel Saint-Loup. If I can get away, I will come and see you.' he promised, while watching the stormy expression on her face as she realised that she had to leave him again.

Merewyn finally nodded and gave in; she was the wife of the Leader of the Horse Warriors, and she knew he needed to concentrate on his men, his King and the ongoing siege.

'Good. Be ready to leave in an hour as we launch a series of attacks this morning, and I need you out of danger. Gerard and five of my men will escort you to Combourg,' he said.

'And my maid, Dorca,' she added.

'You have a new maid?' he asked with a raised eyebrow while pulling her tighter into his arms and kissing her brow and her eyelids.

'She helped me to escape,' she murmured, caught up in the increasing passion of Luc's kisses as he laid her back down and began to remove her linen shift.

'I think we need to make up for lost time first,' he said, running his hands up and over her body to cup her breasts. Her back bowed as she rose to meet his caress, his muscular thighs on either side of her and his mouth descending on her nipples, kissing and sucking at each in turn.

'I have so missed this, Luc. I have so missed you, the feel of your body against mine, the feel of you inside me,' she said, and then gasped as his fingers found and entered the soft wetness between her legs.

'Don't you think I tormented myself every night at Morlaix?' he said. 'Watching you and wanting you, but thinking that I had betrayed you. It was the worst torture I have ever been through,' he declared while kneeling up and untying the laces holding his linen braies in place.

She gazed at the taut, statuesque, muscled body of her husband as he impatiently pulled his clothes off. Her eyes followed the defined muscles, the dark hair that lightly covered his chest and continued in a line down to his groin, where his manhood stood proud in a sea of dark curls, and she waited almost nervously in anticipation. He leaned forward and placed his arms on either side of her, his powerful biceps and shoulders hovering over her as he lowered his body onto hers. He entered her with just the tip of his manhood, holding it there and gazing into her eyes. 'I have thought about this every night I have been without you,' he said, in a husky passion-filled voice.

She nodded. She could not speak, her eyes never leaving

those dark, long-lashed, blue ones above her. Then he could wait no more, and he plunged into her, her body arching to meet him. She wrapped her legs around him and gave herself to wave after wave of pleasure, his hands in her hair and his lips on hers. She found herself repeatedly climaxing until finally, Luc shuddered and gave a cry of pure ecstasy as he revelled in an exquisitely intense and powerful release.

They lay supine, their naked bodies entwined, a light sheen of perspiration on their skin, but they were reluctant to move as he stroked her soft skin in the afterglow of their love. Eventually, Luc stretched and pulled back the fur coverlet.

'I can hear people moving about; I must get up,' he said, kissing her deeply before quickly pulling on his clothes.

She pulled the fur coverlet around her shoulders, sat up on the bed and watched him as he shook himself into the thick but supple leather doublet and fastened the leather cuirasses around his wrists and lower calves. Her heart was in her mouth as she watched him. This was her man getting ready to ride into battle. This was the legendary Luc De Malvais, and she knew that the enemy would part like waves before him on his huge vicious Destrier. However, there would be many enemy knights out there who would want to claim that they had killed Malvais. Her eyes filled with tears, and she ran to wrap her arms around him.

'Take care, Luc, promise you will come back to me,' she cried.

He pulled her tight against him. 'I promise, Merewyn, that I will not do anything foolish. I will be around to see and enjoy our next child and hopefully several after that,' he said, resting his head on her stomach. 'If I am lucky, it will be a blonde, silken-haired beauty just like her mother,' he smiled.

She reluctantly let him go; wrapping the coverlet tightly around her, they drew back the curtain to step into the outer tent. They found both Gerard and Morvan sat waiting for them, and Merewyn blushed as she realised they would have heard everything. Morvan just grinned at her, and she suddenly found herself smiling back, like some young lovesick girl. Dorca stood gazing at Luc with an open mouth as Merewyn pulled her back into the inner tent to help her dress.

'Now that is a proper handsome warrior knight, my Lady, and he is your real husband?' she asked wide-eyed. Merewyn nodded with joy and then laughed and smiled at this amusing girl who had fortuitously come into her life.

While strapping on his swords and shouting instructions to his squire, Luc explained to Gerard what he wanted him to do. He knew that his old friend would be disappointed not to be riding out in the first waves of the attack this morning, but with a grin and Merewyn's permission, he told them about her condition. They were delighted and slapped Luc on the back. Within minutes, he was gone, and the three people who loved him found themselves standing staring forlornly after him as he strode towards the horse lines, this powerful force of energy that was Malvais.

Gerard leapt into action. 'We must leave at once; we must be away from here before the melee begins Merewyn,' he said, shouting for horses to be saddled and for Dorca to get her mistress's belongings packed.

The first fingers of dawn were just filtering through the trees as the party of eight, led by Gerard, rode south. However, they had not gone more than a few miles when one of the outriders came galloping back.

'A large party of enemy horsemen approaching from the east, Sire,' he said, panting with exertion. Gerard signalled the whole party to halt and led them slightly further back into the forest's denser part. He dismounted and crept forward, closer to the treeline. Merewyn was full of apprehension as she could hear the sound of thudding hooves galloping towards them. They were surrounded by shrub, which hid the horses, but there was a stand of thinly spaced birch trees in front of them, so she could see the grassy meadow ahead before the forest encroached once more. She watched as Gerard and the scout tied up their horses and crawled close to the front. Within minutes, the clearing ahead was full of mounted men. Merewyn gasped as she recognised Ronec in the lead with an Angevin. Soon, however, they were gone. Merewyn could not contain herself,

'That was Ronec,' she cried.

'Yes, and I would know that other bastard with him anywhere; it was apparently Luc that sliced his face open. Angevin scum,' he spat on the ground. Merewyn looked at him, surprised by such vehemence from Gerard.

Gerard apologised but then added, 'Luc told me that D'Avray hamstrung two of our best horses, just for the sake of it, when he cornered and captured two of our men. He tied the two young horse warriors to the nearest tree and then chopped their hands off. They had bled out, were dead when he found them. Also, the horses were crippled in the river, youngsters we had reared. Luc had to put them out of their misery. I had never seen him look so grim when he told us the tale. He rode hard and caught up with them, and D'Avray was lucky to escape with just a slash across his face,' said Gerard.

Merewyn turned a shocked face to Gerard at such cruelty, and then she looked puzzled. 'Why were they leaving when there is a battle this morning? Are they deserting?' she asked.

'Good question, but I don't think for a second that they were leaving; I think they are flanking or going round behind our forces. Did you notice that they showed no banners of pennants, no insignia to show whom they are riding for? Some of their helmets gave the Angevins away, but the rest could easily be taken for horse warriors,' he said thoughtfully, waving over one of his men.

'Ride as fast as you can to Malvais. Find him, wherever he is, and tell him what we have seen here. Tell him they are disguised as Horse Warriors, and they are heading west.'

The man nodded and galloped off.

'Come, my Lady, let us get you to Combourg and safety and then I must leave you immediately; I need to be back with Malvais.' Merewyn understood perfectly. She wanted Gerard to be at Luc's side in battle, and she pushed her mare forward into a gallop.

Chapter Thirty-One

L uc, mounted on Espirit, had joined his men on the ridge, waiting for the signal flash from Mont Dol, the signal that would tell him to unleash hell on the enemy shield wall. He had ridden the horse rows initially to inspect and chat to his men, and he was happy with their morale and desire to strike at the enemy. Luc was now fully dressed for battle with a fine mail shirt over his leather doublet, but, unlike some of his men, he never wore a helmet into action; he found it restricted his view and ability to spin with his swords in the saddle. As usual, his trademark crossed-swords were on his back and a long dagger in his belt. He sat, patiently scanning the forces ahead and below him. It felt odd not to have Gerard here with him, carrying out these final tasks.

The first fingers of light were creeping over the tops of the trees in the east, and Luc looked at the scene below. He had to admit he did not understand William's reluctance to use the siege engines and towers to weaken the inhabitants. He had expected an escalade in the early dawn, with the long siege ladders against the walls, but instead, the horns sounded from below, and the front rows surged forward to attack the ranked forces of the rebel Breton Lords. As Luc

346

watched and the light strengthened, it became apparent that the rebels had been well prepared for such an attack. Ralph De Gael and Fulk had arranged for hundreds of men to lie prone in slight ditches, indiscernible in the dark dawn, and now they sprang, fully armed, into a shield wall across the front of the Citadel. Luc was somewhat unconcerned; he knew that although wave after wave could die against that shield wall, William knew enough tactics to break it. He was more concerned with the large Angevin forces and cavalry moving forward in the East; these were his targets.

Luc glanced over at Mont Dol, but no signal came yet. He had strategically placed a hundred of his men in an echelon, a chequered formation hidden in the forest to the east. He had been surprised when his men met with no resistance or patrols. Where was the rebel cavalry, which had patrolled those wooded slopes for weeks? When the signal came, his men would ride out of the forest, at a hard gallop, in their diagonal formation, straight into the flank of the combined rebel forces, while he would lead the main force to launch a frontal assault to attack the Angevin and rebel pike-men.

Luc was pleased to note that Eudo's banners were flying far to the left, on the northwest of the army, close to the Citadel walls. He really did not want to meet the father of Alain Rufus's, his liege lord, in battle if he could avoid it, despite Eudo's decision to join the rebellion against William. His eyes scanned the ground in front of the shield wall. It had not rained for several days, and the going was good; the horses would get purchase on the ground. Many of his men would leap or smash through the front row to attack the enemy from behind, and Luc would be one of them.

Suddenly there was a reflective flash from Mont Dol, the

signal for the Horse Warriors to attack. Luc stood up in the stirrups and raised his fist in the air. He could clearly be seen on the ridge by Beorn and his men in the forest, and he knew they would be moving forward for the gallop down the slopes. He gave the loud Breton war cry, which his men echoed as he led the first wave of Horse Warriors, galloping in perfect unison down the slope and towards the enemy lines. Their attack would coincide perfectly with Beorn's attack from the east, causing panic and mayhem amongst the enemy troops.

As he galloped, he tied his reins in a knot and let them drop on the neck of Espirit; his horse knew what to do and reacted perfectly with direction from Luc's knees and lower legs. The clashing sound of hundreds of horse warriors hitting the enemy lines on two sides was deafening as they punched through the front and flank. The massive warhorses, protected by leather chest and face guards, biting and striking out with their hooves, were a formidable weapon in their own right spreading terror and mayhem amongst the enemy as men were trampled and maimed in their wake, their screams echoing across the battlefield. Mounted on these huge balls of fury were the horse warriors, a sword in each hand, slashing and stabbing left and right, creating carnage and delivering death with a speed that was unmatched in Europe.

Luc, and a small group of his men, had been carried deeper than most, but he could feel the fear rippling through the enemy troops as they turned and fled. He was not surprised; most of these men were peasant farmers forced into service for their lords. Just ahead of him, he could see their commanders beating them with the flats of their swords as they tried to get them to turn and attack again to little avail.

Suddenly, Luc recognised one of those berating the fleeing rebel troops. He caught a flash of auburn hair and realised that it was Fitz-Eustace, the half-brother of Ralph De Gael, responsible for the death of several of Beorn's men and for executing the plan to destroy his marriage.

With no hesitation, he whirled Espirit into a gallop, shouting, 'Horse Warriors to me!' at his men, as he headed straight for Geoffrey Fitz-Eustace and his mounted knights.

Geoffrey saw him coming, and Luc saw the colour leave his face before he pulled his mail hood up over his head and began to turn away. Luc pulled Espirit up sharply, only a foot away, and the great horse reared up, striking out with formidable, deadly hooves at the horse and rider in front of them. Geoffrey's horse sustained a large gash on its neck and immediately panicked, shying away before bolting full-pelt through the gap left in front with the frantic, almost unhorsed rider trying to pull his maddened horse up. Luc set off in hot pursuit, smashing aside the pike's thrust at him by fleeing men. Pulling level with Fitz-Eustace, he leaned forward and rammed the handle of his sword into the side of his head, causing him to fall off the other side, where he rolled, winded, on the ground. Within seconds, Luc leapt from the saddle and was on top of him. He sheathed his sword and instead smashed his mailed fists into the man's face repeatedly, breaking his nose and cheekbones. He had never felt such rage, and that thought stopped him before he killed the man. He wanted Fitz-Eustace to live. This was Ralph De Gael's brother, and he did not wish to start a blood feud for his family. However, he did want to hurt him.

'I swear, the next time I see you anywhere near me or mine, Fitz-Eustace, I will maim you permanently,' he said, in an ice-cold voice as the wrecked man rolled over, spat blood and teeth out of his broken mouth and groaned pitifully.

Luc remounted his wild stamping stallion, gathered his men and started the retreat back to the ridge in time for the second wave to begin their attack. He watched, with pride, from the ridge as the second waves went in, a sizeable wedge-shaped arrow punching through the hastily reformed lines, slashing and stabbing at the enemy around them. Suddenly, they turned and retreated, leaving the shattered bodies and corpses of their enemies behind them. As the second wave returned, the third tranche rode out, a tactic similar to 'retraite en echiquier', attacking and retreating in succession. With top-notch mounted men, the tactic was lethal, the front lines having no time to recover before the next wave was on them and no quarter was given.

A smile of satisfaction lit Luc's face as he watched it unroll. Beorn had ridden over to join him after the success of the attacks on the flanks. He pulled his horse alongside Espirit, who was still pawing the ground in impatience to go again, his teeth snapping at Beorn's horse. As they watched the carnage, Luc noticed a rider galloping down across the southern meadow towards them. As he came nearer, he recognised the man as one of Gerard's men. He also noticed the flecks of foam bespattering the horse's chest; he had obviously ridden hard for some time. Luc experienced a moment of panic; had something happened to Merewyn? He went cold at the thought.

The rider skidded to a halt. 'My Lord! An urgent message from Sir Gerard,' he said, panting for breath.

'Is it the Lady Merewyn?' he asked.

'No, Sire. As we were heading south to Combourg, we

were forced to hide in the trees as a large party of mounted men approached. Sir Gerard told me to tell you that they were led by Ronec Fitz-Eudo and the Angevin Commander with the scar. There were about seventy of them,' he said.

'D'Avray!' spat Luc in contempt. 'In which direction were they headed?' he asked the young horse warrior.

'They were going southwest, my lord, as if they were coming round the back of our forces but quite a few miles out,' he replied.

Luc nodded. 'Well done, young man, go and get you and your horse some water but stay near; I may want you again,' he said, slapping him on the back.

Luc sat in silent thought for a few minutes, visualising the layout of the land to the west. He realised that this was part of Fulk's plan, but where would they attack? Could they just be a distraction? Beorn, beside him, gained his attention.

'Sire, the next tranche needs to go before we lose our advantage.'

'Unfortunately, I cannot ride with this one as planned, Beorn, so lead them out; something else needs my attention,' he said, before turning and galloping back to the camp and the horse lines. He summoned three of his men, who he had used as scouts, and pointed to the map laid on the table.

'Each of you rides swiftly to these areas in the west and north and see if you can locate a large group of mounted men. I believe that they are not showing any colours or flying any pennants. Report back to me urgently, wherever I am. I need to know where they have been and where they are now,' he demanded.

Luc stood at the doorway of his pavilion and watched them gallop away. He remounted Espirit and went back to his position on the ridge, but he was uneasy. He felt as if he was missing something as he watched the lacklustre attacks on the enemy by Hoel's forces.

Beorn cantered back up beside him, blood-splattered but intact. 'We followed your orders, Malvais, the eastern line is broken, and they have retreated as far as their camp, so we have now withdrawn and are regrouping with over half of the force resting in the forest. The Angevin troops fled after the second attack. We were expecting an attack from their mounted cavalry, but it never came.'

Luc nodded his approval. 'You have done well, Beorn, but we have had reports of a mounted force attempting to flank us. I have sent out scouts to the west and north, but we are unsure where they are.'

Both men turned and swept the lands behind them with a searching gaze, but the creeping morning mist that clung to the ground made it impossible.

'Have you alerted the King?' asked Beorn, staring in the direction of Mont Dol, which rose like an island from the early morning mist, the colourful pavilions on the crest flying the Kings colours.

Luc followed his gaze and narrowed his eyes, for, at that moment, he knew where Ronec and D'Avray were going. He shook his head to clear it. Surely, they would not be that stupid. The mount was securely guarded. They could only attack it from the south and west, and that is where most of the King's army lay, around its base. His own knights also guarded the King, and there were twenty horse warriors, led by Morvan, constantly patrolling. Then he remembered the messenger's words; they wore no colours, carried no pennants, they looked like horse warriors. He whirled Espirit around on the spot, almost unseating Beorn in his haste.

'You are to take over command here and direct the next attacks where and when necessary. I must go to the King; they are going to kill him,' he yelled, and he was gone in seconds.

Morvan stretched and yawned. He had been in the saddle for several hours, far longer than he should have been for a man with several broken ribs. He was just glad to be back with his men, so he ignored the nagging ache. He had just patrolled the forests to the southwest of Mont Dol, and all was quiet in the enveloping mist. He had also placed several of his men as lookouts around Mont Dol's slopes; everyone's attention was on the battle raging in front of and to the east of the Citadel. He dismounted and decided to walk the Mount's circumference; he wanted to be above the clinging mist. He knew Luc would be attacking this morning, and he wanted to see what was happening. He handed his horse to a squire and set off up through the scrub brush, nodding to one of William's well-armed sentries who was standing on the direct path to the top, but Morvan decided to cut east and go around the side. As he reached one of his own men, he was pleased to see his reaction, the man whirling his hand over his shoulder, already drawing his blade at the sound of footsteps.

'Rest easy, Petroc,' he said, and the man visibly relaxed at the sight of his Captain. 'Well met,' said Morvan gripping the man's forearm in the warrior greeting. 'How are things progressing?' he asked, nodding in the direction of the melee in the east.

'There have been a lot of horse charges over there for the last hour; our men are smashing the Angevin lines. It is a sight to behold, Sire,' he grinned.

Morvan smiled and stared out over the assembled armies below. The air was rent with the sound of weapons and the screams and groans of men. The harsh reality of war thought Morvan, who could easily recall the gruesome sights, sounds and smells of previous conflicts. Sagas and songs tell of the glory of war, the victories, the thrill, the adrenalin and, yes, he had felt all of that, especially in his first battles. They rarely sing about the pitiful, torn bodies, the maimed, the disembowelled, the smell and tang of blood and emptied bowels that littered the battlefield. Morvan had spent several months as a foot soldier; Luc and Gerard had insisted on it, so every horse rider knew what to expect if he was unhorsed. They were the most brutal months, and he still remembered the squelch of the bodies underfoot as the shield wall moved forward. He cast his eyes back to the Citadel's front, but he could see that Hoel's attacks were desultory.

'What is he playing at? Hoel should have been inside that Citadel months before,' muttered Morvan.

The young man nodded, and Morvan scanned to the west. The mist covered the marshes and still came over halfway up the mount. The sun emerged for a few minutes, and Morvan had a clearer view. He could see that William's forces were driving up the escarpment on the west flank towards the gate.

'At last,' he said, and suddenly, there was a flash of something to his left from the marshlands and again. Then it was gone, swallowed up in the mist. He stared at the spot for a few minutes but shrugged it off, probably a local fisherman or eel catcher in a boat. He slapped the young man on the shoulder in farewell and made his way back along the narrow path. He glanced up at the large pavilions above him and saw William and a cluster of his knights on the edge of the summit watching the progress of the battle below.

Morvan had only met the King on a few occasions, mainly due to his brother's fame, but William had greeted him warmly when he arrived to deploy his men on and around Mont Dol. Morvan admitted to himself he was somewhat in awe of William. The King was a strong, fierce and intelligent man with a prodigious memory. He filled a room with his presence and his rough base voice.

Morvan quickly reached the hill's base and headed to the horse lines to check his young stallion, one of Espirit's beautiful offspring. He ran his hands down the horse's legs, and as he straightened, he noticed three Horse Warriors dismounting; Luc must have sent them to bolster his numbers, he thought. He did not recognise them but presumed they were part of Beorn's cohort from Vannes. He nodded a greeting to them and continued along the horse lines to speak to one of his men about grooming his horse. As he reached the horses of the new arrivals, he raised his eyebrows. The horses were not only liberally mud-spattered but also smaller and in poor condition. He realised, uneasily, that these were not the horses of any Breton Horse Warrior. Morvan whirled around, shouting for his men who came running.

'Three strangers have just arrived dressed as Horse Warriors. Find them and stop them,' he yelled.

Chapter Thirty-Two

Ronec and D'Avray had taken a much wider sweep than expected because of the numerous patrols their scouts encountered. D'Avray, in particular, found this frustrating; he yearned for the chance to raise his sword against William and win glory for himself. Ronec had far more patience; years as a mercenary had taught him that weeks or even months of inaction could precede a few hours of fighting.

Before long, they had rendezvoused with their guide, a young, dark, Breton fisherman, who knew the paths through the marshes like the back of his hand. Ronec dismounted and shouted to his men to do the same, instructing them to hobble their horses, as they would be retrieved later.

D'Avray turned a shocked face to Ronec. 'We are leaving the horses?' he asked.

'Of course, D'Avray, it will be easier and quieter without them; we need the element of surprise.'

D'Avray shook his head and sneered. 'I will be taking mine, as will all of my men. We Angevins do not walk into battle. I am not leaving them for the enemy to take.'

Ronec narrowed his eyes and gave him a long, hard, disbelieving look until D'Avray had to look away. 'As you will, D'Avray, but they are your responsibility, and I will take no blame if you compromise this sortie,' he said.

He was not prepared to argue or to pull rank on the Angevin Commander at this point. On his own head be it. He split the force of sixty men into two, sending the Angevins with their horses to be the rear guard, then he told the stoic young Breton that they were ready.

The young man looked at the mounted men at the rear of the column and shook his head, muttering, 'The mud. They will not make it,' in a thick Breton patois.

Ronec gave a grimace and shrug of understanding as they set off into the marshlands and its deep reed-filled pools.

For the first fifteen minutes or so, the going was relatively easy, with enough room for two men to walk abreast in shallow, sandy, saltwater pools filled with long marsh grass. However, the water became deeper, and the young Breton held up his hand. D'Avray rode forward as the fisherman explained that now the paths would be narrow, this was where the saltwater met the freshwater, and the sand would become sucking glutinous mud. They must be in single-file and not step off the paths. He repeated this several times, and the message was sent down the line. Yet again, the young man told them to leave the horses, but D'Avray refused to dismount, although several of his anxious men disobeyed him and left their poor mounts to wander back to the shore. The mist was much thicker here, away from the sea breezes, and they could see only a few yards in front of them. A flicker of concern raced through Ronec's mind; a man could be lost forever in the mud and mist of the marshes, he thought, as they moved slowly forward a yard at a time. The young Breton pointed out to Ronec the long canes, their tops coated with lime that marked the narrow path.

'Do not stray from the path, my lord; death is that way. The mud will quickly suck you down.' Ronec nodded and passed the message along the strung-out line as he kept his eyes firmly on the ground in front of him.

As he walked, he could hear snatches of the battle in front of them, the screams and shouts distant and eerie in the thick all-enveloping mist. His thoughts turned to Merewyn, and he had time for reflection. He knew that he had betrayed Luc, his past comrade and friend; he knew he had broken the warrior's code. However, wealth, land and recognition had been too much of a tempting prize. Did that make him a weak man, he wondered, taking what he wanted with no thought to the consequences. He shrugged. Not everyone could be the shining example that was Luc De Malvais, faithful and loyal to his women, family and friends. Ronec was not a man for regrets, preferring to live in the here and now, but he wished he had bedded her, even once. He smiled at the thought. Where was Luc now, he wondered, on the ridge with his men? And where was Merewyn, back at Morlaix with her son, heading for England? Did Luc know the truth yet about Briaca?

Suddenly, there was a clamour and cries from behind, followed by splashing and shouts that echoed eerily in the thick mist. Ronec halted the column and made his way carefully back along the treacherous path. He came to D'Avray, still mounted.

'What has happened?' he asked the Angevin Commander, who just shrugged. Ronec sent him a look of contempt and squeezed past him to find out. The continuing cries led him to the narrowest part of the path, surrounded on both sides by bright green, slime-filled pools. Just then, the sun broke through and lit the scene. Two riders and horses were trapped in the pools on either side, both struggling and sinking fast, their eyes filled with terror as they flailed in the water and glutinous mud. Ronec and the others stood on the safety of the path, unable to help them without ropes or solid ground on which to get a purchase.

'Some waterfowl flew straight out of the reeds and startled the horses,' a horrified soldier explained.

Within seconds, one man had gone, sucked down, but the other had managed to scramble onto the neck of his struggling horse and was reaching out his hands. However, they were too far from the path, and as the mud reached his neck, his screams and cries became more frantic, and then he was gone. The stunned onlookers stood in silence, looking at the ripples on the stagnant, green water, where men and horses were lost in moments.

Ronec felt the anger build inside him at such a waste of life, and he shouted at the other mounted men to dismount and turn and follow the hoof prints to return their horses to safety. He turned to make his way back when suddenly, the sun flashed on the helmet of the last, departing Angevin, lighting it up like a beacon. He stopped and drew in a breath, but in seconds, the sun had gone, and the mist swirled back. He reached the front of the column, stopped beside D'Avray, and glared up at the man.

'Your arrogance and stupidity have just lost you two men and their horses,' he spat at him.

For only a moment, he saw an answering flash of anger, and the man's hand moved to his sword hilt, but then he just sneered and shrugged. 'It is an acceptable price to pay for the

359

outcome,' he said.

Ronec forced himself not to reach over for his own sword and turned away to walk to the front to re-join the guide, muttering to himself as he did so, 'I hope one day I meet that bastard in battle,' He waved the column forward down the narrowing path as they moved even deeper into the treacherous marshes.

Chapter Thirty-Three

Gerard successfully delivered Merewyn and her maid Dorca to Combourg, the Lady Saint-Loup being delighted to welcome her. He apologized for his swift departure but explained that he had to return to Dol forthwith. They all understood, especially Merewyn, who had clasped his hands and told him to look after Luc and Morvan. He set off north at a gallop back to the siege, although his mind went to Ronec, where was he headed with his mounted troop of cavalry. An hour later, he cantered into the horse lines behind the ridge overlooking the Citadel of Dol. At a glance, he noticed that both Luc's and Morvan's horses were gone telling him that they were engaged somewhere in the conflict. He made for Luc's pavilion shouting at a squire to bring him a tankard of ale, some food and a fresh horse. Five minutes later, freshly mounted, he rode to the front of the ridge, expecting to see Luc's figure at the end of it. There were a few horses there, but he realised that none of these was Luc or Morvan as he approached.

He greeted Beorn. 'How is the battle progressing?' he asked, scanning the sight below.

'We have driven the rebel forces on the eastern front back

to their camp line. They have sustained many hundreds of casualties; we have very few. William and Hoel's forces finally gained the ground in front of the Citadel and are now on the escarpment with ladders at the ready. No direct attack as yet, Sire,' he answered.

'Where are Luc and Morvan? Did they receive my warning?' he asked.

Beorn nodded. 'Morvan had already left to deploy men around Mont Dol as extra protection for William's command post. Malvais led successful attacks on the enemy, but as soon as he received your message, he set off in pursuit of Ronec Fitz-Eudo. I believe he thinks they are planning to attack and kill the King,' he said.

'Did he take a troop with him?' asked Gerard, shocked by Beorn's words.

'Only six or seven men, I believe, but he was in a hurry,' he replied.

Gerard shook his head as he calculated the odds against Ronec's sixty or seventy Angevin troops and cavalry. At that moment, one of their vedettes galloped up.

'Is Lord Malvais here? I have urgent information for him,' he shouted.

'No, but I am going to him now, so you can tell me,' said Gerard.

'It's a French army, Sire. A vast French army, led by King Philip himself. They are only a few miles away to the north, and they are marching on Dol.

There was a stunned silence as the vedettes words hung in the air, and the implication of the words sank in.

Gerard sprang into action. 'Beorn, recall all of the Horse Warriors and get them back up here on the ridge and ready for action. Regroup them for a full-frontal attack if necessary or a Coup de Main. Make sure men and horses are watered, fed, and all lost weapons replaced. I am riding to Mont Dol, hopefully, to find Luc and Morvan and to share this news with the King,' he yelled as he leapt onto the waiting horse.

Just as Morvan sent his men out to search for the three interlopers, Luc came galloping in on Espirit, followed by his men. As usual, everyone turned to watch the huge, plunging, dappled-grey Destrier as it skidded to a halt, and Luc leapt from the saddle, calling for a horse boy. Espirit, who was trained not to wander, stood stock-still, feet planted, nostrils flaring, snapping at anyone who came close. Luc handed the reins to an apprehensive young boy and ran up to Morvan.

'Where is the King?' he cried.

'On the summit with several of his knights and Commanders. His forces are gaining ground.'

Luc nodded and started up the hill. 'Alert your men and set extra guards; I believe Ronec, with a large force, may try to capture or kill the King,' he shouted over his shoulder.

'Luc, wait! We are at the moment searching for three men who have just arrived. They are dressed as Horse Warriors'. Morvan said.

Luc paused. 'They will be heading for the King,' he said, drawing a sword and breaking into a run up the steep path of Mont Dol, closely followed by Morvan and several of his men. They reached the crest of the hill and ran through the smaller pavilions to reach the large striped tent flying the King's red and gold banner, with its two lions passant. Luc raced across the ground towards the front of the tent. He could see three men arguing with the two guards outside. From his vantage point, he could also see the King and three of his knights walking back from the crest towards his pavilion. William was walking ahead of them, straight into danger, straight into the arms of his assassins.

Luc drew his second sword, and with a Breton war cry echoed by the men behind him, he raced at the three men. The nearest one turned, his eyes widening in terror, his hand reaching for his sword as Luc sliced into his neck. A bright spray of blood covered the young guard, and the tent wall as the man fell backwards while Luc's second sword had already sliced through the throat of the second man, who had only just managed to get his sword out of its sheath. The third man backed away. He knew that very few men took on Malvais and lived. He turned to run and found himself facing William only feet behind him, who, alerted by Luc's war cry, had drawn his sword, and he now cut down the third rebel with relish while his astonished knights were still drawing their swords.

Morvan, sword drawn, reached Luc; his recent injuries had prevented him from keeping up with his brother. He watched as William calmly wiped his blade and then turned with a thin smile. 'Always take the blood off while it's wet,' he said, looking calmly at the panting Malvais brothers.

'Well met Luc. Are you killing your own men now?' he said, looking down at the dispatched assassins. He guffawed at his own joke, and a ripple of relief ran through the group of knights behind him, as William's mood or reaction could be unpredictable.

'Come in, Malvais, and tell me who they were so that I can thank you for your timely intervention,' he said, waving at Morvan to join them as he entered the blood-spattered tent.

A knight poured wine for them all as Luc cleaned and sheathed his swords and related to William the information about Ronec and the large force that seem to have disappeared, although he found that they had been tracked to the far north-west near the coast.

'They were Ronec's Fitz-Eudo's men. I recognised one of them that attacked and beat me,' said Morvan. Luc nodded. 'I suspected so, but I see Fulk behind this, Sire. The other two have Angevin helmets, swords and scabbards; their disguise was not good,' said Luc.

William nodded. 'Yes, it would suit Fulk to have me removed so that he could seize Maine,' he laughed. Then a thought occurred to him. 'So where are the rest of them? Are there a dozen more assassins out there, dressed as my Horse Warriors? The coast? Does that mean that Fitz-Eudo has taken boat to England?' he asked in a perplexed voice.

Suddenly, Morvan spoke up. 'I think I know where Ronec and his men may be,' he said. All eyes were suddenly on him. He nervously licked his lips, but he was sure that he was right. 'I think they are coming across the marshland. They are going to attack the mound from the north side, where you least expect it. When the sun came out earlier, and the heavy mist cleared for a few moments, I saw a flash of sun on metal. Then it happened again as the mist descended.' There was silence for a few moments as they considered Morvan's words.

'That would explain why we could find no trace of them,' said Luc.

The king nodded. 'Clever. Very clever,' he said.

'Sire, we must get you to safety; Mont Dol is no longer safe. Morvan get a contingent of at least twenty men up here immediately and move the rest to encircle the lower and middle mound on all sides, ready to move the King,' he ordered.

At that moment, there were sounds of a disturbance outside. Luc drew his sword and stepped in front of the King while Morvan, sword in hand, swept-back the tent flap to reveal the intruders. A sigh of relief ensued when Gerard was revealed, holding a disarmed sentry by the throat. He dropped the man and left him gasping on the floor.

'Forgive me, but I have urgent news to impart,' he explained, while Morvan grinned but raced out past him to carry out Luc's orders. Luc regarded his old friend, who stood, chest heaving. 'What is it, Gerard?' he asked.

'Urgent message for the King,' he exclaimed.

William stepped forward, 'Then speak, damn you man,' he said in an exasperated voice.

'It's the French, Sire. There is a vast French army approaching Dol from the north. They are led by Phillip himself and are only a few miles away.

William swore long and loudly. 'That damned, interfering Frenchman! He is after only one thing; Phillip wants the Vexin borderlands to the north of Normandy. He thinks that by interfering here, he can push for a parley to persuade me to part with it in exchange for Dol.' He paced up and down in fuming silence for several minutes.

'Damn the man and Duke Hoel for delaying this siege for so long. This Citadel should have been taken over a month ago. It has been an ill-fated campaign from the start and then used by the traitor Ralph De Gael to get his revenge on me.' William continued to storm up and down the tent, venting his spleen while Luc and the other knights looked on in concern.

Finally, Luc had to break in on the King's diatribe. 'Sire, we have to get you to safety. You are vulnerable here, and they may attack at any time.'

At that moment, Morvan burst into the tent. 'We must get the King away; Ronec and the Angevins are climbing the northern slopes. My men are trying to hold them, but there are too many, and they will be here momentarily,' he exclaimed.

The King stood undecided. 'I have never run away from a fight in my life Malvais,' he declared, searching the face of his Horse Warrior Commander.

'I know, Sire. I was by your side at Hastings, and no one would ever question your courage, think of this as purely a strategic withdrawal. Morvan, escort the King and his knights to safety. Get him to Dinan,' he said softly, watching the uncertainty still playing across William's face.

Morvan walked forward. 'Sire,' he said, indicating the doorway and his waiting men.

William put a hand on Luc's shoulder. 'I will not forget this, Malvais,' he said, nodding at Luc and following Morvan swiftly to safety. Luc whirled around on the remaining knights and commanders, who still stood in a state of shock.

'Sound the retreat! Get your men out of there. This will fast become a rout with the enemy on our heels. Leave everything,' he cried.

'But the equipment. The siege-engines. The horses, carts and oxen. What of them?' spluttered an older knight.

'Didn't you hear what Sir Gerard said? Phillip and his army are only hours away. You and your men will be cut down while you are still dismantling them. The Angevin forces are almost at the top of this crest and are heading for this pavilion; get out and save yourselves,' he shouted in frustration.

Within seconds, wine goblets were dropped, and they hastily exited. Luc put a hand out and held the arm of his old friend, Michel Saint-Loup.

'Go to Duke Hoel. Tell him the news of William's departure and King Philip's army, and then flee yourself,' he said, clasping his friend's forearm in farewell.

Soon, only two men were left standing in the chaos of the King's pavilion; Luc looked at Gerard and took a deep breath before reaching up and drawing his sword.

'Now for Ronec,' he said, running through the tent flap, with Gerard in hot pursuit.

Chapter Thirty Four

As they raced out of the pavilion, the clash of swords and cries of men reached them. The Horse Warriors engaged in a fierce fight with the Angevin and mercenary troops, who had just crested the hill. They gave a good account of themselves, but both sides were trained, professional soldiers, so the fight was fierce, with no quarter given. Gerard immediately broke off to help two of his newest recruits, who five Angevin soldiers had surrounded.

Luc scanned the melee and then ran to the edge to look down the slope. More men were emerging from the mist that was hugging Mont Dol's base, and then they moved up into the scrubland on the slopes above. The sun re-emerged for a few seconds as he scanned the slope to the west. To his satisfaction, he saw Ronec clambering sword in hand towards the crest. Luc fought his way through the crowd of fighting men on the summit delivering a well-deserved thrust or blow to the enemy on the way. He reached the spot where he expected Ronec to have emerged, but there was no sign of him as he looked over. He scanned left and right to no avail.

'I must assume you are looking for me, Malvais,' came a deep drawl behind him.

Luc whirled to find Ronec Fitz-Eudo stood several yards away, leaning on his sword. Both men just stared at each other, oblivious to the fighting taking place around them.

'I swore I would find you, Ronec, and I will kill you for what you have done to both my family and to me. I considered you a friend and comrade; you came to my home as an honoured guest,' said Luc, in a cold, even voice. Ronec had the grace to look away for a few moments as Luc, without warning, leapt forward and launched a deadly blow at Ronec's head. Ronec ducked in time but felt the whistle of the sword as it sliced the air just above his head. He jumped sideways to avoid the follow-up thrust that he knew would be coming from Malvais.

The two men circled each other warily. Ronec knew he was fighting for his life, and although he was good, he knew that Malvais was a master swordsman. He saw the hatred in Luc's glittering eyes, the set of his jaw and the thin line of his mouth; all spoke of his determination to kill him. Luc sidestepped and thrust again with the sword in his right hand. Ronec managed to meet it while raising his shield to parry the blow from the blade in Luc's left hand. This is what made Malvais so lethal, his ability to fight with either or both hands simultaneously in a swift, seemingly fluid motion. For what seemed like an age, Ronec fought, met and parried the thrusts and blows from Luc, but he knew he was tiring while Malvais seemed hardly out of breath.

Sweat beaded Ronec's brow running down into his eyes, his dark hair now hanging lank on his forehead. As he rubbed his eyes, it occurred to him that he did not want to die; he wanted to live and enjoy the wealth he had accumulated. He wanted to recognise his child, which Briaca was bearing. For the first time, he regretted the reckless stupidity that had made this fierce fighter his enemy, as the reality hit home that he was not going to survive this.

They circled each other again. Luc suddenly dropped to his haunches and swept the sword in his right hand straight for Ronec's unprotected ankles. The lethal, sharpened blade would have taken off his left foot, but Ronec's reflexes kicked in, and he jumped in the air. Unfortunately, when he landed, his foot twisted on a small rock, and he fell backwards.

Neither man had realised just how close they were to the steep edge of the slope. Ronec rolled backwards, head over heels down to the scrubland and mist at Mont Dol's base.

Luc shouted in triumph. He raced down the slope, his feet sliding on the scree-like surface of the north side. Ronec lay groaning and winded on his back, his sword gone. Luc quickly knelt on either side of him, pinning him to the ground. He put one sword back into its scabbard on his back and placed the point of the other one at Ronec's throat, pressing so hard that it broke the skin; blood welled and ran down the side of Ronec's neck.

'I said I would kill you, Ronec. You have one minute to make your peace with your maker,' he said, holding his sword with both hands, ready to plunge it into the throat of the man who had betrayed him and threatened the life of his King.

'I do regret what I have done to you, Luc,' gasped Ronec. 'I swear that I never touched Merewyn. It was all a ploy by Ralph De Gael to delay and distract you,' he said.

Luc looked down into Ronec's face, and for a moment, he did feel regret for the friend he once had and the comradeship they had once shared, but Luc found that he could not forgive him and his hands tightened on his sword, as he prepared to deliver the killing blow.

Then he saw Ronec's eyes widen as he loudly gasped the word 'No!'

In that fraction of a second, Luc realised that the shout was not for him. A figure had loomed out of the mist behind him. He started to throw himself sideways, but he was too late as the sword, which was held two-handed above him, plunged down into his body, and he heard the voice of the hated Angevin Commander, Pierre D'Avray.

'Die Malvais!' he yelled.

Chapter Thirty-Five

Luc felt the blade slide deep into his body, but he did not react initially. He had moved a few inches to the left, which meant that the sword's downward thrust, which was a killing blow intended for the base of his skull to pierce his vitals, had instead moved to the right. Luc had dropped his sword because of the deadly blow. He could feel the blade embedded in his body, but yet, he could feel no pain, so much adrenalin was still coursing through him.

Fortunately, the thinner Angevin sword had been deflected from its killing path by his scapula. It had gone down across at an angle and, coming out of his body, had entered and pierced his upper right arm. He felt D'Avray step forward and tighten his grip to wrench the sword out. Luc stared blankly down at Ronec's face, who was still lying prone beneath him, grimacing as he stared in horror at D'Avray.

He heard him whisper, 'Move, Luc, the next blow will truly kill you.'

Luc gritted his teeth and gathered all of his strength; he then did what would seem impossible to many men. He unexpectedly and swiftly pushed up against the blade embedded in his body, moving from a kneeling to a standing position. It brought him to his feet but drove the sword down further through his right arm, and he suddenly felt the pain of the thin blade grating on the bone as it came out of the other side. D'Avray, taken aback by the swift movement, let go of the sword and staggered backwards as an ashen-faced Luc turned to face him, the blade still firmly embedded in his body.

At that moment, D'Avray came to his senses and dashed for Luc's sword lying on the ground beside Ronec. However, as he bent to retrieve it, Ronec leapt up to his knees, grabbed the hilt and slammed the blade deep up into D'Avray's chest, who gasped and fell backwards.

'The world will be a better place without a man like you, D'Avray,' he said. Moving up to stand over him, he put his foot on the Angevin's chest and pulled the sword out, watching the blood bubble up and run from his nose and mouth. He turned to Luc, who had now dropped to his knees, blood running down his arm and pooling on the ground beside him. He walked over to him, sword in hand.

'Come to finish me off, Ronec?' Luc whispered with a rueful smile.

'No, Luc. I think there has been enough death, and honestly, I doubt that you will survive this wound,' he said. Before Luc could answer, there was a roar of rage from behind him, and Ronec whirled round as Gerard charged out of the mist.

He had spent some time trying to find Luc, and he had finally fought his way to the bottom of the mound, coming out of the mist to see a kneeling wounded Luc, about to be slaughtered by Ronec. Gerard was a large thickset warrior with massive, muscled arms, and he brought his sword down with a mighty blow on Ronec, who parried it, but the reverberation was such that it numbed his hand and wrist, and he dropped the sword.

'No!' shouted Luc, as Gerard prepared to deliver a killing blow on the unarmed warrior.

'No, he saved my life,' he gasped before falling forward face down and losing consciousness. Both men rushed forward.

'This amount of blood means that he is bleeding badly from a sliced vein, and that must be stopped, but that sword has to come out,' said Ronec.

Gerard nodded. 'From the angle, I think he may have been lucky. I do not think it has pierced a major organ, and there is no blood from his mouth, so I think it has missed his lung, but we must move him from here,' he said, reaching down and picking Luc up carefully in his arms.

Ronec ran ahead of him, sword drawn, as they started back up the hill with Gerard staggering up behind him with his burden. Luc groaned, the blood dripping freely from his arm, leaving a trail behind them. Fortunately, two of Luc's men were coming down the slope, and they carefully took Luc from Gerard, carefully carrying him up into William's pavilion, their faces reflecting their shock. Malvais had always seemed invincible.

The Horse Warriors had mainly seen off the rebel force, with only desultory fighting continuing at the mound's base. The two men carried Luc into the tent and went to lay him on the table.

'No,' said Gerard, I need him upright in the King's carved chair, it has arms, and I need you to hold him down while I pull the sword out. Ronec, tear lots of cloth and find some spirits or wine to wash the wounds,' he ordered

Luc floated in and out of consciousness. He was aware he was seated; he could hear snatches of conversation. Suddenly his arms and legs were held down in vice-like grips. Then there was a searing pain as Gerard gripped the sword's handle with both hands and pulled it out. At that point, Luc blacked out and lost consciousness.

As Gerard extracted the sword, Ronec rushed forward and poured Normandy brandy into the wounds. They padded and bound all four wounds from the path of the blade tightly. This took some time. While they were working on Luc, they were aware of an increasing cacophony of sound, horns and cheers.

'It's the French,' muttered Gerard.

'The French?' replied Ronec in surprise.

'King Phillip has arrived with a huge army, and William has gone,' said Gerard.

Ronec looked thoughtful for a moment, I knew De Gael had asked for support from Philip of France, but no one expected him to come here. 'Then you must get him out of here, Gerard, now. If they capture Malvais, he will die. His wounds will fester in a dungeon, and they will need to be cleaned every day if he is to survive.'

'I know,' said Gerard, turning and ordering the men to bring a cart to the western side of Mont Dol immediately.

Using one of the servant's truckle beds, they carried the unconscious Luc to the cart, wrapping him in blankets. Gerard got in the back with him, ordering his horse to be tied on. Then a thought occurred to him.

'Espirit!' he exclaimed. 'I can't leave him here; Luc would never forgive me if he fell into enemy hands.' He made to get out of the cart, but Ronec stopped him.

'That horse would be a dead giveaway that Malvais is in this cart. I will find him, and I promise I will bring him to

Dinan. With William's departure and King Phillip's arrival, the siege will be over, and people will disperse. I will save my skin by laying claim to wounding Malvais; having his horse will back that up. I will bring his horse to Dinan; I have unfinished business there,' he said.

Gerard nodded. 'Briaca?' he questioned.

Ronec grinned and nodded, while Gerard found himself smiling back as he banged on the back of the driver's seat for them to get moving before the French overran Mont Dol. He shook his head; well, he may be a treacherous, whoring bastard, but somehow you can still end up liking Ronec, he thought, as they trundled along the road towards Dinan.

Chapter Thirty-Six

Morvan had escorted William down to the horse lines, helped him mount one of the big Destriers and then surrounded him with a ring of thirty Horse Warriors. Reluctance seeped out of every pore of Williams's body as he gazed back at Mont Dol. Morvan half expected him to dismount and say no; he would stay to do battle with the French King. However, much of William's success lay in the fact that he could be pragmatic, and he knew that they were now sorely outnumbered. Duke Hoel had also fled, leaving his forces in disarray. It had turned into a total rout, and Morvan needed to get the King to Dinan and away from any possible pursuit.

'Sire, we must leave now,' he said. William nodded and turned the big horse towards the west.

They rode hard and fast; Morvan had set up an entire 'Retraite en Echiquier', a chequered retreat with the main force that meant that the Horse Warriors were attacking any pursuers and then retreating. He felt confident that they would only have to do that for a few miles; the rebel forces would want to celebrate their victory, they would rob the corpses of the slain and pillage the enormous amounts of equipment, horses and animals left behind. Morvan privately thought it would be an eye-watering amount that William and Hoel were willing to sacrifice while cutting their losses and saving themselves.

The King was silent on the journey, only nodding in agreement when Morvan suggested a short stop to rest and water the horses. William stood alone and aloof, unapproachable, a thoughtful expression on his face, but he seemed keen to be back on horseback. A few hours later, the castle at Dinan hove into view, and they cantered over the river and up through the cobbled streets of the town. Morvan had sent a messenger ahead so that Saint-Vere, the Castellan, was prepared for Williams's arrival.

However, as they came to a halt beside the steps leading into the Donjon, there was a further surprise. Standing to greet the King was not only the Castellan and his lady, but also Queen Matilda and one of their daughters. Ignoring Saint-Vere, William ran up the steps and enveloped Matilda in his arms. Morvan smiled; it was well known that William loved his wife and that he was happy to demonstrate that in public. Morvan looked at their daughter, who was plain but with beautiful auburn hair. She held herself regally, and as he looked, he found that he was also solemnly assessed by a pair of fine, blue eyes. He bowed his head in salute and smiled at her. At first, there was no response, but then she smiled back, and her whole face lit up. Morvan was taken aback and the breath caught in his throat; she had an almost ethereal beauty about her when she smiled, a luminescence of eyes and hair. Seconds later, she was gone as she followed her parents into the Great Hall but, at the doorway, she looked back and held his gaze for a few seconds. Morvan stood staring at the empty stone-arched entrance until a polite cough from the Serjeant beside him brought him back to earth.

'Shall we set up the camp in the meadow yonder, Sir?' he asked.

'Yes, of course,' said Morvan waving the escort onwards.

'See the Steward for tents and supplies as we abandoned all of ours,' he added as he turned his horse towards the stable yard.

Merewyn was well looked after at Combourg; the Lady Saint-Loup had been delighted to have her as a guest. As the days went by, the ladies waited anxiously for news; both of their men were fighting at Dol for King William. Both women knew that battles were unpredictable and that even the best soldiers and warriors could easily be killed.

Finally, as the evening was drawing in, they heard the sounds of arrival in the courtyard. Both women rushed down the stairs, hoping it was their husbands. The square was full of men and horses, and the women stood at the great doorway scanning the milling men amid the noise and chaos. Finally, her hostess let out a cry of delight as her lord emerged from the host of men, grey-faced and blood-spattered. Merewyn watched with a smile as his wife threw her arms around him, oblivious to all but each other; the relief was tangible that he had returned uninjured. Merewyn waited patiently for him to mount the stairs and give her news of Luc; she knew that he was not there; Espirit Noir would have stood out, several hands above the others, his noble head held high.

Finally, Michel Saint-Loup stood in front of her and took her hands in his.

'It is not good news, my lady,' he said. Merewyn went stone cold. Luc could not be dead; surely, she would know somehow.

'Malvais has been very badly wounded, apparently stabbed from behind by a cowardly Angevin. I saw Gerard just before they left. They were taking him to Dinan,' he said softly. Merewyn let out the breath that she had been holding.

'I must go to him,' she whispered, her face deadly pale.

'I will arrange an escort for you first thing in the morning. It is almost dark, and my men are weary,' he said.

Merewyn understood, so she nodded and followed them inside; however, her stomach was churning, and her thoughts were whirling. How badly injured was he? Would he live? 'Please, God let him be alive when I get there,' she muttered.

Early next morning, Morvan rode out of the stables at Dinan. He wanted to gallop his young stallion, and he wanted to ride some way towards Dol. The remnants of William's army and knights were arriving, and Morvan had worked tirelessly to ensure that the dispirited men had at least a hot meal and a blanket, albeit under the stars, when they made it to Dinan. William himself came down, and he strode through the camp, having a word here and there with some of his veterans. This defeat was a new experience for these men; William had never retreated or been beaten before, and he could see the confusion and bewilderment on some of their faces. The king had walked with him for a while, making valuable suggestions here and there. Finally, he turned back towards the castle.

'We will leave in three days. I am returning to England,' he said, raising searching eyes to Morvan as if daring him to make some comment or criticism of the rout from Dol. William's two senior knights stood behind him, and they both stared at the ground. However, like his older brother, Morvan was not a courtier and looked thoughtfully at the King.

'It was a good, strategic withdrawal, Sire. With the arrival of Phillip's army, you made the right choice, despite the huge financial loss. Some commanders can be hot-headed and let their emotions rule their decisions, but you acted with prudence. You will, no doubt, deal with Phillip of France and Count Fulk of Anjou in your own time,' he said. William stood back and looked at Morvan as if reassessing him.

'You are wise for your age, young Malvais; you must join us for dinner tonight. Ah, I see messengers arriving; hopefully, they may have news of your brother as well as my enemies,' he said, striding purposefully back towards the castle.

Morvan stood for a while watching as the King crossed the meadow, every man's eye upon him. 'William the Bastard', William the Conqueror, King of England and Duke of Normandy, undoubtedly one of the greatest leaders of all time, he mused, despite this setback. Now, as Morvan galloped past the men and wagons still pouring into Dinan, he knew he was still in awe of William and, while he was pleased with the invitation for tonight, there was not only anticipation but also apprehension. Then he remembered a pair of clear, blue eyes. Would she be there tonight? He now knew that her name was Constance, the favourite daughter of her mother, Matilda, which was why she was still at home and unmarried in her early twenties. As he rode along deep in reverie, he almost did not hear the shouts from Gerard. He pulled up the big horse and whirled him around to stare down at the large cart that was trundling along. What he saw shocked him to the core. Luc lay white as a sheet in the back of the cart, a weary haggard-faced Gerard kneeling beside him.

'What happened? Will he live?' he managed to stutter out while pulling his horse into a fast, loping gait beside the cart.

'I honestly do not know Morvan. I have done my best to stop the bleeding, but he is sorely wounded; he has lost far too much blood. The sword was driven down through his shoulder and upper body and out through his arm. I do not yet know what damage it has done. There may also be much bleeding inside, although it seems to have miraculously missed his lung,' he said. Morvan stared at the lifeless, prone figure of his brother, Luc, who was usually such a vibrant force, laid low with a deadly wound.

'What can I do to help?' he said, in a voice full of emotion.

'Ride ahead and get my Lord's physician to meet us when we arrive,' he said. Morvan nodded and galloped back to Dinan. Lord Saint-Vere was ascending the steps with his Steward as Morvan skidded to a halt and leapt from the saddle. Within moments, Morvan explained, and the Steward raced indoors to summon the physician and servants to help carry Luc inside. By the time the wagon trundled to a halt, a group of people were assembled on the steps. Lady Saint-Vere had arrived with the physician and servants carrying a canvas pallet-bed. They quickly moved a groaning Luc onto it and brought him inside the castle. Lady Saint-Vere shook her head when she saw the deathly white figure.

'He has clearly lost a lot of blood, but we must treat and poultice all of the wounds immediately, before serious infection sets in,' she said. The castle physician nodded, the dreaded word gangrene hanging in the air without being mentioned. It was the primary cause of death in sword and battle wounds, and this was a major wound.

Chapter Thirty-Seven

I t had taken Ronec several attempts to mount the enormous Destrier before he finally managed to get on its back; his body now bore the bruises of several falls and many bites from the stallion. However, he had finally ridden Espirit triumphantly back to the rebel camp. Heads turned as he rode through the tents towards Fulk's pavilion; the horse was almost as famous as Malvais himself. Fulk was stood outside his tent deep in conversation with Ralph De Gael and Eudo de Penthievre when Ronec rode in on the renowned Destrier. All three heads turned to look at him and the horse when he dismounted.

'If you are riding Espirit Noir, I must assume that Malvais is dead by your hand?' challenged Eudo to his son.

Ronec smiled. 'Our mission was not a complete success. We fought with William, his guards and Malvais and his Horse Warriors; they seemed to be aware of our plans, and they were waiting for us when we emerged from the mist surrounding Mont Dol. I fought with Malvais; he is badly wounded, possibly mortally. However, William and his knights fled from Mont Dol; they abandoned everything, and the remnants of his army are fleeing to Dinan after him. We are ready to pursue him there if that is what you request, my Lord,' he said, staring pointedly at Ralph De Gael. Ralph had taken control of the campaign as soon as he emerged from the citadel, and he turned to the other two.

'We have shown our teeth to William this time. He now knows that the Breton Lords will unite against him if he constantly interferes in our matters here in Brittany. He will be like a cornered dangerous bear at the moment; let him return unmolested to Normandy or England,' he decided, running a hand over his grizzled beard.

The other two nodded in agreement until Fulk added, 'and we now have Phillip with his French army camped here at Dol, which we did not expect. We have just driven one wolf from our lands; we do not want another one. His alliance and intervention here at Dol was timely at your request De Gael, but we now need him to return to France.' Eudo ran his hands through his swept-back long hair.

'He will want something in return; Phillip does not take the time and spend the money to bring an army down here without an aim. Let us hope the price he demands is not too high for any of us,' he said.

Ralph intervened. 'It will not be us that are paying the price, Eudo; it will be William. Phillip has marched his army through Normandy and Maine to reach Dol; William will have to come to terms with him soon, and Philip wants the Vexin province.'

Eudo nodded and then turned to leave. He walked towards his son and clasped arms with him in a warriors grasp. 'Well done, Ronec. However, I do hope that Malvais lives; the world will be a duller place without him. Also, I believe he was your friend once,' he said, with a piercing look.

Ronec nodded and watched as the wise old warrior strode

away, his father, still as fit and energetic as ever, despite his age. Ralph waved Ronec to follow him inside the pavilion, so he handed Espirit to a nervous young squire who attempted to stay out of range of the snapping teeth. Within hours, richly rewarded with gold and land, Ronec was heading for two of the most challenging meetings of his life at Dinan, and, in his heart, he too hoped that Malvais lived.

Luc slowly opened his eyes and, blinking, looked at the wooden ceiling above, it was night, and the firelight flicked across the carved beams. It took him a few minutes to realise he was lying in bed as his eyes went in and out of focus. He became aware that he was propped up on several bolsters; he tried to push himself further up but was met with searing pain and the realisation that his right side was tightly strapped, so tightly that he could not move his right arm. He leaned back onto the bolster, a light sweat breaking out on his brow. He cast his mind back over events. He was injured but alive; he remembered racing over to Mont Dol to protect the King.

Then it all came back, the fight with Ronec and the attack by D'Avray. He grimaced ruefully as he remembered that his reluctance to finish Ronec had led to him being attacked. He had done the unforgivable, something he always warned Morvan about; he had left his sword too long on Ronec's throat, channelling his animosity too much onto one man while he talked to him and not being aware of what was behind and to the side of him. This was something he had drummed into every novice. His enmity and fury at Ronec had allowed him to be attacked from behind. For once in his life, he had let his emotions rule his head, and he had paid for it. Then he remembered that Ronec had actually saved his life by shouting a warning and killing D'Avray before he delivered the death blow; it had given him time to throw himself to the left. He remembered, now, the deep sword thrust down into his body. He slowly moved his left hand over to feel down his chest and torso, but he could feel no sign of a dreaded gut wound, the type of wound men usually died a lingering death from when infection set in.

He turned his head sideways; the room was dark, lit only by the light of the fire and in a chair by the fire sat Gerard. Luc smiled. Gerard, the nearest thing he had to a father since his own had died at Hastings. He could smell the pungent, herbal unguents and poultices that Gerard used on all wounds to stop them festering. There was a pallet on the floor as well, and Luc could see the dark head of Morvan asleep in the firelight; he really could sleep anywhere, he thought. He smiled as he drifted back off into oblivion; he felt blessed that he had people like this around him and, of course, Merewyn. He felt a moment of panic and then remembered that she was safe at Combourg.

Merewyn's thoughts were in turmoil as she pulled her horse up outside the Donjon in Dinan. In moments, she was off its back and running up the steps to the vast, carved doorway, where Morvan stood waiting for her.

'How is he, Morvan? Is he alive?' she cried.

'He is Merewyn, but his wound is deep and dangerous, and he has lost a great deal of blood. He is slipping in and out of consciousness. Gerard and Lady Saint-Vere have worked with the physician to ensure the wounds are clean, and he is given juice of the poppy each day to relieve the pain.'

Merewyn nodded. 'Just take me to him,' she pleaded, her

eyes full of unshed tears.

Luc's life was uncertain for several days as his temperature rocketed, and he became delirious. The whole castle waited expectantly to see if the famous warrior would survive what was a mortal wound. Merewyn spent hours beside his bed with Gerard, cooling his overheated body.

The King, who was still at Dinan, thanks to bad weather at sea, had sent to Caen for his own personal physician, a renowned Arab healer and doctor, who arrived with his own box of medicines to offer his knowledge and assistance. At first, the small dark foreigner was treated with suspicion, but his vast knowledge of anatomy and his collection of drugs and potions proved to be invaluable, and fear soon turned to respect. He pounded a concoction of ingredients in his mortar, many of which the other physician had never seen, and after adding wine, this mixture was dripped down Luc's throat.

The next day, the fever broke, and Luc woke to find Merewyn beside him. She was in a chair on his left-hand side, but half on the bed, her arms around him, and her head resting in his lap, fast asleep. Luc lifted his left hand and placed it on the silken silver hair. He closed his eyes, just revelling in the closeness of her as he stroked her head. She was here; she had come to him. He felt tears slowly trickle from beneath his closed lids as he realised that he was still alive and they might still be together with Lusian and their new child, who would be born in the early spring.

At that moment, Merewyn stirred and turned to look at him. Her eyes widened with joy as she realised that he was awake. She grasped his hand and kissed it, and he pulled her gently into his left side, his lips on her hair. They stayed like that, not speaking, for some time.

That night, Morvan sat at the top table with Lord and Lady Saint-Vere, King William, his wife Matilda and the Lady Constance. Since Merewyn had arrived, he had spent more time in their company when he was not sitting with Luc. William enjoyed having the younger knights around him, and he found Morvan's knowledge of horses and his ready wit both entertaining and interesting. He was not the only one, as his daughter constantly turned to watch and listen to this handsome and exciting young knight, who was so different from the fawning and polished courtiers.

Her mother, Matilda, smiled as she watched them. She allowed Constance to walk down to the horse lines with Morvan and William as he showed them the paces of the young Destriers they had bred and trained ready for battle. William had heard much of the bloodlines developed by the Malvais family; he had seen them in action in the distance but had never seen them up close until he was mounted on one in his flight from Dol. The size, speed, power and intelligence of these horses were more than impressive.

As the week progressed, the young couple took walks down by the lake and each evening often saw them sat by the fire talking before dinner if Morvan was not with Luc.

William was impervious to the growing attraction between his daughter and the young Horse Warrior; as he had weightier things on his mind, envoys had arrived from both the rebels and Phillip of France, asking for terms and treaties. Matilda, however, saw no harm in a playful dalliance; it would do Constance good. This daughter was chosen to stay at home with her mother, so she was somewhat unworldly, although very intelligent and well-read in Latin and Greek. However, Matilda knew that the day would come when William would use Constance to secure a future alliance through marriage, which was always the fate of a King's daughter.

Constance entranced Morvan; she was reserved but intelligent and witty when she wanted to be. She had a comprehensive knowledge of the political situation in Europe, and he found himself relaxed and entertained in her company. In his head, he knew that as a landless second son, he was beneath the notice of her parents, as a suitor, but that did not prevent his affections from becoming engaged. Constance was not beautiful, she took after her father, but she had fine eyes, lustrous auburn hair and something else, a presence about her. He was deep in playful conversation with her when Gerard touched his shoulder to tell him that Luc was awake.

William, whose eagle eyes usually missed nothing, waved him over. 'Sir Gerard is there news?' he asked. Gerard bowed. 'Yes, Sire, Malvais is awake, and the fever has broken,' he replied.

William nodded and smiled, as did the other occupants of the table. 'Good news indeed. Tell him I will come and see him on the morrow,' he said, waving dismissal.

Luc had reluctantly let go of Merewyn to clasp a weakened left hand with Gerard and Morvan. The three of them sat around the bed engaged in conversation while a subdued Luc watched them with affection. Before long, though, it was evident that he was tiring quickly and was also in considerable discomfort and pain, so Merewyn chased them out.

'Sleep, my love, you need time for your body to heal,' she whispered, pushing the dark shock of hair back from his forehead as he drifted into sleep.

Luc found the next morning a severe trial as the two physicians examined and cleaned his wounds. He sat up with gritted teeth as they poked, prodded and moved his injured arm. Finally, he was re-bandaged and allowed to rest. The castle physician left, but William's Arab doctor stayed behind. Luc lay back on the pillows and regarded the small, bird-like man with equanimity. He had heard about this man; he knew that he had saved several lives in the past.

'What is your name?' he asked.

'I am Omar Saleh, at your service,' he said and bowed while touching his fingers to his lips and forehead. Luc thanked the man for his services and care, and a smile flitted across the man's face in recognition of this gratitude. He was used to dealing with people who rarely gave him a second thought, never mind asking for his name.

At that moment, the door opened, and Morvan strode in, followed by Merewyn. 'The king is here to see how you are faring,' he said, holding the door wide. William swept in, followed by Lord Saint-Vere.

'Well, Malvais, I am relieved to see that you are still with us. I feared for a while that we would lose you,' he said, as his piercing blue eyes took in the bandaged figure on the bed, sweat still beading Luc's brow after the ministrations of both physicians.

'I must thank you, Sire, for sending me Saleh, such an excellent physician. Merewyn tells me that he saved my life,' said Luc.

William nodded. 'He has been with me for several years;

he is worth his weight in gold.' The Arab doctor cast down his eyes and looked uncomfortable at such fulsome praise.

'So Saleh, tell us of the injuries that Malvais has sustained. Will he make a full recovery?' he asked. Luc narrowed his eyes in interest and alarm as he watched the pursed lips of the small Arab doctor.

'The lord De Malvais was stabbed with a sword, straight through his body from the back of the neck. Usually, this killing blow finds the heart and severs the cord in the spine. However, fortunately, it seems he moved. Which meant the blow was deflected from its path off the scapula, the shoulder bone', he explained, turning to the others, 'thereby doing considerable damage, but missing any vital organs.' The man turned his bright, dark eyes on Luc and continued.

'Unfortunately, the sword continued on its path, coming out of his side and through his upper right arm. My Lord, can you turn your right hand palm downwards?' he asked.

At first, Luc remained immobile, absorbing what he had just heard.

'I remember. I was kneeling and D'Avray, behind me, had both hands on the sword he had plunged into me. However, I pushed up against the sword into a standing position. I felt the blade going out and through my arm as I did so,' he whispered.

Several faces in the room blanched at this description, and Merewyn put a hand over her mouth.

Luc attempted to turn his hand as the Arab physician had asked, which produced excruciating pain in his upper arm. He found the action impossible. In fact, movement in any direction was severely limited, although he could curl his fingers and lightly grip the cover. Merewyn stepped around the bed and took his other hand as she saw the dismay on Luc's face.

'It is as I thought; the blade has severed the tendon in the upper arm, which means, although you will be able to grasp and move objects, holding anything of any size or weight will be a problem,' said the physician.

There was a stunned silence in the room. This was Malvais, one of the best swordsmen in Europe, who had just been told he had lost his right sword arm. Luc could see the shock he felt reflected in the faces around him.

The King recovered first. 'It is a good thing, Malvais, that your left sword arm is as good as your right one,' he said.

Malvais grimaced at that as it was true, but his stomach was knotted as he realised that he could not lead the Breton Horse Warriors with only one arm. He tightened his grip on Merewyn's hand. The small Arab had not finished, however.

'If I may be permitted, my Lord, and of course, with the King's permission, I would like to cut your arm open again and sew the tendons back together. I have had some success with this in the past.' No one spoke as they all stared at Omar Saleh. This was unheard of.

'Some success?' Luc questioned, narrowing his eyes.

'Could they hold and use a sword again?' questioned Morvan, moving forward to stand beside Luc.

The little doctor smiled. 'Well, it was actually on the leg of a goat, but it could walk again, albeit with a slight limp,' he acknowledged.

'My husband is not a goat to be cut open,' cried Merewyn in shock. Luc held up his left hand to silence her.

'If I have this correctly, if I do nothing, I lose the use of my arm; if I let you cut me open, I may not get all use back, but I could get most of it?' he asked.

'Yes, my Lord, but we must not delay because the tendons will be shrinking back into the arm. I need to do it tonight,' he said.

'No!' shouted Merewyn. 'He has not recovered enough; you will kill him.'

Luc calmed her by raising her hand to his lips. He looked thoughtful for a few moments and then looked up at William.

'Sire, you have great faith in this Arab physician, I believe?'

'He is a learned medical man from the Middle East; he has been instrumental in copying and translating Avicenna's Canon of Medicine, a vast tome of Greek, Persian and Arab medicine. I have seen him perform what many would call miracles,' said William.

Luc looked at the worried faces around him, then at the small birdlike Arab doctor. 'Go ahead, but I would like some time on my own with my wife first.'

The doctor nodded. 'I need time to prepare,' he said and bowing to the King and the assembled knights, he left.

William raised a hand in farewell to Luc and summoned Morvan and Gerard. 'Come Malvais is in the best of hands, come and show me these promising youngsters you are going to sell me; I need several warhorses of that quality,' he said as they departed.

Left alone, Merewyn sat down gently beside Luc, who looked exhausted. 'Are you sure about this, Luc? I fear greatly for your life; any surgery is a huge risk,' she said, stroking the side of his face.

'I am prepared to take the risk; the King has confidence in this man,' he said, putting his good arm around her. 'Now kiss me, Merewyn; it has been far too long,' he said as she lowered her face to his.

Ronec galloped out of the trees and over the ford towards Dinan. The huge Destrier had eaten up the miles, and now he was ready to keep his promise and return this beautiful horse to his owner as he had sworn to do. He just hoped that Malvais still lived; the wound he had suffered was traumatic. As long as he lived, Ronec would never forget Malvais pushing himself up against the sword embedded in his body to topple his enemy behind him. He knew from experience that in battle, the bloodlust and adrenaline often numbed the pain of wounds, but he was not sure he would have the sharpness of mind or strength to do what Malvais did in that situation. It was no wonder he was such a legend, the pure courage of the man.

As he rode through the castle gatehouse and into the inner bailey on Espirit, all heads turned to gaze at the huge, dappled-grey stallion with the flowing black mane and tail; almost everyone recognised this as the famous horse of Malvais. Ronec drew rein in front of the keep and dismounted, handing the reins to a squire. He turned to mount the steps just in time to see the king descending with Lord Saint-Vere, Morvan de Malvais and Gerard. Morvan and Saint-Vere drew their swords immediately, but William stood stock still on the steps regarding the young warrior in front of him with a rueful smile.

'Have you come to finish the job, Ronec Fitz-Eudo?' he asked while raising a hand to keep the others back.

Ronec bowed. 'No, Sire, I am delighted to see you safe; I am purely honouring a promise to Malvais to look after and return his horse.' Morvan looked at Gerard, surprised to see that he had not drawn his sword. He turned on Ronec.

'You treacherous bastard,' he spat at him and began to step forward, but Gerard stopped him.

'No, Morvan, Ronec saved Luc's life and killed Pierre D'Avray, who had sorely wounded him and was about to finish him off.' Morvan stepped back, disbelief on his face. He kept his sword unsheathed; he did not and never would trust this mercenary.

'Is he still alive? I would like to see him,' asked Ronec.

'He is, but badly wounded and about to be cut open again tonight,' said Gerard, 'so you will need to wait. That is if he agrees to see you. The Lady Merewyn is with him.' Ronec nodded as the King waved the others on to continue to the stables.

However, Saint-Vere stopped in front of Ronec, sword still drawn. 'I have issue with you, Fitz-Eudo. You have despoiled my daughter and ruined her reputation. She is carrying your child,' he shouted.

Ronec bowed. 'Forgive me, my Lord. Your daughter is very beautiful, and you are right; she did not deserve to be treated so. In my defence, it was her plan as much as it was mine. However, I am here to ask for her hand in marriage. I am now a man of wealth and substance, and with your permission, I would like to marry her before our child is born.'

Saint-Vere looked slightly mollified. 'You had better come in and discuss this. Briaca is not here; she has been sent to the nuns at the Convent de Cordelier; the child is to be taken away and given to a freeman's family,' he said, turning to go back inside. Ronec went pale at the thought of his child being lost and ran up the steps behind the Castellan.

Chapter Thirty-Eight

L ater that day, the Arab doctor arrived in Luc's room ready to perform the surgery. As he unrolled a wrap of sharp knives and began to thread a needle, Luc ordered everyone from the room but Gerard and Morvan. He winced as Saleh unwound the bandages, and Gerard, who had dealt with lots of wounds, watched with the little man interest; fortunately, the wounds all looked clean, although still red and angry in places. The Arab physician had examined the injuries in detail as if there had been any sign of infection; it would have had to be cut out first before the procedure had gone ahead.

Luc gritted his teeth as the Arab proceeded to wash the whole area with a mixture of wine, salt and vinegar. 'I have found that it helps to reduce the risk of infection,' the little man explained to the three men. Luc found it hard to focus on what the Arab was saying, having been given a very heady mixture of brandy and tincture of poppy. Before long, he drifted into a troubled sleep.

Following the Arab's instructions, Morvan held Luc down with his hands on his shoulders and watched with appre-hension as the doctor pulled Luc's arm out straight onto the table that was pulled up beside the bed. Gerard held the arm tightly and firmly at the wrist and forearm to prevent Luc from pulling it back. The physician picked up a small sharp knife and carefully sliced into the arm, reopening the wound and with precision slowly extending the cut from the elbow almost to the shoulder. Luc, although sedated, cried out loudly and repeatedly, but fortunately, did not return to full consciousness.

The little man found and then hooked and pulled the tendons towards each other. The sweat stood out on his bald domed head as he used two long thin sharp bodkins to pierce and then hold them in place while he sewed the two tendons carefully and securely together with catgut that he had soaked in the wine and vinegar. Gerard and Morvan looked on in fascination as the Physician stood up and stretching his back while looking down critically at his work; the procedure had taken over an hour, and at times Luc had thrashed on the bed as his brother and friend held him down. The Arab nodded in satisfaction, and then he repacked the wound and put a few holding stitches in the flesh, pulling it together.

'I will need to clean and wash it for a few days,' he explained, seeing Gerard's puzzled look. This was all new to Gerard, but his mind quickly grasped how this might prevent infection even though it would inflict severe additional pain for several days. He looked at the little doctor with respect as the man covered all of the wounds with a strong-smelling brown paste before rebinding them.

'What is it?' asked Gerard, wiping a small amount on his finger and smelling it.

'It's mainly curcumin, which you may possibly know as turmeric, but it is bound together with salt, honey and vinegar,' he said, not even looking up from his task.

'Is this better for keeping infection at bay?' he asked.

The doctor straightened up and regarded Gerard through bright eyes, obviously pleased to find someone who shared an interest.

'It is, but it also reduces any inflammation. It is a costly spice, but I have plundered the king's stores,' he said smiling. Gerard nodded. He had already learnt so much from watching the little man over the last few days.

'Give him a small dose of the poppy if he wakes; we need him as still as possible. He will have a few uncomfortable and painful nights as we deal with the wound, but hopefully, we will not get another fever,' he said before bowing and leaving.

The following day Luc was awake and fractious. The doctor had left instructions that he was not to use his hand and arm for any reason for several days, which meant he had to stay immobilised, a difficult task for a warrior such as Luc. However, he had people around him to keep him entertained and his mind occupied, although he did sleep a great deal as his body recuperated. Two days later, he refused any more large doses of sedative after the wound was cleaned; he decided he was prepared to put up with the pain in exchange for a clearer mind.

William called in on Luc before his departure for England. He was pleased with Luc's progress, and they talked horses and warfare until the King even shared his misgivings about Phillip of France and his intentions. Then he took his leave, assuring him that he would send tidings to Alain Rufus in Richmond when he reached London. Luc was exhausted by lunchtime and slept, but he woke in the early evening to find Gerard sat beside his bed; he gave Luc more wine infused with hemp to manage the pain while he talked of the men. He had sent a troop of fifty to escort William to St Malo to board his ship for England. He had also sent Beorn, with his troop of eighty men, back to Vannes, as it was pointless keeping them here. The rest of his men were exercising the horses and training each day to prevent idleness, unruly behaviour, or fights breaking out.

'Where is Morvan?' asked Luc.

'He is out walking with Lady Constance around the lake for about the tenth time,' Gerard grinned.

'Constance? A dark-haired girl,' questioned Luc, trying to place her.

'No, she is one of the middle daughters of William and her mother's favourite. She has auburn hair like her father, an attractive girl; you are probably thinking of Adeliza, the eldest daughter,' said Gerard.

Luc looked up to meet Gerard's eyes. 'She is a royal princess of England; what is Morvan about? William will never consider a second son for his daughter, even a younger daughter; he will want a political alliance,' he said in an exasperated voice. Gerard nodded sagely.

'Are his affections engaged?' he asked in a concerned voice.

'They have become firm friends over the last week or so. She is a little younger than him, about twenty years old, but she is exceptionally well educated and seems older.'

'He needs to put her out of his mind; it will never do and can only cause heartbreak,' said Luc, shaking his head while resisting the impulse to flex his right arm and hand.

'You have another visitor, possibly not a welcome one, but he has waited for a few days and has asked for an audience with you.' said Gerard.

Luc raised an eyebrow at him. 'Who is it?' he questioned.

'Ronec Fitz-Eudo. He has brought you Espirit as he promised, and he has been granted Briaca's hand in marriage by Saint-Vere.

Luc did not speak for several minutes as he tried to control and examine his emotions, and Gerard, to give him his due, did not say any more. He gazed across at the sunlight streaming through the window embrasure, remembering all that Ronec had done to him. The lies, the deceit, the seduction and the attempted kidnapping of Merewyn, the plot hatched with Briaca to destroy his marriage. Could he ever forgive him?

However, he had finally faced up to the fact that he had found it difficult to kill Ronec when it came to it, and he still cursed himself for that weakness. However, Ronec had warned him and gone on to kill D'Avray. The silence hung in the room for so long that Gerard finally cleared his throat to end Luc's reverie.

'Has he seen Merewyn?' he asked, raising his eyes to Gerard.

'Perhaps, but she has avoided him. He has not stayed in the castle,' Gerard reassured him.

'Bring him up here,' said Luc and Gerard left, leaving Luc to struggle with his conflicting emotions. Five minutes later, Gerard reappeared with Ronec in his wake.

Ronec paused on the threshold staring at the imposing bandaged figure propped up in the bed. Malvais was pale from the blood loss, and he could see the deep lines of pain etched on his face, but the grim set to his mouth and those hard, steel blue eyes were clear and full of determination. Even severely wounded, Malvais had a dangerous, commanding presence that filled any room. They stared at each other for some time, these men who had once been good friends but had become deadly enemies ready to kill or be killed. Ronec broke the silence first.

'I am relieved to see that you are still alive and on the road to recovery, Malvais. I was hoping that D'Avray had not put an end to your life; I have never seen anyone survive such a sword thrust before,' he said.

Luc regarded the man he had felt such anger and hatred towards, and surprising himself, he found that he suddenly felt nothing, no enmity towards him. The men that had used Ronec and directed him, Fitz-Eustace and De Gael, yes, but not for this mercenary, who had once been such a close comrade. He waved him to a chair.

'I believe I have to offer you my felicitations Ronec, you are to be married,' he said with a rueful smile that did not reach his eyes.

Ronec breathed a sigh of relief, moved to sit on a stool beside the bed, and then laughed.

'Yes, Luc, and before you say it, I know that I will have my hands full with that little vixen, but she is carrying my child, and part of me has a yearning for a real home. I have wandered the countries of Europe for long enough. Like you, I am now in my early thirties, and I envy what you have,' he said.

That sentence resonated with Luc and Gerard, who had spent over five years as mercenaries, but Luc could not help raising his eyebrows and add a rejoinder.

'Even though you tried to destroy and take what I had'. Ronec dropped his head to gaze at the floor; he found it challenging to meet Luc's gaze. 'I am not proud of that, Luc, and I regret my actions believe me.' It was quiet in the room for a while, with only the sound of Gerard poking some life into the fire breaking the silence. Then Luc sighed, determined to move on from what had happened.

'I believe I owe you thanks for taking the time to bring Espirit Noir back to me, as well as for saving my life,' said Luc.

Ronec snorted with laughter. 'That horse is a devil. He nearly killed me. Five times he threw me before he allowed me to ride him, and I think my squire has left me; he was bitten so many times.' Both men laughed. 'However, it was only a small thing that I could do as recompense for what I did to you, Luc. I sacrificed our friendship for wealth and land while trying for recognition and acclaim from my father. This is not an excuse; I know I was blinded to some of the more important things in life, like friendship. However, now I am to be a father shortly, I find that my values and priorities are changing. I thought about that a lot while I rode that dangerous beast of yours back to Dinan.'

Luc regarded Ronec for a few moments. 'We will never be friends again Ronec, too much has happened, too much betrayal and loss of trust, but if we meet again in the future, I hope we can do so with equanimity. Hopefully, we will never meet again on a battlefield as I probably will kill you,' he said quietly.

Ronec stared at Luc, the regret clear to see on his face. However, he had made his own choices, and Ronec found he was resigned to this outcome, and, in some ways, he had received a far better reception than he had expected. He rose to his feet, bowed to them both, turned on his heel and without a word left the room. Luc and Gerard sat in silence for several minutes until Gerard spoke.

'They say that warfare is a great leveller Luc, but it also shows you the true meaning of friendship and loyalty. I do think he may have learnt that lesson,' he said, shaking his head.

Luc nodded. 'Yes, it was a different Ronec that stood there today, but given the parlous condition of my arm, I doubt that we will ever again meet on a battlefield,' he said. Gerard nodded; he hoped that the Arab doctor's solution had worked; however, only time would tell; Gerard was a realist, and he doubted that Luc would ever regain full use of his right arm.

'No, you are right, the pair of you may not meet again in battle, but maybe your sons will one day,' he said.

Epilogue

Over a month later, Morvan cantered down the line of men and carts as they crossed into Normandy. He stopped fleetingly at the large box-like carriage that carried Queen Matilda and her maids to check that all was well. The carriage was slung on poles and strapped to a horse in front and one behind. Morvan had quickly picked up that the ladies preferred this type of transport to the covered wagons on the rutted roads.

They would be approaching Mont St Michel in an hour or so where they would be resting for the night, so he sent scouts and outriders on ahead to notify the Abbot that the Queen was on her way. He pulled his lively, young black stallion in beside the Lady Constance, who greeted him with a shy smile and a tinkle of laughter as the young horse danced and caracoled on the spot.

William had returned with the rest of his force to England, but he had tasked Morvan with taking sixty Horse Warriors to escort his wife and daughter back to his vast castle at Caen in Normandy. Morvan had been delighted to do so, and he calmed the big stallion to ride gently beside the bay palfrey that Constance was riding.

'Your Lady mother is comfortable and happy and asks if

you wish to join her yet, she is worried about the dust,' he said.

Constance stared out over the wooded valley ahead; she could see the sea in the distance. 'I much prefer being able to ride Minette and breathe the fresh air than being cooped up and bouncing along in a box; it makes me sea-sick,' she laughed.

Morvan smiled. She was such an engaging and interesting girl; he had never come across anyone like her before.

'How is your brother?' she asked.

Morvan smiled at her concern. 'He is much recovered, but it is a slow process. He now has more movement and flexibility in his arm, and of course, being Luc, he is beginning to do sword exercises every day when Gerard and Merewyn are out of sight,' he answered.

'So does this mean that we will see the famous, dashing Luc De Malvais galloping at the head of the Breton Horse Warriors again?' she asked, turning those fine, blue eyes towards him. 'He is such a romantic figure; all of the court ladies swoon at the thought of him carrying them off on that huge stallion of his.' She laughed at repeating the daring innuendo used at court.

Morvan smiled and laughed with her. He had lived in the shadow of the great 'Malvais' for long enough for it now not to bother him.

'All of the ladies? Does that also include you and your mother, Lady Constance?' he asked with raised eyebrows, joking with her.

'No. And I think both the Lady Merewyn and my father might have something to say about that,' she said.

He laughed aloud and then added daringly in a whisper, 'I

can carry you off on my huge stallion any time you wish.'

She blushed prettily and then started to giggle.

'To answer your question, my Lady, the Horse Warriors are standing down at present until we are called into action again by our Liege Lord Alain Rufus or at the call of your father, the King. Luc will return to Morlaix with Merewyn this week; they are both desperate to see their son Lusian. Merewyn is expecting a child in the early spring, and Luc is to concentrate on the family lands and the horse-breeding programme for now. That means, for the time being, I will be leading the Horse Warriors if we are ordered into action; I will try to be as dashing as my brother is, he added. Also, Luc has gifted me the large estates at Vannes, so I am now a landed knight and not just a second son,' he said, with a proud lift of his head. She looked at him with shining eyes, her mouth slightly open in an 'o' of surprise and then a smile of delight. 'So you will, in turn, become as famous and as feared as your brother,' she said wide-eyed.

Morvan, as self-effacing as ever, laughed. 'I don't think that anyone could compete with Luc; he will always be the legend that is 'Malvais'. He took on three men in the training ground yesterday while recovering and drove all three off using only a sword in his left hand. I practice for hours each day to have even a fraction of my brother's skill,' he said. Morvan spent a few minutes controlling the young stallion, which had taken exception to some of the village dogs, but he could see from her face that she did not believe him.

'You will be famous, Morvan, as will your horse. My Lord, I have to announce the arrival of 'Minuit', the huge black stallion of the Breton Horse Warriors,' she said triumphantly, mimicking the voice of a squire at court. He roared with laughter; she was so refreshing.

He became more serious for a few minutes, 'Your father has asked for five of our youngsters to be delivered to Caen by the end of the year, so that means I will be riding north again shortly,' he said, watching her face. 'Will you be pleased to see me, Constance, when I come to Caen again?' he said, moving his stallion so close that his leg was brushing hers. She modestly dropped her eyes but then looked up at him, smiling. 'I will count the days, Morvan De Malvais,' she said.

Luc leaned on the fence of the training ground at Morlaix. It had taken him several months to recover from his injuries, and he knew it would take him far longer to build up the muscle he would need in his right arm to counteract the damage. He had significantly improved, but he had finally come to terms with the loss of speed and flexibility in his right arm.

He had made a great show of handing over the Horse warriors' leadership to Morvan, and he was confident that his younger brother would come into his own and inspire his men when he was not constantly riding behind his older brother. He had received a long missive from his patron, Alain Rufus, assuring him that his astute leadership skills will always be needed, but he needed to recuperate for now. Alain had thanked him for his help with his father, Eudo, who had heeded Luc's advice and remained in the background with his troops at the siege of Dol. Alain also mentioned that the King was also eternally grateful for Luc and Morvan's services in those last days at Dol and that rewards would be forthcoming.

Luc smiled. For now, though, he was content to be home

at Morlaix, his wife Merewyn by his side, her advancing pregnancy now very noticeable. His son, Lusian, was shooting up in size and now looked more like a ten-year-old as he cantered his horse over the jumps and logs set up by Gerard. He placed his arm around Merewyn's shoulders and pulled her close, kissing the top of her braided blonde hair, his wife, his Saxon rebel, the mother of his children by his side. At this moment, he did not want more.

'Morvan should be nearly there by now,' remarked Merewyn.

'Yes, they should all be back home by the middle of next week,' agreed Luc.

'That's if he comes home and doesn't stay longer,' she added mischievously. Luc shook his head in exasperation.

'I did speak to him about her. I warned him not to get involved that it could never come to anything,' he said.

'They are in love; it shines out of their faces,' she said.

'The way it shines out of ours,' he said, pulling her closer against his chest and leaning down to kiss her deeply. His kiss left her breathless as usual; even now, after nearly seven years together, he could still send a wave of desire through her body when he kissed her like that.

'Look at us, Luc. We defied all convention. We fell in love; a hated Norman and a rebel Saxon,' she said, smiling.

'I kept telling you all along that I was not a Norman. I am a Breton warrior first and foremost,' he said in a mock-serious voice. 'Seriously though, William and Matilda will never allow it. Constance will have a strategic, political marriage. Those two young people are about to experience their first real heartbreak, a love that is requited by both of them but a love that will not be allowed to flourish,' he said with finality.

'We will see,' she said, watching in dismay as a messenger galloped across the meadow towards them. The young man leapt from the saddle and handed Luc a leather pouch, which he opened to read the content.

'Well, Fulk did not stay quiet for long. Angevin troops have crossed the border into Maine and western Brittany.' He made as if to head to the stables, but Merewyn put a hand on his arm.

'No, it is far too soon, and this baby will be here in a month,' she said, raising her huge green eyes to his face as Gerard ran up. Luc sighed and nodded as she took the missive from his fingers and handed it to Gerard.

'Saddle them up,' she said, as Luc shrugged at Gerard and gave a rueful smile. Gerard grinned and nodded, calling the men and squires as he ran towards the horse meadows.

Two hours later, over a hundred huge warhorses thundered down the road and out of Morlaix, heading for the borders of Brittany. For the conflict never stopped for long in these war-torn lands, as alliances crumbled. Fulk, imbued with his success against William, had turned on Maine but also attacked the lands of his former ally, Eudo De Penthievre, who now called on the Horse Warriors for help.

Luc felt proud but wistful as he stood and watched his men gallop out in perfect four abreast formations. His creation, the feared Breton Horse Warriors, galloped out but without their famous leader, 'Luc De Malvais', at their head.

For now…

Glossary

- **Angevin** – Soldiers, cavalry or citizens from the province of Anjou.
- **Bailey** - A ward or courtyard in a castle, some outer baileys could be huge, encompassing grazing land.
- **Braies** - A type of trouser often used as an undergarment, often to mid-calf and made of light or heavier linen.
- **Chasseurs** - Light cavalry, hunters or raiders, often kitted out for rapid action.
- **Coup De Main** - A swift pre-emptive strike on the enemy.
- **Chausses** – Attached by laces to the waist of the braies, these were tighter fitting coverings for the legs.
- **Destrier** – A knight's large warhorse, often trained to fight, bite and strike out.
- **Donjon** – The fortified tower of an early castle later called the Keep.
- **Doublet** – A close-fitting jacket or jerkin often made from leather, with or without sleeves. Laced at the front and worn either under or over, a chain mail hauberk.
- **Escalade** - The art of scaling walls with ladders during a siege.

- **Echelon Formation** - Cavalry arranged diagonally for a charge on the enemy.
- **Fabian Strategy** - Avoiding pitched battles to wear down the enemy in a war of attrition.
- **Hauberk** – A tunic of chain mail, often reaching to mid-thigh.
- **Investment** - Surrounding and preventing entry or escape during a siege.
- **Liege lord** – A feudal lord such as a Count or Baron entitled to allegiance and service from his knights.
- **Lymers** - A type of hound used in medieval times to scent track game and fugitives.
- **Marechal** – A military officer or noble of the highest rank to control or administer an area.
- **Mead** – An alcoholic drink made from fermented honey.
- **Motte** – An earth mound, forming a secure platform on which a Donjon would be built; initially, this would be made of wood until the earth settled and compacted.
- **Patron** – An individual who gives financial, political, or social patronage to others. Often through wealth or influence in return for loyalty and homage.
- **Pottage** – A staple of the medieval diet, a thick soup made by boiling grains and vegetables and, if available, meat or fish.
- **Prie-Dieu** - A type of prayer desk to kneel on for private use.
- **Retraite en echiquier** - A chequered retreat, alternatively retreating and the facing bout to fight again. The strategy was often used by cavalry.
- **Rout** - A disorderly withdrawal from a battle.

- **Serjeant** – The soldier Serjeant was a man who often came from a higher class; most experienced medieval mercenaries fell into this class; they were deemed to be 'half of the value of a knight' in military terms.
- **Siege en regle** - No bombardment and limited attacks, instead by persuading them to surrender through inducement and persuasion.
- **Vavasseur** - A right-hand man, chosen for his dignity, valour and prowess.
- **Vedette** - An outrider or scout used by cavalry.
- **Vellum** - Finest scraped and treated calfskin, used for writing messages

Author Note

The history of Brittany is troubled but fascinating. The Duchy was subject to Frankish rule for a while and then came under the influence of either the Counts of Anjou or the Dukes of Normandy, depending on who had the upper hand. Unfortunately, very few Breton chronicles have survived from the eleventh century; instead, we have to rely on the monastic annuls or accounts by later chroniclers such as the monks Orderic Vitalis and William of Malmesbury.

The aristocracy of eastern Brittany was proud of its cultural heritage, but they became more involved in Frankish affairs and culture because of their proximity to Maine and Anjou. In contrast, the nobility of wilder western Brittany was more geographically isolated and became more engaged in Anglo-Norman affairs and interests. There were Breton lords in residence at the court of King Edward the Confessor in England. Many Bretons, such as Alain Rufus, participated in the Norman Conquest and had large estates in England. Count Eudo of Penthievre, the father of Alain Rufus, provided 5,000 troops comprising Breton cavalry, archers, crossbowmen, spearmen and axemen, along with a hundred ships for William's invasion of England.

Ralph De Gael, the leader of the Breton forces at the Battle of Hastings, initially supported William's invasion and was richly rewarded becoming the Earl of Suffolk and Norfolk. However, in 1075, Ralph did lead major rebellions against King William as he had never forgiven him for poisoning both his older brother Walter Mantes and his wife Biota. Ralph was part of the significant alliance against William in Brittany at the siege of Dol in 1076. His young wife Emma De Gael famously held Norwich castle for three months against Williams 'Warrior Bishops' after Ralph fled England for Denmark after the Earl's rebellion.

Count Fulk IV of Anjou was a particularly unpleasant character who usurped and imprisoned his older brother to gain the title. He married five times; none of the marriages seemed to be of any duration; Philip of France apparently fell in love with and abducted Fulk's last wife Bertrade De Montfort and married her, even though they both had spouses living and she already had a son, Fulk V King of Jerusalem. Fulk's grandson Geoffrey Plantagenet would establish one of the greatest dynasties in England.

William of Normandy left a profound mark on both western Europe and England. He was one of the most important and influential figures of early medieval history. As a young boy, he survived the anarchy of Normandy to become the Duke and his conquest of England in 1066 altered the course of English history. He faced war and rebellion throughout his whole life, and the events and outcome of the siege of Dol in 1076 would affect his future relationship with not only Fulk IV Count of Anjou and Philip King of France but also with his own sons.....

But more of that in Book Three – **'Betrayal.'**

Read More

The Breton Horse Warrior Series
Book One - Ravensworth
Book Two - Rebellion
Book Three - Betrayal

The third book in the **Breton Horse Warrior Series, Betrayal,** continues the story of Luc De Malvais and his brother Morvan, this time in war-torn Normandy, three years later. King William now faces threats and betrayal from all sides, especially from his own son. Luc's world and family are turned upside down as brother is pitted against brother. Morvan finds himself torn when it comes to his loyalty to his King and family, especially as he struggles with his all-consuming but forbidden love for Constance, the daughter of King William.

Read the first chapter on the next page...

Betrayal

Western Brittany late summer 1078

The group of horsemen galloped down into the village of Saint-Pabu. Luc De Malvais pulled up his great warhorse Espirit and glanced around the small quiet village sitting on the banks of the river Aber-Benoir. He looked around the scattered wooden houses and identified the most prominent house; as he rode towards it, a man emerged from the open door leading to the dark interior.

Luc smiled; the man who appeared was the epitome of a western Breton chieftain with his dark braided hair and long moustaches. This was a remote, scarcely populated and isolated area where little had changed for hundreds of years. The chieftain regarded the horsemen solemnly for several moments and then raised a hand in greeting as Luc's brother Morvan pulled his horse alongside Espirit.

Morvan, who had planned this expedition, waved one of the young Horse Warriors forward, 'Benedot, I believe you understand the Celtic patois in this area,' he asked.

The dark young man nodded 'yes, my mother, she comes from this area,' he said as he went forward and greeted the village leader, explaining the reason behind their arrival. The man looked at them in astonishment, and then running his hand over his moustaches and chin, he gave a great guffaw of laughter and called out his sons to hear the tale. Although they eyed the Horse Warriors on their huge Destriers with wary respect, the two young men were similarly amused and talked animatedly together. The older man then stepped forward and gesticulated at Benedot, pointing down the estuary and describing what seemed to be a sweep south along the coast.

Morvan's black stallion was impatiently stamping its feet, and he whirled it round in a circle to quieten it as he shouted, 'what is he saying, has he seen her, does he know where she is?' Luc smiled at Morvan; after several days of fruitless searches, he knew just how frustrated his younger brother was; Luc hoped this information would be valuable in helping them find her. Young Benedot thanked the village elder and turned back to the two Malvais brothers.

'She was seen only yesterday by the village fishermen, she was in the forest along the cliffs that run down to the beach of the Tres Moutons, but they say we should go now as they think she will be moving inland again for the winter,' he replied with a satisfied smile.

Morvan tightened the reins on his restless stallion; he had waited several years to find her again, so many false sightings, and now they were so close. 'Do you know where this beach is, Benedot?' he asked.

The young man nodded, 'If we follow the banks of the estuary for a few miles, it will bring us to the coast, and we can turn south into the pine forests he describes.' The older man laughed again and added something else. Benedot

419

smiled and nodded in understanding to the chieftain, 'He says you will never take her; if she sees you coming, she will disappear and melt into the forests like one of the ghosts on All Hallows.'

Luc smiled back and nodded; he knew how difficult this would be, but they had travelled a long way, and they had to try to find her. He raised a fist in salute to the man and his sons and slowly led his Horse Warriors out of the village and down along the sandy shores of the wide Aber-Benoir river estuary.

He had only agreed to join his brother's quest to the far west, as things had been unnaturally quiet in Brittany for a time. Many Breton Lords had retreated to their lands after the siege and battle last year at La Fleche. They still had the usual Horse Warrior patrols of the eastern borders to stop the marauding raids by the Angevins into Maine and Brittany, but his right-hand man, Sir Gerard, could handle that while they were away. In addition, he reflected that it was good to spend some time with his brother. Morvan had spent much of the last few years away from his home in Morlaix at the Norman court of King William in Caen, where he was forming and training a new cohort of Horse Warriors.

An hour later, they reached the coast and rode up through the pine and scrub forests and rocky outcrops to stand on a small bluff overlooking the long silver sand beaches of the western shoreline. It was a wild and rocky coast, but scattered throughout were these beautiful beaches surrounded by pink granite cliffs and coves—vast stretches of white sand and crystal clear turquoise waters when the weather was calm. As he gazed at the beautiful vista, the western salt sea breeze sweeping the dark hair back from his face, Luc realised that it had been far too long since he had ridden this way, too many years embroiled instead in the politics and wars of the Lords and King he served.

Suddenly there was a shout from one of the outriders as he pulled up behind them, 'We have found her Sire, to the south-east, we think she is going down onto the beach. High cliffs surround it, and there seems to be just one entrance.'

Luc shaded his eyes, looking south, but it was the far end of the beach they were indicating past a rocky outcrop that went into the sea, and he could see little. However, he could feel the tension in his brother, who sat beside him; Morvan was shortening his reins and peering along the beach at the cliffs and shadows in the distance.

Morvan stood up in his stirrups to address the men, 'you all know what to do, spread out in formation, she must not escape; I refuse to let her slip through my hands this time.'

The group turned back into the pine forests and made their way quietly south, trotting almost parallel to the long beach. Not a word was spoken; not a whinny was heard as they fanned out in a wide circle following the outriders and heading for the shallow gully that led down onto the beach.

They emerged from the trees and picked their way carefully down through the craggy rocks and boulders; a small bluff still hid her from their sight, so she had no idea that they were there. Luc and Morvan rode carefully forward on their own and stopped, raising a hand to keep the rest of the troop back. There she was, on the shoreline, her feet in the surf, staring out across the Atlantic Ocean. As Luc gazed at her, she took his breath away; he had forgotten quite how beautiful she was.

Morvan waited for the rest of the men to catch up and

then whispered, 'She has not seen us yet, so we have a chance to cut across and catch her when she tries to run; the cliffs surrounding the beach should contain her.' He indicated to the three men at the back, 'you three stay here and ensure she does not escape back up through the gully.' He then turned back to Luc, 'we have found her, Luc, finally I will be taking her home,' he said, a grin on his face as he shortened his reins and prepared to gallop down to the water's edge.

The Breton Horse Warriors Series

'Betrayal'
Beguiled
Beseiged
Banished

**The Breton Horse Warriors – Book three
It will be published by Moonstorm Books on
Amazon in June 2021**

To find out more and to join our mailing list and
newsletters, contact us at:
Website: www.moonstormbooks.com
Email: enquiries@moonstormbooks.com
Facebook: S.J.Martin Author
Instagram: s.j.martin77
Twitter: @SJMarti40719548

About the Author

Sarah J Martin... is the pen name of a historian, writer and animal lover in the north of England. Having had an abiding love of history from a very early age influenced her academic and career choices. She worked in the field of archaeology for several years before becoming a history teacher in the schools of the north-east, then in London and finally Sheffield.

She particularly enjoys the engaging and fascinating historical research into the background of her favourite historical periods and characters, combining this with extensive field visits. Having decided to leave the world of education after a successful teaching and leadership career, she decided to combine her love of history and writing as an author of historical fiction. With her partner and a close friend, she established Moonstorm Books, publishing The Breton Horse Warrior Series...

When she is not writing, she walks their two dogs with her partner Greg on the beautiful beaches of the Northeast coast or in the countryside. She also has an abiding love of live music and festivals, playing and singing in a band with her friends whenever possible.

Printed in Great Britain
by Amazon